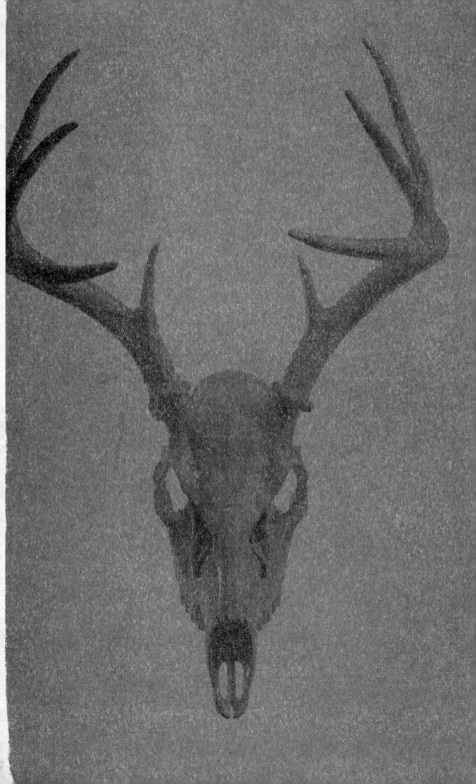

THE FOREST DEMANDS ITS DUE

KOSOKO JACKSON

Quill Tree Books
An Imprint of HarperCollinsPublishers

Quill Tree Books is an imprint of HarperCollins Publishers.

The Forest Demands Its Due
Copyright © 2023 by Kosoko Jackson
All rights reserved. Printed in the United States of America.
No part of this book may be used or reproduced in any manner whatsoever
without written permission except in the case of brief quotations embodied in
critical articles and reviews. For information address HarperCollins
Children's Books, a division of HarperCollins Publishers,
195 Broadway, New York, NY 10007.
www.epicreads.com

Library of Congress Cataloging-in-Publication Data

Names: Jackson, Kosoko, author.
Title: The forest demands its due / Kosoko Jackson.
Description: First edition. | New York : Quill Tree Books, an imprint of Harper-
   Collins Publishers, [2023] | Audience: Ages 14 up. | Audience: Grades 10-12. |
   Summary: When the murder of his classmate at an elite boarding school seems
   to be forgotten overnight, seventeen-year-old Douglas must confront centuries
   of secrets in the school's past and a vengeful creature in the forest surrounding
   the campus.
Identifiers: LCCN 2023000111 | ISBN 9780063260795 (hardcover)
Subjects: CYAC: Boarding schools—Fiction. | Schools—Fiction. | Blessing and
   cursing—Fiction. | Supernatural—Fiction. | Gay men—Fiction. | African
   Americans—Fiction. | LCGFT: Paranormal fiction. | Thrillers (Fiction) |
   Novels.
Classification: LCC PZ7.1.J285 Fo 2023 | DDC [Fic]—dc23
LC record available at https://lccn.loc.gov/2023000111

Typography by Joel Tippie
23 24 25 26 27 LBC 5 4 3 2 1
First Edition

To every marginalized person who survived a PWI—we made it.

Be careful of the curse that falls on young lovers
Starts so soft and sweet and turns them to hunters.
—"Howl," Florence + the Machine

It's an old song
It's an old tale from way back when
It's an old song
And we're gonna sing it again and again.
—"Road to Hell," *Hadestown*

PART ONE

"Douglas."

I ignore Sister Annabeth because there's blood under my nails. It's all I can focus on. Not the polished wood of her office. Or the photos of her summiting six out of seven of the highest peaks. Nothing but the blood.

The good news: It's not my blood. And there ends the good news.

The bad news: The voices are louder this time. Not the voices of the students at Regent Academy, or those of the sisters and brothers speaking in a rapid-fire fever pitch around me, pretending I can't hear them as they whisper how it was a mistake that I was accepted to this prestigious school. Despite how much I dislike these people who stick their noses up at everyone who comes from a different background than them, I'd welcome that. At least those voices would make sense.

But these are the hushed whispers of Atolas Forest, which butts right up against our school and is bigger on the inside than any map or traveler will admit to. A forest that every student knows not to go near. And it's talking to me. It *always* talks to me. And I do my best not to listen.

Usually, if I'm lucky, the dissonant voices hum in the background like white noise. But this time, they're screaming. So loud I can barely hear myself think. A cacophony of twenty-plus voices, all saying everything and nothing at the same time, which blends together into one genderless, consistent, loud, never-ending noise.

I want to dig my bloody nails into my scalp and rip open my head. I want to pull apart my skull flaps, cut the pads of my fingers on jagged pieces of bone, and dig around in my brain until I can grab the voices, strangle them, and toss them onto the floor in a bloody heap. I know how ridiculous that sounds, but perhaps then I'll have peace. Just one freaking minute of peace. Or at least I'll be able to destroy whatever part of my mind makes me believe that a forest is talking to me.

If I listen to the voices, really put my mind to it, and pick out a singular one to hear, I can make out the words, like scratches against stone that whisper a warning.

You're going to die here.
We're going to kill you.
They're going to kill you.
He's going to kill you.

Shut up, shut up, shut up, I mouth to myself, keeping my face down, eyes staring at the red stains that tint my dark brown skin. Funny how anything can be an anchor to reality, even someone else's blood.

The blood in question is Kent Hale's. It stains my knuckles too, and some blotchy specks of it are on my cream-and-maroon Regent Academy blazer. It has already started to dry, which is going to make it a bitch to get out. On top of everything else I have to deal with, tending to my bloody blazer—the only blazer I have, since only one is provided to students and any more cost three hundred dollars apiece—is not how I want to spend my time.

But maybe the repetitive motion, the focus on the suds and the warm water and the way the clear-colored sink turns from light pink to dark red, will do me some good. Repetition and consistency are the cure for so many things. Maybe it'll fix whatever is wired wrong in my brain.

"Douglas."

I don't think I'm insane. *Insane* is a clinical definition, and I would need a doctor, or a nurse like my mama, to confirm before I add that little fun factoid to my Regent bio. I think *crazy* would be a closer word, but that's ableist and just thinking it sends shivers down my spine. I don't know what I am. I don't know how to describe it.

No, I do. *Broken.*

That's the word. I just don't want to say that out loud. Because when you say things out loud, you put energy into the world that you can't take back. Once I say it, once I admit it, there's no hope for me.

But the voices. Oh my god, the voices. They're screaming so loudly today that Sister Annabeth has to slam her hand down on the table to pull my gaze away from the forest where the sounds are coming from.

"Douglas," she says for the third time. At least, that's what I think she says. When someone looks at me with that sternness and flicker of a nerve in their cheek that resembles annoyance, it usually means they're calling my name or I've done something to make them wish I was . . . well . . . not in front of them at that moment.

I focus on her lips, watching the way they part to form a two-syllable word that feels familiar. Ever since the voices started eight months ago, I've gotten good at figuring out ways to pretend I'm actively listening. Reading lips took some time, but it's been the best method so far. Focus enough on the words and they act like an anchor, grounding me through the storm until the voices melt away and the world returns to normal. As normal as being a Black kid in an elite private boarding school can be.

"Sorry, I was—"

"Distracted?"

I read somewhere, probably history class, that in the past they would take those they thought were mentally unstable, lock them away in cold, damp asylums, and do horrific things to them. Ice-water baths. Boiling-water baths. Electroshock therapy. Beatings. Isolation. Lobotomies. Anything to scrape the sick out like black mold that lines attic walls. And though I don't think there's any universe where the sisters and brothers at Regent Academy would do something like that—the parents who pay upward of eighty thousand dollars a year in tuition would have words—it's safe to say that trusting random people with my . . . *affliction* is a way to make me seem even more of an outsider in a place I already fit in about as well as a square peg in a round hole.

"Yes, let's go with distracted," I say. Better than saying I think the forest is talking to me.

Sister Annabeth sighs. If there were a way to visually personify *I'm not upset, just disappointed*, then you'd have the look she's giving me right now. We've been sitting here in her fourth-floor office overlooking the western side of the campus, silently, for the past fifteen minutes. Ever since Coach Watson pulled me off Kent's chest and dragged me down the hallway, kicking and shrieking for everyone to see. I can still hear my voice bouncing off the marble walls, screaming at him, *Who's the bitch now, huh?*

In hindsight, I could have been a bit smarter and classier with my rebuttal.

"You remind me of my brother, Douglas," Sister says. "Have I ever told you that?"

More than once, I think while playing with the faint raised lines inside my wrists. It's a nervous habit I've developed since getting out of jail; those scars from the cuffs never fully healed.

But I don't say those thoughts out loud. Sister Annabeth is one of the nice ones, and being crass and snappy with her doesn't feel right. Sister Baxter, who teaches English, would use the term *self-defeatist*. There's no benefit in losing the only defender I have just to get a quippy reply in. Winning the war is more important than winning the battle. And to me, winning the war means making it out of this school with my diploma.

I shake my head. Sister Annabeth arches her brow. The voices begin to grow quiet. They do that sometimes, just . . . disappear, as if they get bored with me.

Funny thing, though—they are never gone for long.

"No." I adjust the pitch of my voice now that I can hear myself, so I don't sound like I'm yelling. "You haven't."

She turns the photo on her desk toward me, showing a woman who looks exactly like her except fifteen years younger, a man with similar facial structure, and two people who are clearly their parents, standing in front of the Grand Canyon. They look happy, whole. They look *normal*.

"He was a student here too, about fifteen years ago, and then I followed two years later."

"Where you fell in love with psychology, thanks to your professor who did a class on Freud. You did your master's in New York, met Headmaster Benjamin Monroe at a conference, and decided to come back and teach at the school that made your brother into the happy man he is and you into the studious, fair, kind guidance counselor for troubled boys like me that you are today."

Sister Annabeth smiles slyly. It makes her face look younger, hiding her laugh lines. "Someone was paying attention during career week last month. The point is, I know how hard it can be to be . . . the other here. My brother and I were like you."

The words *other* and *like you* make me ball my fist against my slacks. Great, now those have bloodstains too. I have to remind myself again that Sister Annabeth is one of the good ones. She could have easily just sent me to the headmaster's office, or had one of the other sisters handle me. But she's never given up and that means something.

And besides, being called *other* technically isn't wrong, especially here. How many Black students and staff are there at Regent, besides my mama and me? How many openly gay students are there at a school that breeds the top 1 percent? How many scholarship students does Regent actually take?

The answer to all three questions is the same: not many. That's not what makes my skin crawl, though. It's her thinking we're similar. We're the furthest from the same as any two people can be, and her trying to relate to me through some cheap ploy makes me want to clench my jaw until my teeth crack.

When she looks at the forest, what does she see? Bowing trees? All-encompassing darkness? Jagged rocks and ice-hardened stone?

When I squint just right, I see an almost picturesque view from the top of the Regent Academy steps to the main hall, which, together, look like the shape of a skull. And sometimes, the skull looks like its mouth is opened wider than it was before.

Sister Annabeth eventually sighs, shifting her weight in the wooden chair to get more comfortable. She flips open a manila file, scanning the first paper. There's a picture of me—the one from my student ID—information about my family, my grades, and a psychological evaluation. I flick my eyes to the other files on her desk. They're each half as thick as mine.

"Alright, let's start from the beginning. Walk me through what happened," she says, grabbing a pen.

"I'm sure every student at the gym told you."

"I'd like to hear your side of the story," she quietly urges.

Her way of saying, *Defend yourself.*

A wave of anger that morphs into nausea pulses through me again. I do everything to swallow it down. Like my mama says, I'm too old to look at everyone as my enemy. What she doesn't know is that the world makes it so easy.

"He called me a faggot," I mutter, turning to look out the window—the opposite window that faces east, toward Winslow, the nearest town. It's a beautiful, cold October day in Vermont. The leaves have already started to change into shades of fire, and the brisk air requires us all to wear sweaters. It's my favorite time of year. Soon, the weather will turn mercilessly cold. The grounds will be beautiful—the Academy's Gothic arches and eighteenth-century style lean well into pristine whiteness. In more ways than one.

Some students love it. Check the social media platform of any Regent Academy student, and around wintertime, their feeds are flooded with beautiful, homey photos and boring captions reminding the rest of the world how perfect life is as a student here. Yet whenever I look out the window and see nothing but endless white for miles, except for the hazy gray forest in the distance, all I'm reminded of is how truly stuck I am.

"I see." A beat. "You've been called a—that word—before and not lashed out."

"You can say it."

"I'd rather not. And I'd rather you don't either."

I shrug. "He also called me a bitch. And stupid."

"So, that's why you're upset? That's reasonable. I don't think your reaction was—"

"No. F—"

An arched brow.

"The f-word I can deal with. A bitch, sure. But no one's called me stupid before."

Sister Annabeth does her best not to smile, looking down at her folder and clearing her throat.

I don't let the stillness between us last for long. Stillness allows the static to creep in. "I know what you're going to say. That it was my pride talking. But you'll use the word *hubris*. You like those five-dollar words."

"I'd hardly consider *hubris* a five-dollar word, Douglas," she muses, closing the file and staring through me. "But you're absolutely right. I believe you lashed out in an effort to defend your pride. I'd also say two other things."

"That I'm off the hook and you're going to recommend that Kent is the one who gets punished, not me?"

"Close. Number one, you and I both know Kent will never get punished, so this idea of justice you have? That one day you'll be seen as the hero and Kent the villain? It's fraught. And number two, you were one hundred percent justified in your actions, but that doesn't make them right. In fact, it was a stupid choice to punch Kent—or anyone, for that matter—considering . . . "

"My history?"

"Yes, your history."

And by *history*, she means the fire I was accused of setting eighteen months ago, which killed over two dozen people. A crime I *did not* commit. I told the police that. That I couldn't have done it. That I saw someone else there.

But I don't think there's any point in rehashing that. No one wants to believe me anyway, and I'm tired of trying to defend my honor and name.

People say I owe Regent everything. I wouldn't be where I am without them. I say bullshit.

I mean, technically, they're right. Jessica Hale—Kent's mother, funnily enough—came to my rescue eighteen months ago, offering me a free ride to Regent Academy and the use of her law firm to take over my case, since the lawyer my mother bought—the only one she could afford—was going to botch my case. Mrs. Hale was my savior and followed through with every promise she made. A week after our meeting, the charges were dropped. Two weeks later, I was on a plane to Regent Academy with my mother, who was also given a job as head nurse. I was handed a second chance at life that few people get—especially Black kids threatened by the predatory legal system in this country.

But something has always felt . . . off. I'd never heard of Regent Academy before that meeting. I remember scanning the brochure Mrs. Hale had brought me. Analyzing the beautiful photos of the rolling landscape, the perks of this king-and-queen-making school of elite students . . . How had I never heard of it? And more importantly, why did they want me? I'm smart, but not *that* smart.

But I had no choice. Mrs. Hale made that clear, and even if she hadn't, I could see the signs of how my case was going to end. I didn't start that fire that burned the complex to the ground.

But no one believed me. Justice is supposed to be blind, but when a Black kid is an easy scapegoat, that blindness often comes at the expense of the truth. So why not tip the balance in my favor? Why not use the same perks the rich and successful use all the time to get what they want? I know I'm innocent. At least, I think I am.

If Dad was here, if the cancer hadn't come out of left field and mercilessly wrecked his body, he would believe me.

If Dad was here, he wouldn't have let it get this far.

"I'm not going to say thank you again, if that's what you want," I remind Sister Annabeth, pulling myself out of my memories.

"No one is asking you to. We're only asking you to not throw away this opportunity. You know how hard it was for the headmaster to make this happen. You know how much he stuck his neck out for you."

I don't really, but people always like to remind me. Sure, I absolutely would have ended up in prison if it wasn't for Mrs. Hale. But no one, not even my mother, stopped to question how she knew about the case. Or how she went about winning. Or why one of the most expensive and exclusive schools in the country gave me a full ride.

"This is a great opportunity to put all this behind us," Mama had said in our apartment's kitchen when we were packing and I had the audacity to question the gift. "We can't stay here, Douglas. You know that. Either we'll leave or people will make us. It might be good to be somewhere different."

She said *different*, but she meant *safe*. Regent Academy is like its own universe. The campus is over forty acres. Winslow is the nearest town, and the vast majority of the students at Regent live in dorms and go home to their rich families for summer and winter break. There's no better place than here to start over; Regent will give me the tools I need to succeed.

But at what cost?

It's absolutely true that Regent Academy makes successes out of its graduates. But graduates of Regent aren't the type of successful people you would know of. They move in the shadows, manipulating the world like puppet masters. And that type of person, who can afford the Academy *and* get into the Academy, is a specific breed. And a middle-class Black boy who was charged with twelve counts of manslaughter and couldn't even afford one week at the school, let alone two years of tuition, does not click with that profile. I'm not stupid enough or desperate enough to know they aren't getting something in exchange.

And then there's the forest. The always-present forest.

If you ask any student or teacher, it's just . . . there, blending into the colorful background. I get that; I'm from DC. The Washington Monument, the Supreme Court, and the White House are just . . . things to me. They aren't special. It's like that for the French and the Eiffel Tower. Mount Rainier and Seattle residents. And apparently, those in Winslow or Regent Academy students.

But here's the thing: The forest doesn't stay the same. It follows you. If you look at it carefully—I mean really look at it—the trees shift to always face you. It's subtle at first. If you blink, you'll miss it. They move enough so that no one can really tell, like a cat stalking its prey.

Or maybe my mind really is fracturing inside my head. Just a bunch of broken glass rattling around. Maybe I need to keep quiet and focus on school.

Because that's what my mama would want me to do. Put my head down, make good grades, and put the past behind me so her sacrifices aren't for nothing. And how have I repaid her?

Punching Kent Hale in the face. Three times.

"So, what happens now?" I ask. But the real question I'm asking is, *Are you going to tell my mama?*

Sister Annabeth sighs. "You don't make things easy for me, you know that?"

"Maybe that's your curse," I suggest.

Sister Annabeth narrows her eyes. I raise my hands in defeat. "Sorry, sorry. Forgot we don't condone talks of curses in this room."

She nods curtly and once again looks at my folder, licking the tip of her finger to turn the page, before quickly writing down some notes.

"I'm going to let you in on a little secret, Douglas. You're smarter than almost every other student here."

"Tell that to Kent."

"But your mouth, your temper, and your hubris are going to

ruin a good thing for you. If you stay here and graduate, your protection continues. You can get an excellent job, or your pick of colleges and medical schools, or you can win a grant to start your own company. The opportunities are only limited by your imagination. You have the chance to make a real difference for others, and yourself.

"If you keep up like this, though? Going down this reckless path? I can't protect you anymore. *We* can't protect you anymore. And everything your mother sacrificed will go up in flames like that apartment complex."

Sister Annabeth's words are like an arrow with perfect aim, finding the chink in my armor. I squeeze the arms of the seat, doing my best to show as little emotion as possible.

"This is the last time I will help you, Douglas. The sisters will overrule me if this happens again. Headmaster Monroe accepted you and your mother out of the graciousness of his heart."

"You all don't stop reminding me."

"It's worth reminding." She hands me a slip of paper with an ominous and familiar red stamp on it: detention. "The last time, Douglas."

On most days, I'd continue the argument, but a firm knock on her office door gives me pause. A guy with short, blond hair pokes his head in. Ezekiel, a fellow junior who works in the administration office.

"Sister Annabeth, do you have a moment?" he asks. "You're needed."

"I'm with a student, Ezekiel."

"Headmaster Monroe called and wants you in his office. Says it's urgent and regarding . . ." Ezekiel falls silent, looking at me once more before turning back to Sister Annabeth. "He just said you should come now. It's important."

His voice is tight and thin, which isn't unusual for him. Ezekiel is a stick in the mud—in and out of the bedroom. But his voice is colder than usual. There's an urgency behind it he's trying to keep hidden.

Something's wrong.

My eyes flicker to Sister Annabeth, but she doesn't give anything away. She curtly nods to me. "Go to your mother. She's expecting you."

As I leave and Sister Annabeth's eyes turn down to the stack of papers on her desk, my gaze shifts to the forest behind her. The voices aren't screaming anymore. In fact, they're quieter than a moment ago. Now they're snickering at me. Like they know something I don't. Which wouldn't surprise me.

The trees are older than all of us. They've seen things we can't even imagine, and deep within the rings of their bark lie secrets that could break the world. And whatever is happening now is one of those secrets. I can feel it.

2

I have a Black mom, which means she puts up with very little of my shit.

I'm not one to care much about rumors, or what people say about me. I got that from her. Being one of three women-of-color staff members at Regent Academy doesn't help, I'm sure, but you'd never know by the way she carries herself. My mama only cares about three things: me, her job as a nurse, and keeping us safe.

Which is why I know she won't understand why I let Kent get the best of me; an action that threatens all those things.

She's sitting in the lavish office of the nurses, bigger than most schools' classrooms, with cream-colored curtains around a dozen beds and soft ocean music playing through the Google Home on her desk. It's so different from Jefferson High, my school back home. She was the nurse there too, but the windows had a layer of yellow slime on them, the doors never fully locked, and the walls had a lingering scent you just couldn't place. Here, the scent of lavender meant to calm even the most nervous of students hangs in the air. In the eight months I've been here, I've only ever seen maybe five of the beds filled at once—and that was due to some sophomores going off campus and eating bad seafood. Even now, the room is empty save for Mama and a girl I've never seen before.

The student finishes putting on her blazer as Mama hands her a small white bag.

"Take one of these with each meal and you'll be fine," Mama says, smiling.

The girl flashes Mama a hesitant smile back, her eyes flickering to me.

"I didn't hear anything," I promise, crossing my fingers over my heart. The girl rolls her eyes, checking the Regent ribbon all girls must wear in their high ponytails and tightening it a bit before leaving.

The air falls still when it's just Mama and me. She doesn't look up, focusing on the folder in front of her. Strands of her carefully-cared-for locs fall over one shoulder as she's focused on getting all the information down about whoever that was. She takes her job—taking care of me and my fellow students—seriously.

"I can come back later if—"

"Sit."

My body functions without me even thinking, and I lower myself onto the nearest bed. For about a minute, Mama sits in silence, back to me, finishing whatever she's writing. She slides the folder into her metal file cabinet, then locks it. Whoever it was, their last name starts with the letter *Q*.

The metal chair barely makes a sound when she turns to look at me.

"I know you can't tell me why she was here," I say, "but you can tell me if it has to do with her curse."

Students at Regent Academy are like no others. They believe they are predestined for greatness; that they got here not because of luck and privilege, but because they did something to actually deserve the wealth and power they're afforded.

They also believe in curses.

Everyone in school does, like some old wives' tale passed down. The reason someone gets sick once a month? A curse. The reason a student can get As on every assignment but always fail their finals? A curse. It's almost like how people use their astrological signs as an excuse for bad behavior by saying, *Oh my god, I'm such a Gemini*.

I think it's silly. But like Mama said, as a nurse, it's not her job to judge people. It's her job to meet them where they are and operate in their reality, because if that's what helps them get better, then so be it.

Personally? I just think allowing people to believe things like that, things that are obviously wrong and completely out of the realm of reality or possibility, promotes bad behavior. But that's why she's the nurse and not me.

Am I really all that different, though? I think the forest talks to me, that the trees follow your gaze. Say it enough times and you begin to believe it. Say it a few more times and you realize how unsettling and unstable that sounds.

Say it one more time and the forest seems to whisper back *yes*.

Mama pushes off with her feet, the chair sliding over to bridge the space between us. Gingerly, her soft fingers brush against my cheek, the same earthly hue as her own skin—except for the warm redness right under my eye.

"You know I can't tell you that, Douglas. Doctor-patient—"

"Doctor-patient confidentiality, I know. But you're a nurse."

"Still applies," she mutters, taking a beat to turn my face to the left, then to the right. "I'm guessing the other guy looks worse?"

I try not to smirk, but I can't help it. Seeing Kent on his back, clutching his face, blood staining the palms of his hands and the front of his blazer like thick red paint? Worth it.

"Naturally."

She gently taps my cheek with the open side of her hand. It's a weak slap, but it does its job and knocks the cockiness out of me.

She glides over to the counter and grabs some gauze, gloves, Band-Aids, and a few wet wipes before moving back to me and getting to work.

Being a nurse has always been my mama's calling. Taking care of me, though? That's second nature. And I don't just mean physically, or in the way a parent is supposed to, like financially and morally. My mama has always been in my corner. When the fire happened, she never questioned me. She always believed me, even when no one else did.

That's the only thing I feel shitty about: how I let her down, disappointed her by repeating the same violent, aggressive patterns I was supposed to have left behind in DC. It makes her feel like she's done something wrong, even if she won't admit it.

And maybe, just maybe—even though, again, she'd never admit to thinking this—it makes her wonder if everyone else might have been right about me.

We sit in tense silence as she cleans up my busted lip, then checks to make sure the black eye is nothing more than temporary. Soft whispers begin to scratch at the back of my mind, the voices returning. They're manageable right now, barely noticeable. That won't last for long.

"The good news is you don't need stitches."

"Is there bad news?"

"Kent was just here. Before Lydia."

"Really? He dared to show his less-than-perfect—"

Mama pulls back and glares at me, sending a chill down my spine that instantly makes me sit up straight.

"You really hurt him, Douglas."

"Wait, seriously? You're defending him?"

Her steely expression doesn't change.

"Oh my god, you're actually defending him."

"I'm simply stating facts. He's a mess. He might need stitches. He's threatening to tell his parents," she says, peeling off her gloves.

"So says every student in this school," I mutter, swinging my legs while sitting on the bed.

"You know this isn't the same," she hisses. "You know why this is different."

Of course I do. Kent's parents are powerful people, the power couple of the school when they attended years ago. His father is a high-powered CEO who runs a Fortune 500 company, and his mother is an attorney, the youngest named partner at an international law firm with offices in sixteen countries.

Mama checks my face like an artist examining their artwork before pushing back, putting some distance between us. Her face softens. "I thought you left this behind, Douglas."

The disappointment is heavy, like a thick fog, threatening to swallow me whole and drown me. Some kids complain about having too much pressure from their parents: the need to succeed, to be perfect, and to always be the best versions of themselves. I wish I had that problem.

Instead, I'm still making up for a crime that wasn't even mine. A shawl of embarrassment and disappointment I can't even claim. And I know that the only way to truly get us past this is to admit I set the fire. Sacrifice my own soul in order to settle her doubts and move on with our lives. That's what a child should do, right? Pay back their parent for all the good they've done for them in their lives? Some kids buy their parents homes; all I have to do is help my mother move on.

"Why does no one care that he started it?" I say. "Why does everyone only look at me like I'm the bad one?"

I know why. For one, Kent is rich. And two, I'm just some queer Black kid who makes a school look good with its diversity numbers.

Add on the criminal aura that follows me around like a noxious cloud, and you have the absolutely worst-dealt hand in human history.

Mama sighs, standing and walking over to the window. Whenever the conversation shifts to the past, especially the accident, she gets antsy. Mama wins the award for Person Who Wants to Put the Past Behind Her the Most, and her way of doing that? Distance.

Distancing herself from the house where she found my father dead from a seizure, thanks to his cancer reaching his brain.

Distance from the apartment complex that burned to the ground, along with her future.

And, right now, distance from me.

"A little hot in here, isn't it?" she asks, not waiting for my answer as she opens the window.

"I like the heat, helps me sleep."

"I know," she says. "Why do you think the house was always so hot back home? Kept you from sleepwalking out the door. Learned that when I was watching TV one night and you came out of your room. You scared the shit out of me. Thought you were a zombie."

I open my mouth to tell her *obviously I wasn't*, but the rush of cold hits me before I can speak, passing through me like I'm not even here.

But Vermontese cold isn't the only thing that moves right

24

through me. There's something . . . colder. Something that doesn't only chill my bones, but chills my soul.

It feels like empty, bottomless, frigid grief.

It feels like how I imagine dying alone or knowing, no matter what you do, this will be what your last moments feel like.

I grip the edge of the chair nearby so tightly, I think the metal might snap. *Still your breathing, Douglas. This isn't the first time you've felt this since being here.* It'll pass. It'll pass. It'll—

"It doesn't matter who did or didn't start it," Mama reminds me, finally turning to face me, crossing her arms over her chest. "We came here to start a new life. How can we do that if you . . ."

She bites her lip, sighing. She doesn't need to finish; I know what comes next.

"If I keep fucking up?"

Mama visibly winces. She washes her hands in silence. I know she's using the moments with her back to me to collect her thoughts.

"I'm not going to tell you how to live your life, Douglas." She moves to the other side of the room, busying herself by picking up the gauze, wipes, and tissue paper, dumping it all in the biohazard bin by her desk. "That's for you to decide. But what I am going to tell you is that we only get so many chances to make something of ourselves. So many opportunities to make a good impression. You're running out of those opportunities, baby. Maybe you don't see it because you're young. Maybe you don't care. I don't know. But it scares me. As a mother, it terrifies me."

Tension swells in my chest. Mama isn't usually this emotional.

She doesn't waste time with emotions. She isn't coldhearted, just pragmatic. Everything has a purpose and completes some puzzle that unlocks the next step of her one-, five-, ten-, or twenty-year plan. So, when she speaks honestly with me about what I've done and how I've scared her? It means something.

It means I'm more of a screwup than I thought.

I swallow thickly and open my mouth to apologize, to promise—even though we both know it's hollow—that I'll do and be better. But before I can, the door to the infirmary opens with such force, it slides off its hinges and collapses on the ground, the frosted windowpane shattering into a million jagged pieces.

Mama and I jump, but for probably two different reasons. The door, sure, is one of them. But the man who ripped the door off its hinges is mine.

Everyone knows Everett Everley. One of the first things people told me—besides giving me faux compliments on my dreads and asking probing questions like, *No, where are you really from?* and *Why do you talk so proper?* or *Did you really kill those people?*—was *Do not, under any circumstances, talk to the Everleys.*

Much like me, they're outsiders who were lucky enough to find their way into Regent's toxic gravitational pull. Evelyn Everley, their mother; Everett Everley, the oldest of the Everley siblings; and Emma Everley, the youngest, live at the edge of the school, where the forest meets the western side of the campus, where no one is allowed to venture without an adult chaperone due to the weird lack of cell signal—plus jagged rocks and sinkholes that the school hasn't been able to fix, no matter how many land specialists they call. The Everleys keep the school safe from black bears, mountain lions, and anything else that might hurt students or the horses we have. Evelyn Everley runs an elective—Surviving the Wilderness—where she teaches students how to start fires, distill water, shoot flares, and things like that. The family is part of the school, a fixture that has been here for god knows how long.

But I've rarely seen Everett or his sister Emma interact with anyone at school. Around the grounds, sure, out of the corner of my eye or in the distance, and sitting together in the back of our classes, but teachers never call on them. It's like they are here but not *really* here.

And no one seems to care.

So seeing him inside the school with his shaggy hair, dirty jeans, faded checkered shirt, and insulated vest? It's strange. Because for the first time since coming to Regent, I feel like I really see him.

But even stranger? Seeing him with a ripped shirt and what looks like three jagged slashes from a bear's claw on his chest, a grisly image partially hidden by the body he's carrying—a student, with torn clothes and a mangled body like he was tossed around by a pack of wolves and left for dead.

Mama jumps right into action without hesitation. She wheels over and meets Everett halfway as he places the body on one of the empty beds. His steel-toed boots walk in the droplets of blood, smearing the crimson liquid like abstract art.

"I don't know if he's alive," Everett's deep voice rumbles.

"Are you okay?" she asks Everett while scanning the wounded

boy. She opens the remnants of the ripped shirt, gently touching the edges of the wounds. They're deep, I can tell that much; the edges of the boy's skin have turned upward, and I think I can see exposed bone.

"Just a flesh wound. I'll be fine," Everett replies, barely letting her finish.

"What happened to him?" I choke out. I can hardly make out the victim's face. He looks familiar, though. I think I have an elective with him. "What happened to *you?* Holy shit, he's still breathing . . . he's still—"

"Douglas," my mama snaps, not looking up as she cuts away the boy's shirt, "get out of here."

"We need to call the ambulance! We need—"

"I said get out!" she yells. "Now!"

I can't even get out of the way properly. When Everett needs to get around me to fetch something from a drawer, I just stand there. Like a boulder in the middle of a river.

"Babe," Mama repeats. "Babe, look at me."

I look up, meeting my mama's honey eyes.

"Go," she says, softer. "I got this. I won't let him die. I promise."

But there's more blood on the floor than there was before, and the boy's breathing is shallower than when he entered. How can she have this under control? Regent is a school, not a hospital.

The smells, the sounds, and the tension in the air are too much for me. I force myself out of the room, stepping over the glass and the alcove. I turn back when I'm in the hallway, looking at the boy, my mama, and Everett once more—

—just in time to see the half-conscious boy lock eyes with me. Just in time to see his eyes widen as he looks into my soul, to see his mouth open wider than any human mouth should. And to watch him let out the most bloodcurdling scream I've ever heard.

All without ever breaking eye contact with me.

"Did you hear what happened to that boy?"

"Does anyone know who he is? Pat? Peyton? Paul?"

"He's in my art history class. Weird kid."

"Do you think he went into the forest?"

"Serves him right if he did."

The whole school is abuzz with what happened to the boy.
Even in my afternoon classes (Latin, World History, and English
IV) none of the sisters or brothers can muster any sort of classroom management. The boy—whose name starts with *P* by
consensus—is currently the most popular kid at Regent Academy.

A senior, Marsh, turns around in one of the worn wooden
seats that hiss whenever you move more than an inch, and looks
at me.

"Dougie," he says with a type of syrupy sweetness that gives me diabetes.

"It's Douglas." We've been over this before.

"Right, that's what I said. Your mom. She know anything about what's going on?"

Marsh hasn't said a total of twenty sentences to me since I arrived, even though we have almost the same classes. I can't tell if he's gotten into most of these high-tier courses because he's smart, or because his father is the US ambassador to Spain.

Probably both.

"I heard one of the sisters say he was attacked by a bear. That true?" he asks.

"How would I know?"

Marsh doesn't need to know that I haven't been able to get the images of the boy's mangled body out of my head. The boy deserves some level of privacy.

Marsh shrugs. "I dunno. Seems like you would know. Going into the forest is stupid; you two have that in common."

The classroom snickers. A chorus of crackling, hushed chortles dance in the air.

Marsh puts his arms behind his head, propping his ankles up on the back of the chair in front of him. The resident of said seat, Connie, taps Marsh's legs, playfully pushing them away and flashing a flirtatious smile at him.

"Serves him right, then," Connie adds with a tone of indignation that only comes from someone who thinks they've never made a mistake once in their life. "We don't need idiots like that."

I half expected her to add *diluting the gene pool*. But instead, I keep quiet. Because I would have done the same as him, and I have before.

The forest is quiet. No one goes there; maybe he just wanted somewhere to relax. To hear his own thoughts, to nurse his own wounds. Despite what Connie and Marsh and everyone else want to admit, I can think of a million reasons someone would risk going into the forest. Whatever is actually in there is better than the rich brats that make up Regent Academy.

But still, there's a part of me that can't believe he went in willingly. Everyone knows not to go into the forest. Time works differently there, or so people say. People in Winslow take that a step further to suggest reality itself follows different laws in the forest. That you can't find your way out. That sound is swallowed and digested within the darkness. That cell phones don't work and compasses go haywire. That some of the most feral creatures live there. Creatures never seen before. Bears bigger than any normal black bears. Cougars with red eyes. Hell, someone even said they saw a wolf with two heads from the edge of campus.

I think it's just a bunch of bullshit. A folktale that has been kneaded and pounded until everyone just accepts it as truth.

You can't find your way out because the canopy is so thick, light can't penetrate. Cell phones don't work, nor compasses, because of the minerals in the earth. And as for those weird creatures? Simple. Darkness and fear and superstition play tricks on the mind.

Everything can be explained logically if you just take a moment to think.

Some students probably died there years ago and, like with everything else, Regent used the school's money and power to spin a narrative that would keep people from going into the forest so they wouldn't run into a PR nightmare again.

The narrative has stuck. Any students who go into the forest get serious demerits on their record. If you go in more than three times? You're expelled.

I've been in the forest twice.

The first time was the first week I was here, when literally no one would talk to me. It's why I can understand what P Boy is going through. Being isolated does things to the brain. Not only isolated in the sense of being alone, but being alone in a room full of people.

That's a special type of hell.

In a dark and twisted sense, the forest at least felt welcoming. Like I had a weird sort of connection to the earth. The thing that people fear and marvel at, all at the same time. What made the forest so scary that everyone was terrified of it? What made me so scary that no one wanted to give me a chance?

Maybe in the forest I'd find some answers, I'd thought. After all, it spoke to me. There *was* a logical explanation for why this was happening. Even if it was just in my own head, maybe going into the forest would give me closure.

I didn't make it more than three feet before Coach Lainson dragged me out and into the headmaster's office. I got detention for five weeks.

That was the first time.

The second time was six months ago, when I woke up about twenty feet inside the forest. The ground didn't even have a chance to change from lush green to hardened stonelike dirt. The air was drastically colder than on the grounds. The darkness from the overgrown canopy had settled in, an inky blackness so thick I could barely make out the school lights no more than an eighth of a mile behind me.

That time, Everett, Emma, and Evelyn found me with their shotguns and flashlights in hand. Scowling, Evelyn took me back to her home and gave me a cup of tea.

"If you promise you'll never go in there again, and I mean never, I won't tell the headmaster," she said, waiting till I was done drinking. "We'll chalk this up to stress."

Sure, sleepwalking across campus is stressful. That makes sense. Wouldn't that mean during my court hearings I should have sleepwalked? Or when I was dealing with the weight of twelve people dying, I should have walked across state lines? Compared to that, Regent Academy is a cakewalk.

But Evelyn didn't want to hear that. And she most certainly didn't want to hear that when I dreamed about the forest, I heard voices coming out of it, and maybe, just maybe, that's why I sleep-walked there. She was the first person I ever told. And there was a wave of relief in that. Even if it only lasted a moment. Especially with what Evelyn said next.

"It's happening again."

Evelyn didn't give me a chance to ask her what she meant. She sat in front of me, grasping both of my hands, and stared directly into my eyes.

"Listen to me, Douglas. You cannot tell anyone what you just told me. Especially not the headmaster."

"I don't think anyone would listen to me even if I did."

"I don't care," she snapped. "Keep your head down. Graduate and leave this place. That's all you need to do. Do not let this place pull you into its vortex. Promise me, Douglas."

I did. And I agreed never to go into the forest again and to tell no one else about the voices I heard.

Because the way Evelyn Everley's eyes grew wide and then narrowed when I told her that, no matter how much she tried to hide it with anger and force—it looked like she was afraid. Actually, truly terrified of what I'd just said. Or of me.

It's the same look I got when I stood trial in court, spoke to the lawyer, the judge, the reporters, the crowd, and the families of those burned alive, and I never wanted to see someone look at me like that again.

And I didn't even tell her what I saw at the edge of the forest. The two sets of eyes, four in total, all a deep amber yellow. At first, lying in bed that night, I thought it might have been two bobcats, side by side. But that wouldn't explain the square-like pattern of the eyes. Or why they were ten feet in the air, looking down at me, as if to pass judgment. The more distance I got from that moment, the more improbable it sounded. I think I said it enough times to convince myself I was letting exhaustion get the best of me.

Besides, if you tell yourself enough times that it was just stress, you begin to believe it.

"Well, thanks for nothing, Dougie," Marsh says.

"Douglas."

Marsh and his crew return to ignoring me, which I'm fine with. I can't give them the gossip they want. Now we can all go back to pretending we don't know or care about one another.

But for the rest of the day, I can't help thinking about how casually everyone at school just accepted that whatever happened was the boy's fault. After the gossip ran its course, there were new topics to discuss. Subtle humble-brags about where students are summering this year. Talks about expensive vacations. All the usual conversations I hear at Regent.

But this isn't a normal time. A boy was almost killed by something in our forest. Besides the low-hum mutterings of *Shame* and *How unfortunate* or *This is why you must listen when we tell you things*, no one seems to care. No one pushes the envelope to probe for more information. And the Regent faculty sure aren't providing us with any information.

Rumors spin. Fabrications grow. But facts? The truth? None of that trickles down the pipeline.

And my mama is nowhere to be found.

That next morning, after my oh-so-enjoyable interaction with Marsh, is the first time I hear the forest clearly, with one single voice, speaking like it's looking directly at me.

It calls my name, enunciates it so firmly it jerks me awake, thinking someone has snuck into my attic room and is standing over my bed. But it's just me, my small room, and the glow of the five a.m. sun creating a sort of halo around the outline of the dark, endless trees.

I've heard that most students feel a sort of unease when they look at the forest. Sister Claremont said it's because of chemicals the farmers used to use that seeped into the earth. If that was the case, why build a school here?

"They are harmless, but your body naturally knows not to go somewhere dangerous. That unease you feel is your body's defenses. It's what protected our ancestors for generations to help us determine what to eat and what not to eat. Listen to it."

And that was all the explanation we ever got. Just like that, we were supposed to accept that as another reason we shouldn't go into the forest.

I wonder if that reaction is the same one that people have around me. Is that why so many students stay away from me? I don't want to be around those who don't want me; I respect myself enough for that. But up north, in the months of October through April, Vermont gets cold, and these beds are lonely. So many students sit in the large plush chairs, cozying up with other people in spaces meant for one. When the sisters and brothers aren't looking, they sneak off to each other's single rooms.

Sometimes, just sometimes, I wish someone would do that with me. Even if only for a night. Even if we just pretended for a moment that we cared about each other. I'm good at lying to myself.

Besides, it would be nice to have a distraction when the voices are loudest. It's like all the majestic, magical, humongous things in the forest are humming together, at the same frequency, trying to overpower each other to become the loudest voice during the witching hour. But in this moment, at the crack of dawn, it's quiet.

It's just a forest made up of dirt and vines and giant trees.

I'm not prone to staring at it for long—it's like when you look into the eyes of a dog until it bows its head in submission—but this morning, after I heard it call my name so clearly, I can't help but watch it rise from the earth as the fog burns away.

"What do you want?" I whisper. "What do you want with me?"

But it doesn't speak back. Besides jeering just enough to always remind me it's there, it keeps its secrets locked deep within the twisting vines and jagged splinters of wood that make the forest mostly impassable. The low tone of its grumble, deep in the back of its throat, never goes away. As if it's taunting me; daring me to step over the boundary line and take its secrets from it.

"Fuck you."

I have German today, I think, watching the glow of the sun become brighter and brighter. *Biology II, World History, my two electives, and a study period.* I wonder how much learning will be done today and how much time will be taken up gossiping about . . .

"Peter," I mutter. That was his name. Peter.

I expect to hear the same mutters of gossip about Peter crackling around school as I did yesterday, maybe even more. Time is the great fuel of gossip. The more time that people have to fester, the more that people come up with crazy ideas.

But I don't hear anything from anyone. No one in my first two periods—not even the sisters—mentions Peter's name. It's as if we decided yesterday's discussions were more than enough time given to an injured boy. Or that his wounds were just too much of a distraction to the Regent Academy curriculum.

In the middle of World History class, somewhere between the introduction of the Mongolian Empire and the explanation of the fall midterm topics, I raise my hand and stand—customary for when we want to ask a question in class.

"Yes, Douglas?" Sister Kennedy asks.

"Is there any update on the boy from yesterday?"

The class stays silent. Papers shuffle as a few junior and senior boys glance at me.

Sister Kennedy blinks owlishly. "Sorry. I don't think most people would consider King Henry the Eighth a boy. Plus, this year we're focusing on the world, not just white nations. We've moved on to Latin American civilizations now and how primitive their technology was. I would have imagined you of all people would appreciate that."

"You do know that's racist, right? Calling another society primitive?"

Sister Kennedy's round eyes turn sharp. "Are you calling me—"

"I'm not calling you anything. I'm saying your actions are racist. And we don't have enough time in class, or this school year, to discuss the weight of that whole *I imagine you of all people* comment."

"Douglas, I suggest—"

Before she can finish her sentence, I turn to face the class. "Seriously, none of you remember him?"

Still, silence.

"The student who was ripped apart yesterday?"

Silence breaks into whispers and murmurs. Voices flit through the air like dry leaves on the wind, whispers that are all saying the same thing, but nothing specific at the same time. Dozens of different conversations, all about me.

"That's enough, Douglas. Please sit down," Sister Kennedy says. A final warning.

"Wait, you're seriously going to pretend you don't know?" I scan the class, hoping to see at least one expression awash with recognition. The only person I register in the crowd is Marsh, and his objectively handsome, blocky face.

"You asked me about him yesterday. Don't you remember?"

"I have no idea what acid you took, Dougie, but I wouldn't be caught dead talking to you."

"Douglas! My name is fucking *Douglas*. D-O-U-G-L-A-S! I know you have the IQ of a gnat, but even you can spell *that*."

"What did you say to me?" Marsh booms, standing up. "Obviously Kent didn't punch you hard enough."

"Obviously you didn't see what I did to him up close. How about I show you?"

"Douglas!" Sister Kennedy yells. "That is enough. I will not tell you again. Sit down, be quiet for the remainder of the class, and we'll talk after."

Sister Kennedy waits for me to sit down, and when I don't, she flashes me a glare before continuing with her lesson on world history. But his name is right on the tip of my tongue.

"Peter!" I yell. "His name is Peter. He's a sophomore. He has . . . what is it . . . History of Art with me. He sits right there." I point to an empty chair in the row ahead of me.

Sister Kennedy screams, her textbook flying out of her hand. It hits the table, knocking her coffee mug over and onto the floor. The room fills with pregnant silence as the brown sludge seeps into the cracks of the floor.

"De-ten-tion," she says with a quivering voice, speaking each syllable slowly and clearly.

I shove my books into my bag as quickly as I can and storm out of the classroom. I don't care about Sister Kennedy's threats. How can no one remember him? How can everyone pretend he just doesn't exist? What type of sick joke is this? There's one person I know who will be able to vouch for me.

Mama.

She's seen her fair share of violence before, and being a nurse, she'll be unfazed by what we saw. Maybe she can give me some advice on how to push through it. Or maybe she'll have some logical explanation for what's going on.

My heart pounds out of my chest, so loudly the rest of the class's interactions melt away and disappear.

"Peter. Peter. Peter. Peter. Not some boy. Peter. Remember his name," I whisper over and over.

But the name feels like oil in my mind. It's like the memory of his name is trying to wiggle its way out of my grasp and disappear into the depths of my subconscious. But I won't let it. I hold on to everything I remember as tightly as I can.

I make my way to the infirmary. As I push into the room, I brave myself for the lingering smell of blood, but I'm hit with nothing.

Just the typical scent of lavender and honey that my mama uses to make the infirmary seem more like home.

"Mama?" I call. "Mama!"

"Over here, over here. Jesus, don't yell."

I follow her voice to the large armoire-like closet that's stuffed to the brim with medical supplies. She's struggling to carry all the boxes out at once, balancing them precariously in her arms. "Can you—"

"Where's Peter?"

Mama glances at me, a mixture of confusion and strain on her face. Sighing, she puts the boxes down. "Peter? Who are we—"

"The boy from yesterday!"

I don't realize I'm yelling until I see my mama flinch. That's something I'll never forget. Watching my mother back away from me, even if only half a step, because of something I've done. She tries to hide it, but for one moment, there's a flicker of fear on her face. Fear brought to life by *my* actions.

I try my best to swallow down the anger and frustration, but my body won't stop shaking.

"He came in yesterday with Everett. Bloody? Like something ripped into him," I mutter in a hushed, hurried whisper. I'm not sure if I'm talking to her or to myself, saying it over and over so it stays real.

"Douglas," Mama whispers. "Baby, you're scaring me. Are you okay? Do you need . . . ?"

"I don't need a pill or to fucking sleep," I hiss, pulling back as she takes a step forward. "There was a boy here yesterday. You treated him. He was—"

"I only treated one student yesterday, Douglas, and it was a girl," she says slowly. "And I haven't seen Everett for days. He comes by every two weeks for . . . well, you don't need to know the details, but he's not due back until next week."

"Why are you lying to me?"

Mama's face flashes with shock. "Excuse me?"

"I saw him. He was bleeding right here." I point to the bed. "There was blood everywhere!"

I run over to the biohazard bins, turning each of them upside down. Needles, gauze, period pads, and dozens of waste products fall out of each bin, littering the floor. "Where is it? Where is it!"

There have to be bloody bandages somewhere. She couldn't have gotten rid of all of them. There was so much blood. So much.

Mama's arms grip my shoulders, forcing me out of my own mental prison. She turns me to look at her, panic written all over her tearstained face.

"Douglas," she says quietly. "Douglas, please. Let me help you. There was no boy here. Baby, please . . . we can't . . . *you* can't do this again. Do you need to take a few days off? Do you need a lighter load? I'll talk to the headmaster. Whatever you need, I'll do it. But please don't go to that dark place again."

Again? Sure, seeing my mother cry because of me hurts. It tears something apart inside me that I don't know if I'll ever be able to stitch back together. But that single word—*again*—speaks volumes. It's the one thing that stands out.

I rip my body from my mama's grip. "You think I did it, don't you?"

She looks at me, puzzled.

"You said *go to that dark place again*. It's not exact, but that's what the psychiatrist said at my hearing. That my psychosis, my darkness, caused me to set the fire."

I don't want to say it, because saying it aloud will make it real, but Mama has never been able to hide anything from me. She's never tried to lie to me because that's not who we are.

"You really think I did it." It's not a question as much as a statement. "You think I killed those people."

And the look my mama gives me in return? That's all I need to know. Deep down, she really does think I set that fire.

"Doug—"

I quickly put distance between us and walk toward the door. White-hot rage, ice-cold sadness, and electric panic fuel me. My whole body feels warm and frozen at the same time. My mind swims with thoughts. Nothing makes sense. The sound of my mama screaming my name drifts through the background.

People just don't disappear. No one forgets what I saw. What *we* saw.

I push the doors—both doors, because even the sliding door is fixed like it never broke—and rush down the hallway. I ignore the curses from students and sisters I bump into.

There's one person I can talk to.

Everett Everley.

4

Regent Academy's grounds are huge. Like, country-club huge.

Between the dorms, broken up into five different houses, the four academic buildings, two stables, two gyms, and administrative buildings, the campus is about four hundred acres.

It takes me ten minutes to get from the infirmary all the way to the edge of the campus where the Everleys live. The house has a brick facade that matches the same rustic burnt reds that the campus sports, yet it almost looks like it doesn't belong. The earth here is softer under my feet. A broken-yet-respectable fence sets the house apart from the school. There's a vegetable garden on both sides of the walkway, a hastily painted mailbox that looks unused, and a rusted truck under a makeshift tarp, which I sometimes see—and hear—driving around campus.

I swallow nervously, pulling my maroon-and-cream Regent hoodie tight around my body. I don't know why I feel like my stomach has dropped into the soles of my feet. There's nothing to be afraid of. I'm just talking to a fellow student-ish. Regent boys are brave. They take what they want. They know how to be humble but also confident. They make good impressions, and they know how to navigate any social situation. Talking to Everett Everley is the bare minimum.

But it's not the *talking* to Everett that scares me; it's what might happen after. During the walk out of school, down the steep hill, I keep thinking, *What if.* What if Mama is right? What if I made this all up? What if there really wasn't a boy? That means the problem is with me. Means my brain is playing tricks and plotting against me.

It also means that my statement about not starting the fire could be reliant on an untrustworthy memory.

To settle the nerves that make me feel like I'm soaring sky-high, I dry swallow a trazodone. This isn't the first time I've taken pills. My therapist prescribed them after the fire. They helped me sleep, helped my dreams become nothing more than white noise. Maybe they'll help calm me this time too.

I shake my body out when I reach a dingy Welcome mat that's missing the *W* and the *c*. Three deep breaths in. Three deep breaths out. It's just a conversation. Nothing more.

I raise my hand to knock, but before I can, the door swings open.

Everett Everley is a big guy; I always forget that. He easily stands six foot three, and even as a seventeen-year-old, he looks older. He is one of those people who is naturally threatening. He's a solid six inches taller than me, a good twenty or so pounds heavier with muscles, and he naturally doesn't give two f's about anyone.

His shaggy blond hair is unceremoniously cut, like he did it himself, and his angular jaw and broad chest—verging on *gym rat* but staying firmly within the *good genes* area of fitness—makes him even more imposing. He's shirtless when he answers the door, a pair of equally ragged jeans on his body and nothing else.

He studies me, his face showing a flash of recognition. But he doesn't say anything.

"Do you know—"

"What do you want?" he asks, his deep voice cutting through any awkwardness and going straight to the point.

I dig my sneakers into the mat to steel myself.

"I'm here about yesterday."

Another flash flickers across his face, except this time his lips push together in a thin line like my mama's do whenever she's annoyed. And he can only be annoyed if he knows something.

"So, you do remember." I breathe out a sigh. "I wasn't sure if there was something wrong with me or—"

"I don't know what you're talking about. Shouldn't you be in class?"

He turns away from me, and I notice how broad his shoulders really are. Would he have to turn sideways to fit through the door? Maybe. But right now, all that matters is he's trying to put up a wall between us, literally and figuratively. And I can't let that happen.

I place my foot in the gap between the door and the frame before it can close. Searing white pain jolts up my leg, but I don't pull back. Even as Everett's green eyes burn like hellfire.

"Look," I say quickly. "I'm not sure what happened, but I know you know something. I can see it in your face. You remember him, don't you? Of course you do! You carried him. You must have gotten bloody since . . . he . . . he was bleeding so much." I can still smell the hot copper scent. I don't know if it'll ever leave my nose. "I'm not asking you to . . . I dunno, testify or anything."

"Great, cuz I didn't intend to do that anyway," he snaps. "Move your foot."

"I just need your shirt."

Everett raises a brow.

"The one covered in blood? When you came into the infirmary?"

"What is this, some reboot of *CSI*? Move your foot. I won't ask you again."

"Funny. No, I just need some proof to show my mama. To help her remember. Or maybe you caught his name and—"

One second, I'm standing at the door and the next I'm on my back, staring at the grayish sky. There's no pain, just a feeling of wet mud on my back. Everett's body blocks the view of the endless sky as he looks down at me. Barefoot, he squats in the cold mud and leans forward, pressing one hand against my chest to hold me down. But the strength he exhibits pushes me into the dirt, making it feel like my chest is cracking under the pressure.

"Get . . . off . . . of . . . me . . ." I wheeze.

"I'm going to tell you this only once," he warns, his voice a low whisper. "Forget what you saw. Don't talk to anyone unless you want them to think you're crazier than you already are. Yeah, I know your history. And stay. Away. From. Me."

Before I can sit up, I hear the heavy wooden door slam and lock.

There's a part of me that thinks I should demand he open the door. I'm so close to figuring something out. I know it. My fingertips are tingling with anticipation and my heart is racing, though that could be the adrenaline talking. Or the oxygen returning to my lungs.

I stand up, dusting flecks of dirt off myself. The whole backside of my dark slacks is cold and sticky. It's even in my dreads too.

"Seriously?" I groan. I'm going to have to walk through school with mud ass. And mud hair. And mud everything. Great.

I make it halfway up the hill, lost in thoughts of what I'm going to say to Everett to keep this from happening again when I come back tonight, when I hear someone shouting my name. I turn and feel a heavy lump lodge itself in my throat.

Shit.

Coming at a breakneck speed masquerading as fast walking are Kent Hale and his goons.

I brace myself—not for physical impact, but for the general aura of bravado and unearned respect that Kent's existence gives off. He's like a tornado of white privilege and, honestly, I'm half tempted to punch him again. But it seems my first beating did its job.

"Kent." I nod. "How's the eye?"

He's still sporting that bandage on his nose. Both his eyes are black, and his right cheek is a little puffy.

"Shut the hell up, Jones," he snaps as his comrades circle me, effectively boxing me inside. I stand a little taller and tighten my shoulders. If I need to, there's an opening between two of them that I could push through. I can run to school; Kent may be stronger, but I'm faster.

"Look, I know yesterday was not ideal for either of us. But we don't need to do that again. Let's just—"

"Hey," he interrupts. "If I wanted to hear your stupid gay voice, I would have asked you to talk."

"OHHHH!" his friends say in unison, like it was some clever quip. I bet they don't even know how to spell *quip*.

"What were you doing with that freak?" Kent demands. "I saw you coming from his house."

"Why do you care?"

"I don't. Just want to make sure that trash like you and him don't get any ideas."

Trash. So original. "And what type of ideas would trash like me and Everett be getting, hmm?"

"Oh, you're on a first-name basis now?"

"It's literally his name. It's not that hard to remember. Maybe if you didn't take those steroids to overcompensate for—"

I see the stars before I feel the pain of the impact. I stumble, pushing into Kent's two friends, who then push me back into the makeshift circle. Pain erupts from my nose, and I can feel trickles of warm blood dripping down my face.

"That's for yesterday," Kent growls. Another punch, this time to the gut. "That's for always having something smart to say."

My body naturally bends over to clutch my stomach. Kent grabs my shoulder, his knee slamming into the back of my hands, reducing some of the impact.

"That's for always thinking you're better than me. Better than the rest of us when we all know what you are." He leans down, hot breath skimming my ear. "A good-for-nothing faggot who got here just because his mom's useful. Surprised she's in the house, to be honest. She's a bit dark, don't you think?"

I don't care about the pain anymore. Don't care about expulsion or who might see me. I growl out a rallying cry, moving to tackle Kent, but his two years of repping Regent's football and wrestling teams comes in handy. With two easy and surprisingly fluid motions, he spins me around, pins my arms behind my back, and slams me hard enough on the ground that everything falls away into blackness.

5

I don't know how long I'm unconscious, but when I come to, all I
see is darkness.

I know my eyes are open; I feel myself blinking. I feel the cold
ground underneath me, feel the jagged edges of stones pressing
against my skin; how my body has turned to lead, every limb
rusted metal, unable and unwilling to respond to any commands.

Eventually, I force myself to sit up. It's not the back of my head
that hurts but my face. Memories flood back of Kent and his two
friends, blurring together in an indistinguishable pattern. Sounds
of grunts that turn into cries of pains, the loud crisp snapping of
bones, the gurgles of pleas . . . warped begs . . . but who is pleading and begging? And who are they begging to and for what?

I remember, barely, being carried. I remember running to and also from something. Following it deeper . . . deeper into where? Deeper into . . .

"Oh god."

Atolas Forest.

I stand up quickly, pushing through the heaviness of my body. I look around, but there is only darkness as far as the eye can see. I can barely make out my hand in front of me.

"Shit, shit, shit." My chest tightens. Why was I asleep for so long? Why the hell didn't I—

Why are my hands sticky?

My first thought is that caked mud and dirt have made a second layer of skin on my palms, but whatever this is feels thinner and warmer than mud. I try to rub it on my pants, but the stickiness lingers.

I need light. First and foremost, I need to see where I am in the forest. I pat my body down as quickly as possible, searching for my phone. It has to be on me somewhere.

"Come on, come on . . ."

My fingers bump against cool plastic and metal. Perfect. I've seen enough survival movies to know this is usually where the hero drops their phone and loses it. I'm careful with it, clutching the lifeline with both hands like it's the only thing in the world keeping me tethered.

I double-tap the screen with my thumb. Thankfully, it comes to life, still with a healthy amount of battery. The time reads 7:02 p.m.; hours have passed since I visited Everett. At least three, no, five hours. Which doesn't make sense. I couldn't have lost five hours in—

"Time moves differently in the forest," I whisper, reciting the warning one of the students said. I always thought it was a joke . . . that they were leaning too much into the weird. But I still don't know what knocked me out so I could be unconscious for so long.

That should be the top concern in my mind—that I'm lost deep within the forest and have no idea where the past five hours went. But it quickly becomes the least of my concerns when I see the smudge of a thumbprint on my phone screen.

It's a thick maroon red.

Like blood.

I swallow the fear as best I can and tap at my phone, a chain of three clicks, before the light on the back illuminates the space around me. Shakily, I put my right hand in the path of the light—it's covered in more blood than I imagined, dripping globs of it. Same with my left.

I pan the light down, checking my pants, my shoes, my shirt; all of it, covered with blood.

My heart thumps so hard I think I'm going to pass out. I don't feel any pain. I don't feel any wounds, which means it's not my blood. That should make me feel good, but it means the blood came from something . . . someone . . . else.

I scan the area. It's just me, and the forest that always speaks to me—except right now, it's more silent than ever. Almost as if it's not even here, like I'm standing in a gash in time and space that doesn't truly exist.

No. That's not true. There's something else with me. In the

corner, misshapen and hunched over.

I can barely make out its form, but it's not like anything else in the forest. Slowly, with the light pointing directly toward it, I step forward.

It's a person—and not any person but *Kent*, bent over a tree like he's sleeping. The closer I get to him, the more details become clear. His Regent blazer is torn. His pants are ripped at the knees. He's missing a shoe. There's dirt and mud on his face. His cheeks have gashes on them, like a rock cut his flesh.

And his body is riddled with holes. Ten, no, twenty of them. Puncture wounds about two inches in diameter fill his body. And one of them, perfectly centered in his chest, has a pocketknife sticking out of it. A pocketknife with his initials on it.

Before I can stop myself, thick, burning bile erupts from my throat. I'm on my hands and knees, my stomach tightening and body shaking from the intensity of it. Kent's dead. And I did it.

I don't know if that's true, of course, but the evidence is there. I'm alive, covered in blood, with no memory of what happened, and he's not. This is the second time that people have died and I don't remember what happened.

"Oh my god, oh my god, oh my god. Fuck fuck fuck!"

I need to run. That's the first thing that comes to mind, screaming so loudly I can't tell if it's my own voice or the forest. I need to head into town and escape. I don't know how long I can run, but it's something. It's better than staying here. It's . . .

Snap!

Something's here, behind me. Standing quickly, I fumble with my phone, shining the light in the direction of the noise.

"Who's there?"

The figure—now visible as roughly my height—doesn't move.

"I said *who's fucking there*?" I scream, hoping my conviction doesn't ring false. "I swear to GOD if you don't show yourself, I'm going to . . ."

Going to do what? Do what I did to Kent? Something I can't even remember?

I should grab the knife. But if it's another student or a faculty member looking for us, seeing me with the knife in hand will seal my fate. Maybe if I appear innocent, I can plead to them for mercy. Maybe they'll take my side. Maybe . . .

"Douglas?"

I know that voice. The deep rumbling of it, like it's spoken in the pit of his chest, not his throat, can only belong to Everett Everley. When I face him, he's wearing a leather jacket, ripped jeans, boots, and a checkered shirt, with a beanie pulled over his head barely containing his curls. The flashlight he's carrying helps illuminate his features, but even at full brightness, he's still mostly hidden in the black.

I've never been so excited, so terrified, to see a person in my whole life.

"Everett," I breathe out, meeting him halfway. "Everett, you have to help me—"

"Are you okay?" he interrupts, eyes darting up and down, looking me over.

"I'm fine, I—" I look over my shoulder at Kent. "I didn't . . . I don't know . . . Kent is dead . . . I think I killed him. I don't know. I—"

"It's okay," he says, voice hushed and in a hurry. "I know, okay."

"We need to get him help. I dunno if he can be . . . I don't fucking know anything right now, but—"

Wait.

I snap my vision to him and take a step back, rolling my shoulders to pull myself out of his grasp.

"You know what?"

Everett hesitates, but only for a fraction of a second. His eyes flicker to the left and then to the right, like he's watching for something.

"Look, you have to get going, okay?" He points in the direction he came. "I need you to hurry. Keep running straight in that direction. Stay on the path. You'll be able to tell if you're on it by how the earth feels against your feet. If it's rough, you're off it; if it's soft, you're good. Just keep—"

I pull away from him, putting a foot or two between us. "Did you hear what I just said? Did you see what I was showing you?"

"I see it."

"And?"

"There's nothing we can do for him."

The calm finality of his voice leaves no room for interpretation.

"And you're not dead," he adds. "But if you want to stay alive—"

Another snap. The sound of branches being moved aside by something large. The wind howls and dances, pushing deeper into the forest, almost as if it's trying to keep steps ahead of whatever is following it.

Everett visibly tenses. He turns his body to me, gripping my shoulders so tightly I think his nails might dig into my skin.

"I know you don't know me, and you have no reason to trust me, but please, I need you to put your faith in me right now. I need you to find cover, Douglas. Quickly."

"Everett, I—"

"Please," he hisses, "fucking listen to me, Douglas, for your sake and mine, just do this. I promise I'll answer any questions you have."

The desperation in his voice is so heavy it drowns out any other emotion he might be trying to convey. Or maybe that's the only one. Maybe he really is that desperate for me to listen.

I don't know what's true, but I know that at this moment, I'm inclined to believe him.

"Fine," I say. "But the moment we get out of here, you're telling me everything."

"Everything."

I nod and pull back, running past Kent's body. The tree he's leaning against is huge at its base, so wide I can't get my arms around it. It's perfect to hide behind.

I lean my back against the opposite side of where Kent rests, pressing against the tree so hard, it's like I'm trying to topple it over. I pull my knees close to my chest, nestling myself in the grove the overly large roots make. And even though Everett didn't tell me to, I hold my breath. That's not hard, though. A heaviness strangles me, like weights pressed against my chest and throat, making it hard to breathe even unintentionally. Like pressure in the area has increased fivefold.

The howling of the wind kicks up, sounding like a mini hurricane for several seconds before it falls silent as quickly as it came. Large, weighted footsteps replace the wind, so dense that the ground under me pulses. I can tell by the thumps there are four sets of feet—hooves—paws—whatever they may be.

Suddenly, the steps stop. Using the distance between Everett and the tree as a guide, I'm guessing the thing is about seven feet away from me.

"Good evening, Your Emissary," Everett says.

"Good evening, descendant of Everley." The voice sounds both man and woman, both young and old, both wise and innocent.

Except *speaking* isn't the right word. Speaking requires use of vocal cords, enunciation, and diction. This voice . . . it's in my head. Deep within the depths of my mind, almost like how the forest sounds when it talks to me.

"What are you doing within our lands?" it asks.

"I was looking for something."

"Something? Or someone?"

Everett doesn't reply.

"I see foolishness is a trait that passes on through blood."

"I apologize for my stupidity, Your Emissary."

"I care not. There was a death within the forest. A child of the school. I am here for what is due."

"Yes. I know him. He's here."

The thing walks again, its thumps getting closer. It stops

directly in front of the tree, less than three feet from me—I assume to examine Kent's body. I stay as still as possible, so still I'm not sure I'm alive anymore.

"This death was by a mortal tool," the creature says. "Someone delivered this blow. Was it you?"

"It was not, Your Emissary."

"But you know who it was."

It isn't a question, more a statement, as if it knows the answer Everett doesn't say. If the . . . thing can speak in our minds, then can it read our thoughts too? If it does, then that means it knows I killed Kent.

And it also knows I'm here.

"Forgive me, Your Emissary, but I don't see how that matters. My family—"

"Your family is still paying for the sins of your ancestors three centuries ago, son of Everley," the creature booms. Its voice sounds like someone is screaming directly into my ears. "You do not have, nor will you ever have, the position to speak back or question anything I or any other children of the forest ask of you. Do you understand?"

A moment of silence layers the forest, almost as if anything living is holding its breath.

"I understand," Everett quietly says.

"Good. How the boy died doesn't concern us. The conditions of the curse were met; that is all that matters."

The air fills with the sounds of bones cracking and shifting, almost like when someone pops their back, but the popping is tenfold. I hear Kent's body move, hissing as it slides against the dirt, while the creature pulls it into the darkness. The creature's thumps retreat as it puts space between itself and me. Eventually, the creature sounds even farther away from Kent than it was when it arrived.

And then it stops.

"Descendant of Everley, let me remind you that you stink of your ancestors' avarice. The curse placed upon you, their offspring, and yours was a mercy. Do not make us reevaluate our kindness. Your soul will taste just as sweet as any other Winslow resident. Do you understand?"

"I understand, Your Emissary. Thank you."

The wind howls and roars again for only a moment, before it disappears, and the heaviness with it.

I stay still, waiting for that thing to come back. I've seen enough horror movies to know that once I turn, it's going to be looking directly at me, ready to snap my body in half; or carry me deeper into the forest with it.

"You can come out now, Douglas," Everett says.

Invisible shackles around my body loosen and disintegrate. I stand on wobbly legs, rounding the corner. It's the first time I notice there's a warm patch of urine around my crotch.

But the creature is gone. No footprints deepen the earth. Not even Kent's body or the knife remain. Only Everett.

"What just happened?"

Everett doesn't turn around to face me. His body is still, almost statuesque, but with my phone's light, I can see his shoulders slightly rising and falling.

"Everett, what was that? What just happened?"

Still nothing.

"EVERETT!" I yell, grabbing his shoulder. "Fucking turn and—"

Before my brain could process it, he's behind me. His right forearm is wrapped around my throat, his left arm keeping his right arm in place. His grip tightens. I lose my footing. He backs up against the tree, sliding to the ground, bringing me down with him.

It only takes a moment for me to realize he's putting enough force on my throat to cut off my air. I hit his arm, scratch, punch, trying to do anything, but his grip is too strong. The corner of my vision begins to darken, and the sound of his voice is distant.

"I'm sorry," he whispers in my ear. "I know I promised I'd tell you everything, but it won't matter. When you wake up, you won't remember it, anyway."

And then, everything once again goes dark.

6

It feels like I'm falling. Like my soul is being pulled from my body on an express train to . . . somewhere. Every emotion, every feeling, is magnified. And I just want it to stop. But there's one thing that's clear: the sound of the forest.

It speaks to me as clearly as if it's a person sitting across from me in a quiet café. I can't see anything—my mind is still shrouded in darkness—and this time, the voice takes a form and a gender—that of a man—but I know it's my forest. Because despite how terrifying it is to feel like I'm losing my mind each time the forest speaks to me, right now, it's a comfort.

"Wake up, Douglas," the voice says. "This is just the beginning."

I gasp, sitting up so quickly, dizziness takes over. My clothes are drenched in sweat. No longer am I in my bloody Regent blazer; I'm in a pair of sleeping pants and a T-shirt, the same ones that were thrown on my chair the night before.

I look around quickly, scanning my room. It appears exactly how I left it. For a moment, it feels like maybe the forest, Kent's dead body, and everything else was some twisted nightmare that came from over-exhaustion and stress. But the pit in the base of my stomach tells me that's not true.

I pat down my bed wildly until I find my laptop. I type in my Regent login and go to the school roster.

"Hale, Kent," I whisper while typing. "Please pull a result, please pull a result, please . . ."

NO RESULTS FOUND.

"Shit."

Shifting over to Google, I search for Jessica Hale. Her law firm pops up as the first result. Clicking her bio, I scan it quickly.

Jessica Hale is a name partner at Hale, Westwood, and Turner, an international law firm in Washington, DC. She specializes in criminal defense law and has made Hale, Westwood, and Turner's department top three in the nation. A graduate of Harvard, where she majored in political science and history, and Yale Law School, she and her husband—who she met in high school—live in Washington, DC, with their pet dog, Rufus.

No mention of Kent.

I close my laptop slowly, eyes drifting toward the forest. I feel my chest tightening as the memories of his dead body flash in my mind. Kent existed and now he doesn't.

Ever since that thing took him in the forest.

I take a deep, shaky breath. I can't deal with this alone. This is bigger than me, bigger than this school. I need help. I have to tell someone.

My first thought is to tell my mama. She's supposed to be my safe space, my Switzerland. But the conversation we had before I went to see Everett is still a fresh wound on my heart. If I tell her about another student who she doesn't remember, she'll have no choice but to . . . I don't know what she'll do, but I don't want to find out.

My second thought is Everett. Every fiber in my being tells me he's connected to this somehow. What did that thing say? Something about his ancestors' avarice?

The bigger problem is that I don't know anyone in Winslow— at least, no one who would listen to me or care. Someone like me (aka Black) isn't going to go to the cops, if you can call the Winslow Police Department "cops."

And sure, being a Regent Academy student carries some weight, but the school's secrecy is also its downfall. Regent Academy likes that no one knows what happens behind the cast-iron gates; unless they want them to.

Which, in turn, means why would anyone care?

That only leaves one other choice, an option that feels like a mistake, especially since I promised Evelyn I wouldn't. But that was before I saw a dead body and . . . heard that thing. That has to override whatever promise I made, right?

I step out of bed, my legs shaky. While I wait for the shower to get hot, I pull out my phone, go into my email, and call the headmaster's office. The phone rings twice.

"Is Headmaster Monroe free for a meeting?" I ask. "It's urgent. I want . . . I want to tell him about a murder."

"Headmaster Monroe will be with you shortly."

Headmaster Benjamin Monroe's office epitomizes someone who has more money than common sense.

It's like money went to his head, trying to fill the room with everything and anything one could have to give the appearance of being wealthy, but it comes off heavy-handed. Like a sledgehammer of opulence instead of a dusting.

I sit in the uncomfortable leather chair, doing my best to not fidget. Headmaster Monroe's office has a wide window that spans the length of the room, overlooking the grounds. It's almost like he's always watching, always peering down from on high. But more importantly, the room is a perfect vantage point for viewing the forest, and in the distance, I can see Winslow.

The room is quiet. I can hear myself think, even if my mind is racing a thousand miles a minute. Am I happy that the forest is silent? It feels like a god that has forsaken me, decided I'm no longer worthy of its grace.

It makes me feel hollow.

I rub my sweaty palms on my slacks. I'm going to tell him the truth. Everything about the voices and Peter and Kent and what I saw in the forest. Everything. I'm going to let the chips fall where they may, and whatever my fate is—so be it. This is my last, my only, choice now.

The wall behind the headmaster's desk slides open to my surprise, revealing a secret door. Headmaster Monroe briskly walks out, every strand of his black-and-silver hair in place. He looks like the type of man who was handsome when he was younger. Strong face, tall wide-set frame telling anyone who notices he takes care of his body. His eyes have a way of swallowing your soul whole, but also are so lively you swear they're a portal to a world where shadows are sentient.

"Douglas." He nods as I stand. "Please, sit."

I wait for him to sit first. Headmaster Monroe studies me before grabbing the glass decanter on his mahogany desk, pouring me a glass of the yellowish liquid. But that's not what interests me.

Who keeps a human skull in resin on their desk?

"Lemonade?"

My eyes stay focused on the skull, almost like it's a glowing beacon of light in a storm guiding me home.

"It's macabre, isn't it?" he asks, putting the drink in front of me without me confirming I wanted any.

"Is it real?"

"Not at all," he chuckles. "Just an inside family joke. I should probably put it away . . . ," he mumbles.

Headmaster Monroe takes a sip of his lemonade. "My assistant told me you have—and apologies, correct me if I'm wrong—information about a murder?"

I nod, and he arches a brow.

"This conversation is going to be very short and boring if you don't speak, Douglas. You are a student of mine; I know your mother is here with us on campus, but still, you're my responsibility. Anything you tell me, any troubles you're facing, I'm here to help. I promise you that."

I don't trust many people. It's just safer that way. The list ends with one person, my mama, and I'm not even sure I can trust her anymore. But Headmaster Monroe is a close second. Not because I want to trust him or think I can, but the way he speaks . . . it's calming, alluring. It's convincing, even if only for a hair's breadth, that maybe, just maybe I'll be okay. That Regent Academy will protect me. That I'm one of the lucky ones and I should lean in to that.

It also helps that in his office, the voices of the forest are the quietest they've ever been. Almost like the whispers have stopped at the entryway and are afraid to cross over. And for that reason alone, I like the headmaster.

But I remind myself that's not why I'm here.

I take a sip of my lemonade, downing half the glass before the floodgates open. I tell him everything. I go into excruciating detail about Peter, about stabbing and killing Kent. I explain how they were students here, how no one remembers them except me and seemingly Everett.

"Everett Everley?" he asks.

"Yeah, he was in the forest with me."

"And he saw Kent's body?"

I nod. "He saw the thing too."

"The thing you called the . . . what was it?"

"I didn't call it anything, but he called it an Emissary."

"Right." Headmaster Monroe nods slowly. "And he talked to it?"

"I know it sounds—"

"If you were going to say crazy, I would refrain. I'm simply trying to understand and process everything you're saying, Douglas." He pauses for a beat. "And then Everett strangled you and said that you won't remember anyway?"

"Exactly."

"Yet you do, it seems. Remember."

I pause, opening my mouth and then closing it. "I guess I do."

"Any idea why?"

I shrug. "I don't know. The forest . . . it talks to me, Headmaster. At all hours of the day and night. Sometimes loud and sometimes soft. I don't know if I can trust my mind anymore." I hold up the glass of lemonade and say something I've never said out loud before. "I don't know if I can trust *anything* anymore."

"So she was telling the truth," Headmaster Monroe mutters before pressing the intercom button at his desk. "Jenna, are they here?"

"Just arrived, sir."

"Let them in."

"I—what—" My eyes snap to the door, and I'm on my feet before I remember telling my body to stand. Evelyn Everley walks into the room first, then Emma, and finally, Everett. He doesn't look at me directly. In fact, he does everything he can to avoid my gaze.

But that's not what I'm paying attention to. Each of the Everleys has a weapon in hand. Evelyn has a shotgun, Emma has what looks like a braided chained whip with a shoulder bag on her right side, and Everett has a hunter's bow slung over his shoulder.

"Did you kill it?" Headmaster Monroe asks Evelyn.

"Emma delivered the blow."

"So we don't need to sound the alarm?"

"No need."

Emma, taller than Everett with a braid of dirty-blond hair thrown over one shoulder, takes a step forward, putting a cloth bag on the headmaster's desk and opening it. Grabbing the bottom of the bag, she shakes it until the contents drop on the table with a heavy thump.

A head rolls out. But it's not a normal head. It's human-sized, but the left side looks like a bear, while the right side looks like a man. Covering everything from its eyes upward is a masklike crown made of tree bark and bone, extending above the head like antlers. Its mouth isn't where a mouth should be, but offset to the right.

"What the hell is that?" I ask.

"I would like to know too," the headmaster says, grabbing it by its antlers, holding it at eye level, ignoring me. "Did we have just cause to kill it?"

The cut along its neck is clean. Surgical, almost. Looking at the exposed inner flesh, I can see the center bone where the spine should be. Whatever blade was used cut right through it. The flesh that hugged the calcified column is still supple and pink. It hasn't decayed yet. In fact, if I look closely, I think I can see the muscles still retracting, each pulse slower and wider apart than the last.

"I asked it three times if it was an Emissary before slaying it," Emma says. "It didn't respond."

"So, it's a Perversion," the headmaster says, putting the head back on his desk. The blood from the exposed neck wound leaves a pool of copper that stains any papers it touches.

"HEY!" I yell, looking around at all of them. "I asked you a fucking question! What is that?"

I lock eyes with Everett, but he just shifts his gaze back to his family. In fact, no one seems to say anything, completely ignoring me like I'm not even here.

"That's the fourth one this semester," he mutters.

"The second this week," Evelyn interjects.

"The other one killed Peter," Emma adds. "But Everett handled that."

Wait. Did they just say . . .

"Peter's dead?" I interject. "You . . . where is he? Do his parents know? We should call someone."

"No one could have helped," Evelyn whispers. "He was . . . too far gone."

"You mean ripped to shreds."

"She was trying to be nice for your . . . sensibilities," Emma chimes in.

"That's what they do, Douglas," Evelyn says. "They rip and shred and destroy everything in their path. They are poison, to the forest, and to our town. You'll understand . . . in time."

"What do you mean?"

"Now that we got our energies aligned," Headmaster Monroe

mutters, looking over at Emma and Everett. "You two really are following in your mother's footsteps. You should be proud. The grounds are safer with you all here. At least something good came of that petty curse."

No matter what I say, no one seems to pay attention to me. Like right now, my existence is an inconvenience.

So no one stops me as I grab a letter opener from the small coffee table between the two chairs and brandish it at them like a weapon.

Slowly, all eyes turn to me.

"Douglas," Headmaster Monroe says, annoyance in his voice. "Put that down."

"Fuck you," I hiss, voice shaking. "And you three too."

"Want me to knock him out?" Emma asks.

Headmaster Monroe puts his hand up without looking at her, his eyes locked on me. "Didn't you come here for the truth? I know you did. You knew something was wrong and you came here for help. I applaud that. It shows—"

"Shut up!" I yell, turning the blade on him. "I know what you're doing. Trying to keep me occupied while you call the campus police."

"I promise you, I didn't call anyone. Just the Everleys. And they're already here. We're all in this together, Douglas. You might not understand, but we are."

I take a step back, putting some distance between me, the Everleys, and the headmaster. Panic floods my body and makes every sense hyperaware. I look over my shoulder. The balcony to the left is only a two-story jump. Adrenaline might be enough that the impact won't hurt me. I can run if I need to. I don't want to be a part of any of this. Of Perversions and Emissaries and curses. I just want to wake up and be normal.

I just want to go home, go back in time to when none of this mattered. When it was just me, Mama, and Dad. No racist private school. No talking forest. No near criminal record. No dead father. No loneliness. No feeling like I was a burden to everyone around me and would be better off dead and gone.

"I just want peace."

"I know, son, I know," Headmaster Monroe says, snapping me out of my thoughts. "Douglas. I'm sure this is all very scary. I get it."

"There's no fucking way you understand this or anything I'm going through."

Emma snorts. Evelyn elbows her hard, looking at me softly. "He does, Douglas. We all do. Please, just give him a chance to explain."

Headmaster Monroe takes a step forward, his dress shoes making no sound as he steps gingerly. "I can promise you that you're not going crazy. In fact, you're exactly the person the previous headmasters of Regent Academy and I have been looking for over the past two hundred and forty years. And I can prove it to you, if you want."

I see Everett move a fraction of a second before he's behind me, and I try to put some distance between us. But he's disarmed me with a quick three-step move before I can. My right arm is pulled back hard, causing my shoulder socket to burn, as he walks me forward and slams my right cheek against the desk. My vision blurs for a moment, but refocuses when I hear Evelyn speak with a heaviness in her voice.

"I'll grab his arm."

What for, I have no idea, but that doesn't stop me from squirming, to no avail. Evelyn is firm with her grip while I see, from my sideways position, Emma grab the head of the Perversion.

"Everett," Headmaster Monroe says, shifting positions with him, now holding me down with a surprising amount of force. "Will you do the honors?"

I tilt my head enough to see him walk around the side of me, standing next to his sister. He doesn't react, his sullen eyes fixated on me, his jaw tight.

"This is wrong," he finally says in the back of his throat. "Mom, this—"

"If you won't do it," she interrupts, "Emma will."

I can't see Evelyn's face, but her words are sharp. Everett's eyes stay locked on me; I know he sees me mouth *Please* to him.

But still, he reaches down, swiftly pulling a knife from his back pocket. With a cut so quick I don't notice the slice has happened across my hand until I sense the warm, now-familiar feeling of blood against it, I feel the sorrow and pain radiating off him.

That didn't keep him from slicing my hand, though.

"Good," Headmaster Monroe says. "Very good, Everett."

Before the headmaster can finish his sentence, Everett turns on his heels and heads to the door, slamming it behind him before his sister or mother can stop him.

"Leave him," Headmaster Monroe says. "We have a more important task at hand."

Which I'm sure is me. No matter how much I struggle, or whimper from the force of the headmaster's elbow against the nape of my neck, there's no mercy given. Instead, Evelyn grabs the head, laid on its side on the table, by one of its horns, and holds it at my eye level in front of me. Slowly, Emma moves to my arm, grabbing my bloody hand, forcing my palm to open, and presses it against the creature's mouth.

"Ahh, what—" Immediately, I feel something against my palm . . . something like . . . suction.

I look at the head. I'm not sure what I'm expecting to see—but the image that I come face-to-face with makes my mind race. The creature's eyes, rolled back just moments before, look directly at me. Its nose snarls, as if it's breathing heavily while its mouth suckles on my palm, sucking the blood out of it.

Which should be impossible.

I'm frozen in place; not simply because of the forces grabbing me, but because of fear that careens through my body like living ice crawling up my nerves. I can't help but stare at the creature, the hunger in its eyes . . . and the death. It's not alive, I know that; its eyes tell me it's not *really* there. I don't know how to describe it, but it's clearly somewhere in between life and death.

The horror doesn't stop there, though. The voice starts quietly in the back of my head, like a whisper. But with each word it grows louder, until the voice is screaming.

Child of Earth, Truth Speaker thine.

Bound to the forest, wrapped in vine.

A perilous journey lies ahead.

One drenched in blood and bodies shred.

Within Atolas your end awaits.

Past stones and woods that block the gates.

To survive until the moment's end.

Trust yourself and find—

Before the head can finish, the squelching sound of metal meeting flesh fills the air as Emma slices the head in two, moments after her mother drops it. Headmaster Monroe lets go of me, stepping back, but not before speckles of blood stain his suit.

But that's not what's interesting to me. The wound on my hand is gone, like the mouth sucked the laceration away.

"Really, Emma?" He sighs, brushing off his front. "Do you know what this is made out of?"

"Fabric, I'm guessing?"

I'm frozen as Headmaster Monroe debates differences between types of fabric with Emma, still looking at the halves of the head that just moments ago was talking to me. Those words sounded like a nursery rhyme. Like something it had been waiting to say, or had rehearsed multiple times before.

No, Douglas, I think. *It was a prophecy.*

But why did it speak to me? What about me made me special enough? And why did it react with my blood? Would it do that for anyone? And if it would, why wouldn't the headmaster use his own blood, or Everett's, or Emma's, or anyone else's . . .

Headmaster Monroe tilts my head up to look at him, forcing my eyes into focus. He cups both of my cheeks with his soft hands, forcing my gaze to get lost in his endlessly black eyes. He smiles brightly, so widely I feel like the tips of the grin might reach halfway up his face.

"You and I are going to do great things together, Douglas. You and I are going to change the world."

7

My mother had told me you can't trust people who smile too widely.

"It's something about their faces," she'd said, driving back from a meeting with a banker who was going to help us refinance our house.

"Smiling that big takes effort. You gotta break the ligaments in your face. Not literally, of course. But you can tell it's forced. Listen, Douglas, anyone who wants to pray on your weakness like that? Isn't worth your time. Beware of them. They want something."

Even without that advice, I could tell Headmaster Monroe was someone I should keep at arm's length. Sure, he had power, and connections, and money. All of which were like levels of armor that kept him safe and that someone like me could never penetrate. And maybe there was a part of me that envied him. Okay, there was definitely a part of me that envied him.

But that didn't mean I trusted him. Maybe with the information about the death of a student, because that affects the perfectly constructed gilded castle he's created. But with my well-being? No way. He would toss me to the wolves the first chance he got if it meant he could recruit more students or build another wing to Regent Academy.

You can't trust people like that. History reminds us of that. If anyone dug deep and looked beyond that perfect smile, they would find atrocities buried right under the surface. It wouldn't take much to discover them. You'd barely have to scratch under the first layer of pleated Givenchy and Gucci.

That's the one thing I repeat to myself over and over again, so many times that the words worry a groove in between the folds of my brain.

Headmaster Monroe cannot be trusted.

Headmaster Monroe cannot be trusted.

Headmaster Monroe cannot—

"Douglas?"

But I didn't have a choice here when I went to him about Kent. Somehow, without me noticing, Headmaster Monroe has moved to stand next to me and is focusing on wrapping my cut hand with gauze. His touch is gentle, almost like he's sorry for what he just did.

I don't care how fucking sorry he is. If I could get away with it,

I'd punch him in the cheek right then and there.

"Where did you go, son?"

Son. The word flows off his tongue so easily. He thinks it makes us closer; that because my mama came here without a husband, I'm in need of some father figure to help guide me. He wouldn't be the first person to think that maybe Douglas Jones wouldn't have ended up on the path he's on if he just had a strong father figure in his life.

People aren't as good at whispering as they think they are.

"Nowhere," I say. "Are you going to tell me what just happened?"

My eyes flicker to Emma, settling on her for a moment longer than is probably socially acceptable. She's younger than me and Everett, a sophomore at Regent, but she carries herself as if she was Everett's older sister. She wields her confidence as expertly as whatever blade she used to separate this creature's head from its neck.

"Why aren't any of you freaking out? A severed head just talked to us. Through our minds. After you put my blood to it and it drank it. Does that not seem freaking weird to you?"

That was the thing, though. None of them found this odd. Sure, their eyes darted uneasily between each other, as if settling on one person's gaze for too long might give something away, but no one was freaking out. Not like me.

"Okay, let's try this again, then. You called it an Emissary before," I say, doing my best to steel my breath while looking at everyone in the room, and at the same time, no one. "But now you're calling it a Perversion?"

Keep asking questions, I tell myself. *You'll find your way out of this soon enough.*

"That's right." Headmaster Monroe nods. His sharp black eyes never leave me.

"Which means there's a difference between that thing and what I saw before."

I look to Evelyn. I've always trusted women more, and I think the same is true vice versa. Maybe it's because it's been me and my mama for so long. Maybe in some strange biological way, it has something to do with me being gay. I don't know, but when it comes to people I trust—and people in power—I'm more likely to feel my shoulders relax half an inch when it's a woman.

But Evelyn's eyes dart to Headmaster Monroe's and stay for a fraction of a moment before looking back at me. She's dressed in a near-perfect blueprint of Everett and Emma: boots, a flannel shirt, and old worn jeans. She has the dirty-blond braid of her daughter but the height and firm body of her son.

"Go ahead, Evelyn," Headmaster Monroe says from behind me. "He deserves to know."

"It's not going to make sense to him."

"A severed head just spoke in my mind. I think we're a little past that."

Emma snorts lowly, dipping her head down to avoid her mother's glare.

"Very well," Evelyn mutters. "An Emissary is what you and Everett saw last night. They are representatives of the forest.

Think of them like ambassadors, and the forest like an embassy. Whatever is needed, whatever sacrifices have to be made, they do it to protect the forest."

"But why?" I ask. "These things don't exist in every forest."

"You haven't learned by now that there's something . . . special about Atolas?"

Special. What a word choice; she really means something dark and twisted. Something horrific and demonic. But sure, let's go with special.

"Where do they come from? These . . . Emissaries?"

"Like everything else, the forest," she says, nodding to the split-in-half one. "You see those mushrooms on it? The bark? The flowers budding? The Emissaries are as much the forest as the jagged rocks or the looming trees."

"Again, you need to see more forests across the country if you believe that."

"Again, you need to change your perception about what is and is not possible," Emma interjects. "Atolas isn't like any other forest. You know that by now. Or at least, you should. If you want to understand, you need to accept that none of the rules out there in your world apply here. This forest is its own reality."

"You speak like it has a mind of its own."

"Don't all living things?"

Her words sting because she's right. Not about Atolas. Emma seems to speak like the bending of logic and physics is normal and something I should just accept. And maybe I should. But when you've gone for the past twenty months thinking your mind is breaking, and everyone around you doesn't believe you, hearing that *maybe* sometimes things really aren't what they seem doesn't feel comforting.

It feels like I'm more unstable than I ever thought I was.

"Okay, I follow," I say tentatively. "You mentioned something else, a Perversion?"

"That's right." Evelyn chimes in, "It is exactly what the name suggests. A twist on an Emissary."

"Like a corpse that's begun to rot and the rot has gone to its head," Headmaster Monroe mutters, swirling his drink, a glass of brandy he poured from the drink cart in the counter.

"And what role do they play? Are they like . . . the SWAT team of the forest?"

"Absolutely not," Emma says with a sharpness in her voice.

"What my daughter is trying to say is we do not respect Perversions. At all. We try and excise them as quickly as possible. We can't let them get on the grounds. Headmaster Monroe called them a rot, and that's an apt description. But it's a rot that drags everything into its core. Every living thing is easy prey, food, or something to add to its collection, to become part of the rot to strengthen it."

"Even people?"

"Even people."

Before Evelyn can say anything more, Headmaster Monroe rings a small cast-iron bell on his desk. Moments later, his assistant—Jenna—a small woman whose twins are freshmen at Regent, hurries in with an expertly balanced tray, places it on the desk, nods, and hurries out.

"Ask the next logical question, Douglas," the headmaster says while tending to the steaming porcelain teapot. He places the spherical stainless-steel tea strainers in the different cups that match the teapot, slowly pouring the water over the orbs in a circular, clockwise motion three times, until tea fills the cups. "You've already started down this road. Why stop now?"

He's goading me, I think. *Testing me, even. How smart really is Douglas Jones?*

"What does this have to do with me?"

Headmaster Monroe smiles. "Now you're learning."

One by one, he removes the strainers from the cups, placing them on a cloth napkin with the Regent Academy logo on it. He hands each one of us a cup—saucer included, because of course—before taking one himself.

"To new beginnings," he says.

"To new beginnings," Evelyn and Emma repeat.

Once I see both Headmaster Monroe and the others take a sip, I follow. It's not that I think the headmaster would poison me, but seeing them drink first gives me a small semblance of comfort.

The tea tastes earthy, like how a Christmas candle smells, but with traces of honey and natural sweetness, and undertones of something that resembles the floral tastes of grass.

"To answer your question, Douglas, I need to ask you a question in return," he says. "How much do you know about Winslow?"

"I know it's in Vermont."

Emma snorts into her cup. "I like him."

I ignore her and continue. "I know we're about an hour and a half northeast of Montpelier."

"But nothing about its history?" he asks.

"Never made it into my top five priorities. And Mrs. Hale didn't offer a history lesson when she gave me this opportunity."

Headmaster Monroe nods and sets his cup down quietly. He glides across the room to a bookshelf that takes up the full wall, floor to ceiling. Stepping up onto the third rung of the matching mahogany ladder, he pulls a tome from the middle of the shelf.

"My great-great-great-great-grandfather wrote this," he says, placing the book on the desk. "It's the only copy. A list of diary entries, one for every day, ever since people arrived in Vermont more than three centuries ago."

"Does it include how when the Dutch got here, they killed the Abenaki tribe?" I ask without missing a beat. "Or did your great-great-great-great-grandfather leave that out because it didn't make an interesting enough story?"

Headmaster Monroe doesn't let his face betray him, but the corner of his right cheek does twitch for a fraction of a second before returning to neutral.

"Vermont might have been the fourteenth state to enter the union, but there were thriving colonies here before it was unified with the rest of the country. Everyone has heard of Fort Sainte Anne on Isle La Motte, the first colony, but few people know of Winslow.

"Rumor has it, Winslow is special. It resides on the intersection of two ley lines, which is why the area is so unusual. I'm sure you've noticed it. Cell phone service sporadically disappears. And a lush forest that seems never-ending, close to what used to be thriving coal and gold mines? These two things don't normally exist in unison."

Headmaster Monroe opens the book to a specific page without even looking, and holds it out to me. Each page is filled with illustrations of normal things you'd see, like townspeople going about their day, scenes of women churning butter, men helping to erect houses, churches, schools. There's even a full-page spread of some sort of successful hunt.

But in each drawing, there's something . . . off. One figure in particular—a man shrouded mostly in darkness with what looks like an antler skull for a head.

"What is that?" I ask, tapping it.

"Ley lines don't just attract weirdness and oddities, Douglas," Headmaster Monroe says slowly. "They attract those things hungry for power that we humans cannot fathom, control, or harness. They, at their strongest intersections, attract and give birth to gods. That is exactly what you're looking at.

"Rumors, and my great-great-great-great-grandfather's words, say that a god named Etaliein lives among the people in Winslow. He helped shroud them from prying eyes, which is why people never knew Winslow existed until much later. He helped them with irrigation, taught them how to effectively and efficiently hunt. He was curious about humanity, was fond of them, and yearned to protect them. And somewhere along the way, he fell for a mortal girl. The daughter of a simple carpenter.

"At first, the people were overjoyed with the matrimony between god and human. But, like most human things and much like the Emissaries in the forest, emotions soiled and curdled. Accusations were thrown. Out of all the ladies in the town, why had Etaliein fallen for a girl of no name, no stature, and no title? Surely, she had bewitched him. And why would she have done that? There was only one logical explanation—to harness the power of Etaliein for herself."

Headmaster Monroe closes the book slowly. "Humans, since the dawn of time, have always wanted more of everything. More power. More land. More control. More love. The residents couldn't imagine that perhaps there was nothing nefarious about the love between Etaliein and a mortal. That it was the purest and simplest thing of all: true love. But they wouldn't let that stand.

"So one night, when Etaliein—a naive creature who still believed and trusted in humanity—was helping the men on a late-night hunt deep within the forest, the townspeople kidnapped the girl from her bed. Beat her, tied her to a stake, and burned her alive.

"Etaliein heard her screams of anguish, her pleas for mercy, and rushed back to his love, but it was too late. When he arrived, she was on her last breath. Supposedly, rumor has it, another god, shrouded in blackness with a nondescript mask, appeared at the same time he did, leaning over her with dark wings beginning to wrap around her in an embrace."

"A god of death," Douglas says.

Headmaster Monroe nods. "One would think. Again, this is all conjecture and the interpretations of the ramblings of an old man, but there is enough concrete evidence for me to believe what he saw was fact. That the girl was too far gone for her god to save, and so, in an explosion of agony, of grief, of sorrow and magic, Etaliein spirited her away, deep within the forest."

The headmaster pauses and stares out the window at the forest. He clears his throat. "That is the last the people of Winslow saw of the girl, or of Etaliein. But that evening, around eleven p.m., everyone fell into a deep slumber where they stood."

"The Witching Hour," I say.

He nods. "Everyone who awoke, moments later, had the same dream. Etaliein was there, with nothing else but endless white surrounding them, and he said three things. The town of Winslow, due to its ignorance and hatred, was now cursed. Anyone who died within all of Winslow proper would be forgotten. The descendants of the five families who led the witch hunt against his lover could never leave the town. And everyone who stayed too long within the town of Winslow would suffer different ailments— some small, some large. Some people get sick. Some people have nightmares every night. Some bad luck. The town curses every-one differently, descendants and residents alike."

"And you believe him?" I ask. "This . . ."

"Wives' tale? Lie? Melodrama?" The headmaster nods. "You've seen what happens to those who die, Douglas. Peter, correct? That was his name? No one remembers him. Kent either. Except me."

"Except us," Evelyn adds.

"And me," I finish. "I remember them."

"And there lies the conundrum we're facing. No one has come to our school, not been related to one of the original five descending families, and been able to remember the dead. And if you *were* related, before you ask, there's no way you could have crossed the town line. Which makes you an anomaly."

Headmaster Monroe walks around the desk, leaning against the wood, placing the half-drunk tea on the table. "You do see why this is interesting, Douglas? When Evelyn told me you could hear the forest—"

"Wait," I interrupt, turning to Evelyn. "You . . . that's what he meant before pressing the intercom. You told him about me. That's why he wasn't surprised."

Evelyn doesn't show a flicker of remorse, but she does stand up a bit straighter.

"I had to, Douglas. This is bigger than you or me. This is about the future."

"You can't be serious."

"Oh, but Ms. Everley *is* serious. We believe you might have the power to break this curse, Douglas. Do you not see how important—how unique—that is? What an opportunity has come our way. It is our duty to secure it."

"You know, people throw that word *duty* around whenever they want to convince people that their way of thinking is more important."

I know where this is headed. Headmaster Monroe is going to make a deal with me. I do what he wants—somehow, I help him break this curse—and he'll give me anything I want. Which means, at least on the surface, the power is now in my own hands. I can set the terms of this agreement. Assuming I want to help him. Assuming I *can* help him.

But what is it going to cost me?

"I . . ."

I open my mouth to try to test the waters, to see how movable and open to negotiation he really is, but nothing comes out. My mouth is dry, and even attempting to speak hurts. The blur starts at the corners of my eyes, like someone is dropping pure ink directly onto my cornea. When did that start to happen? Why didn't I notice it before?

"I . . ."

Stumbling backward, I feel a tingle in the tips of my fingers and toes, crawling quickly up my nerves. In the span of a single inhale, my forearms feel numb; then my calves, causing me to lose my balance. I brace for the impact, but I feel something catch me right before I hit the ground. Something firm, but far softer than wood. Looking up, I see Evelyn looking down at me upside down, my head cradled in her arms, holding me carefully while she lowers herself to the ground.

"I got you," Evelyn whispers, so quietly I think only I can hear. The soft features of her face are the last thing I see as everything goes black. "You're okay, I promise."

But her voice isn't the last thing I hear. The distinctive footsteps of Headmaster Monroe's wing-tip shoes fill the air. He stops right next to me. I hear the rustle of his expensive suit as he leans down, smell the woodsy scent of tea on his breath as his lips move next to my ear.

"You seem like a man who makes choices based on logic, Douglas. Proof, conjecture, and knowledge are your guiding principles, while others believe in faith, their heart, and a higher power. Allow me to appeal to your logical intuitions. We'll talk more when you wake."

He leans down as he whispers.

"Say hello for me, will you, Douglas? And tell them we'll see each other very soon."

8

The first thing I feel when I wake up is cool metal against my cheek.

I don't open my eyes at first. Instead, I lie there, getting my bearings. I've seen that in TV shows I binged when I couldn't sleep, especially *Alias*; people playing possum in hopes they can get some secret information. If I'm quiet enough, Headmaster Monroe and the Everleys will let something slip.

But the longer I lie there, the more the pieces start clicking into place. There wasn't metal in the headmaster's office, only polished, expensive wood. The air smells different too. Too metallic. Too sharp, like eggs . . . no, like urine.

I know that smell. I'll never forget that smell.

I sit up quickly with a gasp. Sharp pain rockets from my wrists up my arms, the pain of my body being stretched past its limits. I don't need to look down to know what caused it, but I do anyway, partially because I can't believe it.

There are cuffs on my hands.

I look around but know what I'll see. The two-way mirror to my left. The sterile gray walls to my right, and the door with the small blacked-out window in front of me. The interrogation room at the police precinct when I was arrested after the fire.

I'm back home.

Emotions I can't describe swell inside me, like a bubble threatening to explode. Home. The town I grew up in and call my own, not Regent Academy. Sure, there are . . . so many bad things that happened here, horrible things. But this is where I thought I'd spend my life. The good and the bad are here. Even if right now there is worse than good.

I look down and see the same worn T-shirt and sweats I was wearing when I went to bed that night. Black Adidas slides cover my ankle sock–covered feet. No stiff-feeling uniform. Maybe Regent Academy was the dream.

Some psychotic shattering of my mind to help me process what happened with the fire. I mean, that would make sense, wouldn't it? Nothing about Regent made sense. A school I had never heard of. A curse that only I could break? Monsters? It all seemed like a bad twisted fairy tale from the start. Something I made up to disassociate myself from the life I was living and the horrors I witnessed.

I can't just escape my reality and fold myself into my mind. I have to face it.

"That's a very human thought, Douglas."

I didn't notice the door in front of me open, but the voice pulls my focus to it. I can't make out the full form at first, his body shrouded in the darkness of the hallway. But as my eyes adjust, slowly, he steps out.

No, I'm not sure *he* is the right word. It makes him sound too human. And he's definitely not that. Well, at first, he looks completely human. A little taller than me, thin, dressed in nondescript pants and a shirt that wouldn't cause me to give him more than a half glance if we passed each other on the sidewalk.

But that's where any similarities to a human stop.

A bit of revealed flesh—thanks to this short-sleeved shirt he's wearing—bulges grotesquely with swollen, green veins under the skin. The veins pulse and throb with each heartbeat.

And that's not even the most horrifying thing. It's his face. From his shoulders up to his neck, he looks normal, sans the green veins. But his face is something from a Keith Thompson painting. The right side looks normal, almost handsome, but the left looks like his DNA was fused with a rose. His flesh and bone—the fragments that jut out of the skin—are in the shape of rose petals, intricately laid out in the centrifugal swirling style of the flower. His left eye is far from where it should be—it's where his *ear* should be. His lips stretch like someone made them from Silly Putty and wrapped them around the lower half of his face.

Something about him reminds me of the other Emissary in the forest, but more human. It's horrifying. Because it confirms that Regent Academy wasn't a dream.

I take a deep, slow gulp as the man stops in front of the metal table that separates us. He doesn't move. He doesn't lash out. He simply studies me as I study him. Methodically, he pulls the chair out and sits down, clasping his hands in front of him; prim and proper, like he's been taught how to greet a human.

"I'm not asleep, am I?" I finally say.

"What do you think?"

Words leave my mouth before I can pull them back: "You know, for once, I'd like people to give me a direct answer. Everyone is speaking in half-truths and omissions, as if to get the full picture, I have to beat the next level or some shit. I want the truth. Is that too much to ask for?"

My voice ends louder than it started. Anger, which was fear before, molds back into terror.

"I'm sorry."

"You have no reason to be sorry. I imagine a lot has been thrown at you in the last several hours. It's only reasonable you are frustrated and want answers."

"I don't simply want answers," I argue. "I want to be treated like a person."

"Now, that is a harder request. You of all people should know that." He leans forward, his voice dropping to a whisper.

"Tell me, Douglas, truly, when has a person like you been treated like a person in a world like this?"

Before I can counter his statement—I have no idea what I would say to that anyway—the man leans back and speaks again. "I apologize if this isn't the place you would have picked for our conversation. I didn't have much time, and this was your strongest memory."

"It's because it's when my life changed completely. When *this* whole 'adventure' all started."

"I would argue that this is one of the moments your life changed. A moment you decided to go left instead of right. People tend to have many moments like that."

"Did you have one?" I ask. "That made you . . . look like . . ." I nod to him, not able to bring myself to say it. "Who are you anyway?"

The man-thing lets out a humming sound in the back of his throat, as if he's trying to decide if he wants to answer me.

"Are you like that thing I saw in the forest?"

"In a way," he says slowly. "But I'm also you and I'm also me."
Fucking riddles, I think.

"How about you answer something else, then. Directly this time. My body is still in the office, isn't it? The headmaster drugged me?"

He nods. "Tea made from the root of the plants that have been steeped in the magic of the forest since before you were born. For a man who hates the forest so much, he isn't above using it to his advantage."

"The headmaster and the Everleys drank that tea too," I counter. "Are they here?"

"Descendants of the original families are immune to the effects of the forest. It's why they remember the dead and others don't. That includes your precious headmaster and your groundskeeper friend."

Just another way the headmaster has power that the rest of us don't have.

"But I remember the dead too. Shouldn't I be immune?"

"Magic is not a fixed rule, Douglas. It doesn't subscribe to logic like other earthly sciences. The forest requested your presence, and it gave you passage here, to an in-between space where many have come before you."

"Many?" I ask. "Wait, what—"

"What did Headmaster Monroe tell you, Douglas?" the man asks, unfazed and ignoring my question. "About the forest?"

He's not going to answer my questions, I think.

But that doesn't mean I can't get what I need from him either.

"Not much. He was more focused on how I may be able to break the curse put on Winslow."

"That may very well be true," he says. "But did he tell you why he wants the curse broken?"

"It's a curse. Who wouldn't want it broken?"

The man chuckles under his breath. "Fair enough. Do you mind if I give you a piece of advice?"

"You, or the forest?" I ask. "You said the forest wanted me here, which I guess I can understand. But then you decided to bring me back to this place"—I gesture—"where everything went to hell."

"This is where your life changed," the man says intentionally. "When the choice you made set everything into motion."

"You make it sound like I'm special."

"Oh, you are, Douglas. You so very are. You may think you're simply a product of other people's choices, but you have been an active participant since the beginning. You could have said no when Jessica Hale gave you the option of coming to Regent."

"No one would turn down that opportunity. I was going to be tried for a crime I didn't commit."

"You could have fought it."

"I wouldn't have won."

"So, you decided to fight a unique way."

"I decided to run."

The words leave my mouth before I can stop them, but it's the truth. "I took the easy option. I decided that fleeing and hiding in the walls of this school was easier and safer than dealing with whatever was to come."

"You found a way to survive," the creature says gently. "That is a display of strength. You could have simply given in, given up, even, but you found a way to fight back. You're stronger than you think, Douglas. You're better than me."

That simple expression, a small sliver of light that breaks through this creature's facade is all I need to understand him a bit more.

"You died here, didn't you? Not just in the town, but in the actual forest."

The rose-faced man doesn't respond. That's all the answer I need.

"Do you remember it? Your death?"

He shakes his head. "I do not. Not in full. I know it was . . . more than one hundred years ago, then," he says, a hint of surprise in his voice. "Time, Douglas, doesn't work the same in the forest—for those living or those who belong to it. We could stay in this room, in this moment, for days, weeks even, and only a few hours will pass in the real world. Or we could stay here for a minute and two years could pass. We all serve at the pleasure of Atolas, Douglas, even those of us who pretend to not."

I don't know anything about this man—if he deserved whatever death he got, if he brought it upon himself, or anything, but I can't help but feel sorry for him. Trapped in what I can only assume is some hellscape where he can only talk to people through their memories. That's no way to live.

"A word of advice, Douglas, if you intend to go down this path," he says. "Trust no one. Not Headmaster Monroe, not the Everleys—"

"Not even the forest?"

"Especially not the forest. Everyone wants you to accomplish what they have been unable to do because you might just have the power to do so. But just because you can, doesn't mean you should. The door you open by going down that path cannot be closed. Are you sure that is something you want to do?"

"No," I say without hesitation. "I'm not. But I can't go back to Regent Academy knowing what I know now, pretending that I don't know it. People are dying. People have died. Their families aren't given the chance to mourn. The Monroes and Everleys . . ."

"I will say this again, you owe them nothing. This is *their* penance for their own choices . . ."

"For killing that girl three hundred years ago, I know. But

Everett and his sister? His mother? They didn't do that. It's not right to punish—"

"That's what the headmaster told you?" the man asks. "And you believed him?"

Before I can answer, the forest bursts to life with voices. It's the opposite of what I heard when I first got here. Soft, docile whispers morph into sharp, continuous screams. It's like ten thousand people are all yelling at once, at the highest decibel possible, directly in my mind.

"Are you telling me he lied?"

"I'm telling you, once again, to not trust anyone and what they say."

"Then that includes you."

"It absolutely includes me."

Blurred dark faces pass by the window and door. Memories, I can only assume, of my past, pieces my brain and the magic that makes up this place are trying to blend to make it feel more real.

"I'm sick and tired of this," I whisper.

"Pardon?"

"This." I gesture, tugging at my wrists. "I'm tired of always being on the defensive. Tired of never knowing who or what I can trust. Tired of being the one who must react instead of being the one who has to be reacted to."

"You want to be in control."

"I want to be my own person," I admit. "I don't want to be that poor Black boy, or that kid who killed those people, or that scholarship student, or that savior or whatever people think of me. I want to be myself. I want to be Douglas, in control of my own life. Fuck everyone else and everything else."

"Then do it," the man says directly. "What is to stop you, Douglas? Are you afraid you're not brave enough? Not strong enough? I'll let you in on a secret: No one who has ever been strong enough ever thought they were. It's what you do when the opportunity presents itself.

"So, what are you going to do, Douglas Jones? Let other people decide and define your destiny, or take the chance, even if you fail, and attempt to do it yourself?"

For some reason, in that moment, I think back to when Mrs. Hale approached me in Washington, DC, giving me the opportunity to attend Regent Academy. She acted like I was lucky to be selected. That something about me was special, and that Headmaster Monroe saw something in me that no one else did.

That's true. But it's more likely that I never had a choice.

I look down at my wrists, at the bonds of metal that dig into my skin. I will no longer be defensive—I will go on the offense. I feel a warm tingle that starts in the tips of my fingers and moves up my arms, like soothing electricity careening up my body. As it spreads over me, I know exactly what it is: power. Power like I've never felt before. And only one word comes to mind.

"Rust."

I don't speak the words, but I *roar* them with every fiber of my being. My bones shudder. My blood boils. My muscles tighten and release. Every inch of me is behind those words.

In front of my eyes, the metal handcuffs begins to dissolve, hissing as they turn into a pile of silver sand. The man in front of me grins brightly, leaning back in his chair, crossing his arms over his chest.

I flex my hands, squeezing them once, twice, three times. The soreness of the bindings is still there, even leaving indented red rings. But the cuffs are gone; just a pile of dust on the counter.

Like they rusted thanks to a thousand years happening in a matter of seconds.

"What did I do?"

"That right there?" he says, even though with each word his voice becomes more and more distanced. "Is the power of someone taking their own destiny in their hands, someone who has decided to make a choice instead of letting choices be made for them. That is magic, Douglas. Magic to be able to create and destroy all things that come from the earth and are born from it. The same magic that set the wheels in motion for everyone in this town, including you, more than three centuries ago. Consider it a tool to help you . . . even the playing field against what you're going to have to face.

"Win, lose, or draw, Douglas Jones, the road ahead of you is going to be challenging, and you're going to need every tool you can get to survive."

"You can't just . . . I dunno, make it happen?"

The being shakes his head. "This is your journey, Douglas. No one else can end it for you. A journey that started with that fire that night, which has led you here—"

I snap up, my attention focusing on the thing in front of me, even as my vision begins to blur at the corners and turn dark. "What do you know about that?"

My fingertips and toes tingle, the feeling of numbness rocketing up my spine and electrical highways that course through my body. It's hard to focus, even harder to think. But the being's voice rings clear.

"I wish you the best of luck, Douglas Jones. We're all rooting for you."

Before I can ask who, I'm staring upward at the mahogany ceiling of Headmaster Monroe's office, the Everleys arguing to the left of me.

"He's been under for too long, Benjamin," Evelyn says. "We need to take him to his mother."

"And tell her what? Her son took a hallucinogenic drug we gave to him? Two hours ago? How does that end for any of us?"

The arguing continues, but Emma glances over at me. She arches one brow, walks over, and squats, placing the back of her right hand over my forehead.

"You okay?" she asks.

I nod as Emma helps me to a sitting position.

"I'll do it," Douglas says.

"That's not the point, Benjamin, and you know it."

"The point is we—"

"HEY!" I yell. Both Evelyn and the headmaster snap their gazes to me.

"I'll do it. I'll break your curse."

But not for you, I think. There is something horrifically

dangerous going on at Regent Academy, and I'm going to find out why. For once in my life, I'm going to take control of my own destiny—right or wrong, smart or stupid, I'm making a choice and diving into it headfirst.

No matter what becomes of it.

PART
TWO

PART
TWO

9

Headmaster Monroe is very clear about my responsibilities at Regent Academy as he knocks on my door at six a.m. the next morning. I hastily throw on a hoodie and sweatpants and let him in.

"From this point forward, your sole responsibility is breaking the curse," he says, entering the room. "Every resource we have at our school is available to you, without question."

"What about my classes?" I ask.

His fingers dance over my desk, pausing to pick up a photo.

"Don't touch that." I flex my fist.

Headmaster Monroe glances over at me, for only a moment, but does put the photo of Dad, Mama, and me down, even if his eyes, never blinking, never moving, warn me silently what would happen if I commanded anything from him again.

"Every professor has been told, directly from me, that their class is not your priority for the remainder of the semester and will accommodate your needs. You'll receive an A or a B on all your materials while you're working on breaking the curse, no questions asked."

That, I don't agree with, and the furrow of my brow must convey my emotion. It's too early in the morning for me to be sly and cunning.

"Do you disagree that breaking the curse *isn't* more important than calculus?"

"Obviously, I think the curse is important."

"I'm glad we can agree. Because I would imagine that if I was in your shoes, I'd be inclined to believe that finding a way to prevent hundreds, if not thousands, from losing the memories of their loved ones, seems to trump, in my mind, world history."

"And also allowing you to leave the town," I remind him. "That's important to you also, isn't it?"

Headmaster Monroe's eyes are focused on my textbooks as he uses the tip of his right index finger to flip through them. He glances over at me without moving his head, his sharp dark black eyes as focused as ever.

"Of course I won't deny that I have a personal investment in this curse," he admits. "More personal than you know. But my first and foremost desire is to fix what has been broken. This curse has gone on long enough, don't you agree? Don't you think those who should be punished for their indiscretions are long dead?"

Once again, my face silently gives away my thoughts on that matter.

"Exactly. We finally have a chance to do that. You and I, Douglas."

Headmaster Monroe bridges the space between us and, without asking permission, combs his fingers through my black coils of hair. He must think it's some sort of paternal action. Like he's a surrogate father or something.

I don't need a father; not another one. My father, Harold Jones, is dead. But that doesn't mean he isn't still my dad.

I ground myself by clenching and unclenching my fists by my side.

"We have a chance to change the world, Douglas. That's what every student comes here to do. To be given the tools to make their mark. A lucky few will do that by the time they die. But you, my boy, will be able to do that at seventeen years old. How marvelous for you." His hand drops to his side, and he slips both hands into his maroon peacoat. "But I'm not unreasonable. I do understand you came to Regent for a world-class education."

"That's what Mrs. Hale promised me, yeah."

"What if I could do you one better?"

I can't help but admit that snatches my attention. What could Headmaster Monroe possibly be offering that's *more* than what Regent Academy can give me through their carefully chosen faculty members?

"I was actually excited for Regent Academy's curriculum."

That's not a lie. When reading over the folder Mrs. Hale gave me, I was excited that any class I could possibly think of could be taken as an elective. That, besides the core classes, students graduated with a makeshift major of their own creation. Sure, as a transfer student I wasn't given that opportunity—you had to start freshman year to get that—but there were more than three dozen preset majors I could select from. I had narrowed it down to three.

"We do have a first-class curriculum that I'm very proud of. But—I'm going to let you in on a little secret—did you know that education, though of course valuable, is just a tool? A skeleton key, if you want to be exact. It opens doors that are impossible through any other means. I'm offering you the most perfect of skeleton keys.

"If you break the curse, Douglas, I can promise that not only will you graduate top of the class, but every single opportunity awarded to Regent students will be yours, without question. You want to get into Yale and attend Yale Law? I'm close friends with the dean of the undergraduate program and the law school; he was in my class here. You can expect a full ride to both. You want to be a resident at a top neuroscience program? Simply email me the name and it'll be yours by the end of day. You want to be senator or governor of any state? I can make that happen, no political experience or endorsements required."

"And my mama," I add. "I want something for her too."

"Whatever she wants," Headmaster Monroe promises. "I'll even handle any questions she has about you not attending classes. . . . Consider that me showing how invested I am in this partnership of ours succeeding."

Headmaster Monroe walks over to my door and pauses, turning to face me with a three-quarter view.

"Those who help Regent are rewarded handsomely, Douglas. Think about that when deciding what your priorities are."

He leaves me in silence. I turn toward the large window that overlooks campus, pulling the makeshift curtain back, which is really just a towel with some tacks in the window.

Atolas Forest stretches before me, just as expansive as always, so big that with the signature morning fog, it's impossible to see the mountains or the valleys or Winslow in the distance. But right now, the forest is just a forest; a collection of trees and rocks, animals and dirt. Nothing haunting. Nothing sinister. Nothing magical.

And that silence, like it's hiding something, waiting for something to move first, scares me more than any Perversion or Emissary or curse ever could.

With class no longer a priority, there's only one place I can think to spend my time: the Kathleen Singer Library . . . once it opens in three hours.

Kathleen Singer was part of the inaugural class of women allowed to attend Regent Academy nearly seventy years ago. She was smart, quick-witted, and destined for greatness. One of the smartest students who attended Regent Academy, some would say. No, *most* would say.

At least, those who remember her.

If you ask anyone who Kathleen Singer is, students and fellow faculty members will just say it was a clever name selected because it seemed like the type of name you should give a library. No one remembers that Kathleen was a student who was consumed by the forest.

No one, of course, besides Headmaster Monroe, me, and the librarian, the headmaster's aunt.

Shifting the weight of my backpack on my shoulder, I push open the heavy mahogany door.

The library is huge. Three levels, with rings like Saturn allowing access to each ascending level of literature. The library is circular, split into quarters, with two ladders attached to the shelves on each quarter section.

The computers, microfiches, and circulation desk are on the ground floor as soon as you enter. Ms. Regent barely glances up at me, strands of silver hair cut in a fashionable bob that makes her look younger than the seventy or so years old I believe she is.

"Hi," I whisper. I've always liked libraries; I feel safest here among tomes of knowledge, bursting with excitement, ready for their secrets to be unearthed by the right, diligent person. I'm almost glad Headmaster Monroe gave me permission to skip classes. If I could spend my whole time at Regent Academy teaching myself what needed to be taught and living in the library, only leaving to eat, sleep, and take my tests at the end of the semester, I'd be happy.

Maybe I *can* do this.

"Headmaster Monroe—"

"I know what my nephew did," she says. Her voice isn't a

whisper; it's like the below-average octave is her normal volume. "He sent me an email me this morning. You're to have access to any book in the library system. No return date required. And"—she opens a drawer without looking at it, pulling out an old-fashioned key too big for my key chain—"this is for you. Access to the library at any time. Please, Douglas, do not give this to just anyone. I don't trust some of the students to give these books the respect they deserve. Some are older than this country."

I pocket the key and nod. Ms. Regent glances back at her computer, but after two beats, looks back up at me.

"Something else you need? You know your way around a library; I've seen you in here enough times to detect the telltale signs of someone who is comfortable dancing around the Dewey Decimal System."

"No, it's not that. I'm, um, looking for books on Winslow's history," I finally say. "Books that you might not lend out to most students?"

"You're looking for the Sedimentary Section," she says. "The floor below us."

"There's a floor below us?"

"Most people would call it a basement. If anyone asks, it's where we store old computers, textbooks, and memorabilia from previous academic years. But between you and me, the other descendants—"

"It's where you keep all the things that are on a need-to-know basis, and those who need to know have lineage that goes back to the founding of Winslow."

Ms. Regent's cheek flickers for a moment, a faint crackle of a grin. "You never miss a beat, do you? Passcode is 595065."

I nod and take the elevator, one of those old-fashioned ones that requires me to slide a metal-grate door and lock it before the elevator allows me to press a button, down one floor. The temperature drops easily ten degrees. As I step into the hall, string lights flicker on. At the end of the narrow hallway is a single stone door, with the Regent Academy symbol etched into the middle, and metal bolts piercing through its hard granite shell. A keypad, like Ms. Regent promised, is seared into the slab. It looks out of place, like a brand on a wild horse.

"Five . . . nine . . . five . . . zero . . . six . . . five." I quietly say each number out loud as I press the keys. Eventually, the pad chirps its approval. The stone shudders and shifts, sliding to the side with little resistance.

"Holy shit," I whisper.

Polished woods shimmer and twinkle as if they are buffed three times a day. Chandeliers hang from a ceiling that must've cost more than the yearly tuition at Regent Academy. Plush crimson couches with ornate coffee tables are paired strategically. There are even electric fireplaces made to look like real wood-burning ones around the room.

I'm guessing that the Sedimentary Section was created to make the descendants of the first Winslow residents feel comfortable. But it also feels like a bunker. Like if the world goes to hell, or the curse overpowers the town, there's a place they can retreat to and survive the magical storm.

As soon as I step over the threshold, the stone door closes behind me and clicks shut. Involuntarily, I jump.

"Don't worry," a familiar voice says. "That's normal."

I turn to the direction of the voice and come face-to-face with Everett Everley. He's dressed how I've come to expect Everett to dress: dirty jeans, boots, a beanie that attempts to tame his curly blond hair, and a Regent Academy button-down, wrinkled, with the sleeves rolled up and tie stuffed in his jeans pocket.

"Use the same code to exit, just in reverse. Bet Ms. Librarian didn't tell you that."

"She didn't." I pause. "I imagine she just expected me to figure it out."

"Would you have? Figured it out."

"Eventually."

I shrug.

"Of course you would," he mumbles.

I arch my brow. Another annoyance. "What does *that* mean?"

He shrugs and walks toward one of the stacks of books. "Everyone just trusts that you will be our savior and assumes you're the one who will fix everything those before you have been unable to fix."

"Don't be a bitch."

"Don't be an asshole."

"Comes naturally."

That gets a small flicker of a smirk out of him. Everett turns his head down, flipping idly the pages of a maroon, age-worn book in his hand.

"If you're here for the curse, it means you're here on the head-master's orders. Turned into his little lapdog, I see? That was fast."

"Oh, fuck off."

"Thank god you said it before I had to," Everett mutters, turning, signifying this conversation is over.

Joke's on him: I'm not going to let him off that easily.

"What are you doing here?" I ask, walking quickly to keep up with him. "Shouldn't you be guarding the grounds, or tending to the plant beds or something? Speaking of lapdogs . . ."

"Take you a while to think of that one?"

"Depends—how long did it take you to decide you were going to lie to me? Did you know when you asked me to trust you in the forest that this is where we were going to end up, or was that just a split-decision thing?"

Everett stops so abruptly, my body runs into his, face slamming into his back. In that brief second of colliding with him, my body tenses. He's strong, broad shouldered and sturdy, like an oak tree. And even with a tinge of sweat, probably from working, he still smells . . . good. It works for him.

"That . . . wasn't my plan."

I can't see his face, but I can hear him, the voice reminding me of someone drowning, not in water but in guilt. He pumps his fists by his side, just twice, as if he's turning over an engine, before starting to walk again. The moment gone as quickly as it came.

"Emma and Mom are handling the first. And there aren't any plants I need to tend to in October." He glances over his shoulder, crosses his arms behind his head as he walks. "Do you know anything about horticulture?"

"Absolutely not."

He smirks. "I find that surprising. Douglas Jones, the Breaker of Curses, doesn't know something?"

"You still haven't answered why you're here."

"I'm allowed here. I'm a descendant."

"That doesn't mean you *have* to be here. In fact, I'd think that would mean you would avoid it."

". . . Fair."

Everett studies me, as if he's trying to decide if he can trust me or not. He opens his mouth, about to speak, but before he can, the elevator creaks alive again. Heeled footsteps grow louder as Ms. Regent walks down the hall, before she taps in the passcode and slides the door open, looking at us with a puzzled expression.

"Just keep to yourself and don't make too much noise," Everett says instead, turning to walk over to his side of the room. "I don't have much free time and I'm not looking to squander it."

I stare at Everett's back once again, like if I keep glaring at it long enough, two holes will burn in the back of his shirt. A large part of me wants to know why Everett is here.

But it's none of my business, and if he isn't going to offer up the information, then I'm not going to pry. It's not like we're friends or anything, right?

"Of course not," I mutter. Everett Everley doesn't have friends.

10

The Sedimentary Section is large enough that Everett and I don't need to move in each other's orbits. He can stay on his side of the floor, and I can stay on mine—the rest of the library.

But I am interested in what he is researching. Even if it is none of my business. Even if I have more than enough strange relics from the past several hundred years to keep me busy. Plus, with Ms. Regent leaving us only about thirty minutes after she entered, breaking our stalemate, the room feels bigger, colder, *danker*, without any conversation or goodwill to lighten the space.

I wander through the stacks and quickly see that this floor isn't just some refuge for anything the descendants of Winslow want to keep hidden. Sure, that stuff is here. History books, documentary scribbles, photos, newspaper clippings. It's a treasure trove for anyone who wants to dive headfirst into the lore of Winslow and its curse from those who experienced it firsthand—and who are responsible for it.

But there's so much more. There's also the forgotten history of every student at Winslow who was swallowed whole by the curse and tossed down here for their memories to rot. Their book bags, personal belongings, schoolbooks. Each one of them is like a relic, frozen in time. Blocks of history scorched with memories on their surfaces. You can learn a lot about a person when you're given access to their last moments. When you're allowed to see glimpses into their life, the moment before they were scrubbed from existence.

I try to push that to the back of my mind. I don't have any reason to be digging into dead students' memories. If they are dead, then they're gone, and their memories should be protected, honored, and respected.

But the longer I stay here, the more my mind wanders while reading transcribed diary entries from Regent ancestors three-hundred-plus years ago; the more the thought tickles at the back of my mind until soft whispers turn into screaming voices in my head, not that different from the forest. The forest I haven't heard since I had that vision.

I begin the search alphabetically. It's not hard to find his name: *Hale, Kent*. His little box is neatly packed, wedged between *Harper, Marissa* and *Hah, Oliver. Kent Hale. Senior. 17 years old. Consumption Season: Fall 2021.*

So devoid of emotion, of heart. I didn't care about Kent, but that didn't mean I wanted him dead.

Sliding to the floor, my back against one of the sturdy bookshelves, I sit with Kent's box between my legs. The top opens with a soft hiss, as if I'm unlocking some secret that has been kept buried for centuries and something about me was the key to unlocking its hidden knowledge.

The box is unremarkable. At his core, Kent was just a seventeen-year-old guy trying to make his way in the world. Sure, he was an asshole, and sure, he had a head start over everyone else, but still—we were both just trying to make a way for ourselves, as best we could.

Comics, a few old T-shirts, textbooks, his dead cell phone, a pair of over-the-ear oversized headphones, and a few other things within the box gave me a snapshot of the Life of Kent.

"No photos, though," I think aloud. There're no pictures with friends at school, nothing with his parents or family during holidays. Is the box missing things?

"When he died, memories related to him disappeared," Everett says, leaning against the frame of the bookshelf. "Experiences too. Those photos you're looking for don't exist because they didn't happen. There's no reason for Kent to have a photo with friends or family . . ."

"Because he was never there with said friends and family."

"Exactly."

I frown and stand up, putting the top on the box and slipping it snugly back into its allotted space. That must be a lonely way to live. I mean, I guess it's not really living if no one would remember them. Just the idea, though, of disappearing, having every bit of me erased? It's a chilling thought.

"Don't people question that, though?" I ask. "I mean, if I had a photo on my shelf, and someone was missing from it, the photo would look off."

"You'd be surprised how flimsy the human mind really is. And honestly, even if you did notice, and you thought something was off, who would believe you?"

"No one," I admit.

"Right. Humans are social creatures. We yearn to belong, to be seen and accepted. We generally won't do anything that goes against that. Or so I've heard."

"So you've heard?" I repeat.

"I don't give a fuck about people. Do you?" Everett asks, pushing off the wall and leaving me to my isolation like we've been doing the past several hours.

Except this time, I follow him. I don't answer Everett. Of course he's right, but I'm more focused on the scattered papers on the floor of his aisle. Boxes upon boxes are pulled out, precariously stacked atop one another. There's a small notebook with a ballpoint pen lying on top of it.

"I'm going to ask this again, and hope this time you'll give me an honest answer," I say, turning to face him. "It's pretty obvious you're looking for something. Any luck?"

Everett's sharp features turn sharper. His angular jaw becomes more pronounced. His body becomes tighter, and his already-tall six-foot-three form becomes taller as his hackles raise.

"Are you asking as the supposed Winslow Saving Grace, or are you asking . . . ?"

"As a fellow person who is coming up empty-handed," I finish for him. I gesture behind me. "Because between you and me, I haven't been able to find anything I'm looking for."

"What *are* you looking for?" Everett asks. "Hardly anyone comes down here."

I hesitate to think if I should tell Everett. I thought I could trust him before, but he betrayed me when push came to shove. How do I know he won't do it again? Maybe he's spying on me for the headmaster.

As if he can read my mind, Everett says, "You can trust me. At least, with this. I know those are just words, considering . . . everything that happened, but we're both trying to accomplish the same thing."

"And that is?"

"Freedom. Freedom from this curse, this place, and this school."

He's right about that. I'm not sure I would go so far as saying I believe Everett can give me the missing piece of knowledge I'm looking for, but he is a descendant. He's part of this; it's in his blood. It would be stupid to turn down his help.

"I'm looking for something that will give me a leg up on this curse," I admit. "I know that's vague."

"Very vague," Everett corrects. "Not to be . . . what's the word . . . glib . . . but don't you think if it was here, someone would have found it before you?"

"Maybe, but I'm looking at it with fresh eyes."

"And how is that going?"

I let out a bark of a laugh, louder than I expected.

"That good, huh?" Everett grins wolfishly, squatting low and grabbing one of the boxes with its flimsy cardboard handles. His biceps flex for just a moment.

"Your turn. What exactly are you looking for?" I ask.

I'm teetering between actually caring about the answer and just being nice. Everett isn't someone I need to—or *want* to—piss off. He's wrapped up in this curse just as much as anyone else. His family is partially to blame, but that doesn't mean any of it is his fault. Not directly, at least. The sins of his father—or, more accurately, his ancestor—aren't his sins to carry. He isn't my enemy.

That doesn't mean he doesn't annoy the shit out of me.

Everett glances up at me with his green eyes, searching for an ounce of something he can latch onto to justify his mistrust. I don't blame him. I don't think I would trust me either. I don't think I *do* trust me.

Why does it have to be me who breaks the curse? Why can't Everett do it, or Headmaster Monroe, or any of the other students? There's a joke that rich, well-connected people always say: *There isn't a problem you can't throw money at to solve.* Does that apply to the supernatural too? Can we just throw a million dollars at the forest, come up with a think tank or a roundtable or whatever corporate buzzwords rich people think make them look and sound fancy, and let the problem handle itself?

Finally, Everett stands. He slides his fingers over the front of his pants, as if to wipe away something that I can't see.

"I'm looking for files on my ancestors," he says. "Trying to understand how we ended up . . ."

"Stuck here?"

He shrugs. "Yeah."

"Headmaster Monroe said—"

"You should know by now that Headmaster Monroe doesn't always speak in full truths," Everett interrupts. "He gives as much or as little information as he thinks is necessary. *It's a burden to be a Monroe.*" Everett deepens his voice to mimic how the head-master talks.

"I'm guessing you didn't find what you were looking for?"

Everett shakes his head. He squats down, rummaging through a pile of books, pulling out one with a worn maroon cover. Licking the tips of his fingers, he flips open the pages. The book is broken up into different sections, each one having a title page with a name written on it.

By the time I see the second one, *Monroe*, I have a good idea what this might be.

"Did you ever notice Winslow doesn't have any graveyards, Douglas?" Everett asks. "There's no need for them if no one can remember the dead."

He nods. "This book"—he shakes it—"contains the names of all members of the cursed families who have died. Cause of death, age, short bios. Each page is an entry, a person."

I move closer to Everett, scanning the pages while looking over his shoulder. *He smells nice,* I think.

"What are the asterisks for?"

"Anyone who married into the family," he explains. "Once you take the last name, the curse digs its claws into you too."

"What about family?" I ask, glancing over at Everett. "I mean, if you marry someone from out of town, does the curse affect you too?"

"You're asking if someone marries someone in Winslow and they suddenly can't leave, won't their family come looking for them?"

I nod and then pause. Everett keeps his eyes trained on me, jaw tight. The way his eyes darken tells me he sees the puzzle pieces slotting together in my mind.

"They're forgotten, aren't they?" I ask. "Your family forgets about you if you take the name of a descendant."

"It's a pretty shitty fine print, isn't it? Fall in love with someone, want to spend your life with them, but they have to suffer like you? Few families were willing to do it. Unless, of course, you're the Monroes and you use your considerable money to lure men and women into Winslow, then pay them an ungodly amount to help make a kid and sign over all their parental rights."

Everett says that so casually, as if what the Monroes are doing and how they're continuing their bloodline is as simple and common as ordering a black coffee from a famous coffee cart. He doesn't even stop to give me time to process what he just said. Something tells me there are many horrific things the Monroes have done to keep a stranglehold on power, in the name of breaking this curse.

"Half the families have died out," Everett says. "We may not be able to leave the town, or forget, but there's one thing the curse doesn't exclude each of us from doing."

I don't need him to explain any more, but that doesn't stop him from continuing.

"The Weatherbys were the first. Their last descendant, Marta, hanged herself in a home that's now the Goodwill Center on Main Street.

"The Buckinghams—who when this all started tied up Etalie-in's lover and threw the match on the pyre—killed four of President Benjamin Harrison's men when he came to visit Vermont. Buckingham, his wife, and his oldest son were all executed by firing squad."

"That's only four, including your family and the Monroes."

"There's one more. The Meyers," he notes. "Most of them are dead, but one still lives. He works in town. Minds his own business and tries to forget about the curse."

"Must be nice."

Everett nods, not saying anything.

"I know what you're thinking," I say after a moment of silence.

"Do you now?" He chuckles dryly. "And what's that? I'm curious."

"You're wondering if the desire to end it all, that . . . resignation is something those three families came up with on their own, or if it's a part of the curse itself. You're wondering if eventually—be it you, your sister, your mother, or any offspring you have—your family will break and give up like the others did. And if you do, if part of the curse *is* using you up until it's finally done with you, you're wondering what horrible thing you'll do to put your name in this book, and how you, your sister, and your mother will be remembered.

"But deep down, I think you're wondering if you'll leave anything or anyone to remember you by. Or will you just be another name in a book of lost souls for some other unlucky person to find."

Everett falls quiet, but not like before. Before, it was a pensive sort of silence, like he was absorbed and lost in his own thoughts. This feels heavier, like he's holding a dam back by keeping his mouth locked shut, and if he opens it, every emotion will come pouring out and he won't be able to stop it. I know that feeling. I remember sitting in that interrogation room after the fire, willing myself to stay silent because I knew it was the right thing to do. That didn't mean I didn't want to say it all, to say anything, in hopes it would make the noxious feeling in my stomach just a little bit better.

"Do you think I'm capable of that?" he whispered. "Doing horrible things? To myself, or to anyone else?"

The words are heavy, and I wonder how long Everett has been carrying that question around. How long he's been thinking, dreading, dreaming, about what his future holds—and more importantly, how he can stop it.

"I don't think you're that type of person," I finally say. "I've been to jail; you know that, right? I'm not saying that as if it's some badge of honor, but even in passing, I've seen the eyes of killers. You don't have them."

"What do my eyes tell you about me, then?" He laughs hollowly, as if he doesn't believe me.

There are a lot of things I could say. Not only about his eyes, but about the way Everett carries himself like nothing bothers him, like anyone who gets in his way can fuck off, and even if that's not true, I'm envious of it. How the few times I've seen him around campus, I always think he carries himself like nothing can stand in his way. Or maybe I should talk about how he already annoys the shit out of me, but it's more like a welcome burn; one that I want to feel more of against my skin.

But he just asked about his eyes, so maybe I should just stick with that. Besides, I have no idea if Everett is bi, gay, pan, or anything, and he's physically strong. I don't think I could take him in a fight, especially not in an enclosed space like this.

"That you're someone who doesn't give up. Someone who doesn't let the world tell them what they're supposed to be or do, but understands that's a decision you make yourself. Those types of people don't let fate or destiny decide things for them. They make their own path, even if it means turning their back on everyone else; they believe in their conviction. You're someone who was dealt an unlucky hand, Everett. That's it. It's what you do with it that matters."

I feel like a broken inspirational record set to repeat until the end of time. Everett's eyes stay focused on me. I'm not sure if he believes what I say or just thinks it's a pile of crap. I'm not sure if *I* believe the words I'm spouting. But it's enough to get him to focus back on the task at hand.

As Everett's eyes drift to the book, mine follow too. Both our gazes settle on one name, the last name on the list: Thatcher Everley. Male. Asterisk. 1984–2019.

2019. That was two years ago.

"My dad," Everett says. "Died two years ago. A Perversion took him. He was patrolling the grounds with my mother, a routine job, and . . . well . . ." Everett makes a slicing motion over his throat.

It's crude, but from the way Everett's eyes are avoiding me, I can tell he doesn't want to talk about this. It's a sore spot for him. It would be for me too.

"He didn't have to die, you know?" he says. "Mom told him they didn't have to get married. That's the flaw in the curse. If you are just with someone and don't marry them, they aren't affected. I think there's something about the ceremony of marriage that triggers it. But Dad said he couldn't do that. He—"

"If you love someone, then you're with them through the good and the bad," I mutter. "No half in, half out. My mama said the same about my father. He died from cancer. When the diagnosis happened, Dad wanted them to get divorced so she wouldn't be saddled with all those medical bills. But, you know, through sickness and health. Mama wasn't going to have it.

"I don't know if I agree with her. With him. With any of it. I mean, I believe in love, you know? But putting it above everything else? Your own well-being, the financial well-being of yourself and your family? Is it worth it? Risking it all for something intangible? I don't know. I'm not sure if I was in my mama's situation, if I would have done the same thing. But if you ask her, she'll say there wasn't any other choice. That when you love someone, these are the things you do. Without hesitation. That's what real love is. Well, then maybe real love is the dumbest thing in the world."

I don't realize I'm ranting until I look up and see that Everett has turned to face me. It's like he's not only looking at me but through me. Seeing the most personal parts of myself because I've given him the skeleton key that allows him to see my flesh and bone and muscles and nerves.

I hate that feeling.

Before I can backtrack or save face, his phone rings. He fishes it out of his back pocket and turns to take the call.

"Mom? What's . . ."

His back becomes more rigid, whatever his mother says. I strain and try to hear what he says, but I can't make out the words.

"Wait, you're sure? Does the headmaster know? Shit. Okay. Are you going to . . . you're not serious. That's not what we agreed! Mom, I'm . . . fine. Yeah, no I know. I said I'll do it. Tonight."

Everley shuts his flip phone loudly and takes a deep breath, the type that makes his shoulders rise and fall three times. He turns swiftly on his heel, looking directly at me, with a sharpness and coldness that makes me shiver.

"Douglas, I need to ask you a question, and I want you to be completely honest with me. How serious are you about breaking this curse? I mean seriously. Is this something you actually want to do? Put your life on the line for people you've never met and don't even know?"

Everett's words are laced with pain and hurt. Whatever

happened on that call riled him in a way I never thought I'd see. It just reminds me of that thing and what I saw after drinking the tea. The . . . magic, he called it. How I made a pact to be part of this twisted dark game of fate without even knowing what I agreed to.

"I'm serious," I say. "Fully."

"Then meet me at the eastern gates tonight, say around nine," he says, brushing by me. I turn quick enough so that he doesn't bump me, but when he reaches the edge of the bookshelf, he pauses.

"Thank you, Douglas," he says, not looking back at me. "Truly."

That's the last word I hear before Everett leaves me alone. Left to wonder what the hell happened and what is going to happen tonight.

And what the fuck I just agreed to.

That evening, I meet Everett at his home, around the back where his motorbike sits. He's already waiting for me, unfazed that we're sneaking out of school well past curfew, a rule that I'm not sure still applied to me.

"Wasn't sure you were going to make it," he says, opening the pack on the back of the bike, yanking a second helmet out before stuffing his own bag into it. Without looking, he lobs the helmet to me. Luckily, I catch it.

"Surprise," I mutter. "You going to tell me where we're going now?"

"Best if I just show you." Everett doesn't hesitate, swinging one leg over the bike, pulling the helmet off from its position on the right handlebar and slipping it onto his head. With the dark, sun-resistant visor up, only his eyes are visible. But they're expressive enough to tell me he's studying me.

"Have you ever ridden a motorbike before?"

The answer is no, but I don't say that. Right now, my eyes are glued on the forest's edge, no more than ten feet from the house. The way the ground shifts from lush and artificial bright green to a darker hue. How it feels considerably colder here than it did exiting the school.

"Does the forest look different to you?" I ask.

Everett follows my gaze, only staring for a moment. "Looks as creepy as usual."

That's true, but it also looks . . . sharper. The trees have never been welcoming, but the evergreens that make up the flora seem natural. There are more needles and thorns now than I remember. Vines strangle the trees and slither across the ground, making it seem nearly impossible to easily walk through.

It's like the forest is preparing for an invader.

I shake my head, turning my attention back to Everett. I don't need to be thinking about that. Instead, I mimic his actions, slipping the helmet on, swinging my leg over the seat, and gripping his hips tight enough that I won't fly off—but not too tight.

"Tighter," he says, muffled. His right hand moves down, tightening my grip on his waist.

"So I don't go flying off?"

The motorbike roars to life. Everett looks over his shoulder at me, flipping the visor down with two fingers.

"I'm not going to let you fall, I promise you that."

I might not trust much of what Everett says, but I trust that. And the way his voice rings with finality, like there's absolutely no other possible choice in the matter? It's warm, safe.

It's . . . hot.

Pebbles spit out from under the back wheel as Everett does a quick 180-degree turn toward the road. The bike jolts forward with a simple twist of his wrist, my body following suit. And just like that, we're off.

The paved roads morph into the main two-lane road that bisects the campus. The guard barely looks at us when we pass. Or maybe he glared at us. I can't tell; the trees and everything on either side of us melt into a watercolor blur.

Riding with Everett feels like gliding through air, as if the wheels of the bike don't touch the ground and he's manipulating the wind to help us soar down the smooth streets. Leaving campus is a treat; part of what makes Regent Academy so great is that everything you need is on campus. We even have a small convenience store and movie theater. Why would you go to Winslow, a small town with hardly anyone, for anything?

Everett makes a sharp turn, leaning the bike to the right to hug the curb. Instinctively, I hold him tighter. In the side mirror, I see him glance at me, only for a moment. Once the turn is complete, his right hand slides down and squeezes my arm. A silent reaction that reminds me what he promised: *I'm not going to let you fall.*

And though trusting someone so close to the town's curse—who has so much staked on my success or failure, whose family is just as responsible for this mess as Headmaster Monroe's family—might not be the best idea, I do trust Everett to uphold that promise.

I hug him tighter as he weaves through traffic, the wheels of his bike moving fluidly against the pavement. On more than one occasion, drivers honk as the sides of his bike get a little too close to their cars. I tighten my hug-squeeze. His abs tighten in return.

Winslow isn't far from Regent Academy, though the school likes to make it sound like we're miles away. The whole ride, we're parallel to the forest, sometimes passing through a small cross section that someone was brave enough to carve out for an expressway. Though I'm not sure if *brave* is the right word. Make no mistake, Atolas let them do it. Allowed them the grace to excise part of its body, so that the people could go from one small no-name town to another with ease.

Or maybe that was part of its plan all along. To get more people within its grasp to prey on them, like a spider that builds a burrow underground for insects to fall into.

That feels more likely, but at the same time, more horrifying than the people of Winslow might want to admit. But then again, I wonder how many people feel the weightless dread I feel whenever I get too close to the forest. I watch the blacks and browns and greens pass us by. I tighten my grip around Everett a bit more.

"You asked before we left if I thought the forest was different," he mutters as he slows down enough for us to talk.

"And you said you didn't."

"Because I don't. But that feeling . . . I know you feel it. Like something is watching you? Like it's breathing down your neck but you can't actually feel any breath?"

I nod, realizing he can't see me, so I say, "That's a perfect way to describe it. Does it ever go away?"

"No, but it's gotten worse. Since the headmaster put you under."

We navigate through the quaint small-town streets. Winslow may not be a mountain town, per se, but it has the vibe of one. You can still see the forest, no matter where you are on the main street. Most of the shops that make Winslow a reasonable place to live are all on one street, with perpendicular parking along the sides, reminding me of cut scenes from video games that take place in the Old West of America.

That's the first level of Winslow.

Each descending level is like a ring of a tree. Each ring is different; the first being the shops, then behind those the row homes, makeshift apartment complexes, and single-family homes that have been passed down through generations. But Everett doesn't care about any of those. He keeps cruising past those rings, bisecting the town and heading toward a road where tendrils of plant life push up from the concrete, splitting the earth in half, an act of rebellion against human expansionism at its finest.

"We're here."

Everett hops off the bike before it comes to a stop, the soles of his boots skidding against the ground, decelerating the cycle. I'm not exactly sure where "here" is. Sure, we're on the edge of town, but there isn't much to see. Just a dilapidated building the size of a two-story home, with a sign so old I can't make out the words butting against the edge of the forest. The building looks mostly abandoned, but I can see a light through the window.

"You're not gonna ask where we are?" he asks, putting away

the keys and shoving his hands into the pockets of his jean jacket.

"The horror-movie enthusiast in me tells me this is where you're going to kill me."

"If I was going to do that, I'd just throw you into the forest," he mutters. "You asked me before about the cursed families. Here is where that last descendant lives. Taylor Meyers. Or well, lived."

"Lived?"

Everett bites his lip and sighs. "Let's just get this over with."

Walking forward, he uses his shoulder, hitting the door three times to force it open. The sound of the wood splintering washes over us. It's like the forest is swallowing everything whole, anything that might bring attention to it or make people look too closely.

Everett walks into the room first, the pale single light illuminating the left side of his face. I see him look around, his eyes stopping at something to the right that catches his vision.

"Jesus," he whispers. "I'm not sure you want to come in here."

When someone says something like that, of course I don't want to. There's nothing I'm going to see in this house I'm going to be able to forget. But curses aren't called curses because they're fun. I made a commitment. I'm going to see it through.

I take a deep breath and step over the threshold. There's no preparation for what my eyes see. Maybe if we had come from another angle, I would have seen the blood spatter on the window. Or if I had looked down, I would've seen the pool of blood under the chair.

But nothing can prepare you to see the body of a man who shot himself in the head.

Before I can stop myself, I run out of the house, grab the railing that I'm not sure can support my weight, and vomit over the side. The scene . . . the smell. I'm never going to forget any of that.

Everett's hand on my back makes me jump. He pulls it away, taking half a step back too.

"He left a note," he says, holding it between two fingers. It feels odd, such a pristine and perfect white slip of paper with so much . . . blood right next to it. "Not much on it. Just says *I'm sorry.*"

I wipe my mouth with the back of my hand, making a note to gargle as soon as I can. I study Everett's face, unable to detect . . . really anything. Is this something he's used to? Murder is one thing, but suicide? I'm not judging anyone who thinks that life is too hard to live. That's their choice and their choice alone. But I don't know if I'll ever be able to get that sight out of my head.

"Any ideas why he did it?" I finally ask.

Everett shrugs. "He's a cursed descendant. I'm sure he couldn't take it anymore." Everett pauses, like he wants to say more.

"You know how each family has a role? Monroes run the school, we protect the grounds? The Meyers were responsible for dealing with the dead in Winslow."

"What do you mean, dealing with them?"

Everett sighs, running his fingers through his shaggy hair. "When people die in Winslow, we need to do something with the body."

"Yeah, there are no graves."

"Right. And it's not like people will remember their dead loved ones the next day. So whenever someone would die, Taylor let us know. He takes the bodies and . . . calls us to . . ."

Everett doesn't need to finish. "Wait, hold up," I say. "You burn the bodies? Like, you?"

He nods curtly.

"And you're okay with this?"

"Never said I was okay with it, but someone has to do it."

"Someone being you."

Everett frowns, crossing his arms over his chest. He stands a bit taller, like he's trying to peacock me. "Look, I'm not asking for your forgiveness or anything. But I don't need you judging me; I do that enough for myself. Someone has to handle the dead. My family protects the school and the town. That includes from the dead. So we burn them. And I'm guessing, with Taylor knowing everything that happens here, he decided killing himself was the best and he knew we'd handle it. There are worse things than being dead, Douglas. Especially here.

"You wanted to see what was at stake here—now you do. It's not just creatures in the forest or some deal you made with the headmaster. It's real people. Real lives."

I look past Everett toward the room again. From this angle, I can see Taylor's boot. If you didn't look at his face, it looks like he fell asleep in the chair.

"Your mom called to tell you this? Why didn't she do it herself?"

"It's my turn. I'm old enough to do these on my own. Soon Emma will be too. My mom won't be around forever. We have to be able to do all the duties of an Everley."

I cannot possibly understand why a parent would make their kid do something like this. But I'm not in their situation. I haven't been living with this my whole life. The Everleys and everyone else cursed can't even leave town. There's nothing else here for them except, well, this.

"Where do you do it? The burning?"

"There's a furnace in the Meyers' basement. We do it there and then take the ashes and scatter them in the wind."

At least that's . . . nice, I guess. Their bodies might have died here, they might have been stuck here, but at least they get to travel through the air and see the world. They're free.

"I'll help you," I finally say. "Deal with . . . him."

Everett frowns, staring at me without saying anything.

"I'm serious. I'll do it. You can't do it alone."

"I absolutely can," Everett replies, almost defensively.

"I know you *can*. But I'm here—I might as well help you." I pause for a moment, adding, "You shouldn't do something like this alone. Your mom may believe you can do it, but that doesn't mean you should."

"And you shouldn't have to see something like that," he says. "When this curse is done, you'll leave town. You'll have a normal life. Don't let this fuck you up."

"I've seen a dead body, a severed talking head, and a creature in the forest that looks like something from a horror movie. I think we're past the *Don't get fucked up in the head* part of the story."

Everett lets out a small snort, turning his head downward. It's cute, the sound he made and how he almost seems . . . ashamed.

"We'll do it quickly," he says. "And if it becomes too much, you let me know and I'll finish it up."

"I'm not going to chicken out," I promise. "We're in this together, yeah?"

Everett pauses and looks at me. No, not *at* me, *through* me, like he's trying to analyze the deepest parts of me for any sort of lie.

"No one has ever said that to me before," he mutters.

"Not even your mom?"

"I mean, yeah, she has. But it's different. She's my parent . . . and she's . . . preparing me for this shit when she dies. It'll be my job to do the same for Emma, though sometimes I think she's more prepared than me." He waves his hand dismissively. "Thank you, Douglas. It means a lot." He smiles. "Dinner on me after this?"

I nod, but I have no idea how Everett can even think about eating. He leads the way, with me only a few steps behind him. But then I stop. The feeling of eyes on me is so strong, it's like they're right behind me.

I turn, but the street is quiet. There isn't a soul out. It's just me, Everett, the voices that never leave, and the dead body.

"You coming?" Everett says from inside the home.

I give the forest line and the street one more look before turning back inside, closing the door behind us, and locking it. I'd rather be with a dead body than whatever is out there.

And there's definitely something out there.

12

"Whenever Mom would take me on . . . well, a burning . . . ," Everett says, "we would always stop at Hildebrand's. Feel like we gotta continue that tradition."

According to Everett, it has the best food in all of Vermont. Which seems a bit of a hyperbolic statement, considering one of Regent's selling points is that they have multiple five-star chefs on rotation.

More importantly, I think it's his favorite because it's open twenty-four hours. Which seems weird in such a small town. Maybe the owner knows something I don't. Knows there's a need for a place like this, even if she doesn't *really* know why. I mean, she has to have the right idea. We're not the only ones here. There are a few other lost souls, hunched over a plate of food or luke-warm coffee.

I wonder if they can't sleep either.

I wonder if the town haunts them too.

But the way Everett's eyes light up when the plate of food comes out, plus an Oreo milkshake with extra Oreos on top—rivals the joy of seeing a child open presents on Christmas Day. Makes me forget all about that. It must be nice to have some way to decompress after what we just did.

"Thanks, Anna," he says, flashing an almost innocent smile at the server. As innocent as Everett Everley can be. I mean, there's nothing really soft about him. Everything is sharp from working on the grounds for so long, and also as a defense mechanism. The way he walks, talks, and how he sits—he gives an air of *This shop is closed for business and don't ask when it's going to open back up.* But when Anna comes with his food? He's like a kid again, getting to go to McDonald's after acing a spelling test.

She smiles back. Not the type of smile a normal waitress would give. The type that lingers on Everett's features for a bit too long, like she's hoping he'd notice.

Which is how I notice he isn't looking at her but only looking at me.

"And here's your country fried chicken with mashed potatoes and green beans," she finally says, placing the plate down. "Careful, it's hot."

"Thanks."

"You two need anything else? If not, I'm going to head out. Ashley will take care of you."

"Get home safe," Everett says.

Anna puts her hand over her chest. "You're so sweet," she says, walking over and grabbing her coat before blowing Everett a kiss. He chuckles lowly, shaking his head.

I wonder if there's history between the two of them. Everett's an interesting guy, balancing this whole *I can't get close to people* act with the obvious desire for closeness and finding it in fleeting moments. He's charming when he wants to be. Standoffish when he needs to be and brave when he has to be.

I've never met someone like him.

"I'm telling you," he says loudly between bites. "Best food on the East Coast. No, the world."

"You haven't been out much if you think—"

I catch myself too late. Shit. Of course he hasn't been out much. Everett stops mid-bite before going back to scarfing down the food.

He waves it off. "Don't worry about it."

"I should have thought out my words more carefully."

"Seriously, Dougie. Don't worry—"

"Douglas," I correct.

Everett arches his brow.

Just hearing him say that reminds me of the other students at Regent. How they intentionally call me by the wrong name. Something more juvenile. Something cuter. As if giving me an adorable name makes me more palatable for them. I almost let it slide when I first arrived at Regent. Mama wanted nothing more than for this to be a good experience for me, for us both. And if that meant allowing them to call me some cutesy name, the wrong name, then so be it.

But I learned that stomaching small grievances like that quickly balloons into bigger and harder-to-swallow requests.

"Not Dougie. Douglas."

Everett stops eating, focusing on me. He's like one of those psychologists I had when I was first in jail; waiting for me to answer, as if enough silence will make me break. Funnily enough, it usually worked and this time is no different. I hate silence, no matter how much I long for it in my own head. It just makes my mind twist and morph nothingness into every possible thing that could go wrong in the moment.

"Everyone at Regent calls me Dougie," I say. "That's not my name. It's Douglas."

"You're right," Everett replies, to my surprise. "Douglas. Sorry about that. See, we both fucked up and insulted one another; now we're even. In the past, you know, some cultures considered being able to insult your opponent and make up with them the first step to mending long-term conflicts."

"What cultures are those?"

Everett shrugs. "Cultures. Trust me, I read it on the internet. But more importantly," he says, cutting a small piece of chicken and holding the fork up to my mouth. "Bite."

"You can't just force me—"

"*Bite,*" he says, deepening his voice and pushing it forward. The gravy smears against my lips as he grins, forcing it past my mouth when I open it just a bit. The flavors instantly dance in my mouth. The perfect mix of sweet and sour. One bite, and I can tell the meat isn't too tough. The skin on the outside, though drenched in the best sauce I've ever tasted, still has a crunch to it.

"Good, right?" Everett grins. "It's Winslow's Garbage Plate. Chicken with Italian gravy, fried green beans, mashed potatoes, and applesauce." He points to each item as he says it.

"You all seriously call it a garbage plate?"

He pushes his plate into the center, silently offering to split it with me. "Yep. And yet, you still want to eat it. So what does that say about you?"

I open my mouth to say something clever, but nothing comes out. Everett smirks, shoveling another bite of the chicken into his mouth. "Exactly. But more importantly, Mr. Town Savior, have you come up with anything to tell Headmaster Monroe?"

I take a smaller bite than Everett. "Don't call me that. And it's only been a day."

"Doesn't matter. Headmaster Monroe is going to want answers soon. He's not going to allow you to spend hours reading in the library, trying to make heads or tails of this place. Your goal is singular to him: help him break the curse. That's it. Anything else makes you a liability. That's where I come in."

"Oh really?" I ask, resting my chin in the palm of my right hand. "Are you going to be what? My chevalier?"

"I have no idea what word you just said. But I am an Everley. You need me to protect you against Headmaster Monroe if he gets out of hand, just like I need you to break the curse."

Everett finishes his food, completely cleaning his plate and downing the thick Oreo shake like it's water. He doesn't give me a chance to argue, or even negotiate the terms of this arrangement.

He's going to help me and I'm going to help him: no questions asked, case closed.

Part of me feels the burning sensation of annoyance creeping inside me. Him making decisions for me is no different than the headmaster forcing me into a corner. But another part of me likes it. Maybe because it's coming from Everett.

Wiping his mouth with the back of his hand, he pushes the chair out from under him.

"I want to show you something. You done eating?"

I gesture to my half-finished plate, as if that's answer enough.

"Yeah, you're done," he says, throwing a crumpled ten and three fives on the table before walking out to his motorbike.

"Seriously?" I say as I follow him outside.

"Come on, Douglas!"

At first, I think Everett is taking us back to the school. But instead, we head west for fifteen minutes, past the center of town. Run-down abandoned homes, broken stone streets, and remnants of a life once lived make the west part of Winslow a ghost town.

We come to a stop at the end of what would appear to be a makeshift dead-end street. It's clear the road doesn't actually end here. The cracked pavement obviously leads out of town. But it's the definition of the road Robert Frost mentioned when he said the road less traveled. The Winslow sign on the right is broken, twisted like someone bent the metal in anger with their bare hands. The trees and rebellious foliage keep me from seeing how steep the drop is. I can barely make out the handwritten cursive white font of *Winslow! A Perfect Place to Raise a Family! Population: 2,000.*

"Are you going to scatter Taylor's ashes soon?" I ask, thinking about the small pouch in the carrier on his bike.

Everett nods. "Mom will want to do a funeral. She was close to Taylor. They grew up together, and now without there being an heir . . . we'll have to figure out how to deal with the dead," he says, kicking a rock. "A problem for another day, though. We're almost there."

Everett walks to the edge of an invisible line that is parallel with the sign, standing in the middle of the road. He glances over his shoulder at me, strands of hair over one eye. He extends his arm to me, beckoning me forward, palm side up.

"Come on," he urges. "I promise, I won't bite." That doesn't stop him from baring his teeth, though.

"Har har har."

I move forward, taking his hand in the process. His fingers' pads are rough from his days working, but his grip is gentle; firm enough to keep me in place and make sure I don't fall, but not so firm to hurt me.

"One more time," he mutters. "You trust me?"

Before I can answer, he tugs me, harder than I expected, and uses the momentum to effectively yank me past him, turning his waist with the motion to follow through with the movement.

I stumble forward past him, digging my traction-less sneakers against the asphalt, steadying myself. "Seriously?" I bark, whipping around to face him. "We're at the stage of the friendship where we slingshot people now?"

"You'll forgive me," Everett says softly but confidently.

"Yeah? What makes you think that?"

Everett raises one hand, palm facing me. I study it for a moment, noticing how much larger it is than my own hand. How I can see the veins on his arms snaking down from his wrist, winding and hugging his forearm like an overprotective serpent. I notice the calluses again, rough and a few of them busted, probably from working on the grounds.

I also notice how he presses the air—and it ripples, giving off a white flash where his hand touches. It's faint, and if I blinked, I'd probably miss it. He repeats the action with his other hand—the same ripple. As he presses both palms forward, the rippling pulse continues, the white growing stronger, showing the outlines of his hand.

"I know you meant nothing by it," he says, "but I wanted to show you what we mean—my mother, my sister, and I—when we say we can't leave Winslow. You're on the border of the town. About ten years ago, a Perversion attacked. It tore through the town at a little past midnight. Slaughtered a ton of people. You can still see the slash marks in some of the houses it tore through. Headmaster Monroe paid a considerable amount of money to help anonymously relocate the families in Winslow. But the bloodshed? The hollow feeling that something wrong happened and keeps happening? People didn't forget that. They couldn't. That's the curse in this part of town—people remember. The curse no one wants to talk about. The memory, the dark night.

If you bring it up, people will pretend they don't know. No one wants to admit that something is wrong here in Winslow, Douglas. No one wants to accept there is something nefarious at work. Because once you admit that things actually do go bump in the night, you have to admit we're not alone. And that rabbit hole of dark thoughts you begin to go down? The what-ifs? It'll swallow you whole and it's fucking terrifying. It's even more terrifying to live it firsthand."

Everett lets his arms fall by his sides. He raises his right hand, as if his body just can't stay still, and sighs, combing his fingers through his hair, pushing the locks back nervously.

"Australia," he says. "If I could travel anywhere in the world, that's where I would go. Somewhere that doesn't get as cold as it does here. Somewhere I can swim in crystal clear water. The farthest point from here possible."

I step back over the invisible line. Everett steps backward too, like a magnet of the same pole, keeping a short distance between us. Reaching down while continuing to look in his eyes, I take his right hand and give it a squeeze.

"I'm going to make sure you can go there," I promise. "I'm going to break this curse, okay? And you'll be able to take that twenty-two-hour flight to the Gold Coast, fight a kangaroo, and wake up to a scorpion in your hotel, staring at you. You and your sister and your mom are going to be able to do all those things."

I'm not sure if I should be promising that. It feels like I'm promising something that I can't follow through on. That I'm going to let him down. That ballooning feeling of dread and shame feels like an anvil pressing down on my shoulders, causing my bones to splinter under the weight.

But I hunch my shoulders tightly and focus. I can do this. I will do this. *One step at a time, Douglas.*

Everett opens his mouth to say what I expect (or at least hope) is a thank-you, but the words never leave his mouth. His eyes skip to one of the abandoned homes, before he moves swiftly and fluidly, gliding across the concrete to stand in front of me. With a flicker of light, a flash of silver is drawn from his waist—a hunter's knife with a jagged edge and a leather-wrapped hilt. He holds the knife in his right hand, the blade level with his chin, parallel to the ground. His left hand reaches behind him, pressed against my thigh.

"Show yourself," he says loudly. "Now."

There's nothing but silence, but not the normal type. This is an eerie silence that feels like dry air sucking every bit of sound toward its center; that center being the home that Everett's staring at.

"I won't ask again," Everett says. "You've been following us since we got into town. If you make me come in there, only one of us is coming out alive, and I promise you it'll be me."

A moment passes before I see something—no, someone—shuffling. Slowly, a woman walks out, hunchbacked, strands of silvery hair exposed as she pulls her hoodie down, holding up her hands.

Before Everett or I can ask what she wants, she says, "You're looking for answers about the curse, aren't you? Put the knife down and I can help you. I mean you no harm."

The woman's eyes drift from Everett and his blade to me. Her eyes are wise; there's knowledge and depth in those glassy gray-blue pools.

"You've seen him. Etaliein," she says. "You saw the forest, didn't you? The tree?"

I feel my brow stitch into a frown. "What do you mean?" I whisper, turning to Everett. "What is she talking about?"

"I know, because I've seen it too," the woman says. She looks at Everett. "Now do you believe me?"

13

"I want the record to show I don't trust her," Everett whispers.

"Duly noted for the second time."

It's actually the third time he's said that. I don't blame him. A mysterious person says they know something about a hypersecretive curse that only a few people are aware of, and we're supposed to trust them? Yeah, no.

"Do you?" he hisses. We keep our distance as we follow her, Everett walking his cycle while I walk next to it. The woman leads the way back toward town, approaching the border of Winslow's actual inhabited parts.

"I'm not the one who claims to know everything about everyone in this town. What did you say before, it's your sworn duty?"

"Don't be dramatic. But no, that's the thing. I don't know who she is, and that should scare you."

That gives me pause. Everett doesn't seem like the type to lie. If he says he knows everyone, he does. So if he truly doesn't know this woman . . .

"I don't trust her either," I say. "But I also think we've been in town too long to come back empty-handed, and we haven't found anything that I couldn't have found in the comfort of the Regent library. Maybe she has some information that Headmaster Monroe doesn't know about? You said we need to extend our search outside of his reach. What better way to do that than . . . ?" I gesture wildly at the woman ahead of us.

"I didn't mean we should trust a random person."

I understand Everett's hesitation. I feel the same prickles on the back of my neck. "What other option do we have? I can't go back to school empty-handed. Besides, if she does anything, you'll protect me with that knife of yours."

"You're sure confident of that. What makes you think I won't leave you for her to make into a cake in her gingerbread oven?"

"I'm too important to you," I say, knowing he's teasing. But his deadpan scowl makes me pause. No, that's just Everett's normal resting face. "Speaking of which, have you had that knife the whole time?"

"I don't go anywhere without it."

"For situations like these?"

"For situations like these," he repeats. "And Perversions."

"You really think we'd meet one in town?"

He shrugs.

I roll my eyes, letting Everett have that one. I'm more interested in figuring out what this woman wants with us—and how she knew about me. I've learned something about this curse. Everyone connected to it wants something in exchange for whatever they possess. It's like having your life connected to this curse mutates you into a person who lives their life by quid pro quos.

I wonder, whatever this woman wants, if it's something I'd be willing to pay.

She leads us to her house, which we had passed when we drove toward the edge of town. A small one-story home that is the definition of quaint and cute. There's a small yard with mostly barren land, and a lopsided rusted-metal fence with the door partway open. There's a small doghouse, but it looks like it hasn't been inhabited for years.

No one in town—the few people on the streets that spider out from Main Street—seems to care about the shuffling woman, or us for that matter. She holds the gate open for both of us. Everett rolls his cycle through the entryway and places it on the rickety porch. The weight of it makes the floorboards groan.

"Yeah, this feels like a good idea," he mutters sarcastically without moving his mouth as the woman fumbles with her keys and pushes the door open.

"Be nice," I scold. But I'm thinking the same thing, no matter how much I don't want to admit it. I just remind myself that Everett has his knife. We'll be fine.

I close the door behind us, once the woman has welcomed us inside. The interior of her home is just as quaint and cute as the exterior. It's divided into three different sections—the living room, bedroom, and kitchen—each separated by beaded curtains.

"Would you boys like anything to drink?" she asks, leaning

over to throw chunks of wood into the furnace against one of the walls. "I have tea, water, lemonade, and, I believe, soda, though I don't drink the stuff. Too sweet for me."

"No," Everett says.

"Tea is fine, thank you," I add.

"Haven't you learned anything about taking tea from strangers?" he hisses, a bit too loudly.

"Mint?" she asks.

I smile, ignoring Everett. He isn't wrong, but I don't feel the same tight-wire tension I did when I was around Headmaster Monroe. Maybe it's a failed defense mechanism, or maybe she's just that good at hiding her motives, but I'm not worried about her drugging me. Besides, if he's not drinking the tea, then I have nothing to worry about.

"That would be perfect."

Everett glares at me while the woman shuffles into the kitchen, the beads on the curtain bouncing against one another.

"Seriously?"

"It's good manners," I argue. "I know that's probably something you don't know from living on the grounds for your whole life."

"Oh, fuck off," he whispers. "You know what I *have* done? Watched a lot of movies and gained pretty decent common sense. We have no idea what this woman wants or who she is. There is no universe in which taking something from her is smart."

I turn away from Everett and slowly walk around the living room, taking in as much as I can. The house has all the usual things: a couch with worn indentations of one person's body, the other seat barely touched. A knitted blanket of vibrant colors, probably the brightest and warmest thing in the room. An ashtray with half a dozen cigarette butts. Books, old newspapers. There's nothing really abnormal about this place. There's nothing that makes me fear for my life.

Maybe how normal it is should make me fear for my life.

"Douglas," Everett whispers. "Here."

Above the TV, there's a framed photo, with small tears in the corners, and there are specks of yellow to show its age. The photo is of a woman, around eighteen or so, standing with a boy to her left, close to the same age, bright warm smiles on their faces. Fanning on each side of the couple, there are other people: three on the left, two on the right.

"I know this man," he says, pointing to one on the right, two away from the girl. "That's my great-great-great . . . not sure how many greats . . . but that's Edward Everley. He led the hunting dogs that were sent into the forest to chase after Etaliein. Or so the legend says."

"And the rest?"

"The other families," he observes, tapping the glass right where the woman in the middle is in the photo. "That's the girl who was in love with Etaliein and killed."

"But you have no idea who this woman with us is?"

He shrugs. "No. But she's not part of our fun-loving cursed group."

I shake my head, glancing over my shoulder toward the kitchen.

I can still see the woman in there, fumbling with the tea bags and cups.

"She knew about what goes on in my head. That means she has to know something important."

Everett studies me, pushing his lips together in a thin line. "I don't think staying here is a good idea, Douglas."

"What, you afraid you're not going to be able to best some old woman if shit hits the fan?"

"No, I'm worried that shit will hit the fan and when it does come to combat, we'll realize she's not an old woman after all."

That makes me take pause. "You think she's a Perversion?"

He shrugs. "I have no idea what she is, but I've never heard Headmaster Monroe or my mother talk about her, and suddenly she knows about things happening in your head? That doesn't seem oddly convenient to you? Like something that should terrify us?"

Everett is right. We should get out of here. But something keeps me rooted in place.

Flexing my fingers on both hands until my bones crack, I let out a soft sigh. "Go get your bike. Check the oil or whatever. I'll be right out."

"Absolutely not," Everett says. "I'm not leaving you here with a woman who—"

"Everett," I say more sternly. "Go. I got this."

At the hospital a few years back, when my mama and I were called at four a.m. to say goodbye to my dad (we just didn't know that's why we were there yet), I read in a magazine that when you wake up in the morning and don't feel confident, all you can do is fake it until you *do* feel confident. That's what I'm doing right now: faking bravery.

Everything Everett has said is correct. This woman could be a Perversion. She could want to kill me. She could be some weird and crazed cultist who knows a little too much about town lore and now wants to be central to the story. Often the simplest answers are the true ones.

But that voice. The forest has been quieter ever since I saw . . . the man in the dream who gave me the magic I supposedly have. Well, not supposedly anymore. Everett and I both saw what happened with the dead guy. Magic isn't a possibility anymore; it's a reality for me.

Which is why when the forest whispers to me, and I can make out what it's saying, I don't try to push it back. I listen. It's telling me to stay.

"Five minutes," he whispers. "If you're not out by then—"

"You're going to come bursting in, throw me over your shoulder, and drag me out of here?"

"Something like that."

Before I can throw back another quippy response, he closes the door.

"Your friend going somewhere?"

The woman comes through the beaded waterfall with a metal tray: two steaming cups, made of the same metal, and a pot of tea with different fixings in small, cute bowls. It almost makes me lower my guard. It feels like coming home to your grandmother.

Or how Hansel and Gretel felt.

I pause for a moment, deciding how exactly I want to answer that question. It's not like she was in another room behind a closed door; I'm sure she heard our whole conversation. That being said, admitting that we don't trust her might not be the best way to get information from her.

Truth is always better, Douglas, my mama always says. *No matter what happens, bank on the truth.*

"He thought we should talk privately." Not a lie, not the full truth either. "Didn't think what you had to say related to him."

She nods absently, putting the tray down on the table, and then I help her into one of the rocking chairs that flank the couch.

"Your mother taught you well," she says, patting my arm when she's settled.

"She taught me to respect my elders. Kinda a required lesson you have to pass in a Black household."

"Even with those who you don't trust?"

The bluntness of the accusation feels like a soft punch to the chest.

"I don't need to trust you to be respectful."

"Your mother is a smart woman."

"Agreed."

We sit in a comfortable silence for a moment. The oak clock above the couch clicks reliably, setting a steady beat that I could tap my foot to if I wanted.

Eventually, the woman speaks first. "I should apologize." A beat. "For sneaking up on you and your friend like that."

As discreetly as I can, I study the woman. She's easily over sixty years old, though her slightly tan and leathery skin could be lying.

"You can apologize by telling me your name," I say. "That's a good place to start."

"Jane," she says.

"Nice to meet you, Jane." Feels weird to say that to . . . whatever she is . . . but what else do I say? "Let's start from the beginning. Were you born here?"

Jane nods.

"And your family was born here too?"

She nods again.

Alright, now we're getting somewhere, I think. She was born here, which explains why she knows of the curse. But it doesn't answer the most obvious question: "How did you know about me?"

It takes me a moment to realize I'm whispering the words.

"Isn't it obvious?" she asks. "You scream of wild magic and stink of hope."

Before I can ask for clarification, she turns her head, looking toward the kitchen. Judging by the path her eyes take, she's looking out the small circular window, divided by four panels, in the kitchen. Through that, I can see the forest.

"You hear it, don't you—the forest?"

"I always hear the forest." The words come out before I can silence them, but they feel right, saying them to her.

"Does it call to you? Sweetly, horrifically, quietly?"

I nod. Jane's not looking at me, but I know she knows I agree.

"But that's not all of it, is it? You hear it too, like a note layered under the melody. A whisper always present. What does that sound like to you, Douglas?"

"Pain." Just saying that word feels like a stopper has been released. Like it's the one thing I've been itching to say since I came to Regent. "It sounds like something in pain."

"Something?"

That's not the right word. We both know it. Quietly, I whisper what I really mean.

"Someone."

Slowly the woman stands, smoothing the front of her pleated dress.

"May I offer you a piece of advice, Douglas?" she asks as I stand.

"Never taken advice from a ghost before, but sure," I say, giving her a weak smile. "That's it, right? You're dead. That's why Everett doesn't know you."

The words come out before I can smooth them over. I pick up the mug of tea and take two strong sips. It's perfect; just the right amount of hazelnut and milk to be exactly how I like it.

"I am. Buried here in this plot of land, if you can call it that. The people of Winslow didn't actually give me a burial."

"And I'm assuming the reason why has to do with why I'm here."

"See," she says, smiling softly. "You are just as smart as I thought you were."

The woman puts her tea down, the cup making no sound against the tray. Suddenly, the room changes, like every color has been thrown into a blender and we are the blades. As the colors slow and particles begin to come together, slotting into place like a puzzle of a million small pieces, we're no longer standing in the house but outside, watching as the woman's home is burned to the ground, townspeople of Winslow cheering, egging the flames on.

"I was killed for speaking the truth," she says, plain and simple. There's no remorse in her voice, but how can someone not hate people who hurt them? Who killed them? "For not letting the past of Winslow be rewritten like so many people wanted to."

Within the windows of the home, I can see a shadowy figure moving from pane to pane, desperately trying to escape the flames that lick at her skin. I can't make out her face, but I don't need to. I know what panic and desperation look like, sound like, feel like.

A lump appears in my throat as I swallow hard. This reminds me of the fire back in DC; the way the smoke strangled my lungs, the figure I saw, for just a moment, disappearing behind the flames, the screams I heard.

That's how this all started. One mistake that the police claimed I made. One heater left on in a building that was too drafty while my mama was out working, and like the flimsy wallpaper, everything—my future, our home, the other residents' lives, all went up in flames. All because of me. So why can't I remember it? A person should remember something like that, right?

The woman places her hand on my shoulder, squeezing it gently. When my eyes meet hers, I see a soft smile on her face.

"I'm the one who should be comforting you," I say quietly.

"They were horrible to you."

"They were human," she corrects quietly. "Humans are always afraid of what they don't understand and what will threaten their acceptable reality. Plus I am dead, Douglas, and you are alive. There's no reason to pity those who passed; our story is over. Yours can still end in happiness, or suffering."

Jane turns back to the scene in front of us. "Truth, Douglas, is one of the most powerful disinfectants. You were told, I'm sure, that the people of Winslow killed the woman years ago for her love affair with a god. That's only half-true. The people of Winslow did kill a god's lover, except they were not a woman, but a man who was not much older than you. And not just the people of Winslow—the main families each had a role to play."

That wasn't what I expected her to say.

My gaze snaps to her face, but she doesn't stop staring directly into the flames.

"But why? They weren't doing anything wrong."

"You're too smart to be that naive, Douglas. The people of Winslow killed the man because he was a man, Douglas," she says, glancing over at me without moving her head. "They were a proud, God-fearing people. Accepting the help of a pagan god was one thing, but allowing a pagan god to defile the purity of their town with its urges for a man? That they couldn't stand."

"But they weren't urges," I correct. "That makes it sound perverse. Love isn't disgusting because a man loves a man, or a woman a woman, or anyone loves anyone."

"That's not what the people of Winslow thought. That's why

they killed him, burned away his sin to help purify their town, like Eve and her original sin."

"And then they rewrote history," I whisper as, slowly, it all comes together. "The town didn't want the world to know of the . . . homosexuality that existed here. So, they changed the narrative. Everyone can get behind the fable of a girl who was seduced by a god; there are stories written about it. It would be easy for that to become part of the town's lore. And everyone just let it happen. Except you."

"Except me."

In the window, Jane's body slows. The pounding of her fists becomes less frantic until I see her body slide against the glass and out of frame. Moments later, the house groans and collapses in on itself. As a gust of soot, dirt, and flames engulf the surrounding area, including me and the ghost, the scene returns to her home, as if the images before never happened. But the hairs on my arms still feel warm, and the smell of burning wood and flesh still fills my nostrils, like what I saw was actually right in front of me the whole time.

"What else do you know?" I ask.

"It isn't about what I know, Douglas," she says. "All the knowledge in the world won't stop what has already happened or prevent what has to happen."

"You make it sound like all of this is predetermined, or has happened before," I comment. "Like I don't have a say in my next step."

She doesn't elaborate. Instead she just stares at me, ghostlike, without an expression on her face to give away any information about what she might be thinking.

"Is that what you're telling me? What do you know about me that you're not sharing?"

A smile slowly spreads over her face. Her thin, bony fingers move, smoothing wrinkles from my shirt. She leans forward, pressing a kiss I can't exactly feel against my cheek.

"You've seen the tree, haven't you?" she whispers, right against my ear. "It speaks to you, not the forest. It calls to you and has been since you arrived. It will be your north star, Douglas. If you can make it there, everything will be explained, and then, only then, will you have the tools to make a decision that will end your story in happiness or tragedy."

Jane squeezes both of my shoulders, squaring my body like she's going to look at me for the last time and wants to hold my image in her mind.

"You take care of yourself, Douglas Jones," she says, pulling me gently down to her level and kissing my cheek. "And remember two things. One, the forest is unforgiving to those it swallows whole. And two: the dead have more to tell you than the living want you to know."

I won't let her be forgotten. I promise. I'll break this curse and put her to rest. It's the least I can do. For her. And for the others I'm sure that exist who have been affected by this curse and those like the Monroes who will do anything to protect it.

A tug in the center of my chest pulls me toward the door. The rush of cold air from Winslow is a stark difference from the warmth inside the home. It nips and scratches at my skin, clawing at me like a wild animal.

My mind is swimming. This is exactly what I was looking for. Something, a morsel of information, that steers me in the right direction. Did Everett know? No, he couldn't have. He would have told me.

Maybe this will be important to him too?

I shake my head to clear my thoughts. My vision focuses on Everett, who isn't exactly looking at me, but past me toward the woman's house. I step off her porch two stairs at a time, my mind moving faster than my legs can carry me.

"Hey," I say, jutting my thumb back to the home. "Number one, told you I'd be fine and back in less than five minutes."

"Douglas."

"Number two, I don't know if you know this, but the whole *This god loved a woman* thing? A lie. He loved a guy. And the headmaster's family is who led the fire to burn them."

"I know that already, but Doug—"

"How did you know? Of course, you're an Everley, but that's not what is important. What is crucial here is he was—"

"Douglas!"

Everett cuts me off before the words *like me* can leave my lips, which might be for the best. I've never said out loud that I'm gay. It's not like I'm afraid people will look at me different or something, because they already do that. What's one more difference. I think the reason I haven't said it is because it's just another reason, piled onto so many others, that I won't find love or someone for me. Ever. A Black kid who might have committed murder who listens to a forest and likes guys? Who wants to be with someone like that?

"What?" I say instead.

Everett points behind me. I turn around, except when I do, the house isn't there. Only a precariously stacked pile of wood and rubble, with smudges of hastily and haphazardly applied swaths of soot. If you squinted, turned your head to the side, and looked at the wreckage just right, it would almost look like some high-value abstract art piece.

But that doesn't take away from the fact that the home I just spent the past few minutes inside isn't there. And probably never was. It's like the house I was just in was there for me, but not for everyone else.

"The forest is unforgiving to those it swallows whole," I whisper.

"What did you say?" Everett asks.

I wave it off. Everett studies me in a way that feels like his eyes have the ability to pick the locks that protect my heart and my soul.

"You believe me, don't you?" I ask Everett.

"I mean. I saw you walk into a house that a moment later wasn't there after you walked out. In the blink of an eye a whole fucking home I had never seen before, and I know every home here, disappeared and aged. So yeah, I'd say I believe you," he says, nodding toward his bike. "Tell me more about what you were just saying while I take us back to campus. We don't want to be out too much longer."

He's right. The forest looks more oppressive the deeper into night we get. It can't stop me from thinking how the dead are all trying to tell me something. And I can't help but think, deep down, they're warning me to stay away.

14

Like some sort of obsession, I've spent the past week and a half trying to find more info about that woman and the home I saw. The fruits of my labor couldn't even feed a toddler at snack time.

The good news is that Headmaster Monroe did keep his word. There isn't a single book in the Regent Academy library that I can't check out without question. Even when another student has it loaned out for a school project, an email is in my inbox about its availability within the next two and a half hours. It's like everything Regent has to offer is only one short email or request away.

Everything, at least, that the headmaster deems I have the right to know.

I know the woman's full name now: Jane Halstead. I know she comes from a line that, as far as I can tell, has lived in Winslow since the pilgrims decided to take the land from the Indigenous people. The photo on her mantel makes sense now. I know her house was in a fire about twenty years ago because her occult and pagan beliefs made the town uncomfortable.

I know she died in that fire, unintentionally, when the teens who set it as a prank to warn the "old crazy woman she wasn't welcome here" didn't know she was inside. Two teens who were Regent Academy students.

I know no one knows why the house with the rubble hasn't been swept away, or even why the rubble is there. And I know that Headmaster Monroe owns the land. Just one of many questions I want answered by him—but if I ask, he will find a way to weasel out of it and change the subject.

"So do you think it was a vision or something?"

Everett is sitting on one of the tables in the courtyard of Regent Academy, boots on the seat, talking in between bites of the apple he has in his hand. He's wearing a checkered shirt with the sleeves rolled up; many professors have walked by and glared at him for being out of uniform. In typical Everett-style aloofness, he gave them a two-finger wave and they continued on their way.

"I mean, that would make sense, wouldn't it?" I ask Everett. "We saw the house on the inside."

Everett nods. "It looked like someone lived there. Like, currently."

"Right," I reply. "And after I had my conversation with her . . ."

"It looks like rubble," he says. "Like it hadn't been lived in."

"For years." I tap the book in front of me. "At least twenty. Do *you* have an explanation for that?"

Everett shrugs, taking another chomp on his apple. "Magic?"

"You say that so easily. You know, most people don't believe in magic."

"Most people don't come from a cursed bloodline and can't leave a town even if they want to."

Everett jumps off the table and stands tall, like his body is a lightning rod for confidence that passes through him and dissipates.

A pulse of jealousy rockets through me. I wonder what it feels like to just . . . be so sure of yourself. To not care about what the rest of the world thinks or feels. It's probably a defense mechanism, and if I peeled back the layers of his slightly suntanned skin, I'm sure his underbelly would be like that of any Regent student. Afraid. Concerned. Insecure.

I push the thought out of my head, idly flipping through the book on Winslow's history, seeing if I can find anything else about Jane Halstead and her family. Maybe some clue that can tell me where her descendants are, or where her ancestors are buried. Did any of them make it out of the town?

"Speaking of magic . . ." Everett drawls out.

"Nothing good comes from starting a sentence like that."

"Get used to it, savior."

My eyes flicker up into a glare that I hope makes him feel like daggers are stabbing his eyeballs. But there he is, with that stupidly innocent grin that makes the corners of his eyes crinkle and his dimples show.

I don't think it's wrong to say that in a different situation, maybe I'd ask Everett out. It's more likely to think I'd pine after him and make it a significant portion of my personality. But in a universe where I had friends to push me forward, maybe I'd ask him to prom. Maybe we'd have our first kiss, have a happy ending. I could see a world where we could work together. Or at least one where I'd go to sleep thinking about him.

But this isn't that world. This is a world where Everett and I are far too different. And there's no way he would like someone like me.

"But seriously, speaking of magic, if you're going to try to destroy a more than three-hundred-year-old curse, you're going to need to learn how to defend yourself. I'm going to do my best to protect you, but I might not always be around and even if I am . . ."

Everett pauses. A flash of darkness passes over his face, pulling him into the endless pit of memory. I know that look. It's the look of remembering someone you've lost. It's the look of getting caught off guard by a wave of emotion.

When you lose someone, you learn how to steel yourself. What your triggers are, how certain dates will elicit more emotions and force memories to play. But every so often, something unsuspected sucker-punches you right in the gut. It takes your breath away and leaves you at its mercy. The only way to get past fear is through it. That's true. But it's the same for grief.

Mama has that same look on her face when she remembers Dad.

"If I have to deal with a Perversion?" I ask, continuing our conversation.

"Not if, *when*," he corrects, snapping himself out of the memory. "That or an Emissary. They're protectors of the forest. You think you're going to shut down a whole curse and never come across one? Never meet one that wants to give your head to the forest and use your blood and body as fertilizer?"

"That's . . . a little intense, don't you think?"

Everett arches his brow. "Seriously, Douglas. Those things are brutal. You heard one in the forest. Whatever you imagine, add about five feet and at least twenty percent more rage. My family is trained to deal with them and . . ."

Everett rolls up the sleeve of his shirt on his right arm, high enough that the fabric bunches in the middle of his bicep. On his right arm, from the wrist all the way past the bundle of fabric, there's a thick pale jagged scar. It healed as best it could, but from the way the scar is raised from the flesh like a mountain range, I can tell that when it was inflicted, the wound was brutal.

"This one had a scythe, four arms, and four legs. Could swivel on its waist to turn a hundred and eighty degrees in a blink of an eye. It took all three of us to put it down. It slashed me so deep I could see my bone. Headmaster Monroe almost agreed we needed to bring in a doctor from Montpelier to deal with it.

"Imagine facing that by yourself. I can't train you to win against something like that."

I don't disagree with what Everett is saying. I need to learn more self-defense. I'm walking into the belly of a beast that is magical, that no one really understands.

"Okay, you may be right. But can you help me—maybe with some self defense or something?

"Yes, I can train you. At least in the basics."

The moment we arrived at the Everley home, Everett told me to make myself comfortable and disappeared out the back door, leaving it open and giving me a direct line of sight to the small shed about an eighth of a mile behind the home.

The Everley home looks the same as it did before, but right now, more lived in. A small oak table that has enough imperfections to tell me someone made it by hand; a bunch of coats, boots, and cold-weather clothes piled on top of each other by the door; and a small living room. The house is tightly packed, and it doesn't look like three people can live here comfortably. But the longer I'm inside the house, the larger it feels, and the more like an actual home it seems. Like, even though the space is limited, there's love and care here, and really, that's all that matters. The rest is just extra.

There are a few photos on the mantel over the fireplace. All were taken during a hunting trip with a Polaroid camera. Everett with his first slain deer. Emma standing in front of some construct she built. There's even one snapshot of Evelyn and a man I can only guess is Everett's father rock climbing. They're both belaying from a cliff face, a third person responsible for capturing this moment. I wonder if that's Everett, Emma, or someone else.

They look happy, loved.

"Found it," Everett says when he returns, carrying a pack in both hands. It's heavy enough to make his biceps flex and when he dumps it on the table unceremoniously, it sounds like dozens of broken glass shards clattering on the wood. "Stand up straight, I need to see something."

"Please?"

Everett rolls his eyes, dusting off his shirt. "Let me try again.

Stand up straight, unless you want to die and get swallowed up by a monstrously magical forest that is going to do everything in its power to kill you."

"Well, when you put it like that . . ."

"Shut up," he says, but a flicker of a grin passes over his face like the first crackle of lightning during a summer storm.

Obediently, I stand up as tall as I can, pushing five-foot-eight—five-foot-nine if you count my curls.

He circles me twice before standing in front. "You've never fought before, have you?"

"Most people haven't."

"Everyone needs to get their ass kicked at least once in their life," Everett counters.

"Including you?"

"Including me."

He turns to the table and unfurls the pack, revealing all kinds of knives. Light catches the curvature of the metal when he lays all the blades out, evenly separating them like he's putting them on display.

"Knives?" I ask, stepping forward and scanning them. They're all different; some like the hunter's knife always attached to his hip, some smaller, some wider. Even without touching them, I can tell each of them would feel different in my hand, that they would play with gravity in a different way.

"Knives," he repeats. "I'm not going to give you a gun. Or an axe; that's too big for you. You're spritely, you're quick, and you're smart. A knife is perfect for you. Especially these."

Everett grabs the smallest ones, with slightly curved blades about four or five inches long and handles with some thinly cut brown wrapping. He takes the ten of them, hands me five, and juts his head toward the door.

"Follow me."

Handling the blades feels awkward, like they don't fit in my hands. I see these as tools, not weapons. I'm going to be expected to use these to hurt another? To kill another? That makes my stomach turn.

I take a deep, shaking breath, and close my eyes, centering my body and focusing only on my breathing.

"It wasn't my fault. It wasn't my fault. It wasn't my fault," I repeat over and over again. But that doesn't make me feel any better. It doesn't stop the rapid thumping of my heart in my head and chest. Doesn't stop the dizziness from taking over. The only thing that does that is . . .

Everett.

His voice rings clear, like an iron bell acting as a beacon, calling me home. When I open my eyes, he's standing in the entryway, holding the door for me with his elbow. "You coming?"

"Unfortunately," I mutter, following him.

"Come again?"

"Nothing." And I follow him out the door.

15

"Do you know how to play HORSE?"

It's been a week since Everett first started training me. Teaching me how to hold the weapon, draw it without looking, the most important places to slash in order to hurt, or kill, someone.

"HORSE? Like the basketball game?" I ask.

Everett nods, walking across the field behind his house through the sopping wet earth, which makes thick, sloppy noises as his boots sink in and suction out, and yanks a tarp off a round bull's-eye target. The same ones the school's archery club and archery elective use.

"Did you steal this?"

"That doesn't answer the question I asked you."

I shrug. "I think I want to know what type of person I'm getting involved with before I decide if I want to play a game with them."

Everett rolls his eyes. "So let me get this straight: I don't go to class, and that's okay?"

"Mm-hmm."

"I drive like a bat out of hell on a motorcycle."

"Yep."

"I hunt creatures that, honestly, *do* go bump in the night."

"That's right."

"But stealing from the school? That's the line you draw?"

"Bingo."

Everett huffs, rolling the tarp around his arms and putting it off into the corner. "If it really matters to you—I didn't steal this. It was given to us. Funny enough, if you tell the headmaster I need something for target practice so I can make sure my aim will hit a Perversion and not a student, he'll give you anything you want."

"Imagine that."

"Now your turn." He repeats, "Have you ever played HORSE?"

"If you're about to tell me we're going to play HORSE with knives . . ."

"That's exactly what I'm about to say."

Everett picks up one of the knives, tossing it into the air without looking, catching it as it turns 360 degrees in the air. "Rules are simple. We name one of the rings: the red bull's-eye, the yellow middle ring, or the black outer ring. If you pick the ring and the other person misses, but you make the shot, you get a letter. If they make it and you miss it, they get a letter. If neither of you get it, they get a letter."

"I know how to play HORSE, Everett."

"Right, but you don't know how to play *my* version of HORSE," he corrects. "Each person states a question and picks a target. If you hit the target, you win that round, and the other person has to answer. If you miss, then you have to answer. And they can't say no to any question. Whoever 'wins' gets a letter, too. First to spell HORSE wins."

"I thought the point was to teach me how to throw a knife to defend myself? It's not like a Perversion is going to ask me my deepest darkest secret and I'm going to have to land a knife between its eye sockets while answering."

"No, but if you know how to throw a knife under pressure, knowing that if you lose you have to answer some deeply personal, possibly embarrassing question? I'm more comfortable letting you face Perversions alone."

"Comfortable? Heaven forbid the great Everett Everley doesn't think I can hold my own."

But we both know this is just me trying to make myself seem bigger than I actually am. I've seen how Emma carried that head and dropped it on the table like it was nothing but a heap of meat. The Everleys have been training and fighting their whole lives. How am I supposed to learn everything I need to know in a few days?

"Here," Everett says, standing behind me. He hovers his hands over my biceps. "May I?"

"Sure."

"Stand up straight, relax," he mutters, manipulating my body like it's a doll. "Keep your right foot forward and your left foot slightly behind it. Yeah, like that. Good. Now," he whispers in his baritone voice that crackles when he talks right in my ear, "when you want to throw the knife, you should focus on how you *hold* the knife. That's important. Keep the target in the center of your vision. Hold the handle here, in the middle, kinda how you would hold a hammer."

"Bold of you to think I've ever used a hammer," I tease, looking over my shoulder at Everett.

But the fact our faces are so close together? I notice features of Everett I've never seen before. A faint scar right above his lips. The almost invisible freckles that pepper his nose like a secret constellation. How his green eyes have flecks of brown in them, which you can only see in the right light.

Objectively, Everett Everley is good-looking.

He shakes his head, not saying anything to my bad joke. "Are you going to let me continue?"

"I'm not stopping you. Not like I have that power over you."

"You have no idea how much power you have, Douglas." He doesn't give me a moment to process that. "Now, this is important. Be sure to keep your thumb on top of your other fingers when you throw. That's key. That'll make sure none of your fingers will alter the trajectory of your throw. If your fingers get caught, your knife will go off to the right, or the hilt, not the blade, will hit your target."

He guides my hand to show how he wants my body to follow through. Everett keeps his grip on me light, his fingers dancing over my skin. Firm enough so his guidance is intentional, but not so firm that it feels stifling.

"That hurts." *Hurts* isn't the right word. It's like how your muscles feel when you haven't worked them in a long time.

"It'll become second nature," he promises. "The goal is to get to a point where you don't even notice the tightness. Your body is so used to the movements, it just does it automatically."

For the next two hours, we forego HORSE while Everett builds on what he taught me. Now he teaches me different types of throws; specifically the half-spin throw and the single-spin throw. We practice each of those for an additional hour straight, Everett standing at different vantage points to analyze my body and posture from different angles. Sometimes he sighs, sometimes he has a constructive comment, sometimes he says nothing; just nods, a silent way of telling me to go again.

Once I throw five knives in a row with perfect posture, each roughly hitting the intended target, he moves next to me, blowing puffs of white-hot air on his palms. It's warmer than it has been other days in Winslow, but that doesn't mean much. With us being so active for the past few hours? I'm sweating. My jacket is thrown to the side.

"I think you're ready," he says, grabbing his own set of knives. "Move over. Let's play HORSE."

Everett grins and stands next to me, with about three feet of space between us, and the distance between us and the target roughly ten feet or so. Metal clinks against metal as he rolls the knives in his hands.

"We're really doing this?" I ask.

"We're really doing this." He gestures with his knife. "You first."

I grab one of the knives I have in my belt loop and take aim. I let the air flow through me as I take a breath, feel it in my whole body, and wind my arm back, but Everett stops me.

"Name your target first," he reminds me.

"Blue ring," I mutter.

"And your question."

"Are you afraid of dying?"

Before I can let the fear of my own question take over me, I toss the blade with a flick of my wrist. The sliver of silver does a double turn in the air, catching the light and refracting off a puddle, before sinking deep within the balsa wood of the target.

"Hmm," Everett says.

"Hmm?"

"Good form, bad execution. Make sure your left foot is in front of you. You're going to want to react quickly to whatever comes next when you throw the knife."

Effortlessly, he tosses the knife. It does a half turn, sinking into the wood, but not the blue ring, causing me to get a letter.

"*H* for me," he says, glancing at me with a spark of mirth in his eyes. "And your answer?"

I hesitate for a moment. Not because I'm afraid to say it, but because I'm not sure what my answer should be.

"I've never really thought about it," I say instead. That's the honest answer. "I mean, how many seventeen-year-olds actually have to come face-to-face with their own death?"

He shrugs. "I do, every time I deal with those things."

"You're not the average seventeen-year-old."

He flashes a wolfish grin at me. "Damn straight. But I'm not sure that answer counts. Now that you know breaking this curse means you might die, are you afraid?"

I rub my thumb against the blade, pressing my flesh down hard against the angled metal until I feel a light burn. It doesn't break the skin, but it does hurt, enough to leave a thin red line that slowly disappears.

"I don't think I'm afraid of it," I finally say. "I'm curious, if that doesn't make me sound morbid. Curious about what happens after you die. I'd like to know that."

"But not too early, I hope," he says more as a statement, not as a question.

"You saying you'd miss me if I died, Everett?"

He shrugs, tossing the knife into the air again before grabbing it out of the air.

"My turn. Bull's-eye," he says. "And my question . . . Do you think I'm handsome?"

Without much hesitation, he throws the blade forward. In a blink, the metal sinks deep into the bull's-eye.

"Shit."

He smirks, flashing a wink before stepping aside, letting me stand directly in front of the bull's-eye. I flex my fingers, bringing the red bull's-eye into the center of my mind's eye, focusing solely on it. I let the rest of the world melt away, even the distant sounds of Regent Academy students, or the soft rustling of the forest, or the whispering of the woods in my head. Instead, I focus on the task at hand. The bull's-eye.

Inhale . . . exhale . . . inhale . . . exhale. I wait until I feel my pulse relax. Until each thump in my mind is predictable and a comfort instead of a fear. Swallowing thickly, I dig my heel into the earth, raise my right arm, and lean into the throw, flicking my wrist . . . and watch as the knife nails the bull's-eye, resting snugly against Everett's knife.

"Well, shit," Everett mutters. "I didn't think you were going to make that."

"Have no confidence in me? Or no confidence in your teaching skills?"

He narrows his eyes, saying nothing in response at first. He blows puffs of hot white air on his hands, rubbing them together. As if he's prepping himself for the answer. "You're not bad," I say.

"Not bad?" he groaned. "Wow, talk about an ego killer."

"I never knew protecting your ego was part of the agreement." I smirk. "My turn?"

He gestures, moving his hand forward in an *after you* motion.

"My question, since you want to get so personal: Have you ever kissed someone?"

I go through the motions, practicing and executing the throw. It's becoming easier with each toss. The blade sinks into the soft wood, not as deep as Everett's throw, but deep enough to stay there firmly.

"Rebecca Cononley," he says without me having to ask. "She graduated last year. Daughter of a media mogul."

"A student?"

"You sound surprised. Think I can't bag a student?" he asks almost defensively, but with a hint of mirth.

You're right, I think. But not because of the reason he assumes. Again, and objectively speaking of course, Everett is *very* good-looking. Tall, strong, has that brooding quality that people like. But he's also a groundskeeper's son, and the students at Regent are class obsessed.

"I just thought you'd be happier with a townie."

"Smooth recovery," he says sarcastically, sitting on a stump. He uses one of the blades to dig a hunk of dried dirt from the grooves of his boots. "I think it was some pride thing for her. She wanted to prove to her friends she wasn't like other girls. I saw it coming for days. Her visiting our house, asking if she could help, asking probing questions. It was obvious I was just some notch on her bedpost."

"So you slept with her," I blurt out.

Everett opens his mouth, then closes it before any words can escape. He squints his eyes, almost like a cat focusing on the world around him to bring everything into sharper detail. The weight of the words feels like heavy bricks stacked precariously on my chest. That feeling when you *know* you shouldn't have said something.

"That was wrong."

"Yeah, it was."

"I'm sorry."

"I should make you give me that *O* you just got for that."

"I'll do it happily," I say, pulling an invisible letter out of my pocket and handing it over to him.

Everett rolls his eyes, giving me the finger instead. "If it makes you feel any better, no, I didn't."

"It's none of my business."

"But it didn't stop you from asking, so you must care."

The directness in his voice is refreshing. There's no way to hide from his words, and I can't help but reply as honestly as I'm comfortable: with a shrug.

"And you?" he asks. "Have you ever kissed someone?"

"That's not part of our deal."

"Humor me, will you?"

I could easily lie. Maybe I should, but for some reason, there isn't a part of me that even thinks about hesitating, not for a second. It's like I know my words will be safe, sealed away in Everett's mind. Maybe it's because, morbidly, I don't know if he has any friends. Who is he going to tell? Emma? Maybe it's because I trust him.

"I've never kissed a guy before."

Everett pauses his movement for a fraction of a breath, hesitating, twirling the blade in his hand. "You're into guys?"

"Is that a problem?"

My words come out like poisonous bile. I swallow, digging my heels into the earth. I don't think Everett is homophobic, but you never know. You never know anything about anyone.

"Not a problem for me. I would be a hypocrite if there was. You want to finish the game?"

Everett shifts back into our game, gesturing for me to state my bet and to make a throw. He's already moved on; the conversation rolling off his back like a bead of sweat rolling off his brow, while I'm still stuck in the middle of our revelation.

What did he mean by *hypocrite*? Is Everett Everley gay? No, bi? No, he could be gay—just because his first kiss was with a girl doesn't mean he isn't gay. But he could also be bi. I don't want to discount the fact that maybe he does like girls and guys. Or maybe he's pansexual. I can't forget that option either. Honestly, does it really matter if there's a label?

Of course it does! Because how am I supposed to figure out which applies to him? More importantly, why do I care?

"Sure," I say. "Let me beat you and we can get this over with."

Everett scoffs. "You're sure cocky when the game is tied."

"I've just been letting you think you're going to win to help your confidence."

"Is that it? Alright then, you're on."

16

"You seem distracted, honey," my mama says. We are in her room, sitting on opposite ends of the couch, eating dinner together, something we haven't done for a while.

Since the game of HORSE I lost, I haven't seen Everett around campus.

On the list of things I have to worry about, Everett's whereabouts are at the bottom. He's more capable than me when it comes to surviving on his own. There's no reason I should concern myself with his well-being.

But I've stopped by his home three times over the past five days, and he hasn't been around. Always near misses.

"He went into town," Emma said yesterday.

"You just missed him—he's out surveying the grounds," his

mother said the day before that.

And five days ago, the day after our friendly little competition? The door was locked. Not a single light was on in the home when I looked through the window. It's almost as if he's intentionally avoiding me, which feels like I'm reading too much into a simple missed connection.

But my mama is right; I am distracted. She just can't know that.

"Something up?"

I shake my head. If only I could tell her the truth, what is actually happening. Why the headmaster visited her personally a few weeks ago and told her I was excused from all my classes. How the reasoning he gave—a private mentorship with him that will teach me more important life skills than I could ever learn in a classroom—is complete and total BS.

But if I told her why, she'd start prying, and she wouldn't let it go. And something tells me that in the end, no matter how much I'd plead and barter, if she got too close to the truth, Headmaster Monroe wouldn't lose a moment of sleep extinguishing her life to keep his secret safe.

I can't risk that. She's all I have left.

"I'm fine," I promise, forcing a smile that I know she won't see through. "Just tired. Headmaster Monroe's regime is kicking my ass."

"How is that going, by the way? You don't talk about it much."

There's a hint of curiosity in her voice. On the surface, there's something alluring about Headmaster Monroe and his offer. That's how he's gotten as far as he has in life; not just money, but his charm. Additionally, he's preying on the one thing my mother wants more than anything for me: a life. A future. A purpose.

Of course my mama believes him. Look at the gifts he's already thrown at her feet. A job, this amazing opportunity for me, and never-ending kindness. My mama isn't a stupid woman, but she has blinders on when it comes to me.

It's up to me to protect her.

"It's going fine. Just a lot of lessons about business."

"That's what you think you'll go into? Business?" she asks, scooping some of the potato soup into her mouth. She was working late tonight, filling out medical forms, but we still try to have dinner together once a week. And I could use a break from the library.

"I think so. I'm good at it."

The lie is as easy as swallowing water, despite how much deceiving her makes me sick. I don't enjoy this; especially how my mama's eyes light up, thinking I've finally found a path for myself that's safe. How she thinks she made the right choice, and everything is turning out how she's prayed for.

But it's not all fake. I can see myself going into business. Maybe a business far away from here. Maybe even on another continent so the memory of Regent Academy is simply the last line in my bio on a website, but I can see it. And that's what scares me.

Because if I do what the headmaster wants, then that life could easily be mine.

"Well, I'm glad he's helping you," she says. "I admit, I wasn't sure this was the right place for you when the offer came our way."

"But what choice did we have, right?"

My mama doesn't look at me, only nods curtly. "Opportunities don't always announce themselves, Douglas. Sometimes they appear and are gone a moment later. You have to trust that the choice you're making is the right one, one you can make the most of, but most importantly, stomach if it goes badly. When Mrs. Hale came to me, asking for my blessing before visiting you, I knew this was the right choice. But you had to make that decision, not me."

She reaches over, taking my hand that is cold from the condensation on the glass I was just holding, and gives it a squeeze. My eyes drift up, meeting her wet ones.

"I'm so proud of you, baby."

I wish she hadn't said that.

Her pride feels like a hundred additional pounds on top of the weight I'm already carrying, and now it threatens to splinter my shoulders into a million shards. If only she knew what I had to do. If only she knew that if I fail, or if something happens to her, no one will remember.

Or worse, if something happens to me, she won't even remember she had a son. She'd just be another woman, working at Regent for as long as she could remember.

I flash her a quick smile and finish the last bits of the soup so she can't see the way the grin doesn't spark life in my eyes. "I need to get going. I have some homework the headmaster wants me to tackle before our next session."

"Of course, of course," Mama says. "Don't let me keep you from your destiny. Anything I can do to help?"

I know she's just asking to be nice, but I also know there's a piece of her that wants to be helpful, to be part of my journey to greatness. I walk over, kiss her cheek, and give her a squeeze. "You've done enough, promise."

I give her another kiss on the head before leaving her room. Once I'm on the stone walkway, I turn left instead of right, heading toward the Everley home.

There's a faint light on, and I can see three figures moving in the window.

Emma answers the door after two knocks. She doesn't look exactly surprised to see me, nor thrilled. "You're here for Everett."

I nod. "Is he in?"

Emma just gives me a blank stare before silently stepping aside. I wonder what she thinks about me. Does she think I can actually break the curse, or does she not care?

"He's in his room," she finally says. "Down the hall and to the left."

I nod again, flashing a courteous smile to Evelyn. She nods back, but her eyes linger for a moment too long, like she wants to say something.

I force my feet forward, knocking on the ajar door that spills out soft auburn light.

"It's open," Everett says.

I'm about to enter Everett's room. There's something so personal about this. The place where he sleeps. Where he dreams. Where he hopes and thinks. Being in such proximity to him? Away from his sister or mother? From everyone else at school. So many things could happen in this bedroom. And I'm not sure if I want those to happen, or not to happen, with Everett. But I know I can't stop thinking about them.

Walking in, I'm hit with an image I should have expected. Boys are always the same, no matter what century or class they come from. Everett's room is messy, filled with posters of rock and alternative punk bands. Clothes are strewn across the floor, and a stockpile of weapons sits on the table. Knives are wedged on a sharpening board, a gun half-assembled, half-cleaned, and another blade with a longer handle leaning against the wall, the handle halfway in the process of being rewrapped.

On his messy bed, there's a pile of books and notebooks, an old-looking laptop with a screensaver on . . . and then there's him. Standing in front of a too-small mirror, dressed in a pair of boxer briefs, dress socks, and a dress shirt, trying to tie his tie.

Our eyes lock through the slightly filmy mirror. For a moment, he stops fumbling with the ropes of fabric, as if he's caught in some lie and he's trying to figure out a way through it. I know, because I'm feeling the same thing. Why is Everett dressing up?

If you can call it dressing up. It's just a button-down and a tie with a jacket thrown over. Jeans are still on the bed and a nicer pair of boots than I've seen him wear are on the floor.

"I didn't know you owned anything other than work clothes and school clothes," I settle on saying.

"This is the only 'nice' thing I own," he mutters as he lets his hands fall to his sides with a sigh. "Damn it. Fucking tie."

"Here. Let me help."

I move toward him, wedging myself between his body and the wall. My fingers move like they're on autopilot, twisting and bending the fabric to suit my will.

"What type of knot do you want?"

"There's different types?"

I pause. "Mm-hmm. Windsor, Half Windsor, Four-in-Hand, Pratt, Nicky . . ."

"Whatever one you think will look best."

I pull back, gently pushing him so there's some distance between us. The dark suit jacket and white shirt are classic. The tie is the only pop of color—a forest green.

"Let's go with Windsor. Classic."

My fingers go through the motion of tying a Windsor knot while Everett obediently tilts his head up to give me room.

"You're not going to ask me why I'm wearing this?"

"Would you tell me the truth if I did?"

Everett shifts, and I can tell by the way the vein in his neck becomes more prominent that he's frowning. "I'd never lie to you."

"Funny joke," I chuckle.

"No, seriously." Everett pulls back, forcing me to look at him. "I won't lie to you, Douglas."

"How do I know that's not a lie?" I say, trying to break the thickness in the air.

But Everett doesn't laugh, doesn't make a joke, doesn't even try to lighten the mood.

"Ask me," he says. "Ask me again why I'm getting dressed up."

The question is, do I really want to know the answer? There's only a few reasons why, one of which is that it's a special occasion.

But curiosity gets the best of me, and knowledge is better held than free.

"Why are you dressed up, Everett?"

'I'm going on a date." He says it without pause, almost as if he wanted me to ask.

Each word feels like a brick slapping me across the face, especially the last one: *date*.

"Cool, congrats." I finish tying the tie, tightening it a bit too tight around his throat. Everett lets out a small wheeze, clenching his fists by his sides.

My mind is racing, my pulse is throbbing. I don't know why I care. Everett can go on a date. He should live his life, more power to him. I'm happy for him. I think I am? Yeah, I am. But, if I really am, then why can't I stop my throat from turning dry? Why can't I stop my fingers from fumbling the fabric of his tie a little rougher than needed?

Deep down, I know why. But I'm not going to bring that thought to the forefront. I'm here for a very specific reason. Break the curse, get everything I ever wanted. Everett isn't part of that.

"Ow."

"Sorry."

"Do you want to know who?"

I shouldn't care. I shouldn't have this hot burning feeling in my stomach. I shouldn't feel like I want to strangle him, or want to know exactly who he's going out with. It doesn't matter. He's allowed to go on a date with anyone he wants to.

"Done."

Everett turns to look at himself in the mirror. He turns his face, left to right, examining his well-formed, sharp jaw, and tugging slightly on the tie. Finally, he gives a curt nod.

"Looks amazing. Thank you. You never answered my question."

"Why do you care?"

Everett steps back, walks over, and grabs his jeans, slipping them on and tucking his shirt into them as he jumps up three times to straighten out the pants.

"Just thought you might." A beat. "You know, if you don't want me to go—"

"I didn't say that."

"I know, but if you did."

"If I did what?"

He shrugs. "I wouldn't go."

The bluntness of his words feels like a train crashing into my chest. I didn't expect the sheer honesty of his sheer honesty. In fact, they are so frank, it raises my hackles.

"Why?"

"Why wouldn't I go?"

"You're going on a date because you like this . . . ?"

"Girl," he says. "She asked me to get dressed like this."

"To make yourself fit more the type of person she would date."

"Mm-hmm. Exactly."

"So, you're going out with someone who doesn't like you for you?"

"Because the person I want to go out with doesn't want to go out with me."

My voice catches in the back of my throat, forcing itself to stay there. I'm not sure what to say to that. Is it presumptuous to think he's talking about me? Or would it be self-deprecating to think he isn't?

Everett doesn't give me a chance to think it through. "I know she likes me and I would rather be with someone and feel something than be alone. When she graduates, I won't be able to follow her, Douglas. I won't be able to follow anyone. So while I'm young, I want to experience some version of normalcy that most young people at a school get to experience. And that means going on dates."

What he says makes complete and total sense. Live fast and die young. I wonder how many of the Everleys subscribe to that idea. When you're going off to battle every day, who knows which day will be your last? I get it.

He grabs his wallet, slipping it into his pocket. "Again, if you don't want me to go, you tell me. I have the truck; we can go on the date I had planned for her and forget this ever happened. I'm not saying I love you, Douglas. I'm not saying I want us to have some happily ever after where we ride into the sunset. I'm not saying we even have to talk about it tomorrow. I'm just saying, let's enjoy tonight. There is something between us, and we have a shared experience maybe half a dozen people in the whole world can understand. That has to count for something, right?"

It counts for more than he knows. Wanting someone . . . someone to share moments with? That's such a simple human desire. And

Everett is offering it to me. No strings attached. No expectations.

All I have to do is say yes. All I have to do is be brave enough to give this, whatever this is, a try.

A knock at the door breaks the moment. Everett's eyes turn to it, Emma speaking before he has a chance to ask who's there.

"She's here."

Slowly, he returns his gaze to me. "So? What's it going to be?"

I know what I want to say. But those words feel jagged and cut my tongue and cheek, flooding my mouth with blood until I can't speak. I swallow down the stones, muttering.

"I should go practice my knife throwing or something," I say. "I mean, like you said, who knows what I'll have to face. Night-time target practice sounds—"

"No, you're right," he interrupts. "That's smart. Good thinking. Logical."

I don't know why when he says "logical," it sounds like an insult.

He turns swiftly, heading to the door with only two strides of his long legs. "Let me know if you need any help tomorrow, okay?"

Before I can say anything, I'm alone, standing in the middle of Everett's room, listening to the muffled sounds of his mom's truck starting and the happy giggles of some girl he's taking into Winslow.

I guess I'm not as brave as I like to think I am.

17

Why are you such an idiot?

That's all I can think walking back up the hill—how I could have gotten exactly what I think I want if I had just said, *Stay, Everett, don't go on that date.* But no. I had to bite my tongue and take some holier-than-thou monk's vow to put solving this god-damn forest's problem before being happy.

Because of course I have to. There's a lot riding on this solution. I'm not the only one who suffers if I fail. Everett, his family, everyone else connected to this curse . . . Mama. So many people, directly or indirectly, are relying on me. I don't have time to be distracted.

You're right, Douglas, I tell myself. *If you pull this off*—when *you pull this off*—*you can have as much dating fun as you want to have. With Everett or . . .*

I stop in the middle of the road, like an invisible wall is in front of me. Who am I going to be dating out here, really? Who would be interested in me? Sure, graduating from Regent could probably be enough to carry me. It would give me the connections to get the flashiest of jobs I could imagine. Someone would fall for me just for my connections.

But deep down, I want someone to fall for me because of who I am. I want someone to look at me and not look at anyone else. I want the world to stop when they see me, for nothing else in the universe to matter: curses, jobs, salary, nothing. Someone for whom making me smile, or laugh, or snort, or anything in between, would be enough, because that would be enough for me.

Fairy tales don't exist, Douglas, I remind myself, starting up again and walking up the hill. My plan was originally to practice, but there's something about that action that is synonymous with Everett, and just thinking about doing it without him makes my chest tight in a way I can't explain. So instead, I make the most of my time and head toward the library. Once there, ten minutes later, I fish the large cast-iron key out of my pocket, jiggle it inside the lock, and push the door open.

I walk through the library and summon the creaking elevator. My eyes are already widening and adjusting to the change in light.

"Nothing is as it seems," I whisper, flexing my fingers. "Don't take anything at face value, Douglas. You'll be safer that way."

I nail the words into the divots of my soft tissue, forcing myself to remember them next time Everett smiles at me or says something funny that he doesn't know is actually hilarious. The elevator appears in front of me, and I slide the metal grate to the side, pausing before stepping into the cab.

Nothing is as it seems . . .

And the dead let on more than the living want us to know. That's what Jane told me. Maybe it's about time I listen to them. Really listen. And what better place to talk to the dead than where they are burned?

I quickly shut the elevator and book it out of the library. It takes me an hour to walk into town by foot. It gives me time to think about what I'm going to do once I get to Taylor Meyers's home.

The last time I saw the house was when Everett and I finished burning the body. I never thought I'd go back. I don't *want* to go back. But wants and needs are two different things.

Stepping through the threshold makes my stomach queasy, knowing what happened here. Knowing what I was a part of. The air smells stale, the singular light that illuminated half the room before, blown out.

"Great," I mutter.

The house is still. No one has been here since Everett and I were last here. I wonder what happens to homes like this when the dead are gone. Do they just stay abandoned? People don't remember the dead, so logically, they wouldn't remember who used to live here. They are just relics with no one to worship them.

But just because no one lives here doesn't mean no one *is* here.

Focusing on the space in front of me and steeling my mind, I breathe out through my nose three times before closing my eyes.

I feel everything—the pulse of the earth, the vibrations of life, the chill of death in the area around me. I let it all wash over me, every overwhelming bit of it. I don't focus on any of it or try to hold on to it—instead, accepting what it is; parts of a greater whole. If this magic is the ability to create and destroy, then, controlling death seems to be . . . a fair assumption, right? I'm not sure if magic and logic are synonyms, but I'm hoping.

And then, with as much conviction as I can muster, I whisper my command.

"Show yourself, Taylor Meyers."

I keep my eyes closed for a few moments longer, mostly because I don't want to open them and look like a fool with his arm outstretched and nothing to prove of my actions. But slowly, one eye at a time, I open, vision shifting from nothing to blurriness to clarity.

And then, a moment later, there he stands.

Taylor Meyers looks nothing like he did before. This version of him is without any wounds or blemishes on his body. His alabaster skin is ashen, like it's been kept out in the cold, and his eyes are wild, darting from left to right. He looks like the type of guy who when younger, would have broken everyone's heart.

"Hey," I say quietly, reaching out my hand. "I'm not afraid of you. And you don't need to be afraid of me. I'm not going to hurt you. Everything is okay."

"What happened to me?" he whispers.

"You don't remember?"

Taylor shakes his hand and flexes his fingers. He stares at them like even his own body is foreign to him.

"You pour soul," I solemnly say.

"Who are you?" he asks, his wide eyes filled with fear, landing on me. "Why are you in my house?"

How do I explain to someone that they're dead? It doesn't feel like something I can just say. You have to ease them into that. Help them understand. But at the same time, does it really matter? I can't change their fate, can't bring them back to life. I can't . . .

"You're right, Douglas Jones."

The familiar voice comes from behind Taylor, sitting comfortably in the shadows, just out of sight. But not audibly, only in feeling. It's the same chill I felt when we were here before. The feeling of something looking at me—something dark and foreboding watching Everett and me.

Whatever *it* is speaks calmly, no rush or hurry in its voice, like it has all the time in the world. Like it's toying with us.

Taylor turns to face the shadows, taking a step back, trying to get closer to me. As if I can protect him. Maybe it's because I'm living, and there's comfort in that. Or maybe he just doesn't want to be alone.

My body feels rigid. In the shadows I can barely make out the face. Its sinister smile that stretches from ear to ear, like wax that was molded into the most exaggerated grin. There aren't eyes but hollowed-out sockets. The face looks human . . . as human as a Perversion can be.

"Such a poor soul, trapped in this town. But then again, they brought this upon themselves, didn't they? Those pesky descendants."

"People shouldn't pay for the sins of the father," I say as confidently as I can, clenching my fists by my sides to try to still my panic. "It's not their fault."

"Perhaps."

Arms with joints too long and fingertips too bony extend from out of the shadows, grabbing the frame of the house. The Perversion leans out of the darkness, larger and thinner than anything I've seen before. There are parts of its body where actual bones stick out from under the skin, like it was bent and contorted in a way that snapped some of them in half and they healed that way. Its body is mostly human, except for the lower half.

Because it doesn't have one. The body stops at the end of the rib cage.

"But that isn't a decision for you or me to make."

"Who makes those choices? The god who started all of this?"

The Perversion chuckles lowly, a laugh that bounces off the walls and rattles my bones. "Oh, Douglas. You think you know so much when you know so little. Enough to get you in trouble, though. Enough to put you and the people you care for in danger."

Magic boils under my skin, rising like a tidal wave. "You keep them out of this."

Before I can speak again, the Perversion, in the span of a heartbeat, closes in. Its neck elongates like a serpent, its face mere inches from my own.

"Or what?" it asks. "What are you going to do, hmm? Use your magic against me? A magic you don't even understand? Poor boy. Part of a game where he doesn't even know the rules."

The head returns to its normal position, body half-submerged in the shadows. "A word of advice, Douglas. There are things worse than death in this town. Those spirits you've met who have come before you? That girl who burned and the man who became one with the flowers? All those are people who got too close to the curse and paid the price. Do not end up like them. Keep away. That is your final warning. Leave alone what is not yours to be concerned with."

I want to say something so badly. To return the threat with one of equal measure and remind this thing I'm not to be messed with. I want to be as brave as Emma and Everett and Evelyn. But I can't. I just stand there, watching as the Perversion slowly turns its head toward Taylor.

"You're coming with me."

Before Taylor can move, the large hand reaches down, wrapping its bony fingers around his waist, and drags him into the retreating shadows. Taylor claws at the air, trying to grab onto something, his eyes landing on me, filled with panic and fear.

"Help me! Please! I don't want to go! Help me! I'm sorry! I'm sorry!"

I want to reach out and save him, but this is just a soul. There's no body attached; Everett and I burned him and Everett scattered him already. His fate has already been written.

"I'm sorry," I whisper as Taylor is dragged into the darkness. His voice fades away, his begging and pleas swallowed by the maw of blackness like it's a never-ending pit. Part of me wonders where it goes. If on the other side through that passage of darkness the

Perversion came through, the god is there, waiting to feast on the souls of those the Perversions bring him . . . or to do whatever with them that he does.

A bigger part of me doesn't want to know.

Once feeling returns to my body, I dash out of the house as quickly as possible. All those dead bodies. All those people who suffered a curse their ancestors brought upon them. They don't deserve this. No one deserves this. I'll break this curse and put them to rest. I just need—

"Douglas?" a familiar voice says to the right of me. I don't even need to look to know it's Everett. My mind screams at me to run back into the house and hide, to pretend he doesn't see me.

"From World History class?" the girl, Sarah, says next to him, clinging to his arm. She's wearing his jacket, leaving him with his white sleeves rolled up, his tie not as taut as it was when I tied it around him.

18

The ride back to campus may be a lot warmer than it was walking into town, but it's significantly more awkward.

I can't tell who doesn't want me there more: Everett or Sarah. Sarah keeps glancing at me in the back seat, as if she's trying to decide exactly how to start a conversation. I'm pretty sure she wants to ask me why I am here—which is a pretty fair question considering she found me staring at a pile of rubble—and when I am going to leave so she and Everett can go back to doing whatever they were planning on doing with each other.

But then there's Everett. He keeps his eyes on the road, driving slowly, careful of any wildlife or possible boulders that could come bouncing down the hill to the right of us. But at the same time, his eyes keep flickering back at me through the rearview mirror.

Regent Academy finally comes into view, its tall spires that make up the four different wings like four different north stars. Sarah takes off her seat belt and turns, strands of chestnut hair falling in front of her face, shielding half of it from me.

"It's not World History class, is it?"

"It's not."

"Spanish?"

"German."

She snaps her fingers, resting her chin on the back of her hands. "Right, German. What did you get on the last test?"

"Achtundneunzig."

"I'm sorry, what?"

"A ninety-eight," I say, biting my tongue so I don't smile.

"Seriously? I got a seventy. I studied all week for it. My parents are going to kill me."

"Of course he got an A," Everett mutters. A small grin spreads over his face, only for a moment. I can't tell if the smile is a snide one or one of pride.

"What were you two doing there?"

I know they were on a date, but that's not what I was asking.

"Just walking," she says, reaching over and squeezing Everett's hand. "I told him I had never wandered around town. I've heard all the stories, but you know, I wanted to see the creepy vibe for myself."

"I told her it was a bad idea," he says. Everett and I lock eyes for a moment, a gaze that says everything.

"I like bad ideas," she purrs.

"Yeah, there are bobcats out here," I say slowly. "Did you see one?"

"Mm-hmm," Everett curtly says. "In the distance."

"Looked more like a house cat to me." She shrugs. "But too big, you know?"

That's because it wasn't a house cat or a bobcat; both Everett and I know exactly what was looking at them. A Perversion.

Which makes me wonder if it was there stalking me. I can't let that happen again.

Everett shifts into first gear, the truck reducing speed. The gates are still open, with two guards sitting in the posts on either side of them. Everett flashes his student ID, which looks different than ours. Most students' IDs have a maroon border. Alum have a silver one. His has a green one, probably like the earth, to signify he isn't really part of the Regent family.

The guards barely look at it, letting him through. He glides the truck into the gravel parking lot, not far from the target practice range near his home.

"Sarah, can you give me and Douglas a second?" he asks. "I'll meet you inside."

"Inside, as in . . . ?" she asks, arching a perfectly manicured brow. "My dorm room?"

"You do have a single, don't you?"

"Men aren't allowed on the girls' side."

"Trust me, that is not a problem."

Sarah smiles warmly at Everett before turning her eyes toward me for a moment. I can't tell if she's judging me, sizing me up, or threatening me silently, as if she wants me to know that Everett is hers. Well, if she wants him, then have at him.

Sarah slides out of the truck and closes the door behind her, the slightly rusted metal whining in protest. Emotionlessly, I sit in silence, watching her form retreat as she heads into the building.

I'm not sure who should talk first, but sitting here waiting for someone to make a move reminds me of the interrogation tactic a female officer tried on me when they brought me into the DC precinct. It also reminds me of a therapist my mama sent me to after my father died, the one who said she could wait as long as I made her, until I was willing to talk. Four sessions, each an hour long, in silence, and finally the therapist told my mama that she didn't think she could help me and that I needed some type of more serious and specialized therapy; maybe even medication.

The point is that I'm not unfamiliar with the silent treatment, and if Everett thinks he's going to break me or make me spill my heart out to him just by sitting there, tapping his index finger against the worn leather of the truck, he has another—

"What were you doing at Meyers's place?"

"Jane told me something. When I was in her house. That the dead know more than they let on. And the only place I thought I could find a clue about that was there. So I went."

Everett's shoulders relax half an inch, but he's still frowning.

"You think it was stupid," I say. "Look, I get it, but—"

Everett shakes his head. "No. But you shouldn't have gone alone."

"You don't think I'm strong enough?"

"It's not that." He sighs, flexing his fingers into a tight clench that makes a vein on his arm pop for a moment. "It's that there are forces at play that you know nothing about."

"I know," I say, pausing before continuing. "I saw a Perversion take Meyers's soul in the house."

At first, he doesn't say anything, just looking at me through the rearview mirror. Behind his eyes, I can see there's something he wants to say, but he can't bring himself to voice it.

"I'm glad you're okay, but that's my point. You don't know what you don't know, Douglas. There are many more Perversions that can do things like that, or worse. You have to be more careful. *We* have to be more careful."

"Because you don't think I can handle myself if I come face-to-face with one?"

"Not yet, no." He doesn't even try to hide it. "But that doesn't mean you won't be. I'm going to make sure of that."

"Again, I can handle myself and I was fine. I'm alive, see?" I pinch my arm. "Human flesh."

"It's not that," he says again, rubbing his temples. "Do you really understand what you agreed to, Douglas? What you signed up for? Emma, me, and my mother? We didn't have a choice. It's in our blood."

"I didn't have a choice either," I argue.

Everett rolls his eyes in the mirror.

"I'm serious," I urge. "Do you really think when Headmaster Monroe approached me, I could have said no? What do you think would have happened to me if I had? Or to my mother?"

Everett is silent for only half a beat before replying, "I know who he is as a person. Trust me."

"Then you know the answer."

"But whatever he would have done would have been better than what you signed up for, Douglas."

Everett's voice dips, shifting from confidence to a quiet whisper. "There's an expression in those history books you think hold the answer to the curse. *The forest giveth more than it taketh, and its preferred payment is blood.* My great-grandfather coined that. No matter what solution you come up with, the answer is going to be more than you're willing to pay."

"I'm willing to take that risk."

"You say that now, but what happens when you're . . ."

Everett falls silent.

"What happens when I die?"

"I won't let that happen," he says without hesitation. "I'm not going to lose someone to this curse again, Douglas."

Everett turns, leaning over the back of the front seat. One arm reaches forward, gripping the headrest behind me, forcing me to lean back as he closes in the space between us.

"I promise," he whispers. "I won't let anything happen to you."

Warmth bubbles from the depth of my stomach even though I try to push it down. "You're confusing, you know that? You're acting like you're so concerned about me, but then you go out with Sarah."

Everett frowns and moves away, leaning back against the steering wheel. The farther he gets from me, the colder I feel. I want that warmth back so goddamn badly.

"Oh no. I gave you the choice. I told you, if you want me not to go out with her, then just say it."

"That's not really telling me how you feel, is it?"

"You're comfortable going headfirst into destroying a curse, but asking a boy out—that's too much for you?"

A perfect blow. There are no words I can form that feel like the right response, nothing as honest and real as what he just said.

"Why is that, Douglas? Why is it that you're so eager to throw your life away for people you don't even know—but when someone wants to take a chance on you and possibly make core memories in what could be the last moments that you have, you push them away? We shared something during that game of HORSE, Douglas. You confided in me, trusted me, and I did the same. Lord knows we can't trust anyone at this school. When you left, I thought we had a connection that even this forest couldn't take away."

"I'm not having this conversation with you," I say, getting out of the truck, hoping Everett will get the hint and not follow me. Or do I want him to follow me? I don't know anymore.

But no matter what I want, I don't get more than five steps away before I hear the driver's-side door open and Everett's voice trailing after me.

"Why? Because it's too honest for you? Douglas, look at me."

Everett catches up to me, placing one hand on my shoulder while the other is under my chin. I feel the roughness of his finger pads as he tips my face up to look at him. In that moment, there's nothing more than me and him. There's no Sarah, there's no forest, there's no curse, there's no expectations. It's just me and a boy.

"No matter how badly I want this curse broken, or how badly I want to have a normal life, I don't want to lose you in the process of achieving a goal that so many have tried and failed at before. And if I had a choice between losing someone I have a connection with in hopes of something unattainable, or spending the next month or the next year making memories worth keeping, I will always choose the latter—especially when the latter gives me time with you. Time for me to explore whatever this is that I feel between us. And I know you feel the same."

Before I can answer, Emma's voice—a choked plea of desperation—breaks through the still air, her screams reaching us before she does. Panting, covered in scratches, ripped clothes, and bloodstain splotches, she places her hands on her knees, barely standing in front of us.

Everett takes a step forward, moving toward his sister. "Emma? Fuck, Emma are you—"

"I'm fine," she gasps. "It's not my blood. I'm fine."

She takes in gulps of air like she's never going to get the chance to breathe again. And then she says the thing I'm sure none of us ever wanted to hear.

"I knew Emmett was out, knew what road he would come down. I saw the headlights from over there, but more importantly . . . there's a Perversion on campus."

19

"What do you mean?" Everett says.

Everett's demeanor changes almost instantly; even his stance shifts. He's an inch taller now, his shoulders pulled back, muscles tighter. It's like he shifted from casual mode to battle readiness with Emma's words.

"Mom and I were doing the normal rounds in the forest. We came across one," Emma explains. "She was handling it. I saw another out of the corner of my eye and followed it, but I lost it."

"How?" I ask, interrupting. Quickly, I add, "Not to say you didn't do the best you could—I couldn't have tracked it—but those things are big. How do you lose it?"

"Each Perversion is different," Emma says, her voice calming down. "This one had six arms; it could swing through trees. Its movements weren't predictable. I wounded one of its hind legs and followed the blood trail; it led me toward the stables on the east side of campus."

"Shit, shit, shit." Everett doesn't hesitate and opens the trunk of his truck, then spins a four-digit code on a lockbox. As he opens it, moonlight refracts off the metal of a hastily packed pile of weapons—shotguns, revolvers, a crossbow, and a few bladed weapons for the taking.

"Did you send a text to the headmaster?"

Emma nods. "Green Alert, urgent."

The school bell, which is also the center of the grounds, rings loudly. Each vibration, four right after the other, makes my bones and teeth chatter. I remember from the orientation handbook, when the bell rings, it means everyone should get inside. They never said why, though, and left the reasoning to our imagination. I always assumed it was just for a bear sighting, or even worse, an on-campus event.

I never imagined this.

Emma and Everett seem unfazed, focused on checking their weapons.

"Everyone should be inside anyway," Everett mutters. "It's after-hours on a school night."

"There are always stragglers. Case in point—you two are out here." Emma doesn't push any further. "But I didn't see the Perversion heading in that direction. I think the students are safe."

"Good. We should do the rounds, anyway." He nods, tossing her a pack of bullets. "For your handgun."

"Perversions don't usually come on campus, right?" I ask, doing my best to swallow down my panic.

"They tend to avoid it," Emma says, quickly restringing the crossbow. "Even stopping at the edge of the forest line and hesitating. The school is our territory. They know that and respect it. Coming on the grounds is certain death. This one, though . . . The blood trail didn't stop. It's like it didn't care."

"Why? Why now?" I ask. "What's changed?"

"That's what concerns me," Everett says, slinging the gun over his shoulder. "Between this one and the one I saw in town."

"You saw one in Winslow?" Emma asks. "Shit."

Everett waves it off. "I think I saw one. Where's Mom?"

"Last I saw, she was checking the perimeter to the west."

Everett nods. "We should split up. You check the north and I'll head to the east. We need to kill that thing before it attacks any students."

"And make sure there aren't any more on campus," Emma adds.

"I'm coming too," I say, reaching for the weapon case. But Everett slams the chest closed before my fingers can reach it.

"No, you're not. The only thing I want you to do is get to safety."

"Everett, I'm not—"

"Hey. No matter what your choice, breaking this curse or what we just talked about? You can't do either of those if you're dead. You're going to get inside and get to your room. Emma and I will handle this. I'll find you when we're done."

"I can be useful," I argue. "I have . . . magic."

It feels weird coming off my tongue. Emma arches her brow at me, glancing over at Everett, as if he can explain.

"Magic you can't control, not yet," he says gently.

"Wouldn't you rather have a ticking time bomb than be caught without a weapon at all?"

"He has a point," Emma mutters. "We have no idea why the Perversions are on the grounds. It could be a trap."

Everett shakes his head. "No. Long-term goal, remember? You're going to break this curse and then all of this will be behind us."

"But there's no point of all of this if you're dead."

That's not exactly what I meant to say. Of course there's still a point; there are so many people—generations of those affected—who will be spared. But why does it matter if Everett is gone?

Why does it matter if we can't celebrate together?

Everett's eyes soften. He reaches forward for a moment to touch my shoulder, but his hand hovers over me, like he doesn't know what to say or if he should touch me. I really wish he would.

"We don't have time for this, Everett," Emma says.

But Everett doesn't break eye contact with me, even as he pulls his hand back to his side, clenching his fist.

"Go inside, Douglas," Everett demands, tightening the strap that holds his shotgun. "Please."

He doesn't wait for me to answer before he and Emma head out, both of them disappearing into the inkiness of the dark.

"Fuck that," I mumble after they've disappeared. I head around the truck and fall to my knees. I push my fingers into the earth, forcing the dirt under my nails like I'm moving through waves of fabric on a freshly made bed. I can feel the pulsing of the earth's core, like a soft, resting heartbeat thumping far away from here.

I take a deep breath, matching my breathing with the earth. I can feel my heartbeat syncing with the vibrations of the magic, and the inhales and exhales of the forest matching in time with mine. It's a symbiotic relationship, one built just as much on submission as it is respect.

And deep down, I know what I want it to do.

"Show me the grounds of Regent Academy."

Instantly, my soul leaves my body. Within a blink, thousands of snapshots of the campus flash in front of my eyes. Each one of them a microscopic part of a puzzle that somehow my brain is able to piece together as being the whole campus, all seven hundred acres of it.

I see Everett running toward the Perversion, his shotgun in hand, taking perfect aim. I see Emma using her small frame and quick movements to her advantage as she dodges, twists, and slices chunks of flesh and wood off the body of another Perversion. And Evelyn . . . she's leaning against a tree, wrapping a wound on her right arm, using her mouth to pull bandages taut. There's a head of a Perversion that looks like a snake mixed with a rat leaning against her right leg.

And then there's Sarah.

She's talking on her cell phone, pacing in a circle, standing in the boathouse that juts out above the manmade lake on campus. She's talking rapidly, waving one of her hands, like the person on the other end of the phone can see her.

Why is she here and not in her dorm?

What she doesn't see or notice is the Perversion, with the body of a spider and the top half of a king cobra, stalking her from the ceiling, upside down.

I let out a gasp as my soul returns to my body, like it's the first breath I've taken since holding my breath to its limit. My body acts without thinking, and I get up, opening the metal box in the back of Everett's truck.

"Think, Douglas," I whisper, frantically looking at the items. *What could I use?* I shift things around and find a few hunting knives.

Hastily, I grab them, tucking two into the belt loops of my pants and clutching the third in my right hand. I run as fast as I possibly can, ignoring the burning in my lungs as the cold air freezes my insides. I have to get to Sarah before that thing decides it's done just playing with its food.

The dock isn't far from where Everett parked the truck. Sarah knows better than to be there without adult supervision. The boathouse hasn't been renovated, a project the headmaster has always said *is on the list* but somehow never makes it to the top. I never thought much of it, but I wonder if there was some student who died here before my time, and no one remembers.

Except him and the Everleys, of course.

I wonder if there is something living, something horrible, in the lake.

Pushing the thought out of my head, I take a deep breath.

Before I can make it to the boathouse, though, a sharp needlelike jab of pain sticks right between my eyes. I hiss, legs wobbling, as it almost forces me to take a knee.

There's so much pain. Not just in me, but in this town. All of a sudden, I can feel every bit of it. Every pulse. Every feeling. Every struggle. It's nothing like before. It's not a pain I feel in my bones or my body, but in every single atom. I can't even think, my mind is just white.

No person should have this much pain. No town collectively should hold this much sorrow. It comes in pulses, like a heartbeat. After six or so of those throbs of increasing intensity, the pulses each turn softer until I can force myself to my feet again, though every muscle fiber burns.

Something warm drips from my nose, and I feel the stickiness of blood coating my fingertips. It's like the magic is rebelling against me. Is there a limit to how much magic I can use before it takes a toll on my body? It would make sense; whatever type of energy fuels the magic, it has to come from somewhere. Maybe it comes from inside me, like carbs converting into human energy. Maybe I've run out and need to replenish. But how?

These are questions I'll have to figure out later. Right now, I need to focus on getting to Sarah.

I smear the blood on my pants before resuming my run toward the boathouse. The burning becomes a numbing sensation, erasing any feeling or warning that my body is reaching the point of no return. Adrenaline compensates for the pain, balancing to keep me going.

I won't be too late.

I won't let what happened to Kent happen to Sarah.

I won't let another student, another person, die when I could have done something to prevent it.

The boathouse comes into view moments later, but I don't stop running. Maybe I should think this through, actually accept that I'm running into the lion's den. Everett might be right; maybe I'm not ready. This could be my last stand. Maybe Sarah will get away and this *thing* will feast on my innards instead.

Maybe. But what is certain is that if I do nothing, Sarah is going to die. At least by inserting myself into the narrative, I can try to disrupt that.

I turn my body so my shoulder is the first thing that enters the room, bursting through the half-closed wooden door. Sarah screams, loud enough to drop her phone.

"What the—Douglas? What the FUCK are you doing?"

"I could ask you the same thing," I hurriedly say. "Didn't you hear the alarm?"

Sarah brushes it off. "I come out here to think."

"What is more important than the alarm?" I hiss almost angrily.

"Regent Academy, Douglas, has many rules that don't make sense. That shit doesn't matter. It's not like anything bad is really happening here."

If only you knew, I think. *If only you had your memories.*

"Get behind me," I hiss, not looking directly at her but above her. The way the broken rafters are situated and the way the clouds move in front of the moon makes it hard to see what is above us, staring, waiting, watching.

But I know it's there. I can feel its eyes on me.

"I'm sorry? I'm not doing any fucking thing until you explain why you came bursting in here and *why* you have a *knife* in your hand!"

"Sarah, I promise, I'll explain everything once—"

"You'll explain it *now*. And what are you looking at?"

I wish I could make her listen to me. I wish I could stop her from following my gaze up to the ceiling. Maybe that's what the Perversion was waiting for, because the moment Sarah looks up, it makes itself known, dropping from the ceiling with a heaviness that almost causes me to lose my balance.

The barely-held-together boathouse groans and sways for a moment but keeps it shape. Sarah lets out a shrill scream. Maybe Everett and Emma will hear it and come running. Or Headmaster Monroe will and send Evelyn to us.

But until that happens, I'm on my own.

Up close, the Perversion looks different than it did in my vision. Yes, it has eight legs and a large spider thorax for a lower body that morphs into that of a king cobra on its top half. But it has human elements too: shoulders like a man, a head of a woman that looks like someone I could easily see in town. A face I swear I've seen before . . .

The waitress at Hildebrand. The one flirting with Everett. That's her. Anna. This thing . . . this curse consumed her. Blended her flesh with its body.

It must have gotten her when she left for work that night. An iron ore drops into the pit of my stomach. I remember Everett telling her to be safe. We should have walked her home. We knew what was out there, better than anyone else.

I don't have time to process the possibilities. The head darts from left to right, turning toward Sarah. Its eyes are glassy, foggy with death, which makes me think it's blind. The way the tongue flickers out, long and prehensile, dancing against the air, confirms my thought.

It's smelling the air, I think. Maybe her perfume, or her fear. It hears her voice.

I can use that.

Sarah stumbles, losing her footing, and I don't hesitate, looking around for anything I can use to distract it. Something loud enough that maybe Sarah can use the sound as cover to escape.

My eyes settle on a precariously stacked pile of canoes. One canoe is all it'll take for the whole pile to come crashing down. If I'm lucky, it'll be enough of a cascade to even damage the creature. I tighten my grasp on my knife, feeling the slickness of my sweat threaten my grip.

My eyes lock with Sarah's, only for a moment. I mouth *Run* and hope she'll understand what I'm saying and when to do it. I can't wait for her confirmation, though. A fraction of a moment is all that separates outcomes. If I wait too long, the Perversion will spring, pin her down, and rip her body apart with its mouth. She won't stand a chance; *I* barely stand a chance.

I toss the blade, tip first, against the canoe. The old, dry wood splits and splinters, a chain reaction of cracks and snaps following as the pile collapses on itself. Luckily, Sarah listened, running past the creature as its gaze turns to the loud commotion, until she's standing next to me.

The Perversion *squeals* in terror. Its arms and legs flail as it bats away the collapsing pile of boats. Grabbing Sarah's hand, I pull her out of the boathouse, under the pale moonlight of the night.

"What was that?" she asks. "What did you just do?"

"You need to get to the school," I say, looking over my shoulder. "Now."

"Absolutely not. Not until you tell me—"

"Sarah," I say, giving her an urgent tug. "Please. Go." To convince her, I add a lie: "Everett is waiting for you."

"Everett?"

That gets her attention. I nod. "I think he's in the cafeteria with the rest of the students. I'll follow you, I just . . . want to make sure it's dead."

I know it's not.

Sarah hesitates, as if she doesn't believe me, but I know she doesn't want to stay.

"You're going to tell me what just happened the moment you get back inside the school."

"I will."

"Promise, Douglas," she demands. "Promise or I'm not—"

"I promise." I see how easy it is to lie to someone, like Everett did to me in the forest. If it means protecting them, then what does a little lie matter? "Now go. Please?"

This time she agrees, turning her back and running toward the main building.

226

I feel the chains around my chest release a fraction. One thing out of the way, one task accomplished. Make sure Sarah's safe: check.

The shifting wood behind me reminds me of the other task on my list.

I take a step back as two arms reach out from under the rubble, the Perversion pulling itself from its burial ground. With each step backward, it approaches me until we cross the threshold from inside the boathouse to outside onto school grounds. Moonlight bathes us both, allowing me to fully see every wound, all the bones and sticks that have fused and become one. And of course, its grotesque half-human, half-animal face, a mix of Anna's soft features and the characteristics of a raccoon.

The Perversion slides across the ground, standing slowly, struggling to find its footing. Spikes of wood stick out from its body. Green blood drips down, burning the grass where each drop lands. From its mouth, smoke emerges in ragged, broken pants. It sounds almost human. Like the soul of the person fused with the flora and fauna inside the Perversion is more prominent.

"I don't want to hurt you," I whisper. "I know there's a person in there. Someone whose life was taken against their will. Let me help you."

"Pity," it says within my head, much like the Emissary I first met in the forest. Except its voice is deeper in the back of my head, like it's part of me. "Because all I want to do is rip you apart."

I barely have time to react before it lashes out. Jumping back and losing my footing, I stumble, falling onto my back. The

Perversion roars, leaning forward, swiping again, this time close enough to cut my shirt. Struggling to get to my feet, I pull the blade out on my right-hand side fast enough to collide with the nails of the Perversion. A high-pitched note rings through the air; a glint of silver as moonlight catches the blade leaving my hand, landing far out of reach.

I dig my feet into the ground, pulling out my final blade, holding it in both hands to keep from losing it. Panic poisons my body, forcing me to divert any amount of battle focus to ordering my mind and body to calm down.

"You're not as skilled as those others," the Perversion snarls, its eight legs moving in unison, circling me. "It won't be as fun feasting on you. We've always enjoyed chewing on those who put up a fight, like those who have come years before your friends. But the panic I smell? I've found that makes flesh taste so much better."

The Perversion is right. I'm not nearly as skilled as Emma, Everett, or even Evelyn. But I have something they don't. The same thing that helped me find Sarah. And I know how to use that to my advantage.

I don't wait for the creature to lunge at me again. Pulling my right hand away from the blade, I push my palm forward. There's only one word that comes to mind, one order, one command. Much like before in the in-between place where I met the representative of the forest.

"Bind."

Tendrils of roots shoot out from the earth, a dozen or more, wrapping around the legs, arms, and torso of the Perversion. Two of the vines wrap around its throat, strangling its breath and its desperate screams.

Slowly I walk forward, and with each step, the Perversion snarls, bucks, trying to pull upward. Each time I push more energy forward and the dull throb in my head starts to burn brighter. I won't be able to hold this forever.

"I'm so sorry. This shouldn't have happened to you," I whisper.

"Don't be sorry. I evolved. I reached my highest purpose. The forest saw in me to be its soldier, to shepherd in a new, better world. To drink and bathe in the blood of vermin like you," it snarls, clawing at the vines in an attempt to rip them. I focus my palm on the Perversion, clenching my fist, ordering the veins to tighten.

White-hot pain erupts behind my eyes, causing my vision to blur. The same needle prick of pain like before, except this time, it expands outward, dosing every nerve in gasoline and setting it on fire.

I ignore the pain as best I can, ignore the blood I feel dripping down my nose and now from the corners of my eyes, my ears, and my mouth. I can't let go; I can't lose the advantage I have.

"You think the power you wield is yours? You think that you're special because the forest bends to your will? You think the forest chose you? You think you're these humans' savior?

"You are *nothing*, child of man! And while I may not be the one to taste your flesh, my brothers and sisters are many; more than you and your precious human friends."

The words of the Perversion ring hollow, almost distant, as I focus every bit of energy on the magic. My chest tightens, the pain reaching my heart, making it pulse irregularly just once. Then twice. Then four times. Every muscle in my body begins to spasm on its own, forcing me to sway and collapse to one knee.

But I don't let up. I keep my palm faced toward the Perversion, even as my vision goes completely blank. Every part of me wants to stop; every bit of me begs for just a moment to catch my breath.

But I have to finish this.

I take in as much air as I can, and push my body even further past the limit of no return.

"Swallow it whole," I say.

I feel the earth under me rumble and the ground splits open. The strangled roars of anger and pleas from the Perversion aren't lost on me, even if I can't see it. I can feel the creature being pulled into the earth, like the farther it gets from me, the less I can detect it, until the pulse of its existence is such a faint fire that it naturally extinguishes itself.

I sense the earth close, the soil stitch itself shut, not a sliver of a seam left to remind anyone what happened moments ago. And just as quickly as it started, the pain subsides; not because I release the magic, but because every drop of molten fire touching my skin and my soul is too much for me to handle. And I collapse forward, the world changing from white to darkness to nothingness all at once.

20

There's a part of me that doesn't want to wake up, that wants to stay asleep and just let the world move on without me.

Sleeping through all of this would be easier.

But no matter how strong I think the magic in the soul of Winslow is, I know it can't sustain me. And besides, something tells me the forest wouldn't let me sleep that long.

It has plans for me, and it demands my attendance in person.

I wince as my senses slowly come back—feeling in my fingertips and toes, working upward. The color of the ceiling starts to push through my eyelids, the fluorescent lights of Mama's infirmary warming my skin. I feel the scratchiness of the sheets. Smell the tanginess of antiseptic in the air and hear Everett's baritone voice.

"He's awake."

I open my eyes. Everett is once again by my side.

"Slowly," he whispers, cupping the back of my head. "You collapsed hard. You're lucky I found you."

"He's right, you know," Mama says, grabbing her stethoscope from around her neck as she approaches and presses it against my chest. "You need to be more careful, Douglas. Everett told me you went for a run around campus? Didn't you hear the alarm?"

I glance over at him. His face doesn't reveal any emotion, but I know this explanation is only meant to keep my mama from asking questions. And if I want to continue to protect her, I need to do my part.

"Yeah," I whisper, throat sore and scratchy. I grab the small cup of water by me and take three gulps of the cool, clear liquid before continuing. "I was thinking of trying out for the track team. You know, like Dad."

It's a cheap shot, using Dad to make the lie more convincing. But the stronger the lie, the less likely her motherly intuition will be able to barge through and break the illusion.

"Oh," she says, turning her head away. "That's . . . very sweet of you. Well, it looks like you passed out, probably from dehydration and overextension of your body. You hit your head on the way down, but I'm not seeing any signs of a concussion or long-term damage. I am a little concerned about the amount of dried blood on you. Did you hit your head or something? I'm not seeing any lacerations or other wounds."

"I can watch him," Everett offers, diverting her attention. "I'm sure you have other students to deal with."

Mama hesitates, like she wants to ask more, but nods. "Seems some students, like you, wanted to stay outside during the alarm and were drinking. Headmaster Monroe wants me to see if we need to take them to the hospital or if they can sleep off their hangovers here tonight."

Everett and I exchange a look, a mixture of *Don't say a word* and *We both know that's a lie, but we're not going to say anything.* That's fine with me. I don't want to bring her into this any more than I have to.

Mama quickly jots down her number, ripping it jaggedly from the sticky pad, and presses it against Everett's hand. "If anything changes with him, you call me immediately, okay?"

"I won't let anything happen to your son, Ms. Jones, I promise."

Mama nods, studying me one more time. She cups my cheek gently, rubbing it with her thumb. "You're going to be the death of me, you know that," she says, kissing my forehead before grabbing her white coat and running out the door.

Everett's eyes follow her, watching her form retreat while I listen to the clicking of her shoes and wait for the sharp sounds to turn muffled and disappear into nothingness.

"Hey," Everett whispers, squeezing my arm. "What happened out there? I thought I told you to stay with the truck."

There's no malice in his voice. If anything, it breaks just slightly, despite how much he's trying to hide it by pushing the fear down.

"I saw a Perversion," I explain, shifting in the bed. Every muscle hurts. It feels like I exercised every single one to its limit and my body just wants to curl in on itself.

"Emma and I were dealing with them. We dealt with them."

"A different one. It was by the boathouse."

Everett frowns, confused. "How . . . the boathouse is . . ."

"I saw it through magic," I explained. "Just like how I found Jane's home. How I killed the Perversion too."

"That was going to be my next question," he mutters, smoothing the stiff blankets over my legs. "You know that magic almost killed you, right?"

"Don't be dramatic." I try to sit up, but my body still feels heavy and the world becomes dizzy. Everett gently pushes me back down, barely adding any pressure to prove his point.

"You were still when I found you, your breath so shallow I could barely hear it when I put my ear to your chest. You were cold too. So cold."

"It sounds like I was dead," I say, half joking.

But Everett doesn't take it as a joke. "Don't say that," he sternly replies. "Seriously, Douglas, don't even put that into the air. I . . . I don't even want to think about that."

"Hey," I say, squeezing his hand, rubbing my thumb over his knuckles. "I'm alright, okay? I'm here."

He nods curtly, squeezing my hand once. "You're here."

I don't think I'd call Everett's feelings hot and cold, but I'm still not exactly sure where we stand. Maybe he's just being emotional; stress can cause that. He just fought a Perversion, and was putting his life on the line for all of us. There was a real chance of him, or Emma, dying tonight. I imagine that chance is high with every encounter. Each face-to-face standoff with a Perversion, willing to die for the students of Regent and the town of Winslow, probably fries his nerves. I don't blame him for needing some sort of outlet.

He doesn't need to know how I was willing to let myself die if it meant Sarah could escape. Speaking of which . . .

"Do you know where Sarah is?" I ask.

"I'm assuming she's with everyone else, on lockdown now," Everett says, standing up and walking around to the other side of the bed. He grabs one of the pillows from the other bed and fluffs it, waiting for me to lean forward so he can put it behind my back. "If she's not, she's going to get detention. Headmaster Monroe created the lockdown so if something like this did happen, we could deal with the Perversions on campus without risking a student getting hurt."

I lean forward for him, nodding. "Someone should probably talk to her. She saw the Perversion. I promised her I'd—"

"Wait, what?" Everett says, concerned. "Did you say she saw the Perversion?"

I hesitate before answering. "Yeah . . ."

"Are you sure?"

"She was in the boathouse. There was no way to get her out without her seeing. Unless her brain erased it from her memories, which would be lucky for us, she absolutely saw it. I promised her I'd explain everything. I really think she'd understand it all. Sarah's smart. She—"

"She won't get a chance," Everett says firmly.

Heaviness weighs on the room, like a blanket of pressure

pushing down on us, suffocating.

"Everett," I say slowly, swinging my legs over the edge of the bed. "What do you mean?"

Everett walks over to the window that looks out over the eastern part of campus. The clock nearby reads just shy of 1:30 a.m. In the reflection of the window, I see the pain that Everett is hiding deep inside. Like something I said broke a bone or snapped a muscle and he's trying to hold it in.

"Everett," I repeat, louder this time, wincing as I have trouble standing thanks to the burning pain. Blood rushes through my sore muscles and I almost stumble, but grab the edge of the bed to steady myself. "What happened to Sarah?"

"She probably went to the headmaster," he says quietly. "It's the most logical next step. Headmaster Monroe always tells the students, *If you have a problem, come to me. I'm your father when you're away from home.*

"But the headmaster will also do anything to keep Regent's secret buried. He can't risk it getting out. Can you imagine what would happen if the world knew about the forest? Best-case scenario, people wouldn't send their students here and the school would die. Worst case, the government would get involved. The headmaster won't allow that. No matter—"

"Stop," I interrupt. "If you're about to say Headmaster Monroe is going to *kill* Sarah to protect the school . . . ?"

"That's exactly what I'm going to say, because he's done it before."

"That's *murder*, Everett," I say, like that matters.

"Do you really think he'll care? And besides, who is going to remember? Him? Me? My family?"

"That doesn't matter!" I hiss, feeling my heartbeat quicken. "We have to tell someone!"

"Who will believe us, Douglas? What proof will there be that she even existed? No one will *remember* her. You *know* this."

"I will," I say without hesitation. "And you will. That should be enough. She's a person who did nothing wrong. She doesn't deserve to die."

Everett sighs. "I agree. Trust me, I do. But we're not going to be able to stop the headmaster. This has been a tradition for . . ." Everett pauses. "For generations. Anyone who knows too much is killed to protect the school."

"To protect the school or protect the headmaster?"

Everett falls silent and opens his mouth once before pushing his lips into a frustrated thin line. "Both."

I search for my socks and shoes, finding them at the foot of the bed and putting them on. Everett already has my jacket sleeves open so I can slip my arms into them.

I hesitate, staring at Everett, unsure what to do.

"Can I trust you?"

"Always," he says. "I promise. I'm on your side. But I can't move against the headmaster. None of my family can; it's an agreement our families made generations ago." He pauses, then says, "But you can. You're not bound by our rules. If you're going to continue down the path of breaking the curse, after everything you've seen so far, you have my support."

"Just not your weapons."

"Exactly."

I let out a sigh, accepting his help and turning my back to him. I slip my arms into my jacket, adjusting the collar so it fits comfortably.

"Be careful, Douglas," he whispers. "Please."

I lick my chapped lips, tasting blood, as I nod, but don't face him. He doesn't need to see the nerves on my face as I push the sliding glass door open. Because if Headmaster Monroe is so comfortable killing students, what makes it so he won't kill me?

21

"He's expecting you."

Jenna says this before I barely make it up the stairs into the Headmaster's receptionist's area. She nods, gesturing toward the door. I do my best to study her—*really* study her. I've only seen Jenna a few times since attending Regent, but I always thought she was a decent person. One of those no-nonsense people who gets her job done. But I can't help but wonder, if she's really Headmaster Monroe's right-hand woman . . . How deep does the rot travel? Plus, having her here, at 2:00 a.m., the *executive assistant*, tells me something is up. What executive assistant works this late? What headmaster is in their office this late?

"Did you know?" I ask before entering the room.

"Excuse me?" She doesn't look up from her computer, eyes

darting left and right, fingers moving quickly over the keyboard like a dance.

"Did you know about Sarah? About—"

"What the headmaster does inside his office doesn't concern me or you, Douglas," she interrupts, bright blue eyes flickering up for a moment to look at me. "The headmaster is doing everything he can to protect us. That will always be his priority. Perhaps you should remember that and focus more on your own goals instead of others, hmm?"

She's just like him, I think, not breaking eye contact with her. She's okay with the horrors that go on here.

Eventually, her eyes turn back toward her computer. "Please do not keep him waiting."

Part of me wants to wait. What if I can't save Sarah? What if I'm already too late? What's the point of any of this, of even trying? One thing I've learned in World History class is that things that have been set in motion for hundreds or even thousands of years cannot be stopped by one person with good intentions. Wars, conflicts, oppressions, that span the centuries . . . those things rarely change.

But that doesn't mean we shouldn't try.

I take a deep breath, stilling my thumping heart before pushing open the heavy wooden door. The familiar smell of vanilla, oak, and cologne fills my nostrils, sending my senses into overdrive, and not in a good way. My shoulders tighten, and my nerves begin to vibrate at a fever pitch. There's a power dynamic here that I can't ignore, one that makes me feel smaller than I ever want to feel.

"Douglas," Headmaster Monroe says, his voice like the smoothest of silk. His back is toward me, but I can see he's looking over a thick tome bound in black and brown. "I'm glad you're alive. I was worried that—"

"Where is she?"

I do a quick scan of the office but feel foolish. It's not like I actually expected her to be just lying on the floor in front of me, or sitting on the couch having tea with the headmaster. But part of me—a large part of me—had hoped I was blowing this out of proportion.

However, Sarah is nowhere to be found.

Headmaster Monroe doesn't answer. His eyes continue to scan the book.

"Where. Is. She?" I repeat. The live-wire feeling, the burning pain of magic behind my eyes, begins to build inside.

Yet, as quickly as it blossoms, Headmaster Monroe cuts it down. "I saw you, you know. Out there in the fields, wielding magic. I saw the forest bend to your will. I've never seen someone do that before. It was . . . a beautiful thing to watch." He closes the book heavily, turning to face me. "It's a pity you couldn't summon that strength and power soon enough to save Sarah."

Just her name feels like a gong ringing in my head. My vision turns blurry at the edges. I'm not sure if it's because of rage or sadness, but it causes me to lose focus.

"You killed her," I say without hesitation. "Didn't you?"

"I didn't kill anyone," he says. "I made a decision that put the safety of the school first."

Every ounce of me wants to pull the magic from deep down and launch it forward toward the headmaster, but his words keep me rooted to the ground.

"You knew that the moment she saw the Perversion, she couldn't stay here."

"If that's the case, you could have just sent her away! Expelled her."

Headmaster Monroe lets out a cold bark of a laugh. "And what? Let her out into the world, telling people what she saw?"

"No one would believe her."

"That just shows how foolish you are."

The headmaster moves over to his large desk, barely giving me any attention or time. He pulls a large leather-bound book from his drawer, flipping through it by licking the tips of his fingers and moving from page to page.

"Ah, here."

The sharpness of ripping paper cuts through the air. He studies the paper, holding it up to the light, before placing it on the table and pushing it toward me.

"I do what I do to protect everyone, Douglas. Once she saw the Perversion, there was no choice. The secrets of the forest must be kept from mundane eyes. I'm sure Everett has told you our little saying. *The forest giveth more than it taketh, and its preferred payment is blood.* This is what that means."

I pick up the paper, my eyes scanning the neatly written cursive handwriting.

When I look past the veneer of the beautiful cursive letters and actually put each letter together, there's darkness on the page that sends a chill down my spine.

"Check payable to the Medina Family Foundation," I mutter. "Four hundred and fifty thousand dollars."

The check receipt is blank; it doesn't have the headmaster's name on it, or the seal of the school. There's no way to trace this back to Headmaster Monroe or the Academy.

"That's correct, isn't it?" he asks, barely looking at me. "You're the smart one in the Academy; I trust your judgment."

"Correct for what?"

"How much a human body is worth."

He says that so quickly it's like he's rehearsed the line, as if he said it to many others before me. I think back to the resignation in Everett's voice, the heaviness that betrayed how he thought no matter what I did, it was a worthless cause, a wild goose chase. Has Everett tried to stop the headmaster from doing what he did to Sarah to other students before? And if so, how many have seen beyond the veil and had their fortune decided for them by a man who cared nothing about others, besides how they can help him accomplish his own goals?

The forest was right; I can't trust any word that comes out of Headmaster Monroe's mouth.

"I know that look, Douglas," he mutters, closing the receipt book and slipping it back into the drawer. How many receipts like this one were written out to other parents? "You want to kill me, don't you? Hurt me? Take your anger out on me for what I did to Sarah?

243

"Consider this. If you'd done what you'd said you were going to do, this might not have happened. You're just as liable for her death as I am, just like you're responsible for those kids and families who died in that fire you set eighteen months ago."

Like a Pavlovian response, memories of the burning flesh, the smell of bodies and wood and the howling of heated water through metal pipes, fill my mind. The screams of sirens and individuals trapped inside the apartments as I crawled across the floor, feeling licks of flames against my skin. It might have been a year and a half ago, but it feels like it happened yesterday. The screams of death in the house of pain overtake any sound of the forest or thumping of blood in my ears, and for the first time, I find myself wishing the screams of the woods could drown out all other noises and fill my mind with its chatter.

Anything would be better than reliving that night.

"At least I'm doing something to atone for my sins and can live with my mistakes. What have you done? How close are you to breaking the curse, Douglas? These Perversions wouldn't have been on campus if you had broken it by now. Did you think about that before throwing stones at my glass house?"

"It's not the same," I try to argue, but my voice only comes out a whisper. I can feel hot tears brimming against my eyes.

"Oh, why? Because your hand didn't specifically cause her death? Are you any less guilty if you sharpened the blade, even if you didn't bring the guillotine down?"

There's something almost hypnotic about his words. I know deep down that what he is saying isn't true—I'm not directly responsible for Sarah's death; the blame lies solely on him. But with each sentence I fall deeper and deeper down a pit of despair, as if I could have done more, as if I *do* hold some level of responsibility. What if I had been faster? What if I had mastered or understood this magic quicker? What if I had been in town and Everett had still been on his date in Winslow? All of these what-ifs I'll never have answers to, but in the end, Sarah will still be dead.

"You have the power to change this, Douglas," Headmaster Monroe says. "Only you. You can stop others from ending up like Sarah, and horrible events like this from happening. All you have to do is figure out how to break the curse."

He seems to think that's such an easy ask. It's easier said than done.

"If you want to break this curse, Douglas. If you want to change the fate that so many students here are tied to, you have to take matters into your own hands. You can't keep playing defensive. There will never be a right time to act. You have to decide when that time will be. You have to—"

"—go to the source," I interrupt.

"I'm sorry?"

I hesitate to say anything more, but we're already this deep. "I saw a tree, in my dreams, in the center of the forest."

He pauses, as if he has never heard that before. "And you think that's where the source of this . . . magic is?"

"I do," I say truthfully. "And if you want me to break this curse so badly, I need to go there."

Headmaster Monroe pauses again. The air lingers heavy for

longer than is comfortable. I can tell he's trying to think through what he's going to say. Perhaps my commitment threw him for a spin.

"I want you to do what you think is best," Headmaster Monroe says slowly, his careful wording thrown out here to make it seem like he's giving me the power to make my own decisions. "If you think that's how the curse needs to be broken, then that's what you need to do."

It's not about what I want. Just thinking about going into the forest causes a darkness to spread inside me in that anxious way one feels before a test or a speech.

It's what has to happen. That's what none of the headmaster's ancestors have been able to do. None of them knew about this tree, or if they did, couldn't venture into the forest and destroy it.

I can.

I won't let another student die. I won't let the headmaster do this again to someone else who was just caught in the wrong place in the wrong time.

I'll be the storm that breaks the status quo. Even if it kills me.

22

There is only one thing more terrifying than the voices of the forest: the voices in my own head.

Ever since the headmaster and I made the decision that I'd go into the forest a week ago, ever since that Perversion came on campus and the headmaster killed Sarah in order to protect his own ass, I've felt like my body and my mind are disconnected. Like I'm in two places at once and never destined to be whole again.

His words keep rattling around in my head, reminding me that if I want to stop this from happening, all I have to do is break the curse. The power is in my own hands. I can change this. I can stop this.

But I can't, can I? Not really. I'm not stupid enough to not know what he's doing. Putting the onus on my shoulders relieves him of any responsibility. Headmaster Monroe is smart, but he's not as sneaky as he thinks he is. That reverse-psychology BS might work on these other students here, but I'm more street savvy than them. I know when someone is trying to pull the wool over my eyes.

That doesn't stop me from feeling like my stomach is bottoming out.

What if he's right? What if I can actually break the curse, and the only thing holding me back is me? I've been looking for a purpose. Hell, everyone is looking for a calling. What if helping Winslow is mine? What if I really am . . . that special?

"The chosen one," I mutter to myself, putting my right arm over my eyes, blocking out the faint moonlight through my window. God, that sounds so fucking stupid. Chosen ones don't exist, and if they do, they aren't Black boys from Washington, DC. They are the white kids who have life handed to them. They're the families who have generations of wealth.

They're the Monroes of the world.

Sighing, I roll over to face away from the forest, as if just turning my back would be enough to calm the sounds I hear in my head and make the voices stop. The small clock on my rickety dresser reads 2:34 a.m. Too early to get up but creeping in on that uncomfortable time when sleep will be useless.

Part of me wants to go talk to Mom. If I knocked on her door, she'd wake up. Not only because I'm her son, but being the more senior nurse here, she doesn't really sleep. She's always half-awake, ready to help whatever student needs her.

But what would I tell her? The headmaster who is giving us

everything we've ever wanted is trying to get me killed? She wouldn't believe me. I could see the look on her face right now, a look I could never forget.

The look of shame, of her realizing that there really isn't anything she can do for me. I'm destined to be a failure who believes in boogeymen and succumbs to their own paranoia. No, this is a journey I have to take on my own. That's the kind thing.

But right now, all I want to do is sleep, something that escapes me as the door vibrates from a heavy knock.

I sit upright in my bed, thinking it was a trick of the night, or worse, a trick of the forest. But when it happens again, I swing my legs over the edge of the bed, pull on a T-shirt, and slowly open the door a crack, only to come face-to-face with Everett.

"What are you doing here?"

Everett frowns. "Ouch?"

"Sorry," I sigh, opening the door wider for him. "You okay?"

There's no reason for Everett to be here unless something bad happened. My mind is racing trying to figure out what that could be. "Is Emma okay? Mama? Your mom?"

"They're all fine," he says, turning his body to the side and slipping inside. He shifts from foot to foot of his scuffed-up boots, tugging on the edge of his checkered Henley.

I've never seen Everett anxious like this before. This is more than the time back in the library when he told me about his family. It's like something heavy is holding him back and he's afraid if he gives in to the weight, everything will come crashing down around him.

"Hey," I say, reaching out and squeezing his shoulder once. "You're okay," I whisper. "What's up?"

I feel his shoulder muscle relax under me, and I can't help but knead it a little more. He lets out a sigh, like his chest is deflating, but I see him fidgeting in the pale light.

"I couldn't sleep," he mutters. "And. Well. Thought coming here . . . might help?"

A question, not a statement. The power is in my court. I could send him home; I could try to use logic to help him see that there is nothing that could hurt him, an Everley. But that's not what he needs right now. I know because I need the same thing.

"You have any sleeping clothes?" I ask.

Everett gestures to his shirt.

"You're not getting dirt in my bed," I whisper, walking over to the dresser. I look back at Everett, examining him—seeing how broad his shoulders are—and pull out a pair of basketball shorts and a shirt that's a size too big I never returned. "These should fit you."

"Thanks," he says. Everett turns his back to me, and I do the same, letting him change.

"Hope I didn't wake you," he says.

I shake my head, but realize he can't see it. "No, you didn't. I couldn't sleep either."

"The moon is bright tonight."

Yeah, the moon. That's it. But I can tell he's just saying that to save face and giving me the same out.

"Yeah, too bright."

It's funny how easy a lie was for both of us. Neither of us willing to address the actual issue, that the looming terror of the forest that surrounds the school is starting to seep under our skin. It's not only that its presence is massive, it's that its power is massive, and I think, for maybe the first time, Everett, just like me, is recognizing just how powerful the forest is and how small we really are. And that's a terrifying thing.

"Okay, I'm done," he says. Slowly, I turn around, facing Everett posing. "How do I look?"

"Comfortable," I say, pausing as I examine him. The following words slip out before I can stop them. "You look like you belong."

"In your clothes?" he asks, smiling in a soft way that's not confident or cocky, almost shy.

Instead of speaking, I just nod and crawl into the bed, pushing my back against the farthest wall. Everett arches a brow as he approaches with hesitant steps.

"You want to be the big spoon?"

"You mind that?"

He shakes his head. "Just not used to it," he says. He easily slides into bed, slotting his body against me. Without thinking about it, I rest my forehead against the back of his head. It smells like faint cologne and sweat. My arms slide around his body, our legs tangling together. He doesn't pull away. In fact, he pushes against me.

We stay like that, for several minutes, our inhales and exhales beginning to match in time with one another.

"So you're really gonna do it, huh?" Everett finally speaks.

"You're really going to go into the forest?"

The words almost seem to come out of nowhere, and pull me out of the comforting silence that I was drifting in like a saltwater pool. I pull back, just an inch, before resting my head against him again.

"Headmaster Monroe told you?"

"Heard him and Mom talking about it. You didn't answer my question."

"I told you I was going to break the curse," I remind him. "No matter the cost."

In my arms, Everett turns to face me. "That doesn't mean putting yourself in harm's way like that."

"You do it every time a Perversion comes on campus," I whisper.

"I'm different."

Everett raises his right hand, stroking my cheek gently. "I was born for this. This is all I know. There isn't anything else for me out there, not now at least. Protect. Fight. Kill. Repeat. That's not you."

"It could be me," I mutter, nuzzling his hand.

"I pray to God it isn't."

Everett moves his body closer to me, almost as if he's trying to make us become one person. His body feels more relaxed than I thought possible, like he needs this more than he lets on. Which I'd understand. I need this too.

"I'm not going to change your mind, am I?" he mutters.

"I'm a pretty stubborn person, so no, I don't think so."

"You, Douglas, stubborn," he chuckles. "Who would have thought."

"Don't be sassy."

"You wouldn't want me any other way."

He's right, I think. Maybe I should say it? I mean, this could be the last time we see each other. God, I don't want to think that. I can't think that—just the thought paralyzes me.

"Can you promise me something?" Everett asks.

"Shoot."

"This school owes you nothing more than you're willing to give. If you want to go down for these people, then do it. But do not think you owe them. You don't owe them anything, Douglas. Winslow will take and take and take until you don't have anything else to give. Promise me, if a time comes for you to put yourself first, to save yourself, you will."

"Saving myself means not saving you," I admit honestly, whispering practically in his ear like I'm telling him a secret only he should hear.

"I stand by what I say. There's no guarantee you doing everything right will end this curse. Promise me you'll put yourself first."

"I promise," I say, and then repeat it to sound more convincing.

"Good," he mutters. "I'm going to—"

"My turn to make you promise me something," I interrupt, feeling the comfort of warmth and fuzziness begin to envelop me as I drift off to sleep.

"Anything."

"Take care of my mama," I say. "Headmaster Monroe . . . seems vengeful. I want to make sure she's protected. I know she won't remember me if I die, but . . ."

"I promise," he says. "An Everley promise."

"Is that more than a normal one?"

"The best promise in the world. It means I'll lay down my life to do it."

I want to tell Everett *thank you*, but feeling his breathing, his strong chest pressed against mine, makes me feel so safe, so warm, sleep comes naturally. And I know it's going to be the best sleep I've ever had because he's with me.

I remember in English class reading the quote *Man plans and God laughs*. How cruel of him, I think, to bring me a boy like this, right before I decide to do something that might pull him away from me forever.

The gods really do consider us their pawns.

23

"I can't believe you get to travel out west. I've never been to Seattle before."

Headmaster Monroe didn't pull punches to cover my journey into the forest with smoke and mirrors. According to him, I had just gotten a prestigious opportunity to intern at Mrs. Hale's law firm. It's only been a few weeks since my agreement with Headmaster Monroe, but already it's time for me to hold up my end of the bargain.

"Douglas has such a talent with words, I just think it's the right move for him," he told my mother, who hung on his every word. "And why not give him the chance to do it now? That's the type of opportunity we provide our students at Regent Academy."

He had her hook, line and sinker, no questions asked.

My mama is in my dorm room, packing now. I do my best not to look at her. How do I tell her that I'm not actually going thousands of miles away, but just a few hundred feet—into a place I might not return from?

Headmaster Monroe reminded me there was no need for a plan if I died. "Your mother won't remember," he said frankly. He didn't even look up at me, instead focused on the paperwork in front of him. "Seems like a waste of time, no?"

"I don't care," I said. "You want me to do this for you—you're doing this for me. I'm not going to have her wondering what happened to me until she forgets. I want her to know I did something with my life."

"Even if it's a lie?"

"Even if it's a lie."

Headmaster Monroe conceded and, well, here we are.

"Is it going to be cold? You should pack a sweater. Maybe I should get you one from the school store."

"I'll be fine. I'm not going to, like, Aspen," I say, grinning and flicking my eyes over to catch her gaze for a moment. "Plus, I have a stipend. Anything I need I can get while I'm there. And it's only two weeks."

"Right, right," Mama says, hitting the side of her head for comedic relief. "I'm just so proud of you, Douglas. Look how far you've come in such a short time. I knew this was the right move for us. For you."

How do I tell her that this was in fact the worst possible choice she could have made?

I don't—that's how. I keep that to myself. If I succeed, this won't be an issue, and if I die, well . . . I'm sure Headmaster Monroe will make sure she's well compensated. Nearly half a million dollars could go a long way to help her.

"Alright, you've got your underwear, toothbrush, laptop, cell phone, books, notepads, pants . . ." Mama counts each item on her fingers, staring at the two bags: one carry-on and one piece of luggage.

While she's counting, I can't help but stare at the forest. Ever since I agreed to the headmaster's terms, the whispering woods have been silent. And not sleeping silent or dormant silent. Like . . . a normal person's mind. There's no connection to it. Same with the magic; the tingling is gone. The feeling of live-wire energy right under the surface that I can pull forth when needed? Disappeared.

It almost feels like the forest has abandoned me because of the choice I made. As if I'm forced to suffer alone.

I bite my inner cheek until I taste blood. Mama closes my bag and zips it, pressing her full weight into the bag before nodding in approval.

"Ready?" she asks, fishing her keys out of her pocket. "How about we get milkshakes on the way? My treat."

A pang of guilt floods my body like the opening of a dam. Getting sweets every time we went shopping was a thing my father and I used to do. It's one of the best memories I have of him, one of the few memories that isn't filled with haziness and dustiness that clouds his face. I know Mama knows this, because she always used to scowl and comment that my father had ruined my appetite whenever we came back with milkshakes or slices of cake only twenty minutes before dinner was ready.

But before I can agree or shoot her down, there's a knock at the door. Mama and I turn at the exact same time to see Headmaster Monroe poking his head in with an overly friendly smile.

"Am I interrupting anything?"

I'm not sure which emotion I thought I'd feel when I saw the headmaster again. His arrival means he hasn't forgotten or found some lost solution to our problems. It reminds me I need to uphold my end of the agreement. It's also as if he dressed down to soften the blow. He isn't in his usual suit and tie; right now, he's dressed in a maroon turtleneck, a pair of slacks, and boots, his black-and-silver hair washed and pulled back in a slick style.

Mama's face bursts with admiration, so much that the light she exudes makes me nauseous. She idolizes this man because of the opportunities he's given me—she has no idea that this might be the same man who sends her only child to his death.

"Headmaster." Mama smiles. Headmaster Monroe attempts to shake her hand, but she scoffs. "We hug," she says, pulling him into a tight embrace before he can stop her. A look of surprise washes over him before he hugs her back, his eyes locking on mine for a brief moment, an exchange of knowledge passing between us.

We both know why he's here.

"I was just getting ready to take Douglas to the airport," she says. "Thank you, again, for this."

Headmaster Monroe waves it off, playing the part perfectly.

"Think nothing of it. Douglas is a smart man and a real talent. He is the future of what this school can and should be. I'm happy to help foster his education anyway we can, and I know Mrs. Hale will be excited to have him."

"Oh!" Mama grins. "A real talent"—she smirks over at me— "look at that."

Headmaster Monroe lets out a light chuckle. "But, Maria, I am afraid I have some bad news. We have a student who needs medical attention and requires your help."

Mama frowns. I know what's passing through her head. Her defenses begin to rise. "I need to take my son to the airport."

Headmaster Monroe nods. "I know, I'm very sorry Maria, truly. But the on-call nurse is no longer available."

"I'll be fine, Mama," I say with a smile. "It's only two weeks, right? Also this is good prep for you getting ready to send me off to college. Maybe we'll be going across the country. Who knows?"

My mama does that thing that she always does whenever I catch her off guard and cause her to laugh. A snort leaves her lips and she covers her face with her hand, turning her head to the side and causing her locs to bounce against her cheeks. It almost brings tears to my eyes to hear that sound, to think about how I used to roll my eyes or be embarrassed by it. It's even harder to think that if something goes wrong in the forest and I don't come back out alive, my mama is simply going to go to bed one night thinking that I'm thriving in Seattle, living my best life and making a name for myself, only to wake up and forget she even had a son.

I hold on to this moment as tightly as I can. Before she can say anything, I wrap my arms around her, smelling the mix of lavender and patchouli that comes off her. She kisses the top of my head, letting her lips linger against my skin. This will be the longest time that we've been separated—two weeks—except for the time that I was in jail. Our emotions may come from different places, but they end up at the same destination.

She pulls back, grabbing my shoulders and grinning at me. "You're going to do great," she says. "And I am so, so proud of you."

One more kiss on the cheek, a soft thank-you to Headmaster Monroe, and Mama takes to the hallway, her footsteps disappearing as she enters the elevator.

I watch as the soft smile plastered on Headmaster Monroe's face turns into stoicism as he slowly glances over at me, studying me for just a second. He pulls out his keys, one of them exactly like mine, and gestures with a sweep of his hands for me to exit the room first. Once I do, he locks the door behind me; there will be no reason for anyone to enter my room until I return.

"Are you ready?" he asks.

"No." There's no reason to lie. "But what choice do I really have?"

If I ever want Mama and I to actually have a life, I have to do this. If I want to keep people like Sarah—innocent people who exist now and will exist for years, if not centuries, to come—to have a chance at living a normal life, I have to succeed. I have to try. I have to break this curse. The illusion of choice is one of the funniest things society gives us, when in fact, so much of our lives is predetermined. We may have wiggle room, to be able to step out of line a bit to the left or slightly to the right, but most of us will always end up where we were supposed to. Fitting perfectly in a predetermined box that we don't even know exists with its invisible walls. Today I will break those walls. Today I will break the curse.

Avoiding any students or faculty we might see, Headmaster Monroe leads the way in silence, walking across the lawn at a brisk pace toward the Everley home. While he walks, I study his movements. See how he strides across the campus with his head held high, without a single ounce of remorse. This is his kingdom, his domain. Why should he feel like he's done anything wrong? We all just exist as his pawns. Everyone from the Everleys to my mama to the students who have no idea what lingers underneath the surface of their school.

When we arrive at the wooden door, Headmaster Monroe knocks twice.

"You'll take care of her, won't you?" I ask. "If I die."

He glances over at me, not moving his head, only his eyes. "Your mother will be fully taken care of, Douglas. I promise. No matter what happens."

Why do I feel like he isn't telling the truth? At least I have Everett's word. An Everley promise is worth the world, after all.

Everett answers the door, practically ripping it off its hinges. He's dressed in a T-shirt with leather straps that resembles suspenders attached to his pants, looping over his shoulders. His jeans are tucked into military-style boots, fingerless gloves on his hands, and bindings around his wrists and forearms. There's a bandanna wrapped around his head to keep his shaggy hair out of his face . . .

. . . and a bag in the corner.

It only takes me a moment to put two and two together.

"Absolutely not," I say. "You're not—"

"How about we get inside first, hmm?" Headmaster Monroe says. It isn't so much a suggestion as a demand. Putting his hand on my lower back, he pushes me inside, closing the door shut.

Dozens of toolboxes and chests are pulled out, many of them half-open with their contents strewn across the room. Evelyn is standing behind Emma, helping tie straps to Emma's body in the same suspender style that Everett is wearing. Emma is meticulously studying two different handguns, balancing each on her different palms, judging their weights.

I snap my vision to Everett. "I'm—"

"Come on," he says, cutting me off and leading me down the hallway to his room. He waits until we're alone, closing the door behind him to cut off the now-muffled sounds of Headmaster Monroe and his mother chatting.

"What are you *doing*?" I hiss.

"What does it look like? I'm coming with you."

"No way."

"You didn't think I was going to let you go into the forest alone, did you?"

"That was the point of me going! We talked about this!"

Everett doesn't seem convinced. He crosses his arms over his chest. Even under his T-shirt, I can see his biceps straining and the leather straps pulling his chest tight, making him look even bigger.

"I lied. And I need to make sure you uphold your promise you made me that night."

I open my mouth to say something, but nothing comes out. He's right.

"Besides, let's be honest. I've trained you as much as I can, but being inside the forest is a completely different beast. You don't know a thing about surviving against Perversions and Emissaries. You handled one and passed out. What happens if you need help like that in the forest?"

I want to state that I'll be fine, and him joining me doesn't help his case. If we both die, then not only did I fail, but the school will be down a protector. What if they attack again?

"Plus . . ." Everett starts, like he's hesitant about saying something.

"There's a plus?"

"Neither of you know how to navigate the forest."

Emma's voice cuts through before I see her, the door suddenly ajar enough for her to stick her head in, then slither in the rest of her body, her blond hair pulled back into an efficient ponytail.

"Emma's spent more time than me or Mom in the forest," Everett argues. "If a student wanders into the forest, she's usually the one to retrieve them. She knows the wildlife, the trees, everything, perfectly."

"You know where to go?" she asks, looking at me. "I can get you there."

"And I can make sure you get there in one piece. You help no one if you're dead, Douglas. None of this will matter."

I purse my lips, flexing my hands by my side. They're both right. I didn't even bring any weapons with me to enter the forest. I don't know my way around. I was hoping magic or whatever would guide me.

I let out a groan. "This is going to end badly," I mutter. "This is such a fucking bad idea."

"More importantly," Emma says, leaning against the wall, "you're acting like you have a choice. We're going with you. We're Everleys. Once we set our minds to something, nothing can stop us."

"Think of us like your own personal battering ram."

I want to tell them that analogy sounds horrible, but before I can, the headmaster knocks on the door, opening it without asking.

"The assembly at school has started," he says. "I've been told everyone is accounted for. We need to move, now."

"We'll be right out," Everett says. His eyes lock with Emma's, that unbreakable sibling bond kicking in, a silent exchange of words no one but they can understand. Emma gives a small nod before slipping between the door and the headmaster, who keeps his gaze trained on us.

"Two minutes," he says. "We can't afford anyone seeing you." He closes the door behind him, leaving Everett and me alone.

"Douglas, listen," Everett begins, but I cut him off before he can continue.

"I want you to know you don't have to do this. I can handle this."

"That's not why I wanted—"

"I'm serious, Everett. You don't have to be some savior or whatever. I know you don't think I can fend for myself."

"This isn't about that. I promise, if you just let—"

"What happens if you and Emma die? Then who's left? Your mom? Is she really on board with—"

"Douglas, if you don't shut the hell up and let me say what I want to say so I can kiss you already, I'm going to scream."

Well, that shuts me up.

Everett walks past me and sits on the edge of his bed. The weight of his body causes the metal box spring to groan as it dips around his body. I follow suit, sitting next to him, waiting in silence for him to speak.

"I'm not someone who is big on words," he finally says.

"And we only have two minutes."

"That too. So I'll keep it simple. If you go down, I'm going down swinging with you. And if we die, I want to experience kissing you one time. You said you've never been kissed before, right? Why don't we make this a first for both of us, and make it a memory we can find asylum in, whatever may happen?"

I don't take Everett's words as a resignation that we're going to die. Though, if you asked me what I thought our chances were, I would say they're not very high. I think that's the first time I've admitted it, even mentally. I'm going into this forest thinking, hoping, that I can stop the curse, but if I do and it costs me my life . . . maybe that's okay. Maybe leaving my mark on the earth in a positive way—my soul and body just a scorch mark on this planet but something good coming from my sacrifice—is worth it.

Maybe kissing Everett and making that memory is worth it too.

"So," Everett says, hitting my leg with his own. "Douglas, can I kiss you?"

But first, I need to tell him something.

"Before you do," I say slowly. "I need to tell you what happened, what brought me here. To Regent."

His shoulders relax, and his face seems to soften, as he nods.

"I haven't told anyone this. Besides those who need to know." Everett is the first one I've told voluntarily, and it feels like the wrong thing to do. Like I'm going to ruin everything if I open my mouth. But it's only fair, right?

"I killed people," I mutter. "At least, I think I did. My mama was gone working, it was winter, and I left the heater on in our apartment. I knew not to while I was sleeping—it was faulty—and next thing I knew, a fire started in our building. Over twenty-five people died, unable to get out. Women. Children, mostly. I . . . I killed them."

The words come out thick and heavy. I haven't allowed myself to say that, always been trying to replay the memory and find some fraction of truth that absolves me from my sin. I don't think I've ever said before that I killed them.

Everett's rough hand reaches over and squeezes mine, lacing

his fingers in between. "Regent Academy may be a place for rich students, but it's also a place for those who have done bad things to find a path forward. No matter what you did, Douglas, it led you here. To this school. This curse. To me. I don't like to believe in destiny or think that people died so that you could fulfill yours, but I have been alive long enough to know that we are not as in control of our lives as people like to believe. And the only thing we can do is live the best life we can, when we can, and remind ourselves we're doing our best."

"You don't think . . ." I hesitate, not sure what I want to say. "You don't think I'm a horrible person?"

"I'm not one to judge," he said. "And it sounds like, at worst, it was an accident. You can't blame yourself for accidents, Douglas. Remind me one day and I'll tell you all the shit I've done—most of it on purpose. But right now, I just want to kiss you. Would you like that?"

"Yeah," I choke. "Sure. I mean, I'd like that."

Butterflies riot in my chest as Everett turns to face me and I follow suit. He raises one hand, cupping my cheek, gently turning my face until we're looking in each other's eyes. Moving forward slowly, he tilts his head to the side, closing his eyes as his lips touch mine.

I'm not sure what I expected from the kiss, but from TV and movies, I thought it was going to feel like electricity coursing through my body. It doesn't feel anything like that. It feels warm, safe—like home. There's no time stopping. There's no secret equation to the universe opened up in front of me. It feels right and welcome, and I don't think I ever felt as at home at Regent Academy as I do in Everett's small cluttered bedroom.

I deepen the kiss, adding pressure that he reciprocates. I wish we could stay like this forever, his lips against mine, his hand against my cheek, our bodies touching and hearts beginning to synchronize. I wish this was an awkward first date, a goodbye kiss before college or summer vacation. I wish we had more time.

Everett pulls back at the same moment I do. He opens his eyes after me, his tongue flicking against his lips.

"You ready?" he mutters, hand still cupping the right side of my face with his rough fingers, stroking my cheek slightly.

I nod, unable to find the right words. Or maybe I can, but if I answer him verbally, maybe he'll move, maybe he'll get up and walk out that door and the world outside will become a reality. Because right now, with neither of us moving, nothing else but this room matters. It's just me, Everett, and that kiss.

I wish that could be enough.

PART
THREE

PART
THREE

24

The forest looms before me, Everett, and Emma like a beast with its jaw unhinged and wide open. Two bags sit by Everett's side— one a side satchel and one a large hiker's bag—with one backpack on my shoulder and one backpack on Emma's back along with a fanny pack around her waist.

The three of us stand in front, Evelyn and Headmaster Monroe right behind us, almost as if they are too scared of getting too close to the forest, like it might swallow them whole.

"You okay?" Everett asks, smiling at me. The smile doesn't reach his eyes.

"I can't hear it," I whisper. I want to reach out, as if I can grab the voice of the forest and pull it from its throat. "The forest . . . It's been silent."

"For how long?"

"Since what happened to Sarah."

Everett makes a sound in the back of his throat; I can't tell if it's a sound of approval or concern.

"Before we go," he says, pulling the bag from his shoulders, "I got something for you."

Everett removes a leather pack with a string on it. As the string comes undone, the pack unfurls. Light catches the set of seven knives placed equidistantly apart. Each knife is about six inches long, with a wooden polished handle and a cross guard with letters spelling out D-O-U-G-L-A-S.

"You'll need these, if you're going to defend yourself."

"Did you make these?" I ask, taking them from him, examining them one by one.

"I have talents, you know." He grins. "I'm not just a killer."

I smile and nudge his shoulder. "Thank you, Everett. Really."

He nods. "Just make sure you're safe, especially if Emma and I aren't with you. And promise me—*promise* me, Douglas—if you need to, you'll run back home. You'll leave the forest. Leave me and Emma. You have a chance to live. Don't throw that away."

The words feel heavy. But the look in Everett's eyes tells me that I don't have much of a choice.

"You really want to die in here?"

He shakes his head. "No, but I've known it's a possibility. Emma too. I want you to live. Not only to have a life, but if retreating means trying again . . . That's better than you dying because you think it makes you a martyr."

Before I can reply, Headmaster Monroe clears his throat. His vision bounces from one of us to the next.

"I am very proud of you three," he says slowly, his voice smooth and easy. "Not many who know what waits for them inside the forest would so willingly walk into it. Stories of the past are not only fictional; they are warnings. And yet, you three enter freely. If I could leave you with one piece of advice . . . Remember, we do not truly know what is in the depths of the forest. It is a universe within itself. Trust in each other. Do not trust what you see."

"The forest giveth more than it taketh," I start.

"And its preferred payment is blood," Emma finishes.

"Exactly," Headmaster Monroe says.

"One more thing," Evelyn interjects. "Be careful. We don't fully know the extent of what the forest will do when someone threatens it like this. You're going for its heart. It will fight back to protect itself. I've trained you both for this, Emma and Everett. But Douglas, you need to be prepared for how this forest will toy with you."

"Evelyn and I will do everything we can to ensure your mother is safe and thinks you're at your apprenticeship, no matter how long you're gone. I can promise you that," Headmaster Monroe says.

My eyes drift away from him, looking behind him at the school. I wonder what Mama is doing right now. Is she concerned about me, worried if I got to the airport okay? What is she going to think if it takes months for me to return and she hasn't heard from me?

It won't matter, I think. As long as I make it out of the forest, we can move on from this. Headmaster Monroe promised—anything I want is mine if I succeed.

And I will succeed. If not for me, for my mama and the life she deserves.

"Douglas," Everett says. When I turn, he and Emma stand at the edge of the campus where the lush, verdant grounds end and the cold, brown, hard dirt of the forest begins. "You coming?"

Not like I have a choice.

"One moment," Headmaster Monroe says, reaching forward. Before I can protest, he pulls me into a tight, fatherly-like hug. It makes me weak for a moment.

"You are under my employ, Douglas. We have made an agreement, a pact if you will. A contract has been signed between the two of us. I would advise you to remember that when you're in there. How much you have to lose and who is counting on you to succeed. Not just me, but the other people in your life. Do not try to be a hero. Do what you need to do and get out, for your sake and those around you."

Headmaster Monroe adjusts my collar, smiles, and pats my shoulders. It's a thinly veiled threat, but serious enough to send shivers down my spine.

"Go on," he urges. "You have a world to save."

I take a deep breath as I join Emma and Everett. I hold it until we cross the threshold. The temperature drops almost instantly as we enter the forest, like it's a completely separate world with an invisible membrane that keeps everything within the forest lines.

But once we cross over? The dread, the heaviness, the sadness, all of it weighs down on me. On us. Emma stumbles first, taking what looks like a fractured breath for just a second. Everett grunts, breathing through his mouth while it hits me like a weight pushing down on my chest.

"You get used to it," Emma says quietly.

"That feeling like every bad thing that has ever happened or could happen is right around the corner?"

She nods. "It's like having the bends. At least, I guess it's like that. Never been diving."

"You didn't feel it before?" Everett asks. "When I found you in the forest?"

I shake my head, not looking back as we walk deeper inside. If I turn around, I know I might go running back to the safety of the school. "No. Just the cold."

"You said you were connected to the forest before," Everett interjects. "Maybe it was protecting you."

"Sure wish we had that now," Emma adds.

She's right. I never thought I'd miss hearing the forest in my head. It's like a friend who is no longer there with me, someone who just decided one night that our relationship was broken and left me to fend for myself, to pick up the pieces. The only thing I have etched in my mind is that tree.

"Emma," I say as we lean forward, hiking up a hill. Everett pulls out three flashlights from his bag, handing one to each of us. "You said you know this forest better than anyone."

Emma nods. "I've spent more time in the forest than Everett or our mom."

"She's killed more Perversions too," Everett adds. "She's ruthless. In a good way."

"So . . . if I need to find a giant tree? One that extends into the skies high above the tree line?"

"I know exactly where that would be," she says without hesitation. "The forest may seem cold and dead, but I've been deep enough to see where it's vibrant, lush, and thriving. That's where that would be."

"I've seen it in my visions. Large tree, in the center of the forest. It felt almost . . ."

"Safe." Emma nods. "Yes. I've seen it. In the distance. An Emissary stopped me from entering, but . . . I know where it is. I can lead us there."

"And I can get us there safely," Everett chimes in.

I nod, a sense of calm passing over me. The forest might be imposing, but having these two by my side makes it feel like maybe we'll make it out alive. We at least have a chance. It's not just me against the world, it's *us* against the world, and though that doesn't mean much, it provides us three chances to succeed. If worse comes to worst, like Everett says, then one of us can make it out of the forest. That's something.

At least, that's the plan.

But almost as if the forest heard my thoughts, a loud crack rips through the air like thunder. Everett springs into action, pulling a blade from his back, standing in front of me and Emma. The sound makes my bones shake; even if Everett and Emma pretend it doesn't faze them, I know they feel the same. A howling bellow of pain and anger comes from the forest itself, like the miles and miles of trees and hard earth and darkness are coming to life, awakening with a lionlike roar.

Wind rushes. The ground shudders. The trees bend and snap as if a monstrous force is charging through them. Everett stumbles. Emma digs her heels into the earth, grabbing my shoulder while Everett puts one hand in front of his face to block the howling of the wind.

You shouldn't have come here, Douglas, a voice ripples inside my head. It feels like the voice of the forest, a whisper that skims the edges of my ears, but it sounds hollower, more haunting, more . . . damaged. *We told you not to come here; we warned you.*

I open my mouth to say something, but in the span of a blink, the forest turns silent and everything disappears, leaving just me alone, as if Emma and Everett were never there.

"You knew better," the voice says, clearer this time. A single vine turns into two, then two turn into four as they braid around each other, twisting upward until they take the form of a man, much like the man I saw in the vision before, when Headmaster Monroe drugged me. "You knew coming here meant death."

"I'm trying to break the curse," I softly argue, not actually speaking, but thinking it in my head.

The man doesn't react at first. He gestures to the right of him, then the left. Tendrils of vines rise from the earth once again, this time revealing a large bulbous flower on each side. The flower blooms, bloodstained petals unfurling to reveal a body inside each of the flowers.

Emma's and Everett's bodies.

Everett is ripped to shreds, with pieces of wood and thorns sticking out of his body. His eyes are gouged out, his intestines exposed, his heart open and barely beating. Emma is only half a body, one arm missing, a slithering vine coming out of her mouth, a flower blossoming from it. Half of her skull is gone, a chunk of her brain missing.

My knees sway, feeling like lead. My stomach burns with vomit and bile that suddenly rises up my throat. The smell of death and rot from their bodies, mixing with the sweet floral scent of the plants . . .

"This isn't real," I whisper, closing my eyes and clutching my head. "This isn't real. This isn't real. This isn't real."

"It isn't real . . . yet," the man says. "But your fate is sealed, Douglas. You and your friends, all because of your choices—your folly. These deaths are on you. These deaths that will come to pass will be because of your hand," he says clearly, unflinchingly. "You will all die in this forest. You will be the fertilizer to bring the next generation of Emissaries to life. Your souls may have been wasted on this quest, but your bodies will go to use. For that, the forest thanks you."

And just like that, the world returns to normal.

Everett is kneeling by my side, shaking my body. Emma has her canteen in hand, pouring water on my face.

"Douglas," Everett whispers, concerned. Swathes of panic and fear cover his sharp features. "You're okay, you're here, you're alive."

"We're . . ." My voice feels scratchy, like the words don't want to leave my throat. I grab the canteen, gulping down the water. "The forest," I finally say. "It gave us a warning."

Before I can tell Everett and Emma what the forest said, though, the ground hisses again. The trees around us shift, and everything that looked familiar just moments ago changes. A tree to the right has now moved in front of us, the type of trees changing as if the bark has been folded inside out, and the canopy rises, actually rises, swallowing us more in darkness.

"I'm guessing," Emma mutters, "it says there's no way we're getting out of here alive?"

I don't have the courage to tell her she's right. But on the plus side? The whispering of the forest is back. And it continues to say to me, *Run, run, run, run.*

Run as fast as you can, Douglas.

25

Time truly does work differently inside the forest.

I'm not sure how long we have been walking. Sometimes it feels like hours, other times like minutes. My phone doesn't have reception, and the watch on Everett's wrist isn't ticking anymore. When Emma holds her compass level, it just spins, never landing on a specific direction.

"I didn't think it would work anyway," she says when she catches me looking at her. She shrugs once. "Dare to dream, right?"

I give her a thin-lipped smile, zipping my jacket tighter around my body. Everett is ahead of us, using his flashlight to bathe the area with light, preventing us from stumbling over any stones, roots, or bones.

And we've seen more than enough bones.

Puffs of air from my mouth turn into white smoke. The tips of my fingers are starting to tingle as I lose feeling. I flex, forcing blood to rush to my fingertips. The burn is a welcome feeling; it reminds me I'm still alive.

Emma doesn't seem affected, at least not outwardly. She keeps walking forward, her steps never faltering.

Emma and Everett's determination pushes me to go farther. I can't be the one who holds them up. They are here for me; I will not be dead weight.

I fight through the burning in my legs, bridging the gap between myself and Everett until I'm keeping pace with him.

"Hey," he says, a bright smile on his face, though a part of me thinks that smile is just so I don't freak out. "How are you holding up?"

"Thinking I need to try harder in gym class."

He snorts. "Trust me, it isn't usually this hard. It's like the ground is actually trying to keep us from making any progress." He pauses. "Which isn't unreasonable."

"I mean, it is," I counter. "Who would have thought that our lives would come to this?"

"Fighting a supernatural curse in a forest? Me. It's been my whole life. I just didn't think anyone would be brave enough to try to break it."

"Brave enough or stupid enough."

"To each their own," Emma bluntly says. "Has Everett told you it's not too late to turn around?"

"I have, multiple times."

"So then I think you're leaning closer to stupid than brave."

Emma's bluntness is refreshing. I wonder what caused her to be so . . . direct.

"I need to do this," I finally say. "I—"

Everett puts his arm out in front of me moments before it happens, like he felt it coming in his bones. The ground in front of us cracks and groans; the earth caves in on itself, leaving a gaping hole so deep, the light that Emma shines doesn't reach the bottom. The chasm is so wide it's impossible for us to walk around or jump across.

"Come on," Emma says, walking parallel to the hole, unconcerned by anything that might be within it. "This way."

Everett and I let her take the lead. Eventually, I continue what I was thinking.

"I need to do this. I need to set this right."

"You can't change what happened, Douglas. I don't know if you're hoping you can, but—"

"I'm not," I interject. "But what happened to Sarah? Jane? Kent? All of it centers around this curse."

"Kent left you in the forest for dead."

"But he didn't deserve to die."

Everett is silent as we walk. "You're a bigger person than me," he finally says. "I would have let him rot."

"Like Emma said, I might just be stupid." I grin. Suddenly, a sound to the right of us, like a bone breaking in half, makes me grab a knife from the set wrapped around my waist.

Everett puts his hand on my shoulder. "Keep moving," he mutters without moving his lips. "They've been following us since we came into the forest."

"They? Perversions?"

"Emissaries," Emma hastily whispers ahead of us. "They are the guardians of this forest, after all. And we are intruders."

I stumble, and Everett glances over at me and frowns. His fingers brush against my cheek. "You're freezing cold."

"And you're not," I say.

"Again, trained for this. But"—he glances around—"the temperature *is* dropping."

"And quickly," Emma adds.

"Is this normal?" I question.

"Yes." She pauses. "But not this cold. Not this much. We need to find shelter. It's only going to get colder and darker."

She doesn't need to elaborate. If everything in the forest functions with its own laws, I bet even the darkness here is different. Thicker. Stronger. Making it easier to pick us off one at a time.

I do my best to distinguish between the Everleys' conversation about what's best to do next, and the taunting of the forest—its snide snickers that lick at the back of my mind.

You're going to die here.

You've seen the visions.

You know what happens next.

I bite my tongue until I taste blood. The pain quiets the voices a bit.

"We have a tent," Everett says. "We can find someplace to

pitch. Hunker down for the night."

I nod and push forward. Will a tent be enough? The chill in the air feels like it's crawling against my skin, scuttling up my body.

Sharp pain moves from the base of my skull, ricocheting down my spine, making my whole body feel like it wants to tense up. I grit my teeth, holding the pain back as I continue to walk. The whispers of the forest get louder until they sound like a symphony of screaming people, everyone speaking over one another, right against my ears. This sounds different than usual. I can't usually make out individual voices when I hear the forest—it just sounds like a garble of people. But right now it's like individuals, each distinct and different in their own right, are whispering the same thing.

"Shut up," I hiss. "Shut up shut up shut up."

"Douglas?" Everett asks.

I feel his warm hand on my shoulder, as if right under the skin of his palm there are hot iron holes. I want to lean into it and self-ishly take his warmth for myself. Even with my eyes closed, I can picture the concerned look on his handsome face, the way his angular features are studying me. I know in the back of his head, he's probably debating if we should turn back.

"I'm fine," I say, cutting it off before he can even suggest it. "Just a headache."

"From the forest?"

It's not so much a question as a statement that drips with annoyance and distain. I open one eye. Even with the weak light from his flashlight, I can see the scowl on his face.

"I'm not turning around."

"I didn't say you should."

"Your face says it."

He hesitates. "All I'm saying," he finally says, "is that no one would blame you for giving up. Many people before you have failed. Even Headmaster Monroe, with all of his resources and money and his family's generational vendetta against the forest, has not been able to get as far as you have."

"Headmaster Monroe is one of the richest and most driven people I know," I say. "I find it hard to believe that if he didn't want to enter the forest on his own, he couldn't do this himself."

"That's the point. He's scared."

"Of what?"

Everett shrugs. "Million-dollar question, isn't it? Maybe he's the smartest one out of all of us."

He sighs and continues. "I just want you safe. You can't be that in this forest."

"A bit late to tell me, isn't it?"

"Would you have listened any other time?"

"Probably not."

"Hey, guys," Emma says, far enough ahead of us that her voice echoes off the trees, making it hard to determine where she actually is. "Come here."

It's less of a request and more of a command. Everett squeezes my shoulder one more time, his hand sliding down to lace between my fingers, leading me toward his sister. It's a simple gesture, a silent way of him telling me that he isn't going to let me go.

I don't know what I expect as Everett and I walk up the hill. Perhaps a wounded Perversion, or an Emissary staring Emma down. A small part of me was hoping that maybe this tree we're looking for was in the distance. Since time works differently inside the forest, perhaps we've been in here for days or weeks.

But after Everett and I take ourselves to the top of the hill, what stares back is the furthest thing from what I expected.

"That's my apartment." The words come out more as a gasp of desperation than sheer astonishment.

"What?" Everett asks.

"The apartment complex where Mom and I lived after Dad died," I elaborate, my voice choking. But it's not only that—it's the place where the fire happened. Where everything changed. Where my life went to hell. It's just standing there, covered in soot with more than two dozen of the eighty-plus windows on the twenty-plus stories blown out. It looks exactly like it did on the news, after the fires had been extinguished. Like someone just picked the complex up and dropped it right here in the forest, the top of the building extending so half of it is swallowed by the darkness of the canopy.

Everett stands in front of me, his chest flush with mine. "Douglas, you know that's not actually your home, right?"

"The forest made that to trick you," Emma says carefully. "To distract us."

"I know . . . but . . ." I swallow. "It looks so real. Every detail, even the sign in front of the building missing the *s* at the end of *Willow Homes*. All of it. Is here."

"It's real because it's coming from your memories," Everett urges. "You say the forest can speak to you, right? Who's to say it's not pulling this right from your memory to *make* it look real, so you believe it's actually here."

"Maybe it's trying to tell me something," I reason, taking a step forward.

"Or maybe it's trying to lure you in and keep you here," Emma counters. "Douglas, think. A home symbolizes safety and comfort. What better way to keep you here than to give you that?"

"Then why wouldn't it give me a home I actually want to see?" I ask, turning to both of them. "This place is filled with horrible memories. We moved here when my father died of cancer. If the forest wanted to keep me here, it would give me something comforting, not this."

Everett opens his mouth to reply but closes it, brow furrowing. He shoots Emma a glance. "Back me up here?"

"He might be right," Emma says slowly, like she doesn't want to admit it.

"You cannot be serious."

"I'm not saying the forest is on our side, but his logic makes sense. Why show us something he would avoid if it wants to keep us here? There's something here it wants us to see. Something tied to Douglas's memories."

"Bullshit," Everett says, pointing to the apartment. "There's nothing good in there. At all. We need to keep going, find a place to camp."

"I don't know if we have much of a choice," Emma says slowly.

She's right. The skies are getting darker, and the chill in the air is starting to produce a frost on the ground.

But Everett and Emma can't hear what I can hear: the soft whispers of Kent, Jane, and Sarah, all telling me to come home. To trust what's behind the door.

They can't hear the forest telling me to go inside. That what we seek is right on the other side of the door if we're brave enough to venture in.

Even my mama's voice is there, clear as when she used to sing me a lullaby or read me a bedtime story.

Emma's and Everett's voices fade into the background, but the voice of my mother takes center stage. It's like she's with me. Like I never left her behind. Like I never let her down.

I'm not stupid; I know it's not real. I know, like Everett said, this is the forest playing a trick on me. But don't I deserve to be happy? Even if for a minute? To take a breath, to be at peace, to remember what it was like before everything went to hell? Even if it's just an illusion, I can live with that if only for a few moments.

My hand is on the doorknob before I even notice my legs have carried me to the door. The knob feels warm—like there's sunlight, peace, happiness.

My mama is waiting for me on the other side. Sarah is waiting for me on the other side. Kent is waiting for me on the other side. All those people who died in the fire are on the other side.

And something important is waiting for me on the other side. Something we need to know and I can't avoid. A truth that will change everything. I just know it.

And even if I'm wrong? I'm willing to risk it all to find out.

Before I can open the door, Everett's hand is on my shoulder again. I can tell it's his by how he squeezes me.

"You sure about this?" he asks. "There's no turning back once you open that. We have no idea what's in there."

"I know . . . I don't expect you to understand, but I have to do this. I have to go in here. I feel like we have to go in here."

I feel Emma's shoulder slide against mine as she stands to my right. "Then we go," she says. "Together."

Both Emma and Everett put their hands over mine on the doorknob. I don't count down out loud, but I can tell they're counting with me, backward from three, holding their breath as we turn the knob, no idea what's waiting for us on the other side.

26

"This isn't the home I remember."

There's nothing but death for us here in the apartment complex. The moment we step inside, Emma closes the door behind us, locking it quickly. Everett looks around frantically, finding a weathered cabinet and pushing it in front of the door.

The inside is nothing like the apartment complex I used to know. There's no lobby, but instead, the entrance goes directly into my apartment.

The bones of the structure look like my home in DC. Looking around, I remember the chair in the corner, even though it looks like it's been devoured by moths and rodents. Floorboards creak underneath our footsteps, to the point where I don't want to put too much weight on the wood, afraid that I might fall through.

"I never saw it like this," I clarify. "Burned and abandoned. I was gone by the time . . . this happened."

"What do you remember?" Everett asks, rubbing his hands together and blowing on them.

I never told him any specifics or details about the fire. It still hurts to think about. Hard to form the words and put them into the universe.

"I remember going to sleep. Mama had to take a night shift to pay for a school trip I really wanted to go on. I made dinner and passed out while doing homework and then . . . flames. I ran down the hallway, trying to get out. But the smoke was too thick and then . . ."

I close my eyes, trying to focus. "I can still hear their screams." They sound louder this time. Like they're right on the other side of the door.

"I hear them too," Emma says. When I open my eyes, she and Everett are looking at the door we just came from. Under the door, red and yellow lights pulse, like strobe lights. At least, that's what I think at first.

But then smoke seeps in from under the gap and I realize, outside the door is exactly what happened before. Those screams aren't in my head. They're actually screams of the people burning alive from the fire. Just inches away.

I take a step toward the door, raising my hands, already beginning to bubble inside. But Everett stands in front of me and wraps me in a tight hug.

"It's not real, Douglas," he whispers in my ear. "You can't do anything. The forest wants you to open the door. It's tempting you. Don't give it the satisfaction. Don't let whatever is out there in."

Deep down I know that. The logical part of me understands this is all a test. But I know those voices. They were my friends. People who took care of me and welcomed me into their lives. When my mama and I came, one of our neighbors helped us move in. Another made us food for a week. They were the reason we got through Dad's death.

And I killed them.

Everett holds me until the tears start to fall down my face. I cling onto him tighter, just watching the flames under the door. Hearing the distinct voices, saying I'm sorry to each of them in my head. Slowly, the flames die out, the smoke disappears, and the voices grow silent.

"We can stay here for the night," Emma finally chimes in once I pull away from Everett and wipe my face. "Or at least until it warms up."

"You sure you're okay?" Everett asks.

I nod, forcing a smile. I can't bring myself to speak.

Everett doesn't believe me, I can tell. It's why his gaze lingers on me for a moment or two longer before he squats, opening his bag and pulling out some turkey sandwiches and small bottles of water.

"Eat," he says. "It'll help."

We sit and eat for a few silent moments, no one knowing what to say or do. Halfway through the second half of my sandwich, Everett speaks.

"We're missing something. The apartment complex was placed here to tell us something."

"You want to think there's logic to everything," Emma mutters. "Maybe the forest is just an asshole."

"So you think this was placed here to what? Simply show me the horrors of my past? To remind me what I did to end up here? That doesn't make sense. There has to be more. "

Emma shrugs, shoveling the last bit of food into her mouth before standing. She walks around, scanning the room. Spaces on the mantel where photos should be, a bookshelf that should be filled to the brim with stories . . . All of them are here but echoes of themselves. Shadows made to resemble a home, made by someone with hate and pain in their heart.

"You okay?" Everett asks.

"Are any of us okay?"

"Fair enough."

I should be doing something useful, I think. Trying to talk with the forest, or making a map, or trying to understand some of the visions I've had over the past few months. Everything in Winslow is a clue. Everything is a piece of evidence that I can use to my advantage. I just need to be smart enough to piece it all together.

But right now, all the pieces are broken and separate. It's like I have a third of the puzzle, but not enough to see what the final image should be. And I hate moving forward like that. I hate being on the defensive.

"Did you keep a diary?" Emma asks from behind me. "When you were younger?"

"No." I shake my head, turning to see her squatting in front of a bookshelf. "Never found it useful."

"Then why does this have your name on it?"

Emma holds up a leather-bound book, her back still to us, while she scans the rest of the mostly empty shelves. Frowning, I walk over to take the book from her.

The book burns to the touch. It feels like evil drips off it, as if the darkness between its pages is palpable. I take a deep breath, steeling myself as whatever is within the pages clings to my soul. It's as if touching it allows whatever is malevolent inside it to soak into my body through my pores, past my bones and muscles and veins and deep into somewhere intangible.

"Leave something to help the next one survive," I read from the first handwritten page.

"Any idea what that means?" Everett asks.

"Was hoping you did. You know all the town's lore."

"That went out the window when we entered here. This is your apartment," he counters.

I know he's right, so I do not answer. Instead, I flip through the pages, one at a time. Each page has a different name on it, a different date, and different styles of handwriting.

"This goes all the way back to a few years after Winslow was founded," Everett mutters, looking over my shoulder. "I've never seen these names before, though. Amy, Elijah, Ernesto, Jack . . ."

"There aren't any last names," Emma notes. "This could be anyone's. Maybe someone who entered the forest and left it? Fell out of their bag like some English project?"

"That doesn't explain the dates and different styles of writing," I argue. "Each one of these is a different person."

I make that declaration like I actually know what I'm talking about. But it makes sense; I only skim the first paragraph or so of each page, but all the entries are the same. People begging for forgiveness, people asking for a second chance at life. People promising they'll do better if they make it out of the forest alive. Every single one of them wishes for a second chance and regrets entering the forest.

And though they all share a commonality, linked by regret in fear and pain, there's something else that ties them together more neatly. Instead of last names, each has a stain right by their name, a fingerprint pressed into the paper in blood, as if it's some sort of calling card they've signed off with when they finished their letter.

"We should put it back," Everett reasons. "Or take it with us. I don't care, but I don't want to keep reading."

"It's making my head hurt," Emma agrees, turning back with her brother toward the makeshift campfire she set up using spare wood and a lighter in the living room.

Leave something to help the next one survive. That sentence echoes in my head. There's one blank page at the end of the book, as if it's reserved for the next person who finds it. I keep staring at the paper, heart thumping in my chest and crawling up my esophagus, nestling itself in my throat. There's nothing good that could come from entertaining whatever magic drips off this book. I wonder if Emma and Everett are feeling the same thing I am, just to a greater degree. I wonder if the magic of the forest is keeping me from putting the book away, urging me silently to continue reading, to take the next step.

Leave something to help the next one survive.

The forest demands payment in blood.

Those two statements are not exclusive. They can't be.

I pull one of the knives from my waist and press the tip of the blade against my thumb. The pain is only momentary, and the adrenaline rushing through me masks it. Without waiting for Everett or Emma to try to stop me, I quickly press my thumb against the page.

Immediately, pain more intense than anything I've ever experienced jolts down my spine. For a second, it's as if I don't really exist, the pain shocking every nerve and fiber of my being, burning it to a crisp. I only see white, and my ears ring so loudly that nothing else can penetrate. But as quickly as it happens, it disappears. I find myself on my hands and knees, my body shaking, sweat pooling around my brows and the sour taste of vomit in my mouth, staining the floor in front of me.

I'm not in my home anymore. I'm not even in the forest anymore. Somehow I've been transported back to Regent Academy. The familiar oak walls and photos of graduates and the founders line the hallways, but they're different from the ones I remember seeing just hours before. These photos look younger, as if they haven't been touched by time. The brass-and-gold letterings on the wooden picture frames are polished and new. There are fewer photos too. Down the main hallway of Regent Academy, there are nearly twenty-four photos that line each wall, twelve on each side. There are only four here now.

That's not the only thing different about the school either. The students who rush by me are dressed differently, like something you'd see in a reenactment of the 1800s. None of them notice me as they run by, heading to their classes, moving around me like some invisible boulder they know not to touch.

"Odd, isn't it?" a voice says directly in front of me. "Seeing the school through the lens of time."

The voice causes my hackles to rise. It's a familiar voice. A voice I haven't heard in years.

My dad's voice.

The man standing in front of me looks exactly how I remember him. Dark skin like me, same bright wide grin like me. He has the locs I always wanted to grow out and the vibrant expression that shows how much he loves life.

My father is here with me.

I take a step forward, desperation driving me to wrap my arms around him and hold him close, something I've missed for years. But halfway between where I stand and where he is, I stop. Something is off.

"How are you here?" I ask. "In this forest? You didn't die here. You never knew this place existed . . . You can't . . ."

There's a small smile playing at the edge of his lips, like he finds this all funny but he's trying to hold it back. Nothing about him looks threatening, and the longer I stare, the more my shoulders relax. He just looks so much like my father.

"I thought this would be a more comforting look for you, am I wrong?"

That simple sentence shatters the illusion. I dig my right foot into the earth to steady myself. It doesn't matter how comforting and relaxing seeing my "dad" here is. It's not here. It's something else. Something darker . . . like everything else in this forest.

But that doesn't take away the feeling of love and safety I feel. The sensation of sun against my skin, or a warm embrace keeping me safe. The sound of laughter, the notes of nature. Memories through emotions and feelings that I never experienced but feel so real. That has to come from somewhere. That can't just be fake. It has to be coming from someone who knows what love feels like.

All of them that belonged to . . .

"You're his lover. You're the one who was killed."

The grin grows a little brighter. My "dad" smiles. "Please, call me Henry. I'm glad we can finally meet face-to-face."

Henry and Etaliein. The two lovers who started all of this. Two men in love who couldn't just be left to be happy.

"Would you like me to change form to something more appealing? If this causes you harm . . ."

"No," I say before he can finish. "No . . . This . . . This is good." A beat passes. "You've done this before? Reached out to people?" I ask. "There have been people before me, right?"

"That's not the question you want to ask."

"How do you know?"

"Because it's not the right question. Ask another. I promise, before our time is up, you'll know everything you need to know."

I've learned since being at Regent not to trust people when they say things like that, but right now, I feel I don't have a choice.

"Fine, another question, then. Why did you bring me here?"

"I didn't do any such thing," he said. "You answered the call. When you decided to take on this task. You could have refused the gift."

"It didn't seem much like a gift in the moment."

"The most important gifts rarely do." He grins. "Do you trust me, Douglas?"

"No."

The word leaves my mouth before I can stop it, but Henry doesn't seem offended. He keeps his palm up, facing me. "I'd be concerned if you said you did. But I'll ask you differently. Do you think you can find it in your heart to trust me?"

"You know . . . ," I say, pause, and then pick up again. "I've been doing a lot of trusting people and things lately. And no one has trusted me. Why should I stick my neck out again for you when you won't even trust me and expect me at every turn to follow you blindly?"

Henry doesn't speak. The way he stares at me makes me wonder if he's frozen, like some computer software that's corrupt. But slowly, a smile spreads over his lips.

"If you follow me, I'll answer all your questions about the Monroe family and those who came before you. You want those missing pieces filled in, don't you? Come with me, Douglas, and I'll explain the magic at the center of this curse."

Since this whole thing began, I've learned that magic is a tool;

something that can be used for good or for evil, depending on who wields it. I've seen how Headmaster Monroe uses magic; staying within the gray areas of the curse to get away with acts that should lead to his execution. Is there a way to change things? A way to make things better?

I guess I'll have to take a leap of faith to find out.

27

"Why a book?"

I've never been in the presence of a spirit before coming to Regent Academy. This one seems different from Jane or Taylor. More powerful, for one. Or his power manifests differently. Should I be afraid? Should I try to barter with him?

"I'm sorry?"

"When I touched the book, I came here. That's because of you. Why a book? Why not anything else?"

"I wanted to be a writer," Henry mutters, so quietly I can barely hear him. "Etaliein knew that. He made the parchment himself. Took the hide, dried it, and bound the notebook for me. He could have fashioned it from magic, but . . . he took the time, worked with his hands to create something from nothing. I think it was the last gift I received from him before . . ." Henry doesn't finish. He takes a deep, pained breath, glancing over at me.

"I told him I wanted to be a writer so I can make stories that help the next generation of people who come along. That's what stories are for. And spells are just another form of stories. Spells need a host to hold it, a catalyst to activate it, and a spark to fuel it. The book, the blood, the magic. What better way to honor our memory than to use the gift to do just that?"

Henry pushes the door open, the world swirling around us like a dozen watercolors dumped into a vat and poured out. When the colors separate and take form, we're standing in a familiar room, the expansive view of the forest to the left of us, the polished mahogany desk to the right of us, and a thin bookshelf in front of us.

I would never forget this room. I don't think I can ever forget this room. This is Headmaster Monroe's office. And more importantly, we aren't alone.

Five students my age are in the room. A Hispanic boy sits on the couch, a Japanese girl leans against the desk, a light-skinned African American girl stands in front of me, an Indigenous individual scans the bookshelf, and a South Asian boy has their face buried in their knees in the corner. Each of them looks see-through, like ghosts going through the motions.

There are also five adults, each one sitting close to a student. The one on the couch has a man with a ponytail sitting next to him. A man in military dress talks demandingly in muted words to the African American girl, dictating something to her, based on his hand movements. A woman with sharp features shows the Japanese girl something within a book—the same book that Headmaster Monroe showed me. An older woman with silver hair watches over the student scanning the shelf. And the Indian boy is held by a woman resembling someone I saw in a photo on Headmaster Monroe's desk.

Five teens who look out of place. Five teens of color who seem like they have mentorship from Monroe, someone to guide them and help them through their experiences.

Five teens just like me.

And then it clicks.

"You get it now, don't you?" Henry asks. "Each of these students are like you, Douglas. Disenfranchised teens who came before you to Regent Academy, who were promised the world, lured by a Regent, and sent into the forest to break the curse. Each of them told they were special, promised something they couldn't refuse, and thrown into a world they didn't understand. And each of them . . . are nothing more than a memory." Henry snaps his fingers and the world, within a blink, changes from something pristine and crisp to what can only be described as a horror. Where the African American girl stood, there is only a pile of flesh. Where the Indian boy crouched, only the lower half of his body remains. Where the girl scanned the bookshelf, there's a shadow of red blood, like an explosion has left the imprint of her body against the books. Claw marks inch-deep line the desk and disappear behind it. The couch is prickled with bone fragments: some shards, some half the length of a femur, snapped in half.

I can't scream. I can't stop it. The images flash in front of my eyes, one by one, of how brutally each of them was killed in the forest. How loudly they screamed. How they begged and pleaded for their parents. The sounds of their bodies ripping, their bones snapping, their voices swallowed by the blood caught in their throat.

I'm not sure how long the visions last, but when my body becomes mine again, I'm gasping for air. My legs want to betray me, but Henry catches me before I collapse.

"I've got you," he whispers. "I've got you, Douglas. You're safe."

"Am I?" I choke out, my voice laced with anger and a bit of fear. "That's why you showed me this, right? To tell me how I'm anything but safe?"

Henry says nothing at first. The room slowly morphs back to normal, a hollow office, with not a single soul in it except for me and Henry.

Ripping my arm from his grasp, I take a step back and wipe the sweat from my brow, forcing my breath to calm.

"Why did you show me that?" I hiss. "To scare me off?"

"I wanted you to understand who and what you are up against," he says. "To show you that some forces are more dangerous than the ones in the forest. The Monroes have done to you what they've done to so many other children like you—lost, desperate, scared, and lonely children—for years. Luring them to Regent Academy, sending them out to the forest expecting a miracle. And when they fail? They forget about them, and move on to another.

"You don't think you were simply lucky, do you, Douglas?

That Headmaster Monroe saw your court case and decided you deserved a place in the school, then decided you would be perfect to help him break the curse? No. You're too smart to think you're *that* special."

With another wave of his hand, the room morphs into the apartment complex hallway back home. Nostalgia roots itself in my body for only a moment before I see the familiar sight of flames licking the walls, smoke billowing above us, skimming the ceiling. My body tenses, instantly wanting to sink as low to the floor as possible, to stay far away from the flames and the smoke that left me unconscious before.

"It's just a vision, Douglas," he whispers. "A snapshot of your memory. This is what you contribute to the story. This is what you leave behind."

"I don't care!" I yell. "I don't *want* to see this again! I don't want to participate in whatever twisted game you're playing, thinking this is going to teach me some lesson or make me a better person or help me understand whatever the hell it is you want me to understand! Stop giving me half-truths! You want to make the world a better place? You want to give one of us something that helps? Then tell me everything. Let *me* decide what is and isn't important, because as long as you don't? You're just as bad as the headmasters!"

Each word is like a dagger as it leaves my mouth. I see Henry wince as each lands a perfect blow. Half of me expects him to lash out, but the other part of me knows the truth.

He's trapped in the memory as much as these students are.

"Look, Douglas," he says gently, tilting his head toward the hallway. "Really look; see what you didn't see before."

My gaze is blurry, thanks to tears forming in the corners of my eyes. A pain shoots through my chest, starting from my heart and expanding outward like a shock wave. This is where it all started; where everything went to hell. The fire. The deaths. The . . .

The person, the person I swore I saw before but couldn't be sure if it was just a trick of my mind.

The same person I swore I saw in my testimony. This time, though, as the flames and smoke begin to billow and crawl up the walls and against the ceiling, I can see them clearly.

And the Regent Academy ring that catches the light against their pinkie finger.

"You see, Douglas," Henry says, pausing the scene. "You were never to blame for what happened. But who was?"

"Obviously whoever that is." I point. "I knew I didn't do this. I *knew* it!"

"Yes, you're right. But think bigger. Who put this man up to it? Who put this all into motion?"

"Headmaster Monroe," I say slowly.

"Exactly. You were simply a pawn forced to play a game."

The room returns to the school I've grown to hate. Slowly, Henry moves in front of me, taking his right hand and tilting my gaze up to his.

"I'm giving you the same offer I have given every single other person who has come before you, lured into the Monroes' world. You can say no. You can leave. I can open a door, and you'll appear in Winslow. There's nothing for you here, no reason for you to stay."

"I'm not doing this for him," I seethe. "You don't get it, do you? Those people died. Because of me, because of some twisted game Regent was playing. It doesn't matter. People are dead. And it all still goes back to this forest, and me. He did that to get to me. To frame me. Throwing away dozens of lives, people who had families, hopes, dreams, all cut short because a man with too much power wanted more. I'm as much to blame as you and Etaliein."

Henry frowns. "I'm sorry?"

"The curse that is on Winslow . . . It's yours and his. Both of you are responsible for this. I understand why you did it. The people of the past who hurt you and him deserve to suffer. But there are so many people now who don't. People who haven't done anything. The descendants of those who hurt you should not carry the sins of their fathers. The students of Regent don't deserve to pay."

"You are not wrong," he says. "In fact, I agree."

"Then end this," I hiss, a pained whisper leaving my mouth. "End this for everyone. Stop this cycle of pain."

"You do not think I would if I could? Like you said, I'm just a memory, a snapshot in time. I was never magical; that was Etaliein. I'm a victim of this just like you, trapped in the school, a trophy for the Monroes, unable to move on until I'm buried, until this curse is broken."

"What do you mean?"

Henry opens his mouth, as if he wants to speak, but a dull,

distant sound catches our attention, forcing us to turn toward the window. It sounds like someone's screams. A pained voice feet away, spoken through a layer of water.

It sounds . . . familiar.

"You don't have to stay here, Douglas," Henry says. "You can turn around and leave this place. Forget it ever happened. This isn't your fight."

The option is worth considering. It feels like the most tangible of choices, like the one thing that makes sense. Regent Academy isn't my school. Winslow isn't my home. I'm only here because of lies and manipulations that have been served to me on a platter I fed from willingly and blindly. I don't owe these people anything.

But I can't just leave.

"There are people waiting for me," I whisper. "Emma . . . Everett . . . What happens to them?"

"They will stay and fend for themselves. They are children of Everley, talented and strong. I imagine they, out of anyone, have the most chance to survive."

"I'm not leaving them behind," I say quickly, my words blurring together into one word. "You take me, you take them too. That's what my dad would do."

Henry slowly shakes his head. "I cannot do that—and remember, I am not your father."

I know, I think. *And that makes this hurt even more.*

"Cannot or will not?"

"The difference doesn't matter."

"You say you're not magical like him, but you made all of this.

You're stronger than you think, Henry. A part of Etaliein is inside of you."

"I died, and then I was here. Stuck in this loop, only ever concious when someone like you comes along. There is no life for me. No happy ending. Forgiveness requires a two-way street, Douglas. What have the descendants done to deserve it?"

"The sins of the father are not the sins of the child."

"Tell that to my dead corpse."

There's no reasoning with him, I can tell that. There's too much history and pain to parse through. "They risked their lives for me. They came here to protect me and to help me. I'm not just going to abandon them."

"Then you are as stupid and foolish as everyone who came before you."

Before I can try to argue my case, the world loses all of its color, turning black in an instant. My breath and heartbeat skip, like when you're half-asleep and half-awake and stumbling in a dream. Except this time, it's my breath that stumbles, a hiccup forcing me back into my body—my real body, back in the living room.

The notebook is still in my hand, and though I can't prove it, I can tell only a few minutes have passed. But in the forest, a few minutes is all it takes for everything to change.

And inside the apartment—and outside—everything has indeed changed. Starting with the door ripped off its hinges and the screams I hear in the other world, as clear as day. Screams of Emma and Everett in pain, agony, and most importantly, fear.

28

I don't give myself time to process what I heard inside Henry's dreamworld. Instead I shove myself through the front door, running toward the screams.

Everett and Emma have their backs toward the door. Their weapons are poised in their hands with their bodies slightly hunched forward in a battle-like position. No more than maybe ten feet ahead of them, stand three different Perversions of three varying sizes. The first hovers a few feet above the ground, with bony eagle-like wings half-decayed and a face that is half human, half bird skull.

The one in the middle is on all fours with two additional arms protruding out of its shoulders. It looks mostly wolflike except for the hands, which are clearly those of a man. Its face looks more human than any of the others, even though it has the most lupine-like features. I think it's smiling at them, like it's hungry to devour their bodies.

And finally, the one on the right stands on two legs, and it's thin like a gaunt woman. Strands of black hair drip down its shoulders. It's covered in a shawl that looks like it was dragged through the mud and burned, but I can see something slithering under it. A momentary glimpse shows me the tail of a scorpion.

"Are you all okay?" I whisper, standing between Everett and Emma.

Everett glances at me without moving his head. In his right hand he's holding a sawed-off shotgun while in his left is a machete. Emma has a hunter's rifle and a longer blade on her hip.

"Could be asking you the same thing," he mutters. "You going to tell us what you saw?"

"I dunno, maybe we should deal with what's in front of us first?" Emma hisses. "Or do you want to have a meeting with these freaks too? Bring them into the conversation?"

Everett chuckles darkly, like he needs to add something into the air so that he doesn't let nerves get the best of him. "Fair point."

"Are these Emissaries or Perversions?" I ask quietly. None of the three of them are moving, like they are waiting for us to strike first.

"The latter," Emma says.

"That's good, right? We can kill them?"

"No," Emma whispers. "I mean, yes, but no, it's not good." She nods past the tree line. "Something else is watching us. An

Emissary. It let them go past. I think it wants them to handle us instead of getting its own hands dirty."

"And if they fail, we'll be too tired to fight, and then it'll rip us apart," Everett adds.

"Can they do that? I mean, do they do that? Emissaries and Perversions? Team up like that?"

"No," both the siblings say at the same time. "That's what's concerning."

"Douglas," Everett says, never breaking his gaze with the crew in front of us. "You need to promise me, no matter what happens to Emma or me, you keep going."

"What? I'm not leaving you."

"I'm not saying you should," he hisses. "I'm saying our goal in this is to make sure you make it out of here alive, and get to that tree. If us holding them off buys you the time you need . . ."

"You mean dying. You two can't face these things and win."

"And you think you can help?" Emma asks. Her words are sharp, but I know she doesn't intend it to come across as mean as it does. "You're not trained for this."

"But I do have magic."

"That's not mastered and very unpredictable," Everett argues.

"But unpredictability is good. You think they expect that? I'm not saying it's the secret weapon that helps us win, but it at least maybe puts the battle in our favor."

"You staying here is dangerous," Everett reminds me.

"Him in the forest alone is dangerous too," Emma notes. "There's no good answer here."

Everett sighs. I see him narrow his eyes and follow his gaze.

"Shit," we both say at the same time.

The Perversion in the center is suddenly gone.

That realization is all the three of us need. In fact, it's all the remaining Perversions need. The two at their post spring into action, launching forward. Emma and Everett roll to the side, Everett firing his shotgun, with expert precision. It hits the multi-armed Perversion on its elbow, causing it to roar in pain.

Emma follows up with three shots back-to-back, each one hitting the same spot her brother did. By the third shot, the arm breaks in half, falling off the creature onto the forest floor and burning away like it was dropped into acid.

"Fuck you," she barks, her voice barely audible over its screams.

I keep my eyes on the birdlike Perversion, zipping through the air so fast it's a blur. Everett can't get a good shot on it, and with Emma keeping an eye out for the missing Perversion, we only have so much time before they regroup and strike.

"We have to bring it down," I mutter. "We're never going to get a clear shot with it in the air . . ."

What could make a creature have to land? Rain? No. Thunder? Lightning? Possibly, but nothing's going to get through the canopy. The Perversions know this forest better than we do. They are literally part of it. We can't beat them at their own game.

So, we have to take away that advantage.

I remember what the being said when I fell unconscious after the Headmaster drugged me. About the type of magic I have inside me. It's linked to the forest. Linked to nature. I can use that to my advantage.

Rubbing my hands together, I focus on the moisture in the air, the dampness of the forest, the way it fills our lungs and makes our coughs wet. I take a deep breath and push my hands outward, exhaling as I do.

"Blind them," I whisper.

Moments later, the air begins to thicken. Blankets of white fog rise from the ground and fall from the skies, meeting and mixing halfway. With each passing second the visibility decreases. Emma and Everett are smart enough to close in, flanking me on either side. I keep my vision trained to the skies, watching that dark mass zipping around the trees in through the shadows. Its movements are erratic, and it roars in frustration as it becomes disoriented in the air. And then, almost as if it came from nowhere, I hear the sound I was hoping to hear when I cast that spell. Moments later, with a sickening snap of bones breaking, the being falls from the skies and lands in a heap in front of us, wheezing, unmoving.

"One down, two to go."

Both Emma and Everett shift back to standing in front of me, like knights guarding a king. The creature with its missing arm lunges forward out of the white fog. But not before Emma and Everett both fire their weapons. Once. Twice. Four times. Each of them unloading the magazine of their shotgun into the beast. The force is enough to send it falling backward, landing next to the flying creature.

The second beast wheezes in pain, much like the first. Except this time, it sounds more human, like a person crying out. Perversions are, or once were, people. We all know that. Everett didn't have to tell me that seeing them *as* people would make the job harder. He didn't need to tell me because I swallowed that thought the minute we entered the forest. How could I do what I had to do if I knew I was killing a person?

But in that moment, seeing one of the beast's arms reach out to the flying beast, I couldn't help but wonder, did a fraction of their humanity still remain? In the moments as they died, did they know each other? Family members? Lovers? Friends? What were they to one another?

"I'll put them out of their misery," Emma says, smoothly pulling the blade from her waist.

"No," I say, stepping forward. "I'll do it."

Emma doesn't fight me. She gestures with her blade in a sort of *after you* fashion, before offering it to me, handle first. It's heavy in my hand, weighted so that when a person swings, gravity assists them and slices are clean.

Slowly, I approach the dying Perversions, keeping my distance until I'm sure they aren't going to lunge at me. I'm not sure why I feel it necessary to be the one who kills them. We are all equally responsible for what happened, and when they attacked us, it was pure self-defense. I can't imagine how much pain these people are in. Being pulled back from the brink of death to become something grotesque and filled with darkness and rage feels like a fate worse than death.

I feel like if I was in this situation, I wouldn't want to just lie here in pain, dying.

But at the same time, it's a fate that doesn't seem that out of reach. There was a time when my father died that I hated the world. I was lucky enough to have my mother to be able to help me claw my way out of that. But when I was arrested for the fire and no one believed me . . . when it was easy to just assume that a Black boy wasn't telling the truth, that rage and anger came flooding back tenfold.

"I know what it's like to give in to that pain," I whisper to them. "I know how easily it is and how comforting it feels when there's only darkness around you. And I also know what it feels like when you think you have no other choice and when someone who seems like they care about you makes a choice for you that really only helps them. I'm just sorry there was no one here to stand up for you."

"Save us your pity."

At first, I think the voice comes from one of the dying Perversions in front of me, but when I hear Everett and Emma cock their guns behind me, I know that's not the case.

From the darkness in front of me, where I see the Emissary's glowing eyes still watching us in the distance, the missing Perversion steps out. She looks more human than the rest of them, as if her creation is only half-complete. Pain covers her half-formed face, the other half of it blank like a mask. She stumbles out, long lanky arms with fingertips and nails that are easily a foot long leaving drag marks on the ground. It only takes half a second for my heart to sink into the bottom of my chest when the face comes close enough in the mist for me to make out its features.

"Oh my god, Sister Annabeth."

She looks nothing like she did a few weeks ago. I suddenly realize that after I left her office, I didn't see her again. Before I left for the forest, I never said goodbye, and considering that my duties at Regent Academy changed to being focused only on breaking the curse, I never had any follow-up meetings with her. I didn't think anything of it, but I should have. There was never a time while I attended Regent that Sister Annabeth wasn't on my side, checking in on me, trying to help me. And this is how she was repaid.

"Is that my name?" she asks. "I don't remember."

"How did you . . . You know better. You knew not to go into the forest."

"I . . ." she whispers with a wet voice, thick with blood. "I don't know what happened. I don't know who I am, or where I am. All I know is this is all your fault."

"Wait." I take a step back. "What?"

Sister Annabeth lumbers forward, stumbles, and collapses, her limbs too long and thin to hold up her twisted body. Bones break and protrude through the flesh. Blood as black as the night pours out as she groans in a wheezing gasp of pain.

"Every voice in my head, every thought, every instinct, tells me if I kill you, then the pain will stop."

"That's not . . ."

"Careful, child of man." The voice of the Emissary surveying us booms so loud, it feels like he is speaking all around us. "You were warned of what would happen if you stepped foot in this forest and did the bidding of a descendant. The forest warned you. *We* warned you. Your foolishness and hubris are only to blame for the death and pain of others. And just like the descendants who came before, who brought down this curse on this town, you have put yourself and your own ego above everyone else. And that, like the men who came before you and the men who will surely come after you, will be your downfall. Except this time, it won't only be you who pays the price of blood and pain. It will be every person who has ever helped you."

The Emissary takes a half step forward, and I can see the features of his face, see how he's easily twelve feet tall, with a face much like a horse and eyes that glow like the devil. His lips are curled into a human-like snarl that's a mix of anger and confidence, as if seeing Sister Annabeth in pain brings him joy.

"You will die here, Douglas Jones. You and the descendants of Everley's blood and flesh and bone will lay the groundwork before a new grove for flora to live and for fauna to thrive. At least some good will come from your wretched existence."

The Perversion lunges forward with its claws, but not before I jump back. The tip of one slashes at my shirt, cutting deep into my shoulder. The pain burns like nothing I've felt before, but it doesn't break my stance. I only stumble a bit.

And that is all the Perversion needs.

I brace myself for another attack, knowing Emma and Everett won't get there in time, but the Perversion only gets one step forward before a flash of red from a flare shot by Emma explodes in its face. She fires another, this time lodging it in one of its eyes, causing it to roar.

"You DARE strike an Emissary of the FOREST?" the Emissary roars so loudly, my bones chatter.

"Yeah, well," Emma muses as she and Everett flank me again, pulling me back without breaking eye contact with the being. "Felt good to do it."

Once we're a safe-ish distance away, Emma turns to Everett and me. "You both have to go. *Now.*"

"What? No, we're not leaving you."

"She's right, Douglas," Everett says. "If we want to have any chance of making it out alive, someone has to stay behind."

"I have magic, you have weapons—we can beat these things."

"No, we can't," Emma says. "Maybe the Perversion, but not a fucking Emissary."

"Then why are you . . ."

The look on her face tells it all to me.

"No."

"Douglas, this isn't a time for discussion," Emma sternly says. "You're here to do one thing. Break the curse. My brother and I are here to do one thing. Make sure you make it there alive. We both accepted this might happen when we came with you."

"Everett, she's your sister," I strain. "You cannot be okay with this."

"I'm not. But Emma's right. She's better at fighting than me. She can keep them busy longer, which means we'll have more of a chance to put distance between us. It's . . . the right thing."

"You both are fucking crazy. We're *not* splitting up."

"Stop being fucking stupid," Emma barks. "Do you understand what will happen if we stay? We all die, and then what happens? This will all be for nothing."

"You're only assuming we'll die. There's a chance we can beat them!"

"There's a higher chance of us succeeding if we leave, Douglas," Everett says. His eyes flicker upward. From the corner of my vision, I can see what he's looking at.

The flares' lights are dying out.

"We have to go," Everett says, pulling me back. "We don't have time to discuss this. Emma?"

"I'll come back, I promise." She grins, though the corner of her cheek wavers. "I always come back. If I don't, who is going to keep your ass in check?"

"We're not doing this!"

"We are," Everett says, grabbing my wrist so tightly I think he might snap it in half. "I'm sorry, Douglas. But I'm not going to let my sister's sacrifice go in vain. I'm getting you to that tree if it's the last thing I do."

Before I can argue, Everett hits me hard in the gut, enough to make me wheeze and double over. As I'm trying to catch my breath, he hoists me over his shoulder and begins jogging away from his sister.

Even with my blurred vision, the darkness, and the fog, Emma's face is the last thing I see, and I've never seen someone's face hold so much confidence and so much fear at the exact same time.

29

"Here, let me help with that."

For the past five minutes I've been struggling to get some gauze wrapped around my right shoulder. The cut, now bubbling white from some hydrogen peroxide I poured on it, is in an awkward location, making it hard to get the wrappings securely around the wound. Everett has been eyeing me from across the fire we built. Around us, shadows lick at the campfire, as if they are trying to pull the heat from the safe space and leave us cold and alone.

More alone than we are now.

"I'm fine," I mutter through gritted teeth. I tug at the tail of one piece of gauze with my hand, the other with my teeth. I'm trying my best to not let the burning anger inside me direct itself toward him, but he's making it damn hard.

"You don't look like you're fine," he adds softly, pushing up from his seat on a log and moving closer to me. "May I?"

"I said I'm fine."

"You're not going to get that tightly wrapped. And it's not cleaned well. You're going to get an infection."

"I know how to clean a wound, Everett. My mama is a nurse, remember?"

Everett frowns but doesn't move, knowing I'll eventually cave and let him help me.

He would be right. The gauze isn't tight like it needs to be, and I still need to deal with another slash on my right leg. It's not as deep as the one on my shoulder, but it's been causing me problems since we escaped.

"Fine," I concede, sighing. "Thank you."

He slowly peels back the fabric, grabbing a fresh piece of gauze and drenching it in antiseptic. "This might hurt a bit."

He dabs gently at the wound. The flesh is bright pink, the edges slightly white. The pain is minor, a light stinging like needles tapping against the open wound.

"Did you know?" I ask quietly.

"Sorry?" Everett asks. "Did I know Emma was going to make that choice? No, I don't ever know what . . ."

I shake my head. "When I looked in the book at the apartment, I saw other kids before me. Others who had the same fate as me. Were brought here with a promise made by Headmaster Monroe. Tempted by the forest and . . . let's just say they didn't make it."

I turn to look at Everett seriously. "When I first was cursed, I told your mom. She told me not to tell Headmaster Monroe, but she also said this has happened before. She knew. Did you?"

"No," Everett doesn't even hesitate to answer. "Absolutely not. I didn't. My mom never told me anything more than I needed to know. There was never another kid like you on campus, not while I've been here."

I just needed to hear Everett say it. Hearing his words makes my shoulders relax, just a bit. The tingle of nervousness inside me, thinking that Everett might actually have known, dulls the pain of my wounds, but it also quiets something else in my head.

Emma.

Everett pretends not to notice as he examines the wound on my leg. His fingers stop for a moment, rough pads hovering an inch or so above the three gash lines.

"The good news is that it looks like a surface wound. Can you put weight on it?"

I nod. "Hurts a bit, but yeah."

"I'm going to flush it with some water and wrap it."

He pulls out one of the canteens of distilled water and with three shakes of the bottle, cleans the wound as best as possible. Grabbing a fresh piece of gauze, he dabs at it lightly enough to remove any excess water before putting on a thin layer of antiseptic. Like the wound on my shoulder, he wraps it tightly before putting a small clip on it. He checks the edges, making sure no parts of the fabric are folded over before giving me a nod of approval.

"You should be good," he says. "If it gets worse, you let me know, okay? Those slashes can be filled with bacteria. I don't want you getting an infection."

"If I do, I want *you* to cut off my leg, not my mama," I say morbidly.

"I thought you were just boasting how she's a nurse and you learned so much from her." He grins slightly.

"I did." I pause. "I do, but that doesn't mean I want her to have to cut off my leg. No parent should have to do that."

He nods. "Don't worry, I won't let that happen. We're both going to make it out of here. Alive."

But not Emma.

"Promise?"

"Does this look like the face of someone who would lie?"

Everett flashes me a bright, wolfish smile as he gives me a thumbs-up. I have to admit, if the situation was changed—if we were on a date or something at a movie theater—and he looked at me like that, I might've kissed him. But with the specks of blood dried on his face, the bruise over his right eye from being punched, the way his clothes are ripped, and the scars that pepper his body—some old and some reopened—he looks like a cat's scratching post. That ruins the moment. The smile he's giving me isn't only to try to make me feel better, but also him mustering up the energy to keep going.

Right now, we are in hell. And all we can do is push through it.

"Your turn."

"What?" Everett looks at me, puzzled. I gesture to his body with a wavelike motion.

"I'm not going to let you go into the forest like that," I say. "I don't want you slowing me down."

"Oh." He chuckles. "You're worried I'm going to slow you down? That's rich."

"Mm-hmm, sit."

I use this as a chance to test out my leg by putting weight on it. I hobble over to the bag, opening it and scanning its insides before pulling out all the tools I need. I walk over and kneel behind him, slowly lifting his shirt up to examine the extent of his wounds. Everett lets out a light hiss, his body coiling in on itself.

"Sorry," I whisper, carefully attempting to take his shirt off again.

"It's fine," he grunts out, taking a deep shuddering breath. "Gotta push through it."

The good news is that the majority of wounds on Everett's body are small. He was quick enough to avoid most of the slashes and cuts that came from the Perversion, leaving nicks and scrapes from near misses and collisions with the ground or trees.

All of my mama's training comes into focus. I work on each wound individually, meticulously cleaning them one by one, ignoring Everett's hisses and grunts. We sit in relative silence, the sounds of the forest and Everett's labored breaths turning into steady, calm inhales and exhales.

I don't like the fact that Everett is hurt, but I do like the fact that I can focus on something other than the growing thought of the choice we just made. But, the more I try to push the thought away, the clearer it becomes. The more my brain replaces the previous moments, wondering if I could have done something or said something to stop Emma.

Finally, the dam breaks.

"We let her go," I whisper. "We just . . . we let her go."

"Douglas . . ."

"She is your sister, Everett."

"You don't think I know that?"

"Honestly, I don't know, because you're acting like it doesn't matter that we left her."

I shouldn't have said that. I know that the moment I say it. A flash of anger ripples over Everett's face for a moment before he clenches his fists tightly, stilling himself, as if the action grounds him to the earth. He takes a deep breath and forces himself to his feet, wobbles for a moment, and begins to pace a circle around the fire.

"Emma knew what she was signing up for."

"Everett, that is not enough of a reason to—"

"Listen to me!" he snaps. "Fucking *listen*. She. Knew. Okay? We both knew. We came in here knowing neither of us could make it out alive. I told you that at my house. We probably knew better than you did. We've trained for this our whole lives, Douglas. Every action or test you can think of to prepare someone for the fact they may lose their sister? Their mother? I've been through it. Even the most horrible things you can think of—my mother has done to prepare me for this. Breaking the curse is all that matters, and if Emma was here, she would say the same thing. I know you don't understand, I know it doesn't make sense to you, but you have to trust me—moving forward is what Emma would want."

"I don't believe that," I push, shaking my head. "You can't tell me you're not afraid for her, or that you don't care."

"I never said that," he replies loudly. "I said that breaking this curse is more important."

"Same thing!"

"It isn't!"

Everett's voice booms loudly enough that it echoes through the forest, bouncing off the trees before returning to us.

He growls, running his fingers through his hair, kicking the log hard enough for it to roll away. "This is about more than me, or Emma, or you, Douglas. This curse affects everyone. You told me there were others who came before you, right? Other students?"

"Other students who all died."

"Exactly. This is about them, Douglas. This is about stopping what's happening here so it doesn't happen again if you fail. There are always sacrifices when making change."

"Even if that sacrifice is someone you care about, or you?"

"Especially if it's someone I care about or me," he says without hesitation.

"So you'd sacrifice me, too, if it broke the curse?"

The words come out before I can stop them, and the moment I say them, I regret it. What answer am I hoping to get? If Everett says yes, will we ever be able to be who we were before?

Everett frowns, like I hurt him. "I would never do that to you," he says with an amount of depth and weight that tells me he believes it wholeheartedly. "You should know better than that."

"How can I trust you? If push comes to shove, Everett, and sacrificing me would end this curse . . ."

"I wouldn't do it."

"How do I know?"

"The same way I'm believing you can break this curse: trust. That's all we have, Douglas. Do you trust me? Because I trust you."

"You just told me the curse is the most important thing."

"Not more important than you."

At first, I'm not sure how to answer. Just like Everett could lie to me, I could just as easily lie to him. But seeing the look on his face breaks something inside me. I give myself a moment to think, flexing my fingers, trying to decide how I want to answer. But more importantly, I'm trying to decide what I believe.

"We should rest," Everett says. "Everything is better in the morning. We need to sleep."

He walks past me, grabbing the sleeping set and setting it up. He puts the insulated mat down first before inflating the two pillows. He grabs the blanket and, toeing off his boots one at a time, crawls onto it and pats the spot next to him.

"I have my own," I say, showing him.

"I know, but I want to lie with you. Are you cool with that?"

I take a deep breath and nod, slipping off my boots and lying next to him. Gently, Everett shifts our bodies, spooning his chest against my back, strong arms wrapped around me. I feel his breath tickle against my neck while he rubs my arms in a circular motion.

My body is tense at first. Part of it is the fight we just had. Part of it is fear. Another part is just pure exhaustion. But deep down, I know Everett is right. Emma made her choice. She knew what she was getting herself into. Every Everley does; it's a solemn oath they took.

But to have someone who would put me above . . . the world? Even if Everett is lying to make me feel better, just having someone say that to me . . . it makes everything feel a bit better. It makes all of this more tolerable.

And I can't help but just let it all go.

"I've got you, Douglas," he whispers. "I got you."

He chants that over and over again. He doesn't question me as I quietly sob, holding his arm tightly, burying my face into it. Feeling him against me as I drift off to sleep, the last thing I hear is him whispering sweet nothings. And even as my body releases all the tension I've been holding for . . . what feels like forever . . . it's the most relaxed I've been in weeks.

And all because of the boy holding me close.

30

I'm not sure how long I'm asleep.

I take a deep breath, rolling onto my back. The air feels richer as it fills my lungs. No longer does the forest stink like death and mold, but it smells . . . almost sweet.

I stretch out my body, reaching farther than my limbs can touch and digging my heels into the earth. A rush of blood floods me, and my vision becomes, for a brief second, hyperfocused. If I didn't remember why I was in the forest, I'd think for a moment I was on a Regent Academy–sponsored camping trip. Or maybe everything I've seen has been a twisted, dark dream.

But I know better than that. As I wake up, the voices return. They start as near-silent whispers, scratching at the back of my brain, but with each passing second, they grow louder.

I sigh, looking up at the canopy. Slices of light break through the dark ceiling, and for a moment, the forest looks like a normal forest.

Every bit of my being wants to rally against that. This is just enough lulling of false security. But I know better.

I force myself to sit up, using the heels of my hands to rub at my eyes. The first step is to keep moving.

I scan the nearby area for Everett, the imprint on his side of the blanket still there. Rubbing at my exposed forearms and my legs, I cup my hands in front of me, forcing out a breath of warm air and holding on to it. The fire next to us died some hours ago, embers in the depths of the stockpile of leaves and twigs still burning faintly. Maybe that's where he went?

It doesn't take long for me to find his boot prints. Putting on my own boots, I follow the prints, weaving through the maze of trees.

"Everett," I call out, not too loud but loud enough that if he's nearby he'll respond. "We should get going soon."

The words bounce off the trees until they drift into silence. There's no call back, no response from Everett telling me where to follow. It feels empty in the forest without him, like a piece of me has been crudely hacked and separated from my body, tossed just out of reach where I cannot grasp it.

A dark feeling of dread clings to me like a shawl as I walk deeper into the forest. I should have picked up one of the knives before looking for him.

But right now, the only thought on my mind is finding him.

I follow his trail until the darkness is so thick, I can't see more than a few inches in front of me.

"Where are you," I whisper. I can't see the embers behind me, or the sliver of the forest that was bathed in sunlight, anymore, only darkness. There's no sense of direction either. I could be anywhere, completely turned around and walking in the wrong direction.

"Show me Everett," I hiss desperately, calling out to the forest for aid. There's no revving of magic in my mind; only an eerie, solitary stillness.

"Okay," I mutter. "Show me a way out."

Nothing.

"Show me the direction of the tree."

Refusal.

I go through a list of commands, each one more frantic than the last.

But even if the forest doesn't speak to me, something does respond.

I whip my head in the direction of the sound; snarling, clicking of teeth that fills the darkness. It's not far ahead, I'd guess about ten to fifteen feet. The sharpness doesn't sound like something baring its fangs at me, but more like teeth sliding against something smooth. Like it's . . . chewing on something.

Before I can move, the darkness swirls around me, pushing outward like a sunbeam in the center burns the blackness away. Instantly, I see it in front of me: a Perversion that's half bear, half wolf, leaning forward, protectively hunching over something it's eating.

That something being half of Everett's body.

The scent of blood fills my nose, rich and sweet like copper. The sounds of Everett's bones snapping, crisp and clean, mix with the squishy sounds of his flesh being ground under fangs and claws. The beast's eyes turn to me, ruby-like orbs glaring, as it keeps Everett's arm in its mouth, half dangling between its teeth.

A bird flutters in the distance, causing a tree branch to fall. The creature jumps, disappearing into the forest, dropping Everett's arm as it does.

My heart threatens to rip my chest open. I stand there, unable to move. He's dead. There's no hope of him being alive, no chance I can save him and carry his body back to the school.

"Everett," I quietly plead into the air, stumbling forward and falling in the blood. His warm blood stains my jeans, seeping into the blue, turning the denim purple. I can feel how warm it is; he was alive just moments ago. If I had gotten here five minutes earlier . . .

Like a puzzle shattered from falling on the floor, I do my best to put his body back together. Maybe if I can make some semblance of a person . . . maybe I can call on the forest to fix him, to stitch him. It doesn't make any sense, but I have to try something.

My fingers shake while I move his broken body parts around. My eyes blur with salty hot tears. How do I tell his mother? How do I tell Emma I failed them both? Sure, breaking the curse is the most important thing. Sure, they were ready to die, but were they *really* ready?

Because I'm not ready to be alone.

I sit back on my heels, looking at his chilling body. "I don't know what to do," I say as tears fall from my eyes.

Another sound, this time to the right. It's louder than before, crisper like a bone snapping in half. I turn quickly, half crouched to keep my center of gravity balanced. My thighs burn while I'm balancing on my toes, waiting to defend Everett's body against what lives in the forest. One minute turns into two, then five, but nothing comes. But I can feel something watching me; probably the thing that did this to him, deciding if it's going to strike.

I slip onto my butt, looking at Everett. His eyes have begun to glaze over, his skin not as warm and bright as it was just moments ago.

"I'm sorry," I say under my breath, talking to everyone and no one at the same time. "I shouldn't have brought you in here, I shouldn't have even thought I could do this."

I'm tired. So fucking tired.

Maybe I should just give up. Let it consume me and stop fighting. I can't win. If Emma and Everett can't do it, what hope do I have?

As the heavy steps come closer, I close my eyes, accepting what is to come. I don't know if I believe in reincarnation or any of that. I don't know what I believe will happen in the afterlife, but I hope whoever rules over the next world doesn't judge me too harshly. Because I tried my best. It just wasn't enough.

"Douglas!"

Everett's voice breaks through my mind like a mirror being

shattered. Before I can even open my eyes, he's slapped the blade out of my hand, kneeling in front of me, grabbing my shoulders. He forces me to look at him and stare directly into his eyes. His face is covered with dirt, a few scratches on his cheeks and dried blood spots that weren't there before. But most importantly, he's alive. And the body lying in front of me is gone.

"You're . . ."

"I'm alive. "I promised you I wouldn't leave."

I study Everett, really study him. His shirt is slightly ripped, dirt and mud caked on his jeans. His boots show me he's been deep in mud, wandering through who knows where looking for who knows what.

No, I know what he was looking for: me.

Everett touches my face and I can tell, just slightly, that his fingers are shaking. The twitches are momentary, and every time it happens, he clutches his fist, trying to still his shaking.

"It's fucking cold out here," he reasons. "Got the shakes."

"Mm-hmm," I reply, wrapping my arms around him, squeezing tightly. "Cold."

"I'm here," Everett promises as he squeezes me. I can feel the warmth seeping out of him and into me. Not only does it make my body warmer, but it feels like the darkness that seeped into my skin is burning away too. Like his presence is some sort of magical spell that can push back demons.

"You can't leave me, Douglas," he finally says. "You can't leave me here alone. I've already lost Emma; I can't lose you too."

I nod, knowing he'll know what I mean without my actually

having to say it. Slowly, Everett pulls back so we can look at each other.

"Promise me. You won't do something like that again." He pauses. "You can't give up because I'm not giving up, and I'm not doing this without you. We made a promise, right? We succeed together or we fail together. There's no other option. We're not going to let the forest and its fuckin' twisted magic get the best of us, or prey on our fears anymore. We're getting out of here, I'm taking you on that date, and we're going to win. You and me."

The weight of what Everett says sends chills down my spine, but I nod slowly.

"Promise."

There's relief on Everett's face. But it's not the comforting kind. It's the look of a man who realized what he just agreed to. That suicide really might be the only option if we fail. We won't become part of this forest. We won't let it take us and twist us into something that hunts and kills the people we love. We won't play this forest's fucking game.

We'll be in charge of our own destiny. No matter how it ends.

31

"We have to be getting close. It can't be too much farther."

I know that applying logic to a situation that isn't, in fact, logical doesn't exactly make sense, but in my mind, it does. The illusions that Everett and I saw were created to keep us from getting any farther. If they had succeeded, we would have died. That makes me think that we're almost there; a final-ditch effort to keep us from finding the tree within the forest.

But I can't be sure. The trees and pathways constantly shift. An opening we see fifteen feet ahead of us might shift to disappear as we close in, forcing us to go left or right. Are we making any progress?

The magic inside me tells me we have to be doing something right, though. The sounds of the forest are louder, more staticky, like dozens more voices have joined the room, all saying different things in different keys. It's so loud I have to ask Everett to repeat himself when he asks me a question, and really focus on his words to hear him.

I have to block out all the voices, and I finally understand what they are: the voices of those who have been claimed in one way or another by the forest over the years. And there are hundreds of them.

"Are you ready?" Everett asks, his hand on my back to keep me from falling backward as we walk up a hill made of jagged rocks and twisted vines. "When we get there, do you think . . ."

"I'll be able to do what has to happen?" I finish for him.

Everett nods. "I mean, we have no idea what we're going to see. Or *who* we're going to see. If that illusion was any example of the power of this forest . . . it's going to throw everything at us. It could be anyone . . ."

"I know." I like to *think* I do, that mentally I understand what could happen. But I won't until I see it. No one really knows how they'll act until things like this happen.

"What about you?" I ask once we reach the top of the hill. I look back, surveying the area we've climbed. The darkness swirls around us, making it nearly impossible to see anything farther than a few feet in front of us, but I know we've climbed for at least ten minutes. I wonder, if the darkness wasn't here and the trees were gone, how far we'd be able to see. "You might see Emma, or your mother, or your ancestors, or—"

"August," Everett says. "If it would be anyone besides my

family, it would be him. He was a student here when I was a freshman. I was head over heels for him. He's how I figured out I was bisexual. I thought . . . I dunno, that we got each other, and we would find a way to make it work. Love conquers all, you know?"

I'm not jealous or upset hearing that Everett liked someone before me. If anything, I'm happy he had someone in his life, even for a fleeting moment, that made him happy. So much of his life has been pain and isolation. I wouldn't wish that on anyone, especially someone I cared about.

"What happened to him?"

"Same thing that happened to Sarah. It's how I knew what happened to her when you told me. August saw a Perversion one day. I tried to explain it to him, to convince him to pack his bags that night and leave. To get him away from the headmaster's reach." Everett shrugged curtly. "I was too late."

Everett cleared his throat. "If it was going to be anyone who could stop me besides my family or you, it would be him."

"Are you going to be able to do what has to happen?"

"I don't know," Everett says honestly. "I mean, I could lie and say yes, but . . ." He sighs, running his fingers through his hair frustratedly. "I almost let it all fade away, Douglas. For a moment, I thought of just ending it too. I . . . It just seemed so peaceful."

"I get it," I whisper.

"Would you think less of me, if I say I thought about giving up?" I ask.

Everett shakes his head. "I think that makes you human. No matter what 'magic' you have inside you, you're still just a teenage boy, Douglas. You . . . we shouldn't be dealing with this. We should be worried about SATs, colleges . . ."

"First dates?"

He chuckles. "Yeah, that. Which reminds me, when this is all done, I still need to take you out on one."

"Oh?" I ask, grinning. "And where are we going on this date?"

"Well, if the curse is broken, anywhere you want," Everett promises. "You want to show me your home in DC? You want to get as far away from here as possible? You want to cross the ocean and go to London? Anywhere and everywhere. We'll get in my truck and go. No questions asked."

"I don't think we can take your truck across the Atlantic Ocean." I grin, nudging him. "But that sounds nice. Just you and me. Going . . ."

Everett suddenly stills and slides his left boot against the ground to stand in front of me. He takes a blade from his back, standing tall and straight, looking off into what I think is a thicket of brambles. His pose is tight, but his body is massive, as if he's trying to use his broad form to body block me.

"What is it?" I whisper.

"I don't know," he mutters. "I . . . It sounds familiar."

I'm guessing he means it's footsteps. But that doesn't mean what he hears is actually what it is. The forest is on the offensive now. We have to be more careful.

In response, I pool as much magic into my palms as possible, ready to strike as needed. But all of that energy, like electricity lost when the power goes out, disappears when whatever Everett senses comes bursting out of the forest. A woman, taller than the two of us, covered in scars, both fresh and old enough to be raised and scabbed over. A woman who looks . . . familiar.

"Emma?"

Everett's voice is laced with desperation. His shoulders lower, the defensiveness of his posture like a wall cracking under pressure. I don't need to see his face to know how relieved he is.

Assuming it's Emma.

Before Everett or Emma can take a step forward to embrace, I raise my hand and utter a command.

"Barricade."

The earth splits like whispers as thorns rapidly rise and tangle together. Between the two of them, a wall appears, stretching left and right as far as the eye can see, easily ten feet wide. The magic makes my vision blur and something deep inside me feel like a nail sliding against my inner walls, but I keep my arm out until the wall is tall enough and thick enough that Everett or Emma can't break through it.

Before I can lower my hand, the cool taste of metal slides against my neck and I freeze, in shock.

"Douglas," Everett says coldly, somehow moving within a moment to stand behind me. "Lower it."

I swallow carefully, the expansion of my throat causing the blade to burn. "You have no idea if that's her," I whisper. "Trust me—I want it to be her too. But that doesn't look like your sister, does it?"

Everett doesn't answer me, but the blade against my neck does tremble.

"Everett, listen to me. This wouldn't be the first illusion the forest has cast. It showed me your dead body, and I almost made its wish come true. Why not show you your sister in order to let your guard down? Who else would be able to do that?"

"How do I know you're real? How do I know ever since I found you, you're not some trick of the forest?"

"But I'm standing right here," I urge. "You've touched me, FELT me. You know I'm real. I'm not saying it's *not* her, but . . ."

"He's right," Emma says, her voice muffled from the wall. "I have no reason to believe it's you both either. But, just hear me out. I'm trusting you. You can trust me."

Nothing about that sounds like Emma. Emma would swing a sword and ask questions later. But when she came out of the bramble, she didn't look poised to fight. She looked . . . surprised, but also thankful to see us.

"I'm going to lower it," I whisper. "But if I suspect she's an illusion, or a part of the forest . . ."

"I'll do it myself," he says, not saying what *it* is, but we both know. "I promise."

Nodding to Everett, I clench my fist. Letting the wall down hurts at first, but quickly something smooth and cool falls over me. I brace myself, ready for Emma to have a gun pointed at us, and equally as ready for shrapnel to fly and impale our faces.

But instead, Emma's standing there, with her arms raised in a "white flag" position. There are no weapons on her, and the clothes she's wearing look a size too small, torn and tattered with makeshift stitches and ties to keep things in place.

"When did you last see me?" she asks, her voice cracking.

"The Perversions in the forest," Everett says. "Outside of Douglas's apartment complex."

"And what did you say to us?" I ask. "Before you . . . disappeared?"

"I always come back. If I don't, who is going to keep your ass in check?"

The words were only spoken a day or so ago for us, but for Emma, it seems like that was years ago. Staring at her, really examining her, it's the small things that remind me of Emma Everley. Her posture, the sharpness in her eyes, the slight two-tone color of her hair that is natural and would make most girls envious. Even the shape of her face, more sullen than before, but still the same.

Before I can stop him, Everett lunges forward, wrapping his arms around Emma. He lifts her off the ground and twirls her twice, not letting go for what feels like a minute. He finally puts Emma down, holding his sister at arm's length.

"What happened to you?"

"Time," I mutter. "That's it, isn't it?"

Emma nods solemnly, lowering her hands. "Mom told us, time works differently here. It's been how long for you?"

"I think about a day," I say. "Maybe two. But again, who knows."

Emma nodded and paused before taking a breath. "I've tried to keep track as best I can, but I think it's been . . . three years for me."

"Three years," Everett says, less as a surprise but more like he needs to hear it to convince himself. "That would make you . . . a year older than me."

"Always knew I should have been the big sister. More on that later." Emma turns to look directly at me, her jaw tightening as if it takes courage to say what comes next.

"I found it, Douglas. The tree."

"What?" both Everett and I say.

"Surviving for three years in this hellscape teaches you some things. The forest isn't as big as we think it is."

"No, it's bigger," I say.

Emma shakes her head. "It's smaller," she explains. "The forest plays on your senses, and your fears. We can all agree on that?"

We nod together.

"That's the whole point. That confusion makes it seem bigger. But when you're focused, and I mean *really* focused, on a single task, you can find anything you want. That's how I found you two. I think it has something to do with the magic you were talking about, Douglas. The forest makes us think it's bigger to confuse us, in order to have power over us. I don't think it would take more than half a day's hike to go from one end to the other. But when everything is shifting, you can walk in the same circle for days . . . because it's not *really* the same circle."

"That means," Everett says, "we could have been walking parallel to you the whole time, or to the tree, and never found it."

"It also means we haven't been as focused as we thought," I chime in.

"How could you?" Emma asks. "Like I said, the forest confuses

344

you on purpose, to prey on your weakness, to distract you. You could spend your whole life wandering in a circle, get discouraged, become hopeless . . ."

"And kill yourself to end it," I mutter.

Emma holds my gaze, like she knows that wasn't just a sentence I threw out, but she doesn't say anything. "I'm sure you both have seen some things you don't want to ever see again?"

Everett and I glance at one another.

"Exactly. Same here. You can't blame yourself for not focusing. But if you trust me, I can get us there."

"You made your way back to us." I smile. "Like you promised. I trust you more than your brother."

"Hey!" Everett barks. "Rude."

"But accurate," Emma says, smiling at me. She turns. "Don't be more than a step behind, and follow exactly in my footsteps. Focus only on the tree as much as you can."

Like before, Emma and Everett both flank me, Emma leading and Everett taking up the rear. I focus my mind exactly like Emma says. I even mimic her slow breathing as she leads us through the thicket. As we walk, dark thoughts begin to bleed in from the corners.

But I still my mind. Reaching forward, I grab Emma's shoulder with my right hand. With my left, I extend it backward and feel Everett's fingers lace with mine.

We will get through this. We will survive. We've come too far to not.

Everett and I do exactly what Emma says: we stay focused. No matter the sounds of something—or somethings—creeping along-side us just out of our eyesight, no matter how strong the whispers are, or how I swear they sound like Mama and Dad asking me to *just get a little closer*, we keep walking.

Finally, what feels like two hours later, though I can't be sure, Emma stops, causing me to almost bump into her.

"We're here."

As she pushes through the thicket, light expands from a place that doesn't seem to have a source. Standing in the center of the grove, with a base thicker than most houses, is the tree; an oak that extends so high into the sky, I can't see its tips. Hundreds of branches spool out, and the floor of the forest is lush with fallen leaves, a menagerie of bright colors.

And in the center of the tree's trunk is an archway that doesn't seem to have an exit on the other side. The archway is pure, never-ending darkness. So thick it feels like it would be hard to walk through, like the endlessness would resist you.

"Holy shit," Everett whispers as we walk forward. "Do you feel that?"

"It feels like warmth the closer we get to the tree," I say. "Like its pulsing spring."

I hesitate once we both reach the tree. Life pulses off it, like a heartbeat I can not only hear but feel inside me.

"You feel it, don't you?" Emma asks. "It feels like peace."

"Life," Everett says under his breath in awe.

"Magic," I add. "It's magic. Magic that can create, and magic that can destroy. Like the start of spring and the end of winter."

It's the same magic inside me. The god that's linked to my magic is right through that archway. I can feel the power coming through it, a one-way doorway that pushes the energy out and into the world.

What lives on the other side is linked to every bit of hell everyone in this town has experienced. We just have to find a way to open the archway and go through. This is what we've been looking for. This is our finale. This . . .

"Is where you die," a familiar voice looms from behind us. The voice of the Emissary who separated us before.

PART
FOUR

PART

FOUR

32

In the fight for our survival, Emma, Everett, and I each have our roles to play.

Emma and Everett are going to do everything they can to keep the Emissary that spoke to us and the one that appeared behind it busy, while I figure out how to communicate with Etaliein and put an end to this curse.

No pressure, right?

The tree looks like any other large oak tree. It reminds me of Yggdrasil from Norse mythology, except it has a split down the middle, its large trunk bisecting into two different sections. There's nothing within the negative space except for the smell of rot and death.

No, that's not true. There's something else there.

It's hard to pinpoint, but it feels like a vibration, one that goes all the way down to my bones. It's faint, barely noticeable, rooted deeper than my body, or the depths of the tree, or the cold hard ground. It's coming from somewhere else. Somewhere . . . not of this world.

I press my palm against the bark, and I can feel a faint pulsing throb of magic.

We've been through a lot, this magic and me. A push-and-pull, ebb-and-flow relationship that I don't really understand, and I don't think I ever will. According to Headmaster Monroe, he thinks my ability to control the forest is blood based. According to Jane, it's something deeper. What if both are true . . . or neither? Does it really matter?

A heavy thump sounds behind me. Before I can turn, knife brandished in my hand, Everett is spitting out blood from his mouth, rising to his feet.

Instinctively, I move toward him. I can tell he's wounded, and badly. His right arm is dripping blood, tendrils of scarlet ribbons twirling around his arm in a group of three. There's a large thorn protruding from his right shoulder.

"Everett . . ."

Before I can take another step, he blocks my path. With a forceful thrust, he buries the scythe he's been holding into the dirt and uses his free hand to rip the thorn out, tossing it to the side.

I take a step forward, forgetting about the tree, focusing on Everett. If I have the power of this god to create and to destroy, I should be able to heal, right?

Mama would be proud of me. Following in her footsteps.

But Everett holds up his hand to stop me. "I'm fine," he growls out, not even looking at me. "Can you still do it?"

"I . . ."

"Douglas," he says more firmly, half turning his face to look at me. Darkness clouds his vision, his features sharp and focused. "Can you still open the archway? Yes or no."

I only hesitate for a moment. There's no real other choice, is there? We've come too far and sacrificed too much for me to fail.

"I think so. Yes."

"Then we'll keep fighting."

Everett's voice sounds broken, and I can't tell if it's from sheer exhaustion, actual physical pain, or the fact that there's a real chance at breaking this curse that has dictated his life for so long, right in front of him, so close he can taste it.

I won't stop now.

"Everett!"

Emma's desperate voice is like before, a scream that is uncharacteristic of hers, laced with fear. Everett doesn't hesitate, yanking the scythe out of the earth and dashing toward his sister.

He won't make it, I think, watching Emma stretch her arm out to him. He's still more than twenty feet away and I can't tell if he doesn't see it, but a third Emissary is coming out of the forest to the left of him to help the first two in combat. It'll cut him off before he can reach her.

I pull a knife from my holster, gripping it securely in my left hand. My body moves into autopilot, and I slide my blade against the palm of my right hand. White-hot searing pain erupts, spreading instantly through my whole body, blinding me for a moment. Rich red blood splashes on the earth, bathing the silver of the blade in blood. Slamming my hands against the ground, I push as much magic into the earth as I can. Not just magic—my intent, my hopes, my desires, my soul. If the gaping slash on my palm gives access to the deepest, purest parts of me for the forest to see—to use—then so be it.

"Stop them!" I roar.

For a moment, there's nothing. I can't even hear my own breathing or feel my own pain. But deep under the earth, slowly, something rumbles, rising up like a pulsing wave that's growing in intensity. Sharp whistles, one at a time, fill the air, shooting up like rockets from the earth. In the darkness, it's impossible to see what it is.

At first.

One by one, I hear the Emissaries snarl in pain. I watch them stumble, turning from controlled to desperate; panicked.

"Oh my god," Everett says. "How . . . you . . ."

And then I see it. Spires of thorns have risen from the earth like pillars of flora buried deep and long ago, called by my voice to rise. More than a dozen of them, slanted in different directions, skewering each of the Emissaries, stopping them in their tracks.

"It's not enough."

I pull fists full of earth into my palms and stand.

"Rise."

Slowly, each tendril pushes upward, rising two, five, ten,

fifteen feet, effectively suspending the Emissaries in the air. Emma squirms frantically, pulling herself out from the static bramble, her forearms, cheeks, and legs covered in small cuts, but her eyes are completely focused on the guardians suspended above us.

Pain radiates through my body, the sensation feeling like lightning shocks coursing through every nerve. I sway, almost falling over, but dig my feet into the ground. I see Everett's boots approaching me but extend my hand, telling him silently to stop. My palm shifts into my index finger pointing in the direction of the forest right in front of us. The forest itself speaking in unison as ten voices, telling me exactly what's happening.

Something's coming.

Moments later, a fourth Emissary—larger than I've seen—bursts through the trees. It is double the size of the ones before, a mix of three different heads: two men on each side of a woman's, with several arms and legs, bony bat-like wings with lesions on them, with a flicking scaly tail. The three heads roar all at once, a deep, guttural screech that makes my bones rattle and my teeth clench.

"You humans," the creature growls. "Children of Everley and man. You are foolish, naive. What makes you think you deserve an audience with Etaliein? What makes you believe you have sacrificed enough for your sin to be released from your purgatory?"

Everett helps Emma up with one hand, keeping his eyes locked on the creature, his scythe brandished. "This has gone on long enough, for a crime our ancestors—"

"You have their blood!" it roars, the earth shaking. "You exist because of them! And as long as your bloodline continues, until it is cleansed of every bit of your ancestors, you will continue to pay what is due to atone for what they have done to *me*!"

To me. Not to the forest, to me. That was different. We always knew, I think, that these Perversions and Emissaries were a manifestation of Etaliein, an extension of him. But to actually speak as if part of him . . . What if they weren't just summons or servants? What if each Emissary had a piece of Etaliein inside them, created from him?

"So, I will give you one more chance, Douglas," the Emissary says, looking at me directly. "One more chance to make the right choice and leave. I will even let your friends go with you, a modified version of my offer before. What say you, child of man?"

No, not using the piece of Etaliein's magic against the Emissaries. What if I could use the magic inside them to help me?

The man I met when this first started told me the magic I have is to create and destroy. But nothing in nature is created or destroyed, just changed. That's a basic principle of science. What if the same rules apply to magic? What if I can take magic and convert its purpose to be something else?

What if I can use their magic against them?

"I need its heart," I tell Everett and Emma. "Get me that thing's heart and I can open the archway."

"Are you sure?" Emma asks. "That thing . . ."

"It's huge, I know. But if you can get it for me, I can end this. One way or another, I know I can. Trust me."

Everett and Emma look at one another for a brief moment. Emma takes a deep breath and pulls off the shotgun, holstered on her back, and checks its barrel.

"Then let's get that fucking heart," she says.

Everett and Emma move in fluid unison, playing off one another as they engage in combat with the Emissary. Using Everett's shoulder as a leverage point, Emma jumps up, lunging at him like some sort of Valkyrie taking down its prey. Her jump puts her at chest level, shotgun brandished. The Emissary swings at her wildly, roaring in anger, ready to strike. But before it can swipe at her, she aims and fires, the recoil sending her flying back as shrapnel slams into the creature's face, the bullet pellets enough to make it stumble back in pain.

Everett runs forward, swinging his scythe wildly and cutting one of the Emissary's legs. It takes three quick hacks to cut its hoof off before twirling the blade effortlessly and moving onto the other one. A half dozen rapid and forceful chops later, the Emissary wavers before falling to its knee.

Once the Emissary is off-kilter, I throw my hand out again, forcing as much energy into the air as I can. I ignore the pain, pushing through the throbbing in every cell of my body to summon the forest again.

"Pin him down."

Vines immediately rise from the earth and wrap around the Emissary's limbs, holding him in place. The more it struggles, the more vines appear, until its body is pinned on its back. It growls in pain and frustration, dark purple ooze coming from the wounds that Everett and Emma inflicted.

Burning pain, like a hot iron being driven into every nerve of my body, overwhelms me in a way it never has before. I collapse, coughing, bright red blood staining the ground. I feel the warm thick liquid dripping out of my nose, my ears, even the corners of my eyes, my vision turning red.

Every bit of magic has a cost, I think, looking at my wounded hand. I can barely feel the pain anymore, but when I try to clench my fist, it doesn't fully close.

"You're almost there, Douglas," I whisper to myself, spitting out a glob of blood. "You can't turn back now."

I repeat that until it becomes a mantra in my head, giving me the energy I need to stand. Stumbling forward, I see Everett standing on the chest of the Emissary, his scythe in hand, hacking away. The black-and-purple blood stains Everett's shirt and face, a thick coating covering him with each thrust of his scythe. The Emissary's roars and thrashes turn quieter each time.

And then, there is nothing.

Squaring himself securely on its chest, Everett reaches down and with three heavy, struggling tugs, pulls out the heart. It's still throbbing as he's holding it over its head, a twisted mix of human and animal pathways. The black-and-purple liquid drips out of the arteries, further coating Everett's hands.

"You ask for weird gifts, Douglas." Everett smirks as he walks over to meet me halfway, concern covering his face as he looks me up and down.

"You good?"

I nod, jutting my head to the entrance of the tree. "Put it there."

Everett nods and places the heart at the foot of the parted tree, standing off to my right, while Emma approaches on my left.

"You sure this is going to work?" Emma asks, loading two more cartridges into her shotgun.

"No," I mutter, falling to my knees. "But I don't have any other ideas."

"And what is your idea?" Emma asks.

"Magic flows through me for whatever reason, but it's not enough to open the gate," I explain, putting both palms on the heart. It's warm and soft to the touch. "The magic this heart has is the same magic that comes from Etaliein. I can use that connection like a skeleton key to open the archway."

I reach inside myself, feeling the deepest core of magic inside me. This magic isn't mine, it's Etaliein's. In that regard, in the smallest sense, we are connected. He has to be able to hear me.

"You brought me here to do something. To help you. Let me help you," I whisper, talking to him. "I believe in forgiveness. I believe we all deserve second chances. What happened to you and Henry was unfair and unjust. But staying here, punishing these people, won't solve a thing. You need to move on, both of you, and I can help you, if you help me open this gate. Your lover made this gate. He closed himself off when you died; this is as much yours as it is his.

"Help me help you. Help me give you the happy ending that was taken from you both."

At first, nothing happens, the uncomfortable stillness in the forest seeping into my bones and my chest. But then, slowly, the heart begins to glow a faint yellow. As I push more magic into it, despite the pain, the heart glows more. Slowly, the archway in front of us begins to glow. It flickers once, twice, three times, like tinder catching fire, before it opens with a burst of warmth.

Through the portal, Emma, Everett, and I can see a large open field, with an array of beautiful flowers of different colors. The sky is blue, puffy white clouds dancing in the air. The only thing separating our world from that one is a thin layer of film.

"You did it," Everett gasps.

"Everett," Emma interjects.

Two Emissaries push their way through the large open field, smaller than the one that Emma and Everett took down, but brandishing weapons made of wood: one a spear and the other a bow. Their hollow eyes settle on their fallen comrade, one of them letting out a snarl as it looks toward us.

"You need to get going," Everett mutters to me, gripping his scythe. "We'll hold them back."

"Make sure you two don't die."

"Make sure you come back alive," Emma adds, smirking at me for a moment.

Everett's eyes linger on me for a moment longer than Emma's, flashing me a nervous smile before following his sister. I want to stay, to help them like I did before, but my job is specific. Helping Etaliein understand his grief, and convincing him to cross over with his lover, can and will end all of this. Everything rests on me.

33

The first thing I feel when I step out into the new realm is peace.

Time stops, much like before when I first entered the forest. I take in a deep breath, feeling the sweetness of the air flood my lungs. There's something calming here, so calming that I don't feel panic, or concern for Emma and Everett.

What happens out there will happen, and I'm here.

But all of that comes crashing down as the world around me comes into view. As my vision adjusts, I originally think something's wrong. I'm still in the forest; nothing has changed. Until the minute details become crisp. Hovels. People walking in the distance, chatting in something that sounds like English but isn't. The smells of meat being cooked, sweat, and a stench I don't want to think about.

And as I look around, seeing the people dressed in clothes so different from mine, I realize where I am. I'm still in Winslow; just not in my version of Winslow.

"Shit."

Panic floods me like a dam breached. Can anyone see me? How would a person like me fare in the past? Will I be able to get back? There's no door behind me; the archway I walked through is gone.

"Don't worry," a voice behind me says. "You're still in your time period."

Digging my heel into the earth and using it as leverage, I spin around as quickly as I can, ready to punch if need be. I won't have some Perversion ruining everything Emma, Everett, and I have fought so hard for. I'll go down swinging if I have to.

But what stares at me isn't a beast but a boy, half a shade lighter than me but the same height, with a deer skull that covers half of his face. Through the exposed part on the right side, I can see his eyes, deep and green . . . just like the forest.

But his clothes are clean, not a speck of dirt on them or his body. His skin, brown and rich, almost sparkles as the sun catches it.

"Etaliein," I whisper. He doesn't look much older than me, maybe a year or so. It makes my heart burn—to think what he and Henry went through, how short their lives were cut and how their love was met with such hate.

No person, especially no teen, should deal with that.

He smiles and tips his head in a bow. "I'm so glad you could make it. It's not the Winslow of your time, but I'm fond of it. After-all, I fell in love here."

Slowly, Etaliein turns his head and looks at the version of Winslow from his time period, nearly three hundred and fifty years ago. The angle allows me to see how bright his eyes really are. Before, they were sullen, pushed into his skull, like he was malnourished. But now they twinkle like the stars.

I follow his eyes to scan the whole town. No one can see us, and I'm guessing that's by design. The two or three dozen towns-people are going about their day, completely ignorant of what will happen in the future. They might not even know about Etaliein now, and what's to come.

"What do you think about this town?" he asks.

"I think it needs to be burned to the ground," I mutter.

Etaliein arches his brow. "Really? I wouldn't expect—"

"I'm not finished," I say quietly but confidently. "But these are people's homes. They live here, have families here. You can't just destroy that because you don't like something. It might take years, but Winslow can be something . . . beautiful."

"If you break the curse, would you stay?"

"I haven't thought that far ahead."

"No better time than now to start thinking," he teases. "Would you stay, Douglas? Would you help make this place better?"

"For the right reasons," I say. Everett's face appears in my mind's eye. Images of what-ifs flash in front of me. Cooking in his kitchen with him, studying in my room, listening to music as we do spring cleaning. There's a life to be had here. With him.

"I didn't come all this way to talk about what-ifs, Etaliein." I turn to stand in front of him so he has no choice but to look at me. "I came here to find you."

"And you did. Congratulations. You did something many before you have tried and failed to do. Why do you think that is?"

"Because you wanted me here." I hesitate, then add, "Because Henry wanted me to find you."

Through the crack of his mask, I see his eyes widen, then narrow.

"You saw him?"

"I spoke to him," I say slowly, thinking of each word before I say it to make sure I don't speak incorrectly or out of turn. "A fragment of him. Inside a book you left."

Etaliein smiles fondly.

"You sound surprised."

"Of course he still kept that book. Not surprised. Jealous. It's been almost three hundred and fifty years since I've seen his face, Douglas. Since I've been able to leave this." He gestures wide to the grove where we stand.

"Not the worst place to spend eternity," I say. "You mentioned it yourself—Winslow was something marvelous before."

"I'm here because there is no place else for me to be, Douglas," Etaliein says, his voice suddenly cold. "Do you know what this moment is? It might look innocuous to you, but this is one day before they killed my love. In that building in the distance, the men of this town are scheming how to strip the skin from my lover's flesh and burn him alive.

"I'm here, for all eternity, because this is a punishment for myself. To remind myself what I did. Who I hurt. And who I lost."

The sadness in Etaliein's voice is palpable. He blames himself for all of this, for everything that has happened to Henry. But I'm not here to absolve him, nor to discuss semantics. Right outside this . . . micro-bubble of a world . . . my friends may be dying. I have to stay focused.

"Speaking of punishment. You know why Headmaster Monroe sent me, don't you?"

"I do. I know he charged you with a task, like so many before you, and you accepted."

"And I'm guessing simply asking you to end the curse isn't going to be as easy as saying please, huh?"

Instinctively, I look at my right palm, expecting to see the cut from before. But there's nothing, not a single blemish, the skin perfect.

"Your headmaster is a fool, Douglas," Etaliein says. "Thinking you could do his bidding instead of facing his own punishment. Power blinds people to the truth, Douglas. The quest for it, the desire to hold on to it, and the things we'll do to keep it. Each of those override any sort of logic. It's a toxin. But not one that has poisoned you."

"I wouldn't say that," I interrupt. There's no point lying to him. "What else do you know?"

"I know Headmaster Monroe promised you something. I can see that in your heart. But I don't know what. All I know is it's something near and dear to you. It will help the people you care about the most. A woman, and a boy."

"My mother. And Everett."

"Ah," he says. "An Everley."

"Yes." I pause, then say, "Headmaster Monroe told me if I convince you to break the curse, I can have anything I want."

"A bargain with the devil never ends well, Douglas."

"I know. And I know I can't trust him. But one problem at a time. How much I trust him won't matter if we don't break this curse. So I'm not, like you said, immune to the 'toxin' of power because Headmaster Monroe is offering me that in exchange for you."

"And I'm guessing he said he doesn't care how it's done?" Etaliein asks quietly. "Do you plan to kill me, Douglas? If I don't do what you want? Is that what you're telling me?"

"I don't know. But I'll die trying to protect those who can't fight for themselves. Too many innocent people have been hurt because of this, Etaliein. You have to end it. Please."

Etaliein raises a finger, the tip stained black. "See? That's exactly what I'm saying. You, Douglas, are a good person. Plain and simple."

"Don't say that."

The word *good* sends a dizzying surge through my body. I don't deserve that title and if I could, I'd throw it right back at him.

Etaliein keeps his eyes level with me, as if the sharpness in my voice doesn't faze him.

"I'm not a good person," I repeat, swallowing down my pride. "People have died because of me. Here. Back home. Directly or indirectly, my involvement has hurt people in ways I can't fix."

"I never said you were a perfect person; I said you were a good one. Those are two different things. You're willing to sacrifice yourself, to endure pain that no human could imagine, just to save those you know and those you've never met. You may be getting something out of it, but it's not wealth, or riches, or power—it's the chance to live. That's the most human thing of all."

Within a blink, Etaliein is standing directly in front of me. He smells like the seasons all combined into one scent. Slowly, his right hand rises, resting firmly but warmly on my right shoulder.

Etaliein stays silent, his eyes drifting back to the tree. The leaves have begun to change, starting at the top and at the edge of the landscape, shifting from bright spring and summer colors to rich red, yellow, and orange autumnal hues, like someone is going layer by layer and flipping the tiles over.

"This tree is what I think your people would call a ley line," he says quietly. "It's what my people would call a nexus."

"Your people being other gods?"

He nods. "In every universe, every timeline, it exists, right here, right now, in the same location."

"Wait, there are other universes?"

Etaliein smiles. "Let us stick to just one magical revelation per lifetime, don't you think? If you overlaid thousands of universes, the tree would be here. Be it a forest, a war zone, a barren planet, a citadel, always here. Right now, Douglas, you are the closest any human has ever come to experiencing other worlds. Besides the other versions of you who have come here."

Before I can probe, he continues, turning to face me.

"I still believe and stand by my statement that you are a good person, Douglas. That's why you were selected. You see every choice like a human. Right and wrong. Good and evil. The world is not that simple. Humans like to think what is right and what is good are the same. They are not."

With a wave of his hand, like before, the colors dance and twirl, showing scenes that are far too familiar and raw to me. The first is back in Jane's home.

"The right thing to do would have been to distance yourself from here. You cannot help ghosts, Douglas. They live their lives on repeat, on a loop only they can exit when they are ready. Not knowing that or what was in store for you, you still promised to help her."

Another wave, this time back in the forest, clutching Kent's dead body. "The man who bullied you, who carried you to your death? Who insulted you and your mother? You could have left him. You owed him nothing, and yet you wanted to help."

Two more waves, this time, standing in front of Sarah against the Perversion. "You didn't need to go and help her. In fact, Emma and Everett most likely would have gotten to her in time, no matter what. They are Everleys, guardians of the campus, after all. But you took it upon yourself to save her, and to make sure the Perversion didn't follow."

Finally, the scene changes to Emma, Everett, and me standing in front of the woods.

"You entered here, yes, to help yourself, but also, to help break the curse for someone you love. To make it so they can have a good life. That is a good choice, Douglas, even if the right choice would have been to protect your own flesh and blood. You were willing to risk that to help another.

"Time and time again, your choices prove you make good decisions over the *right* decision. You might not be related to my love, Henry, but you show signs of him. Your virtue, your bravery, your care for others. That makes you a good person, and I will not let my curse hurt those who are an inherently good."

"But that's the problem," I interject. "You're assuming no one else is good just because they what? Live here?"

"Because they benefit from the system," he says coldly. "Every person is judged independently. But the moment they see that twinkle of power that the school provides, they change. Everyone does."

"That's not fair. You're holding people to an impossible standard."

"You didn't succumb to it. The other students whose names you read in the journal, they didn't succumb to it."

"No, they were just consumed by the forest."

Etaliein hesitates to answer. "The Monroes put them out to be slaughtered, like lambs, knowing they could always find another student, another child, who needed a break. You were just as likely to be killed as them, and the Monroes wouldn't have cared either. Each student, including you, has been given the same tools. The visions, the voices, all of it a collective package that I hoped would scare them away, help them find a better life away from here. And when they couldn't, when they didn't, I gave them magic."

"To arm them against the forest."

"To arm them against the Monroes," he corrects. Etaliein's hand reaches out, cupping my cheek gently. It feels warm, but as I instinctively tilt my head toward it, his palm feels hollow, like if I squeeze too tightly it'll shatter like glass.

"You were never in any danger, Douglas. Not from me, or the forest. Until you decided to come within its boundaries, with the intent of killing me, you were never seen as a threat."

"Does that still make me a good person?"

"Your willingness to sacrifice your life for the world? Makes you the best of people."

Slowly, his hand slips down, falling to his side. "I have done my very best to protect you. Even when that boy Kent brought you into my embrace, I had the forest deal with him to keep you safe. But what I cannot protect you from is a Regent. Time and again, I've failed at doing that. It's why you're here, like every child who has come before you. A tale as old as time I cannot stop from being told."

I shake my head, reaching out with my right hand, squeezing his wrist.

"You can. You can stop this. Listen to what you said. These visions, the voices, the magic. You put all of that in my head. You can control this forest. You can move on and see Henry again. He's trapped here too. Anchored by your grief, caught in the curse you created for those who hurt him and you. That's what grief and pain does, doesn't it? Pulls everyone into its vortex without reason? Don't you want to see him again, Etaliein?"

"More than anything," he says without hesitation.

"Then you have to stop this, Etaliein. You have to—"

"What makes you think I can control it?"

The words come as a punch to the gut that directs all of my attention to Etaliein. He stares at me, a sadness behind his eyes. The weight of someone who knows their actions are responsible for ended lives and changed timelines.

"The Emissaries, yes, are mine. They follow my command, and they protect this tree and make sure the descendants of the original families pay for their crimes. But the Perversions? Those are not under my control. They are . . . what would you call it, Douglas, when your emotions take control of you and make you do unspeakable things?"

"Trauma manifested."

He nods. "They are a manifestation of my pain, my anger, my grief, for what those humans did to me and my love . . . and I can't stop it. I've tried—trust me, I've tried. Each day it grows. It takes every bit of energy to keep this rot from growing exponentially."

"You make it sound like you think this rot will take over all of Winslow."

"No," he says, shaking his head. "The world."

He says the word so simply and directly, as if I should have understood his words myself and not questioned him.

"You underestimate the power of a god, Douglas. We come from this earth, and are as part of the earth, the water, the air, as anything else. We can change the fabric of time and space with a snap of our fingers. And when that balance is thrown off, there are dangerous consequences. It is why gods are not supposed to feel human emotions, to be above them, and most certainly not fall for a human."

"But you did," I note. "And don't you think you're better off for it? Isn't a life that has experienced love better than one without it?"

"Would you still stand by that if I told you I couldn't hold the rot back anymore and it swallows your friends, your family, your town, whole? If it all folds in on itself and succumbs to the night?"

I chew my bottom lip, looking in the direction I came. If time actually does work differently inside the forest, I bet it's even more out of sync here. How much time has gone by where Everett and Emma exist? Are they still fighting? Have they died and turned to dust by now?

"What I don't understand is, if you have so much power, why don't you just stop it all? I know you said you don't control the Perversions, but I've seen what your magic can do, just a small sample of it channeled through me, a human. I've summoned vines, I've overturned earth. You are a god of life. If anyone can burn out the darkness, it's you. You just need to try." A moment of silence passes. "Are you afraid to try?"

Etaliein takes a deep breath, exhaling through his mouth. "If I were to fail at doing what you said, the rot would consume me too. Everything in this town, Douglas, is connected to me. The roots of this curse run deep. The water the townspeople consume, the food they eat—there are small particles of the magic inside them.

With a snap of my fingers, a simple decision, all of that dark energy will awaken; this place will be nothing but ash and ruin. What if I can't stop that?" He shakes his head. "No, it is better to stay here. The price for the curse to exist is far less than the price the town, the world, will pay if I cannot control it."

Slowly, I reach out, grabbing his hand again, lacing our fingers together with a soft squeeze. His body tenses, eyes drifting down to my hand. "But what if you did? What if, instead of thinking of the worst possible result, we put our faith in the best?"

"Are you really willing to risk that? Are you willing to put that much faith in me?"

"Didn't you put faith in me first? That I'd make it here, that something about me would be different than the others who came before me? We can break this curse. I'm not sure what I believe happens after death. But I'd like to think everyone, even your lover, is somewhere at peace. Wouldn't you like to be there with them? To meet them? You're a god; traversing between realms doesn't seem impossible for you. But you have to leave this"—I look around—"this safe room of magic if you want to do that. You have to trust in yourself enough to believe you can. Wouldn't that be something Henry would want you to do? Isn't the best way to honor his memory, to try to fight for happiness?"

The people in the town have disappeared, as if they melted away with the passing of time. Only the town remains, a hollow husk of itself and what it used to be, with Etaliein and me standing in the middle.

"Perhaps three hundred and fifty years is enough time of

sorrow," he slowly says. "Maybe it's time to heal. Maybe it is time to be with my love."

"I think he would like that very much."

He squeezes my hand, looking in the direction I walked from. A seam appears in front of us. The line extends to the ground, peeling itself open, revealing, through a film of gray and black, the forest from which I came.

"Are you ready?" he asks, looking at me.

"I should be asking you that."

Before I can ask for an explanation, Etaliein takes a step forward, pulling me with him through the darkness. But unlike before, this time, I'm not alone. A familiar presence is with me, wrapping me in a warm embrace. It's not my mom. It's not Everett. It's not Etaliein.

It's the forest, saying the same thing I heard the morning Everett brought Peter's body to my mom's infirmary.

You're going to die here.

We're going to kill you.

They're going to kill you.

He's going to kill you.

34

Pain. Death. Suffering. Those are the three things I note when we return to the human world.

The pain in my hand comes back instantly, like a fire has been set under my skin.

The scent of death lingers heavily in the air, causing me to focus my vision on one thing to keep from falling over. Human blood smears the ground. Sounds of anguish bounce off the trees, the twisting and breaking of wood adding to the symphony. Pieces of Emissaries litter the ground. Droplets of sweat and human flesh lead my eyes to the scene in front of me. Horrific. Horrible.

It takes a moment for my eyes to adjust, but they soon settle on the sight in front of me: Everett and Emma suffering.

Everett is pinned against a tree, struggling with one arm to try to grab a weapon, as a spire of wood points down at him, getting closer to his head. Emma is kicking, punching, doing her best to keep the crawling vines from ensnaring her.

Both of them are fighters; both have held on for as long as I've been gone. But both are also on the brink of losing.

I turn to Etaliein, squeezing his shoulder. "Help them."

He doesn't move. "They are Everleys," he says. "They—"

"I don't care what their ancestors did. They don't deserve to die. Not like this."

Still, he doesn't react. Etaliein watches as Everett grabs his blade, swinging at the Emissary, but inches from making contact, gets stopped by another vine. Emma cries in frustration as a tendril wraps around her throat, strangling her voice.

"If you want to move on, if you want to start down a path of forgiveness, that means letting go of that pain. That starts here," I whisper frantically.

Etaliein hesitates before raising his right hand. He waves it, and slowly, the Emissaries stop moving, the spire of wood only an inch from Everett's face while Emma's skin has turned almost completely blue, her eyes rolled back in her head.

"Release," Etaliein whispers.

One of the Emissaries turns its head, the sound of strained breaking wood echoing in the air, looking at Etaliein directly. Before it shatters completely, I swear I see pain in its eyes, as if it's asking, *Why?*

Everett and Emma collapse to the ground, panting raggedly. Emma coughs, on her hands and knees, breathing heavily. Everett grabs his blade, holding it close, expecting another Emissary to come out of nowhere.

I run over to him, sliding to my knees, holding his face with my hands. "Hey, it's okay. You're okay. You're safe. I promise."

It takes a moment for him to focus on me. His right hand touches my face, patting it on both sides before sliding his dirty bloody fingers against my forehead.

"It's you," he whispers.

"I'm back." I smile, leaning forward and kissing him quickly.

His eyes look over to Emma, who waves her hand weakly. "I'm fine," she says, throat hoarse. "Barely."

I give Everett a quick scan. A few new wounds, cuts that can be stitched, and bruises we'll want to get checked out when we get back to the school, but overall, he's okay. *We're the lucky ones*, I think. We're going to make it out alive. This is almost over. Soon, Everett and Emma will be able to live a normal life. I can . . . well, do whatever I want. Assuming Headmaster Monroe keeps his end of the bargain.

That's an issue to face once we get out of here.

"Here, let me help you," I say as Everett tries to stand. Putting his right arm over my shoulder, I help him, watching him hiss as he puts weight on his left foot.

"We need to get you back," I say, looking at Etaliein as he approaches us. "Can you do something?"

"I can." He nods. "It is probably best we get you three far away from here before I—"

"It's you," Emma chimes in, joining us. "You're actually . . . real."

Etaliein glances at her, silently looking her up and down for a moment. "Emma, yes? That's your name?"

She nods. "I should shoot you, you know. For everything you've done to me and my family. This is all your doing, after all."

"Emma," I say. "That's not—"

Etaliein raises his hand.

Emma crosses her arms over her chest. "I know I'm right. Are you actually going to do anything about it? Or did my brother and I almost die for nothing?"

"What do you think?" Everett asks.

"I think Douglas is too trusting and too hopeful. I think nothing and nobody is as nice or self-sacrificing as he thinks they are, and I think most of all, he's putting too much hope in someone, or something, he doesn't know. So, forgive me if I'm waiting for the other shoe to drop."

Etaliein chuckles quietly, raising his hand in an apology before Emma can say anything. "Forgive me. It's not funny. You remind me of your ancestor, both of you. Headstrong and brave, you two personify him perfectly. You're right, Emma—completely. And I respect your hesitation. I would think the same if I was in your position."

"But you're not," she counters. "You're not the one who's cursed to stay in this shitty town. You're not the one who forgets the dead or is forced to remember them when no one else can. So, I don't care what reason you have for it, or why you did it. I just want to know you're going to do something about it now. Because if you're not"—she cocks the shotgun, the spent bullets popping out—"I really have nothing to lose."

378

Looking over at Everett, I can't tell if the sternness on his face is in agreement with his sister, or if he feels the same tension as I do. Etaliein doesn't seem threatened.

"Perhaps actions speak louder than words?"

Before Emma or I can speak, he raises his hand, extending a pointer finger. He draws the shape of a door without a bottom, snapping his fingers once, and the air within the space ripples, a vision of Regent Academy slowly coming into view.

"Home," Everett whispers.

Etaliein nods. "Isn't that where you want to go? Home?"

Everett and Emma glance at one another, their silence speaking volumes. Once again, Emma speaks up first.

"What's in it for you? What do you gain from helping us?"

Etaliein hesitates. "Atonement," he says.

Emma's shoulders lower half an inch as she stares at him.

"I'm not expecting you to forgive me," Etaliein says. "I have put you and your ancestors through so much pain. I will do what I can to put an end to this curse."

"Why now?" Emma interrupts. "Why didn't you do this weeks, or months, or years ago?"

Etaliein glances over at me. "Things change."

He juts his head toward the rippling doorway. "This isn't a trap. You take that door, and it will take you home and I will do what I promise. By the time that wound of yours, Everett Everley, gets stitched up, this will be done. The curse will be lifted, and you can live your life. A full and normal life."

"Nothing is that easy," Everett mutters.

"Perhaps when you're a human, no, but you forget, I'm a god."

Everett nods and pulls himself to his feet.

"Emma, you go first. Who knows what type of world we're going to enter? I want a warrior there if needed."

"So, you finally admit I'm stronger than you." She smirks.

"I never would have denied that."

Emma's smirk softens into an honest look of slight surprise. She sighs softly, running her fingers through her long blond hair. Last time I saw her, she had a ponytail. Just another sign she's different thanks to the change of time.

Glancing at her brother, then Etaliein, then me, she settles her gaze on my face.

"Take care of my brother," she says. "Who knows how much time will pass from when I walk through this portal and when you all come after me."

"I promise," I say. Everett reaches out, taking my hand.

Emma's eyes drift down to our intertwined fingers, rolling her eyes as she turns on her heels, giving us a half wave. One moment, she's on this side of the barrier. A blink later, she's gone.

"Can you heal him?" I turn to Etaliein. "You made that portal like it was nothing. Maybe you can . . ."

"I cannot undo those wounds," he says. "Magic can neither be created nor destroyed, only changed. Plus, this is my first time in the mortal world in . . . nearly half a millennium. I am, in some ways, weaker than you two."

"I thought you said you were a god?"

"I'm a being of magic, Douglas. All magic, like a beacon, pulls to me. I am the epicenter of it, just like this tree was when I was within it. Plus, I need all the magic that exists in this forest to have the strength to break the curse."

"So then can't you rewrite reality?"

"Even gods have limits. That wound was made from my sorrow, a part of me. My magic will have no effect on it. It's the same magic that made the wound; it cannot undo it." Etaliein studies Everett, but looks like he's looking through him, past him . . . into him, even. "But I can tell you, he'll be fine."

I trust Etaliein. I don't know why, or if I should, but I do. I give Everett a weak smile and a squeeze of his shoulder. Like a wave coming in from the farthest reaches of the ocean, exhaustion is beginning to flood every fiber of my being. We're almost done. We're almost there. We can soon rest. Just a little bit farther.

I turn to look at Etaliein. "How can I help put an end to this?"

Etaliein lets out a deep breath as he surveys the shadowy area around us. He's silent, but the weight of the silence doesn't escape me.

"I haven't even considered what could happen . . . what would happen . . . when I let the curtains fall."

"Shouldn't you know all?"

Etaliein chuckles lowly. "Even gods are fallible, Douglas. We see what we want to see and turn a blind eye to what we don't. Especially those who have aligned themselves so closely to humanity as I have."

Love will do that to you, I think. *Change everything about you.*

"Plus," he adds. "I never let myself imagine that. Thoughts

have power, Douglas. You of all people should know that."

If only I could make my thoughts have enough power to put an end to all this.

"I imagine, once you end this curse, you'll cross over," I finally say. "If there's another side."

"There is."

"Then I imagine that will be your next stop. You and Henry will be together. All you have to do is be brave enough to take that step forward."

Etaliein grins. "That's easier said than done, don't you think?"

"We made it through a cursed forest to a god locked in a tree in order to break a curse," Everett mutters. "Not sure it gets harder than that."

Etaliein grins. "Fair enough. And you two, and your sister, have done more than enough. Both of you deserve to be at peace. The rest falls on me. Now, I must—"

Etaliein's voice cuts out. At first, neither Everett nor I know what happened, Etaliein's face frozen in mid speech. But then, as a dribble of blood, deep red and black, drips out of his mouth and he falls forward to his knees, coughing, we see.

Headmaster Monroe, standing with crossbow in hand, pointing directly at where Etaliein once stood but now bows in penance with an arrow through his heart.

"Fucking finally," the headmaster says, lowering his weapon. "I've been waiting years to be able to do that."

35

"What are you fucking doing?!" I shriek.

Etaliein almost falls face forward in the dirt. If it wasn't for me grabbing him before he hit the ground, he probably would have. Headmaster Monroe doesn't seem to care; instead, he checks his crossbow and loads another arrow into it.

"I'm going to be honest; I was never a hunter. My dad wanted me to learn how to use a gun, but it wasn't my cup of tea. Preferred politics and money as a method of manipulating people. Not weapons. So crass, you know? But I have to say, I'm beginning to understand the value of them. Especially with an arrow crafted from a tree drenched in the power of a god itself."

Headmaster Monroe looks up slowly, a newfound coldness in his eyes, as he settles his gaze on Everett. "Tell your mother thank you for the crossbow, Everett."

Everett doesn't move, but I can tell by the tension in his body he wants to. Fighting is out of the question. And with Emma gone . . .

That mantle rests on me.

"Are you okay?" I ask, looking at Etaliein.

Etaliein says nothing, his breathing labored and heavy. His eyes dilate open and close, like he's trying to focus; the bone mask he wears, which, up close, I see is actually fused to his face and is part of him, is beginning to crack, like ice splintering.

"Douglas," Everett says.

My vision snaps to Headmaster Monroe as I hear his footsteps approaching. "You didn't need to do that. I was doing what you asked. He was about to break the curse!"

"Douglas," Everett adds more firmly this time.

"You should have let me finish! No one had to die!"

"First of all, that's a god, not a person. They are very different things. And second, you should listen to your friend, Douglas," Headmaster Monroe says once he's standing directly in front of me. "He understands. Impressive, for an Everley."

"It was never about you succeeding," Everett finally says, not once breaking his gaze from Headmaster Monroe. "It was never about actually stopping the curse, was it?"

Headmaster Monroe's face, typically so stoic and sharp, so refined and put together, twists into something . . . horrific and demon-like.

"Again, on the money. Well, at least part of it."

"Have you been following us the whole time?" I ask. "How did you get in the forest? You said—"

"I never said I couldn't enter the forest, Douglas. I simply inferred that I couldn't. Or wouldn't. Depends on how you want to read into it. I just needed someone to lead me to it. Someone to be a bigger target for the forest to focus on. Someone with magic and not only determination to break the curse but the possibility to do so. That made you a larger priority for the forest than me.

"And look at that; you exceeded my wildest hopes for you, Douglas. Despite some annoyingly minor detours, but you did. Congratulations."

Headmaster Monroe squats forward, balancing on the toes of his boot. I feel a chill trickle down my back, and pull Etaliein closer, careful to not shift the arrow in his chest, but also trying my best to keep him away from the man who just tried to kill him.

Headmaster Monroe doesn't take offense. His right hand, gloved in black, traces over the outline of the bone mask that Etaliein wears.

"You know I never had children," he says quietly. "Not because of any medical reason. But by choice. I couldn't bring myself to force someone else to live with this curse like I was. My father . . . he was a horrible man. Didn't care who he hurt. Didn't care that he forced himself on my mother and forced her to give birth to me so he could have an heir.

"I killed my father for what he did to my mother. A woman I never met but my aunt told me about. Supposedly I have her smile. Well, until my father took it away from her. So, I don't think killing this person . . . no, this thing, is too much of a jump, do you?"

Headmaster Monroe looks at me with a blank expression, vacant of any remorse or pity. "This god, his curse, his own selfishness, took away my ability to marry the woman I loved. To have children. To watch them grow and have a fulfilling life. He forced me into this disgusting cold cage that I never wanted to be born into. I'm taking back control of my life, Douglas. You of all people should understand that."

"We are not the same," I hiss. "I would never kill someone to—"

"Would you not?" he asks. "Come on now, Douglas. Truly, would you not? If you had to kill this god to save your mother, you wouldn't? If you had to kill me to save Everett, wouldn't you? You came here, at my behest, yes, but of your own volition, to right what was wrong. A part of you, deep down, always knew killing might have to be an option. If not, then why did you train with Everett, here?"

"To defend myself."

"Which can often mean having to kill," he notes, standing up with a grunt. "You seem to think we are so different. And if that makes you feel better and helps you sleep at night, then so be it. I have no qualms with what I've done to get here. I will not apologize for protecting not only the students at this school, who have been entrusted to me, but also my family line. Because there is nothing more powerful or sacred than family."

Headmaster Monroe checks his crossbow once more, loading a second arrow into it.

"Let me take that a step further, then. If you could change the world, and all it took was killing one being who deserved it, would you?"

My eyes flicker to Etaliein, then Everett, and finally Headmaster Monroe and his crossbow. I just need to find the right opening . . . and that means I need time.

"What are you saying? You would need to have the power of a god to undo . . ."

A sinister smile slowly spreads over Headmaster Monroe's face. "No."

"You get it now, don't you?"

"You cannot do that."

"Oh? I can't?" he asks. "You understand, Douglas. Matter cannot be created, nor destroyed. I imagine godly energy is the same. Something has to take it. Might as well be me."

"You changing the world to make it fit your own ideal of what it should be has consequences! Things you won't even be able to predict."

Headmaster Monroe nods. "I'm willing to take that chance. To create a world where that god doesn't exist. No Henry. Maybe no Winslow." He pauses. "Who knows, maybe no you, Douglas. Depending on how the next few minutes go."

My eyes turn to Etaliein as he lets out a strained cough. Flakes of bone begin to fall off his face, revealing red-and-pink flesh. His body twitches; his voice wheezes.

"What did you do to him?" Everett asks. "He's a god, a simple arrow shouldn't—"

"And I thought you were the smart one in the family,"

Headmaster Monroe sighs. "Shame. I guess even idiots can have a moment of brilliance. A normal arrow wouldn't hurt a god, but an arrow made from the blood and bones of a Perversion? A part of him? Now that would."

Before I can say anything, Headmaster Monroe quickly points his crossbow. My body tenses, only for a moment, as the arrow fires, lodging itself into Everett's thigh, just above his right knee.

Everett lets out a scream that sounds like the earth shattering, and I move to him, but Headmaster Monroe shifts the focus, aiming the crossbow at me.

"Don't."

His voice is direct and clear. He keeps the arrow pointed right at my throat.

"You have to understand my side of this, Douglas," Headmaster Monroe says. "If you had a chance to change your fate, wouldn't you?"

"You're killing people," I hiss. "You and your family have been doing this for—"

"*Exactly!* Don't you see? If I rewrite the world, none of them had to have died. No one. We can start anew."

"But there's no promise they'll be alive either. You think you killing—"

"Restarting," he corrects.

"Killing people is helping anyone? Who would agree with this plan, Headmaster? No one. You're not helping anyone but your own ego."

"I'm helping EVERYONE, don't you SEE?" he roars, pointing

the crossbow at my face. "I know your small stupid mind can't understand, but everyone will be better off in my new world. None of these horrors . . . no gods to judge us and play us like pawns. None of you will remember any of this. I'll take that burden, for you! Don't you see how much I want to help you? How much I'm giving up to save you. Don't you see, Douglas? I'm not the villain of this story. I'm the real savior. I'm a prophet. I'm a messiah."

Headmaster Monroe says that last sentence like he isn't sure if he truly believes it, but if he repeats it enough times, he will.

"Son of Monroe," Etaliein whispers quietly, his voice wet with blood. "You and your family have always been clouded by your own greed and avarice. You are just as stupid, foolish, and closed-minded as your ancestors."

My body tenses when I see the anger flash over Headmaster Monroe's face. My eyes flicker over to Everett, clutching his wounded leg, doing his best to stem the blood loss. *This could be it,* I think. I can't see a plausible way out for any of us.

At least Emma made it out alive. At least—

"Douglas."

The voice in my head is right at the forefront of my mind, like the person speaking it is speaking right against my ear. The voice, belonging to Etaliein, is soft and comforting, much like when we were in the other world.

"How long can you hold your breath?"

Long enough, I think.

"Good. Three. Two. One."

Without questioning, I take a deep breath in and close my eyes.

I feel time slow around me. My soul separates from my body like I'm looking at everything happening around me, and Etaliein, still within my body's arms, is looking past Headmaster Monroe, at me.

I can still feel the world around me, the earth under my feet, the chill of the air, the smell of blood and dank earth.

"Douglas," he says slowly. *"I'm dying."*

"What do you mean? Can't you just heal yourself?"

"The arrow was made from my own magic. Those wounds are like the wounds from my Perversions. I cannot heal them. I cannot heal myself."

"There has to be another way. We can think through this. I can think through this. Just give me time."

"We don't have time. I am like a container, my body, my mind, my soul. All of it has been keeping the darkness controlled. Without me, that darkness will spread unchecked. There will be nothing to hold it back. But I can get you and Everett to safety."

"And then what?"

"And then the rot will spread like a darkness throughout the world, rolling across, feasting on magic, and fear, and anger and rage. It is depression personified, mixed with the emotions of a god. It is carnal. It is pure. It will consume everything. These Perversions you've seen will exist all over the world. It will be what you humans call damnation.

"I can give you a piece of my magic. You will have what you need to defend yourself and your family and friends. You have found a solution once before; I'm confident you'll find one again. I will

remove Headmaster Monroe from the equation. *The rest is up to you.*"

I shake my head, feeling my lungs begin to burn. I know once I take a breath, this magic will end. I have to hold on.

Quickly, I take a breath, a small one just enough to lessen the burn. In that fraction of a second, time accelerates, Headmaster Monroe moves forward a fraction of an inch.

"Will that break the curse?"

Etaliein hesitates. *"I don't know. But I'm not sure we have any other choice at this point. The headmaster cannot get my power. There is no worse ending than that. You've seen what he's done to people with wealth and power on the mortal plane. Imagine that on the cosmic scale."*

Etaliein's right. The rot that's creeping all around us is growing. And the darkness that pulses out from Headmaster Monroe . . . That's the darkness Etaliein is referring to. That's what the future of the world would be. One of rot and ruin or of submission without resistance.

There has to be a way to stop it. Those can't be our only outcomes. All of this goes back to the magic within Etaliein. Without it, with that out of reach or controlled, none of this can happen. There has to be a way to control it. Magic can't be created or destroyed, but it can be transferred. That's what Headmaster Monroe wants to do anyway. What if we could find another vessel? Something that we knew could contain it or at least wouldn't use the power for evil? What if . . .

"Douglas," he says firmly. *"No. That is not an option."*

"Why not?"

"Just like the headmaster, you are human. You cannot be the vessel for this darkness. It will destroy you from the inside out. That is exactly what I was saying about your headmaster. You two may be different in spirit, but you are the same in flesh."

"It sounds like we don't have any choice. If you can't heal yourself, and the darkness is going to spread anyway, we might as well try. If there's a chance one of us can take it, shouldn't it be me rather than him? Plus, I have all the things you said were needed. I can be the source; I've proven before by my control of magic that I can jumpstart the reaction. I can do this."

"Even if you pull this off, we have no idea what sort of ramifications there will be. You are essentially saying you want to become a demigod of the forest. That isn't—that has NEVER happened, Douglas. The chances of this succeeding are low. Minuscule. You're more likely to die and burn out before even having a second to wield my magic. And if it does succeed, you will never be able to leave. You'll be the only thing keeping my darkness from escaping. You'll have no life outside this town. Forever."

"We don't have another choice," I remind him. "We are past the point of having another solution or having the luxury of time to think of one. We have to try. I have to try something."

"It is better to live and fight another day than to—"

"There is no promise there will be another day! You're hoping I can find another solution, get another chance, but you don't know. You won't be here. You don't know what form the darkness will take. I can't control these variables. I can at least try."

Etaliein says nothing; it's almost as if I'm alone again. Just me in this endless space between life and death.

"You were hurt, Etaliein. People who hated you and Henry killed you and took away the chance you had at happiness. So you did something in retaliation, out of pain. I don't blame you for that. But you shouldn't have to suffer forever for your mistake.

"Keeping this darkness at bay, stewing in it, is just prolonging your suffering. You have to move on. You have to let it go. In an effort to contain it, it's eating you alive. Let me help you move on. Let me take your pain."

"My pain, as you call it, might kill you, Douglas."

I don't hesitate before answering. *"That's what pain does when it goes unchecked. It hurts everyone it comes in contact with. Even if it kills me. At least I had a purpose. That's the only thing I've ever wanted."*

I glance over at Everett, his frozen-in-time body just feet from me. I wish I could say goodbye, say something, but I know if he was here, he would try his best to talk me out of it. No, this is best.

I just wish we had more time.

Etaliein doesn't say anything for a moment, his voice now distant. I can't tell if he's doing it on purpose, or if my body is losing its ability to hold its breath.

"We will only have a moment. Headmaster Monroe will give us no longer than that. One moment, one shot to make this work, once I return you to your body. You have to give yourself to me. Completely. Mind, body, and soul. There cannot be a moment of hesitation or an ounce of fear. You have to let the power wash over you and through

you. Any bit of resistance could trigger an adverse effect. And even then, I'm not sure if this will work. I'm hoping it will. But . . ."

"I understand," I say.

Etaliein sighs. *"Take a breath whenever you're ready. And no matter what happens, I want you to know, you are, and will always be, marvelous."*

The words are a comfort, but the burning in my lungs is finally too much. I take a deep breath of the forest's air, feeling the world rush around me as my soul snaps back into my body. Etaliein said we need to be one. He also said we only have a moment, a fraction of a second.

So, I do the only thing I can think of, the most simple and honest act that could create a connection between two people.

I lean down, turning his head toward mine, and press my lips against his, close my eyes, and brace for whatever happens next. I don't regret what I'm doing; I know that now. I'm doing, for once, the right thing, without any concern for what happens next.

I only wish the last sound I heard wasn't Headmaster Monroe's roar of anger at my actions, and instead Everett's voice saying . . . well, anything.

But mostly, *I love you.*

36

Fire burns through my veins like acid, every nerve inside me seared to a crisp.

I know I'm screaming; I can feel the rawness in my throat, taste the blood, as my vocal cords snap, restitch, and snap again. I'm nothing but a live wire of pain I've never experienced, pain that no human should ever feel.

Distantly I can hear Etaliein's voice telling me to hold on . . . no, telling me to give the power back. To let him take the burden of the pain.

"He can take it," I hear Etaliein tell someone, "I'm assuming Everett. He's strong enough. I'm not."

Maybe I'm not. Maybe everything I've been trying to do, every person I've been trying to help, has been for nothing.

But I have to try.

I can sense the ground underneath me, the earth in between my fingers—hoping to feel anything. The forest is dark and cold; perhaps the coolness of the earth will push through and soothe me.

"Breathe, Douglas."

The voice is distant, so far away that I think I imagined it. But when it repeats the order, a soft soothing instrument, I know exactly who it is.

"You have to breathe."

I try my best to listen, but all I feel is pain. All I taste is copper in the bits of flesh. My body is burning around me, pieces of me dripping off. When all is said and done, whatever makes me, well, me, won't exist anymore.

This is my penance.

But then the voice speaks again. This time clearer than before, and I realize it's not Etaliein that's speaking to me. It's Everett.

"Look at me," his voice says, louder than before. "Douglas, come on, look at me."

I tilt my head in the general direction of the voice; I can make out Everett's figure in front of me. It's as if he's absorbing all color, which in turn gives him the rough shape of a person. I can see his strands of hair, his arms, his strong biceps. I can see and feel his palms against my shoulders.

"See, I knew you were strong enough," he says, support in his voice like scaffolding.

"I can't hold it," I whisper. I'm not even sure if I'm speaking. I know I'm telling myself to speak, ordering my body with the right commands, hoping words come out. But Everett seems to understand. At least, the way he squeezes my shoulder tells me that.

"You're doing great," he whispers.

"You have to get out of here. Etaliein was right, you—"

"I'm not going anywhere," he interrupts.

If I could control this magic, even for a moment, I'd use it to push Everett and Emma as far away from the school as possible. I'd break the curse, shatter it like a hammer hitting glass, and bring this whole fucking place down. I'd follow through with my promise, even if it killed me.

"So, what are we doing?" Everett asks. "Are we going down together or are we making it through this? Your choice, Douglas."

But right now, all I want to do is see him. To hold him. To kiss him. All I want to do is be with him and focus on his face, focus on the peace he brings and get lost in the what-ifs and possibilities we never got to experience. At least there, in that space where nothing is real or matters, I can dream we're going to make it through this alive.

But if I can dream it, I can make it a reality. Even if for just a minute, or a second. I can find that peace I've been fighting for, for so, so long.

I swallow through the pain as much as I can, forcing my vision to focus on Everett. He's the only thing that matters, the only thing I can clearly make out. The rest of the world is just colors and shapes, roughly resembling their real forms. I pool the energy like I did before, seeing the darkness in the distance like blackness on the edge of campus. It moves like waves, flicking and dancing at the edge of my vision, getting closer, then retreating, then close again.

I take a deep breath that feels like fire in my lungs. I see Headmaster Monroe, standing off in the distance, frozen.

"This . . . ends . . . now."

I put all my energy into those words, letting my mind run wild.

I don't know how long it takes for me to burn every bit of dark magic, but I go as far back as the start of this curse, and I see Etaliein and his lover, standing in the forest. I see snapshots of him holding his burned magic, see tears of black-and-red blood streaming down his face as he chokingly sobs into the man's mangled body.

I see each student, once again, the smiles on their faces as they join Regent and then the last expressions they have before they die. I watch Everett's and Emma's births, see them grow up, watch as they first meet me in the forest. I see it all, I cleanse it all.

Enough.

Instantly, the darkness begins to disappear, and be replaced with the beautiful colors of light that make up the new color spectrum I can see. Bright pinks, vibrant oranges, beautiful yellows, and roaring reds all take over my vision. The pain is there—and something tells me it will always be there—but it's like any other part of me now. As I swallow down the darkness, with every gulp, the world becomes clearer. The colors dim, until they are pastel, and then they turn translucent, and then, finally, the world around me becomes clear.

Everett locks eyes with me, fear and concern dancing behind his pupils.

"Are you . . . Douglas?" He pauses. "Are you my Douglas?"

I look at the palms of my hands. How do I answer that? I feel the same, mostly. But there's something else inside me, something burning deep that keeps me warm. I can't feel my heartbeat anymore, but I can feel *everything* else. Time. Space. The other realities layered on top of this one. I feel it all.

And I see it all too.

I press my hand against Everett's chest, pushing magic into him and stitching the wound in his leg, healing him in only a matter of seconds. Once done, I walk past Everett, toward Headmaster Monroe. He takes a step back, stumbles on a root, and almost loses his footing. But with a wave of my hand, a thick vine rises from the ground, catching him. I want him to look me directly in the eyes when I speak to him.

"You did this," I snarl.

"I have no—"

"Shut. Up," I order. His mouth snaps shut, thin lips pushed together into an even thinner line.

"I see everything, Headmaster Monroe. Anything this forest touches, any soil its roots permeate, I see what happens there. Including . . ."

I snap my fingers and much like when Etaliein did it, the world around me shifts like sand and smoke turning over on itself. The forest turns into the headmaster's office, a man dressed in a perfect suit glancing at the file in his hand, then back at the headmaster.

"Are you sure?" the man asks.

"Of course," Headmaster Monroe says without looking at the man. "Washington, DC. There's a girl there whose mother reached out to one of our recruitment officers. I think she'd make a perfect addition to our school. But I need her to have no other choice."

Headmaster Monroe glances up at the man and says, "You said you have a commitment to our academy, Mr. Hale. That's the commitment you made when you graduated, to do anything to protect and better the school."

"I still hold that commitment," Kent's father says.

"Then I need you to do this for me." Headmaster Monroe quickly writes down something on a piece of paper, tears it off, and hands it to Mr. Hale.

"Go here. This man will have all the tools you need."

Mr. Hale scans the paper, mouths words silently, then burns the paper via Headmaster Monroe's candle. He tips his hat, turns around, and leaves, stopping at the door when the headmaster calls his name.

"Arson," the headmaster said. "Covers your tracks the best. And have your wife on speed dial. I imagine the girl will need a lawyer."

The vision disappears, the silence of the forest returning.

"It was never supposed to be me, was it?" I ask. "You always were going to target another kid. Have Kent's father do your dirty work, and then have his mother show that there was no other way."

Headmaster Monroe is silent. He shifts his weight, straightening his back in an attempt to add a few inches to his height.

"You should be thanking me," he seethes. "Look what came from this. Look at you. You have power, Douglas. Magic! Isn't that what you always wanted? To be someone worth respecting, fearing, admiring? If I hadn't done that, where would you be? Now you have the power I've always wanted. To reshape the world. Your father can be brought back, don't you see? Don't you understand what type of—"

"No," I interrupt. "No more of your lies. No more of your fucking manipulations. You and your family are done hurting people."

Before Headmaster Monroe can try to plead his case, the ground shakes. Slowly from behind him stalks an Emissary, with antlers and strong hind legs, making it easily fifteen feet tall. The creature, with a face of a hawk and the bony half-eroded body of a wolf, stares at me, then back at Headmaster Monroe, then back at me.

"What is your wish?"

Headmaster Monroe stumbles backward, but Everett cuts him off, pulling out his blade and pointing it directly at the headmaster with his good arm.

"You are the problem, Headmaster," I say, turning to him. "From the beginning, your family line has repeatedly put your own well-being over that of others, even to the point of spilling blood. This curse has taught you nothing. Out of all the families who have suffered, yours continues to repeat the cycle that put you here, sacrificing others because you view them as less than you, instead of learning, moving on, and accepting your role in the atrocities of the past. That ends now."

I turn my head to the Emissary. "Erase him."

"You cannot do this!" Headmaster Monroe roars as the Emissary takes one large step forward. Two of its four parts grab him, dangling him several feet off the ground as it turns toward the forest.

"Douglas!" he roars. "Listen to me! We can reach a deal! Douglas!"

I stand still, watching the space in the forest where the Emissary disappeared, where the trees have parted, bent and broken in its path. I swear I can see the outline of two people, standing in the center, holding hands. I can't make out their faces, but something warm inside me tells me who they are. At least, I like to think, Etaliein and Henry are finally happy.

"You're free," I whisper as they slowly dissolve. "I hope you're finally at peace."

As the wisps disappear, Everett's right hand squeezes my shoulder.

"You're warm," he says with concern in his voice while standing next to me. "Burning up, actually."

"Probably the magic burning through my body," I mutter. "I don't know how long I have."

"That's okay," Everett says. "We can make the most of the time we do have."

I wish I could. I wish I could spend my last moments looking into Everett's eyes.

"I have one more thing to do."

Kneeling down, I push my fingers into the dirt, burying my arms up to my forearms. The deeper I go, the colder the ground is, but at the same time, the closer I feel to the magic, as if I can feel the thumping of its heart. Taking a deep breath, I focus on their faces.

"Sarah, Kent, Peter," I say while taking in another breath. "Live."

The magic pushes out of my body and into the earth, every bit of the energy I got from Etaliein, even the magic that I can feel intertwined with my life force. I have no idea where it goes, but hopefully, maybe, it'll find their remains and be able to bring them back to life. If this godly power can erase the past, then perhaps it can rewrite the future.

"Douglas . . ."

"I'm not done."

My mind wants to be done, though. The magic needed to bring someone back to life, even for a god, feels like it's ripping apart something deep inside of me. But I can't stop. Those students from before, the ones who were lured here like me? They deserve a chance too. To live a life that was cut short. I can't change what happened in DC, but I can save some people. I can make this right in my own way.

"Come back to me," I whisper, repeating the command three more times, each time my voice growing louder until it's a scream. I push my mind and my soul out until it touches them through time and space. I wrap my magic around them and yank them back from the beyond. I'll deal with any consequences later, but what's the point of being a god if you can't chance things that are unjust?

I command the ground, the flora, and the fauna to stitch their bodies back, to use the magical earth and the rich soil to make bodies for them that mimic their previous ones. Somewhere around the school grounds, those students are taking in a breath of new air, in a new world.

Once done, I pull my hands out of the earth, collapsing onto my back. Suddenly, all the energy I had feels like it was sucked out of me, and even sitting feels like a dozen bricks are pushing down on my shoulders. Everett sits down next to me, wrapping his arm around me, holding me close.

"I got you," he whispers. "I've always got you. Until your last breath."

I know, I want to say, but even speaking takes too much energy. Something tells me Everett knows, even without me having to say it.

Still, as I feel my body relax, and my heartbeat slow, I wish he hadn't gotten the last fucking word.

37

"Be careful with that log there."

It's been about ten weeks since the incident in the forest, but it feels like maybe ten minutes.

No one at school was the wiser; no one even noticed I was gone. Headmaster Monroe, a forgotten memory for most of the students and residents of Winslow, was true to his word; at least that much I could say. For the two weeks I was gone, my mama received texts from me, fake updates, even a few audio messages that made it seem like I was having a great time. She didn't need to know I was staying with the Everleys, just a hundred feet from here. Sharing a bed with Everett and using whatever free time I had when I wasn't sleeping to try to understand this new status of mine.

A god. Me. A Black boy from DC, now . . . a god.

Ever since I returned to school, the sounds of the forest have been even louder. It's not the same as before; not like they are actually talking to me. But when I close my eyes, I can feel everything the forest feels. I can sense where Emissaries are, patrolling the depths of the forest. Every animal, every tree that shifts and grows, is like an itch inside me. I'm not sure if I'll ever get used to that feeling. The sensation is growing and expanding like vines in my chest cavity, but it's nice to feel like I'm not alone.

"Sarah!" I shout. "Please, can you stay focused and finish up that section?"

Sarah rolls her eyes at me, adjusting her hard hat. She gives me the finger, turning back to the boy, one of Kent's goons, and passes him a small slip of paper, probably with her number on it, before returning to shoveling trash into her can.

Taylor Meyers's home is mostly clean now. Once I was able to walk again, finally feeling as close to a person as I could feel, I convinced the school to let me spearhead a project cleaning up the town of Winslow. Regent Academy, even without a headmaster— and no one seems to question how the school has functioned so long without a headmaster—still has the sway needed to get Winslow to let a student lead a restoration project. And besides, Regent Academy should give back. All the pain the Monroes have caused this town? Something should be done to revitalize it. To make it a place to be proud of.

"You shouldn't handle that by yourself," Peter says. "The wood's rotted and—"

"I got it," Kent replies, not even giving Peter a chance to explain himself.

"Here, let me help you. My parents run—"

406

"I said I—damn it!"

I turn my gaze toward the noise, along with a half dozen other students who joined in the volunteer service activity, and come face-to-face with Kent, covered in dirt. The rotted dresser he was trying to manage himself is now in shambles. A smile threatens to break out on my lips, but I tuck my face downward and clear my throat.

"You okay?" Peter asks.

"Fuck you," Kent snarls.

"Maybe next time, when someone offers you help, you'll take it?" I shout, bridging the gap between us to give Kent's leg a quick scan. He'll be fine, just a bruise. Something I could easily make go away. But . . . it's Kent. He doesn't deserve any more sympathy than I've given him.

"You know what, Douglas," Kent growls, stumbling over the haphazard pile of wood. "I have had more than enough of your attitude."

There was a time—not that long ago, actually—I would have been afraid when Kent puffed out his chest like that. Even if I didn't admit it before, even if I hid behind my bravado, there was a part of me that understood who had the power here and who didn't. I knew, squaring off against Kent, what could happen when we met on the school grounds. But my pride and need to save face overrode any logic. I thought being powerful, or appearing to be powerful, was more important than being smart.

Now that I have real power? I'm not so sure.

With a discreet flick of my finger, a vine shoots up from the ground and wraps around Kent's ankle. He loses his footing, trying his best to catch himself, before falling face-first in a puddle of mud, loud wet suction sounds filling the air as he groans in annoyance.

"Sorry, were you saying something?" I ask, rolling up the blueprints. Grinning at Peter, I nod to him. "You want to lead breaking down any of the other objects you find on the lot? Just make sure you have some help while doing it."

Peter's eyes flash like when a kid wakes up on Christmas morning to the exact presents they wanted under the tree. Who doesn't love getting their hands dirty and taking out their frustration on the world? But I think it's more than that. I think it's also that someone looked at him, actually saw him, and gave him responsibility. Saw more than just his thin frame, his awkward lanky body, his overgrowth of pimples and wild hair, and said, you can be responsible for something on your own. I trust you to handle this.

He was seen—and I've learned just giving people the chance, even if they mess up, fail, or go in a completely different direction than you expected, is worth it.

My phone vibrates once; a message from Everett appears on the screen.

Can you meet me at the border?

I type a quick response, slipping the phone back into my pocket. Walking over to the row of bikes all the students rode into town, I sift through them like fabric to find my own—a red-and-black one that Everett made for me about six weeks ago. Tilting the kickstand up, I mount the bike, surveying those who came here to volunteer. Everyone is doing their part, like a set of automatons running their commands in unison. At this rate, we'll be done cleaning out the remaining wreckage by the end of the week.

They can spend a few minutes without my supervision.

The bike ride to the border of town takes less than five minutes. I see visions of Everett and me, walking down these same roads, trailing behind the ghost of Jane just three months ago. Life is so different than it was back then. Night and day, really.

I shift gears, skidding to a halt at the town sign that reads Welcome to Winslow. Emma, Evelyn, and Everett stand right at the border, Evelyn's truck packed to the brim with suitcases. Emma and Evelyn exchange what seems to be a hug that neither of them wants to let go from.

Everett pushes off the side of the truck when he sees me, smiling as he walks over, wrapping his arms around me in a tight hug similar to the one his mother is giving his sister.

"How is the restoration going?"

"Should be done by the end of the week."

"And how are those new students doing?"

The new students being the kids who came before me, who were prey to the Monroes, I brought back.

"Your mom has been a big help in integrating them into the school," I say. "No one really questioned it. Just said they were new transfer students."

"No one who goes to this school is going to give two shits about some Black and brown kids. That would mean they would have to care about other people. Except you. You cared."

I shrug. Everett frowns. "Don't do that."

"Do what?"

"Belittle yourself. You cared; enough to do all this. Most people wouldn't have paid the price you paid."

"Most people aren't me," I say before I can rethink the words.

"And that's why I . . ." Everett closes his mouth before he can finish the sentence, quickly shifting to saying something else out of the blue.

"I want you to come with me."

Hidden under the folds of his words, there's a desperation that he's trying to fight, trying to find the space where he doesn't sound like he's pleading for me to give this all up, but at the same time wanting me to know this is the one thing he wants more than anything else.

And I wish I could give that to him.

"You know I would if I could," I whisper. "But . . ."

"I know." Everett reaches forward, squeezing my hands. "When you took Etaliein's power, you became the guardian of the forest, and if you leave, this whole town falls apart. You're tethered to it."

Everett says what I can't say because, if I'm being honest, I'm still trying to wrap my head around it. In an effort to help others and to break this curse, I've taken on a curse for myself; bound to this town, its fate tied to mine and mine to it. As long as I exist, the town will thrive, and as long as the town thrives, I'll live. A symbiotic relationship.

"Etaliein was right," I say, trying to grin through my words. "The forest demands its due . . ."

"And its preferred payment is blood, I know," Everett finishes. "I just wish you didn't have to pay it."

"I'm okay with it." I know that sounds weird and it probably sounds like a lie, but it's not. "I'm fine with the curse that's been placed upon me, as fine as someone can be, being tethered to magic. The one thing I've always wanted is a purpose, and in some twisted way, being bound to this town, fixing it, guarding it from whatever lingering darkness is in the corners right outside my periphery, gives me that purpose."

I turn, gesturing to Winslow. "This town can be something, Everett. There can be a thriving community here. I can feel it. And maybe I can do my part in making that a reality. And hey, I'll be able to live long enough to see that. Maybe in one hundred or two hundred years, this will be the most prosperous town in the country."

"If anyone can, it's you," he says, wrapping his arms around me from behind. Everett rests his chin on my shoulder. I lean into the strength of his chest, taking in his charcoal-scented cologne.

"I'll come back," he whispers. "I promise. I'll visit often."

I shake my head but don't say any words at first. "I want you to live a life. There's a whole world out there for you, not here. I want you to experience that."

"My favorite world is the one with you."

"And I'm not going anywhere." Turning around to face him, I smile, cupping his face with my hands. Slowly, standing on the tips of my toes, I press a soft kiss against his lips.

"It'll be okay. I'll be here, always and forever."

"That doesn't make me feel any better," he chuckles sadly.

"The truth often doesn't, but that doesn't mean we should hide from it."

Everett arches his brow, looking at me, studying me. "Is that Douglas or Etaliein talking?"

At first, I don't know how to answer him. Luckily for me, I don't have to.

"Everett," Emma says, leaning out of the driver's window of the truck. "We should get going."

Everett doesn't look back at his sister, as if his whole world is in my eyes. Funny, because my whole world is in his.

"You should go," I whisper, forcing myself to take a step back. "Don't be a stranger, alright? You have my number."

"And you have mine," he says, stepping backward. We never break eye contact, even as he slips into the passenger side of his truck, looking at me through the window. Emma waves at her mom and I see her eyes settle on me, as if she wants to say something. But before I can focus on her, she slips back into the driver's seat, revs the truck to life, and peels off.

A large part of me wants to follow him.

But for now, at least today, I've accepted my choice.

38

"We haven't done this in a while."

Mama's right. Movie nights used to be a thing for us back home. But once Dad died, and we moved to Regent Academy, neither of us had time for it. But after Everett leaving a week ago, being around her is all I want to do. Especially considering what I'm here to do.

"And you cooking dinner? What special occasion is this?"

I roll my eyes, poking at the mac and cheese that's still left on my plate. *The Holiday*, one of my mama's favorite romantic comedies, plays in the background, about halfway through.

"If it makes you feel any better, I made it from a box."

She rolls her eyes back at me. "How would that make me feel any better? Next time, you have to make it from scratch. I have a great recipe."

Family recipes passed down from generation to generation is a badge of honor. I should then pass that recipe to my children. Children I won't have.

I take a deep breath, licking my lips, still tasting the savory spices on them that my mama added to put her own spin on the meal. I take my plate and hers, balancing the glasses on top of one another, and put them in the sink of the adjoining kitchenette every staff member at Regent Academy has. While cleaning the plates, I can feel my mama's eyes boring into me. It's only a matter of time before—

"Douglas," she finally says.

"I know when something is bothering you. Are you missing Everett? Is that it?"

I shake my head. "No. I mean, it *is*, but that's not what has been keeping me up."

"Then what?" Mama reaches forward, squeezing my hand.

"You've done so much for me. Keeping this family together when Dad died, supporting me at Regent, always believing in me. You've always put me first before yourself."

I sigh shakily. "I think it's time for you to put yourself first. You can't stay here forever in this town. You need to have a life that isn't tied to me, isn't based on how you can help me."

Mama's beautiful face twists into confusion. "I appreciate your concern, but once you graduate, I'll—"

"I know. You'll do something for yourself, right? Maybe see the world, maybe go back to school and get your doctorate?"

"Exactly."

Reaching forward, I take both of my mama's hands, threading our fingers together. Her hands, despite how much work she's put into bettering our lives, are so soft. I'll always remember the feeling of those fingers carding through my hair when I couldn't sleep.

I tilt my head down so Mama can't see the tears forming in my eyes. Tendrils of magic push through my veins into her body, using our connected hands as a bridge.

"I love you, Mama. I love you so so much. And I want you to know I appreciate everything you've done for me. But it's time for you to live a life for yourself. To go out and be someone whose choices aren't defined by supporting other people."

"Douglas, what are you . . ."

"I want you to know one thing before you go," I say quickly, pushing more magic. I can feel it scratching at her mind. Faintly, around me, I see memories we've shared through her vantage point. The first time I talked. Her standing with me at my father's funeral. Us driving to Regent Academy together. "I want you to know how proud I am to have you as my mother. And I'm going to always, always support you. I'll always be your biggest fan, and I love you more than anything in the world. I hope I've made you proud."

Mama opens her mouth—I'm sure about to tell me I'm scaring her—but before she can, I take in a deep breath. The tendrils have latched onto every memory I can find of me and Dad, and as I inhale, the magic pulls them from her mind, through our hands, and inside me. Slowly, her eyes begin to close, and her body becomes limp. I catch her before she can fall over, gently placing her on the couch. When she wakes up, all memories of me will be gone. She'll finally be able to move on, having no reason to stay in Regent anymore. She can focus on her own happiness, for once. But at least those memories we've had will be inside me forever.

Standing up, swallowing back the pain, I take a shaky breath. Tapping into the magic of the forest, I breathe out a single word.

"Erase me."

All across campus, memories of my mama and me are pulled from existence. Photos she has in her house begin to gray out, becoming simply solo photos of her at landmarks. Images from students' minds of me and her walking around campus burn away. I watch all around me as anything that could link me and my mama together disappears. If we ever bump into one another, us sharing the same last name will just be a funny coincidence. Something two Black people can bond over.

And I'm okay with that.

I stand in her room, watching her sleep peacefully one more time. Grabbing the quilted blanket draped over the armrest of the couch, I tuck her in, leaning down and kissing her forehead.

"I love you, Mama," I whisper, grabbing my bag and slipping out of her room. Once the door closes, I press my back against the wall and slide down it, hugging my knees.

I'm alone. Everett is gone, Etaliein is gone, my mama is gone. There's no one else but me.

"You never told me how alone it is to be a god," I say to the air.

"Sounds like you're being a little dramatic, if you ask me."

At first, I think it's the forest talking back to me. But then the voice registers in my head. Snapping my head to the left, I see Everett standing halfway down the hall, a shoulder bag slung over

416

his shoulder. He walks over to me, standing in front, extending his free hand to help me up.

I look up at him, not taking his hand, just looking at him. This has to be some trick, some byproduct of using too much magic at once or some dark twist of the forest to throw me off guard.

"What are you doing here?"

Everett frowns. "Ouch, that's rude, don't you think? I've been waiting at your room for an hour, trying to surprise you, and that's how you greet me?"

"You should be with Emma . . ."

"Yeah, I should be," he says, balancing on the balls of his feet as he leans down. "But then I got to thinking, I want to see the world, and then I realized, I have everything I want here. So why should I leave?"

Everett shifts his weight, sitting next to me, mimicking my body and hugging his knees too. He nudges me with his shoulder, smirking.

"I expected you to be happier to see me."

"I don't want you to regret coming back," I blurt out.

"I made the choice to come back. We made a promise, remember? To go through this together. That includes whatever happens next. For better or for worse, I'm here with you until the end. And besides, with my mom taking over as headmaster of Regent."

"Interim," I correct. "Until the vote."

"Interim." He grins. "You're going to need an Everley on your side in case the darkness returns. Think of me as your royal guardian."

"I'm a god; I don't need a guardian."

"Everyone needs someone by their side, Douglas. Just like I need you. Think you can accept that you need me?"

Needing someone feels a bit weird, especially considering what that means. Tying Everett's fate to my own feels . . . unfair.

"You're going to die before me."

"Talk about morbid," he mutters.

"I'm just saying, you won't—"

"As much time as I can have with you is good with me," Everett interrupts. "I promise. And if my decision changes, that's my choice. Right now, this is what I want. The question is, do you want me?"

"I always want you," I blurt out. "I want nothing else but you."

"Then let me want you too."

There's a large part of me that feels like this is a bad idea, that Everett is going to grow to regret his choice. But being alone, thinking of Etaliein, is how darkness festers. Maybe having someone will keep the cycle from repeating itself.

"You have to take me on a date first," I say. "And then I'll make my decision."

Everett smiles, hoisting himself up, extending his hand to me again. This time, I take it.

"How about now?"

"Now is good."

Now is all that matters.

REGENT ACADEMY DISTINGUISHED GRADUATES

The Forest Demands Its Due *wouldn't be what it is
without these stellar individuals.*

AGENT	JIM MCCARTHY
EXECUTIVE EDITOR	KAREN CHAPLIN
EDITORIAL DIRECTOR	ROSEMARY BROSNAN
MARKETING DIRECTOR	AUDREY DIESTELKAMP
MARKETING MANAGER	SABRINA ABBALLE
MARKETING COORDINATOR, SCHOOL AND LIBRARY	PATTY ROSATI AND THE SCHOOL AND LIBRARY TEAM
PRODUCTION MANAGER	SEAN P. CAVANAGH AND VANESSA NUTTRY
COVER DESIGNER	JOEL TIPPIE
MANAGING EDITORIAL	MARK RIFKIN AND SHONA MCCARTHY
COPY EDITOR	JEN STRADA
SALES	KERRY MOYNAGH AND THE HARPERCOLLINS SALES TEAM
PR MANAGER	JENNIFER CORCORAN AND KATIE BONI
AGENCY	DYSTEL, GODERICH & BOURRET LLC

ACKNOWLEDGMENTS

In 2002, I wrote my first book.

It was only, like, 130 pages but to me, at the age of eleven, it was the best thing I had ever written. It involved dinosaurs, and spies, and teens who rode dinosaurs and solved crimes. Thrilling stuff.

In 2004, I wrote my next book, basically *Final Fantasy* meets *Avatar the Last AirBender* meets *Magic Knights Rayearth* for all my anime fans. *That* one was three hundred pages double-spaced, and I still think about those characters.

In my heart of hearts, I've always been a fantasy kid. Sure, fantasy wasn't how I started my YA writing career, but I knew, one day, I'd want to write one. To me, to make that little kid who read books by flashlight, who imagined worlds for hours while practicing tennis outside, who devoured anime and fell in love with the stories, I knew writing a fantasy book was a bucket list item for me, as a writer, I'd have to complete. I'm so glad I got to make that younger version of me proud.

The Forest Demands Its Due, like so many books, wouldn't be here without so many people. Books, like many forms of art, take a village to be created. I'll make this as short as I can.

To Karen Chaplin, my editor, who saw this book and loved it from only sixty pages, and has pushed me with each edit to make it the best book it can be. I've never been more proud of a novel I've written, and that's in large part to you, the team at Harper-Collins, and every person, especially editorial director, Rosemary Brosnan, who took a chance on me and believed in me.

To my agent, Jim McCarthy, who listened to a first draft of this book's magic system and said, *Whew, that's a lot. Let's see if we can truncate that*, this book is as much yours as it is mine. To Katie Locke, the first person to read the first sixty pages and tell me, *This book is good*, I'm so honored to have you as a friend. To Mary Averling, for always being an amazing alpha reader and editor, your talent is amazing and I cannot wait to read your words so soon. To Holly Black, for telling me in our hour-long chat session one time, *Write the damn werewolf book!*, this book isn't that but the first version of *The Forest Demands Its Due* was that, and this book wouldn't be a book without that wake-up call.

To Hannah Whitten, the first reader to blurb this book and remind me that I'm a good writer when I needed it the most, your words and your praise mean so much. To Ryan, Caleb, Kevin, and Damian, my boys, thank you for always being a sounding board, a friend, and just an awesome group chat.

To the friends and family in my life, Jordan, Mom, Dad, Talya, thank you for putting up with my near manic habits when it comes to my books.

And, of course, to the HarperCollins Union. I'm not sure what the state of publishing is when this book comes out, but standing up for what's right isn't always easy, and I appreciate every single one of you, especially those who worked on this book, for standing up for what's right.

The Forest Demands Its Due is a story about power, love, pain, and the effect we have on one another's lives, even if we don't know it. I think every author needs to shoot for the moon with at least one book. This is my rocket launcher aimed at the moon.

I hope it hits and even if it doesn't? I did that damn thing.

This is your sign to do that too.